BY JEFF SHAARA

THE
EAGLE'S
CLAW

THE EAGLE'S CLAW

A NOVEL OF THE BATTLE OF MIDWAY

JEFF SHAARA

BALLANTINE BOOKS

NEW YORK

Published in the United States by Ballantine Books, an imprint of Random House, a division of Penguin Random House LLC, New York.

BALLANTINE and the HOUSE colophon are registered trademarks of Penguin Random House LLC.

LIBRARY OF CONGRESS CATALOGING-IN-PUBLICATION DATA
Names: Shaara, Jeff, author.
Title: The eagle's claw : a novel of the Battle of Midway / Jeff Shaara.
Description: New York : Ballantine Books, [2021]
Identifiers: LCCN 2021003764 (print) | LCCN 2021003765 (ebook) |
ISBN 9780525619444 (hardback; acid-free paper) | ISBN 9780525619451 (ebook)
Subjects: LCSH: Midway, Battle of, 1942—Fiction. | GSAFD: Historical fiction. |
War stories.
Classification: LCC PS3569.H18 E24 2021 (print) | LCC PS3569.H18 (ebook) |
DDC 813/.54—dc23
LC record available at https://lccn.loc.gov/2021003764
LC ebook record available at https://lccn.loc.gov/2021003765

Printed in the United States of America on acid-free paper

randomhousebooks.com

2 4 6 8 9 7 5 3 1

First Edition

Book design by Caroline Cunningham

THIS BOOK IS DEDICATED TO GEORGE LOWER

Sometimes the greatest wisdom and insight

stands right in front of you.

CONTENTS

LIST OF MAPS

TO THE READER

One of the challenges I've discovered in writing this story is that, unlike so many other campaigns in so many wars, the most significant events of the Battle of Midway take place within a single day—June 4, 1942. Thus, you may notice that the date and time that start each chapter might not be in perfect chronological order, one chapter taking place at the same time as (or slightly before) the one after. That might sound confusing, but I feel it actually works. You have to know what each side or each character is doing at any given moment, because in this story, many of those moments are some of the most dramatic and important in our history.

As always, I have included maps, which I hope will be helpful. Immediately, you will notice that the map of Midway shows a place that is quite simple geographically: a wide lagoon surrounded by a narrow coral reef that embraces two small islands—

little more than hilly sandbars. That such a place should have such a role in the history of World War II defies logic. But that is the story.

I hear frequently from readers who wonder why I chose to include a certain historical character or the details of some particular event. I'm sure it will be that way here. For me, it's another challenge, always: what to leave out. Tens of thousands of sailors and marines on both sides participated in this fight, and choosing the voices for this story was difficult. It is a story told through the points of view of perhaps more characters than I've included in the past, so that I could cover as many of the details as possible without muddying the narrative. I hope I'm right. That judgment will be yours.

I won't describe each character here, since each is introduced as the story moves along. There are five principal voices on the American side, from admirals to pilots to gunnery sergeants and a code breaker (who alone changes history). On the Japanese side, there are three admirals, very different men who play very different roles. And they too are responsible for changing history.

I mentioned in my previous book, *To Wake the Giant,* that I am aware of the proper usage for Japanese names: last/first. For clarity's sake, and to stay consistent with English usage, I have used the names as we would: first/last. I expected considerable grief from Japanese readers for this, but their tolerance thus far has been most appreciated.

So many, on both sides, who were a part of the Battle of Midway, whose heroism and sacrifice determined how this story would play out, deserve to be remembered. This is my offering. As I have said many times about my books, this is not a history book. But I hope that you will learn something you might not have known, as I certainly did. But even better, I hope that you will find these characters and this extraordinary event to be a *good story*. Midway changes the entire war, and so it changes history. In some ways it changed me as I wrote it. I hope you enjoy this book.

—JEFF SHAARA, APRIL 2021

ALASKA

ALEUTIAN ISLANDS

Attu

Kiska

Dutch
Harbor

PACIFIC OCEAN

Midway

French Frigate
Shoals

HAWAIIAN
ISLANDS

Oahu

Pearl Harbor

Wake
Island

MARSHALL
ISLANDS

LINE
ISLANDS

GILBERT
ISLANDS

EQUATOR

The Pacific Ocean Basin

0	MILES	1000
0	KM	100

INTRODUCTION

In early 1942, the American navy is still reeling from the impact of the Japanese surprise attack on Pearl Harbor. In Washington, D.C., and in many American newspapers, there are dramatic calls demanding revenge. These cries are loud and strident, the Japanese becoming a far more despised enemy than the Germans. Some of this stems from pure racism; the Germans, after all, look like "us." Fueled by the news media as well as Hollywood's portrayals, the Japanese are depicted as a vicious alien race, and so for most Americans it is easy to accept them as the most evil enemy we face. After nearly a decade of brutal conquest and atrocities in China, the Japanese do very little to blunt that image. However, the regrettable result of this will be the establishment of internment camps, mostly in California but also spreading elsewhere, where American citizens of Japanese descent are herded together, imprisoned behind barbed wire, to "protect" the rest of the country from their predicted treachery.

For the American military, particularly the navy, the power of these official and public calls for action against the Japanese causes a problem. Prior to December 7, 1941, most Americans believe with certainty that the Americans simply can't be defeated, in any war, against any opposition. At Pearl Harbor, that perception changes. America's defeat there is absolute. The result, of course, is a movement within the military to find an effective way to strike back. But the admirals know they are outgunned, and that any large-scale assault on Japanese forces is simply foolish.

Under pressure from Washington, American ships and planes engage in minor battles throughout the South Pacific, but the results are meager at best. In early January 1942, American submarines sink three Japanese freighters near the coast of Japan. The event is a brief morale boost for the navy, though it has no effect at all on Japanese military planning. To emphasize that point, less than a week later a Japanese submarine torpedoes the carrier USS *Saratoga,* barely five hundred miles from Hawaii. Though the carrier survives, it is put out of action for several months.

Throughout the winter and early spring of 1942, the American navy engages in hit-and-run raids on Japanese ships and island bases, some of which are moderately successful, none of which will change the course of the war. Throughout these engagements the Japanese give as good as they get, sinking a number of American warships along the way. The most costly fight comes at the Battle of the Java Sea, near (present-day) Indonesia, when the Americans lose three destroyers and three cruisers without sinking a Japanese ship.

The Japanese are arrogantly aware of their dominance of the seas, and as part of the expansion of their Greater East Asia Co-Prosperity Sphere, plans are made to strike directly at Australia, or at the very least to sever supply and communication lines between that country and the United States. In addition, moves are made that result in driving the once-mighty British navy completely out of the region, at considerable loss.

The Japanese navy is spearheaded by the ships of their *Kido Butai* ("Mobile Force"), commanded by Admiral Chuichi Nagumo, a sullen and disagreeable man, who had commanded the same fleet during its assault on Pearl Harbor. The *Kido Butai* consists of most of Japan's larger aircraft carriers, plus a significant number of supporting ships, far outmuscling their American counterparts. The Japanese rely on airpower and speed, and they operate with plenty of both. For several months, the Japanese people are told, and the emperor and his military believe, that they are utterly invincible. Later, this belief becomes known by Japanese historians as their Victory Disease: the concept that no matter your planning or your actions, you will defeat your enemy, simply because you always have. That comforting philosophy does not sit well with men like Admiral Isoroku Yamamoto, commander of Japan's combined fleet, and others around him who are charged with planning and executing Japan's next moves.

In spring 1942, two events create a flow toward what will follow. On April 18, sixteen B-25 Mitchell bombers, under the command of Colonel Jimmie Doolittle, launch from the carrier USS *Hornet*. Their one-way mission is to drop bombs on Tokyo and other Japanese cities. There is no great strategic goal intended, the raid serving as more of a symbolic move, but it sends a message to the Japanese that America had a claw that could reach them, and that the Japanese might not be so invincible after all.

The second event takes place in early May: the Battle of the Coral Sea. Powerful naval task forces on both sides engage in what amounts to a clumsy and futile search for the other, resulting in only minor victories each way. The Japanese lose a light aircraft carrier, but the Americans lose the combat carrier USS *Lexington*. Though ultimately the Americans have as much claim to a victory in the Coral Sea as the Japanese, the loss of the *Lexington* is a devastating blow to a navy with limited carrier strength. For a naval force seeking a morale boost, the sinking of the *Lady Lex* is anything but.

In Hawaii, Admiral Chester Nimitz accepts the position of commander in chief, Pacific (CINCPAC), replacing Husband E. Kimmel, who is widely regarded as the scapegoat for the disaster at Pearl Harbor. Nimitz understands that his command is under a microscope, but he knows his subordinates well, and he appreciates the skills and daring of men like Admirals Frank Jack Fletcher and William Halsey (later nicknamed Bull). But the challenge for Nimitz is to combine his limited carrier force, manned by many brown-shoe pilots and flight crews, with commanders who understand naval tactics, most of them Naval Academy graduates, the men who wear the black shoes. The brown/black shoe rivalry is, to Nimitz, ridiculous. But to the men onboard the carriers, the prejudice flows both ways.

From a strategic point of view, the Americans have an urgent need to regroup, to plan some new tactic against the increasingly powerful Japanese. The Japanese for the most part continue to suffer the arrogance of their Victory Disease, since no one has yet been able to defeat them in any major confrontation. But Admiral Yamamoto knows such illusions cannot last. The Doolittle raid makes its point, and though the Japanese government blatantly lies to its public about the impact of the raid, the military knows better. Yamamoto understands that with time, the Americans will continue to strengthen. It is essential that his navy strikes the deciding blow, eliminating the American aircraft carriers, those ships that were spared Japanese bombs at Pearl Harbor.

As he does during the planning for the attack on Pearl Harbor, Yamamoto relies on the young aviators and staff officers to fashion a plan to draw the Americans out from the safety of the fortified port in Hawaii and lure them into a fight they cannot win. There must be bait, a trap. Yamamoto agrees with his planners that the bait will be a noisy invasion of a small atoll, twelve hundred miles northwest of Hawaii, the home of a minor and isolated American naval and marine base. It is called Midway.

PART ONE

"Japan stands today as the premier naval power of the world. It may well presage the rise of Japan in the future history of the world."

—*Japan Times & Advertiser*, May 27, 1942

"Neither side in this conflict can build warships as fast as aviation can destroy them from the skies."

—Major Alexander de Seversky, May 1942

"If the enemy is efficient—prepare for him. If he is arrogant, behave timidly, to encourage his arrogance. Advance when he does not expect you."

—Sun Tzu, *The Art of War*, 500 B.C.

ONE

The Co-Pilot

The flight deck seemed to dive straight down into the waves, great plumes of seawater surging up and over the bow of the carrier. The wind took hold now, blowing the spray back toward them, across the wooden flight deck, and embracing the planes themselves. As daylight slowly rose through the dismal gray of the rain, the saltwater had already bathed each of the bombers with a wet sheen.

Through the blinding fog of windy spray Cole could see the lone sailor at the far end of the ship, the man disguised by foul-weather gear and gripping a checkered flag, standing as still as the waves would allow. He was the flight deck officer, and for the moment, he was the most powerful man on the carrier. The order had already come down from the bridge—the ship's captain, Pete

Mitscher, sending word to the FDO, passed to Mitscher by the task force admiral Bill Halsey: *Get these planes in the air.*

The FDO's signal would bring each of the bombers to life, the first command given to each plane to start their engines. It could not happen all at once. The B-25s were far larger than any of the carrier's own aircraft, some with their wingtips and elevators protruding past the deck itself, with nothing below but rolling ocean. There were sixteen bombers parked together in a tight mass, a necessary arrangement to fit all of them against the stern of the ship, and the only way any of them would have the length of wooden runway to allow them the speed they would need to fly.

For now, the engines were still for another reason: the safety of the sailors still waiting beneath each plane, the ship's ground crews whose job was to pull away the wooden chocks that kept each plane's tires from moving. And so, the FDO's signal would come to each plane in turn, engines engaged one at a time, allowing the first aircraft to surge down the flight deck, clearing the way for the second, until all sixteen were in the air.

In front of Doolittle's B-25, Cole could see the flood of water washing across the deck, the ship still digging low into the waves, then up again, a stomach-churning ride for men who had rarely been at sea. He tried to ignore that, and kept his stare on the FDO, the lone officer who stared back at them. Doolittle's B-25 was the first in line. That was about not rank but Doolittle's own experience and skill. Out in front of the others, he was the closest to the far end of the carrier's flight deck, and thus the pilot with the shortest distance to put his plane in the air. The other fifteen were behind him, each one with just those few extra feet of distance, and the slight advantage of a longer runway.

"Keep your eyes on the flight officer, Lieutenant. He's in charge."

"I see him, sir. The sailor. Guy with the flag. He's gotta be miserable. Hope he don't fall off the ship."

Doolittle kept his eyes on the instruments in front of him, said,

"He's tethered, a rope around him. He's an officer, Lieutenant Osborne. Ozzie, they call him. Worry about what's in here, Dick."

Cole brought his gaze back into the cockpit, nothing more to see now beyond the nose of the plane. The preflight routine had been rehearsed so many times before, but then, it was mostly on dry land and level ground. He had rarely flown in weather like this, certainly not at sea. The winds still came, blowing the sea spray over and past them, soaking the skins of the B-25s, creating a blinding fog across the windscreen, like a wet hand closing around them that made the plane feel so much smaller.

Through the earphones came the voice of the engineer, Sergeant Leonard: "Sir, we just received a brief message from the bridge. A signal flashed to *Hornet* from the *Enterprise*. Admiral Halsey, sir."

"Well? Is it a secret?"

"Um, no, sir. The admiral says, *To Colonel Doolittle and Gallant Command: Good Luck and God Bless You. Halsey.*

"He's got enough *Gallant* for all of us. Nice words."

Cole pointed to the far end of the flight deck, and with too much volume in his voice, said, "He's waving the flag, sir."

Doolittle said, "Easy, Dick. I see him. Time to go to work." Doolittle put a hand on his mic and said, "Navigator. Switches in *on* position?"

Cole heard the response in his earphones.

"On position, roger that, sir."

Doolittle glanced toward Cole now with a sharp nod, and Cole knew the meaning. He began his own routine, priming the number one engine, then a slow mental count, four long seconds, then engaging the pressure and energizing switch, another few seconds, the prop turning slowly. The engine erupted into life, and the magnificent shivering roar shook the plane, blowing salt spray in a dense fog over the bombers that waited behind them. The co-pilot's routine was repeated, the second engine adding its own thunder, the raw energy that Cole loved, that feel of power that engulfed him now, a part of him. But the routine continued, Cole eyeing the oil pressure indicator. He urged the needle higher, twenty, thirty, *forty pounds*. A silent prayer always flashed through his mind, willing the oil pressure to reach that magic number, knowing that if the engines didn't reach the necessary pressure, the flight would be aborted. Any pilot knew that if you ignored it, the engines would simply destroy themselves. And today, shutting down the engines meant the plane's crew would quickly evacuate the aircraft, while the ship's deck crew would scramble out, shoving the B-25 off the side of the carrier, dumping her into the ocean. And so, as Cole kept his eyes on the oil gauge, he offered a silent *Thank you*.

Cole continued his checklist, Doolittle doing the same, with quick positive responses coming through the interphone from the plane's other three crewmen.

Cole fought to see through the windscreen, knowing they would have to focus again on the flight deck officer, whom he could only think of as Lieutenant Ozzie. Doolittle glanced at Cole now, and Cole saw a smile, the first one he had seen from Doolittle in weeks.

"What do you think, Dick? You feel like bombing some Japs?"

"Yes, sir. Absolutely, sir." Cole stared to the front again and through a break in the spray caught a clear view of the wooden flight deck. There was a sudden tumble in his gut. "I just . . . I didn't think it would look so damn short. Sir."

"It's short. But it's all we'll need. You've done these takeoffs before, dozens of times. No different now. We'll be all right."

Another splash of seawater burst over the windscreen, the bow of the carrier rising up from a deep trough, the wind still whipping the spray down the entire deck. Cole tried to take a breath, felt himself shaking from the rumble of the plane's two engines, his hands gripping the yoke in front of him.

"Yes, sir. We'll be all right. That Ozzie fellow down there, he's gonna wait for the right second. The ship drops down, we'll go. Right, sir?"

"We'll go when he tells us to go. The ship's been turning, and she's just about square into the wind. The captain will jam the engines as hard as this boat will go. After that, it's up to us."

Cole kept silent now, nothing else to do. The engines on either side of him seemed to settle into a rhythm, calming, the shaking of the plane matched by the buffeting of the wind around them. He released the grip on the yoke, knowing that it would be Doolittle's job to guide the plane straight down the flight deck with no room for error. At least with the wind in their faces, the plane should stay true—a straight line. Any swerve, any shift of the tail, and they might end up in the drink. Cole kept that to himself, and took a deep breath. He knew that the colonel had more on his mind than the nervous chattering of his co-pilot.

The wind seemed to increase, rocking the plane, and Cole looked to one side, out toward the ship's island. He saw the black numbers written large—the wind speed shown to all the pilots, with sailors changing them as the wind changed. With the carrier now pushing straight into the wind, the wind speed was increased by the carrier's own acceleration and Cole saw what Doolittle saw: fifty, now fifty-five.

Doolittle said into the interphone, "Fast enough. That should get us airborne. We ready?"

The responses came quickly, any fear the others had tucked away in some place they would never admit. Behind the lead plane, fifteen more pilots and their crews were impatiently waiting their turn to bring their engines to life and to aim the nose of their own planes down the flight deck.

Cole leaned as far as he could to the right, watching the sailor beneath him, the man hidden by his rain gear. He focused on the panel, checked the instruments yet again, and stared through another haze of salt spray that whipped across the windscreen. The plane rocked again, seemed to lift on its own, and he thought of the deck crews and mechanics who had swarmed over the plane earlier, topping off the gas tanks, loading the auxiliary tanks, then jerking up and down on the wings to break up any bubbles that might be in the gas lines. But those men were nowhere around, just the lone sailor below him, one of the two men holding the lines that would jerk the chocks away. The sailor looked up at him, a wave of his hand, some kind of salute, but Cole's view was wiped away again by the blowing water. The voice shot into him now, the command each man had heard from Doolittle so many times, so many flights, through so much training.

"Do your jobs. Let's go!"

Cole stared forward, saw the sailor waving the flag in a circle over his head, then faster, and suddenly the flag came down, the final sign, the signal to *go*. The plane vibrated, a hard quivering shake as Doolittle revved the engines, the throttle sliding forward, and the RPMs increasing. Down below, the sailors held tight to the rope that wedged the chocks hard against the wet tires. Cole wrapped his fingers around his safety belt, the brief punch of panic he couldn't avoid that the plane would come apart.

The plane seemed to scream at them all, a violent protest, and Cole watched as the RPMs neared the maximum Doolittle dared to push for. Cole looked to the bow of the great ship, another deep fall, another sheet of water coming up and toward them. But it was time. The chocks were suddenly yanked away, Doolittle releasing the brakes. Cole's eyes went to the bow as it rose up from the deep pit of the wave. Now the carrier would begin the slow rise, the plane surging forward. There were no words, no commands, Doolittle's hard stare focused toward the bow of the carrier, the flight deck absurdly short. Cole stared toward the line, the boundary between ship and sea, pushed himself back against his seat, a ridiculous gesture, as though he could help the plane's nose come up just a bit quicker. Doolittle waited till the last few feet, the ship's bow rising up in the rough seas, a gentle toss upward as the plane cleared the bow, open ocean below, the bomber settling down a few feet, the crew's stomachs rising, hearts racing. Doolittle yanked the yoke hard against him, keeping the nose of the plane upward, as the great engines now took over, the speed increasing, the nose coming level, and Cole saw the horizon, a faint line between the sea and a dark and rainy sky.

They were airborne.

Jimmy Doolittle was in his forties and had flown every kind of plane on nearly every airfield where a plane could land. Sometimes they didn't land, as he had learned as a fledgling aviator building his own glider from a mail-order kit. The thirty-foot tumble off a cliff left him bruised but miraculously alive. The lesson came quickly: If you want to do it right, do it yourself.

He had been born in California, but was hauled to Nome, Alaska, by a father whose greatest dream was to strike it rich in the Klondike. His father's dream was never realized, and Doolittle, somewhat undersized as a boy, had to learn boxing, or any other kind of physical competition in which guile could help where brute force could not. That passion, and an astonishing fearlessness in aircraft of all kind, eventually earned Doolittle several speed and endurance records in aircraft that stood for years. By the end of the 1930s, Jimmy Doolittle was one of the four most famous aviators in the world, rivaling Charles Lindbergh, Billy Mitchell, and Amelia Earhart.

Dick Cole was not Doolittle's first choice for co-pilot, but injuries to two others vaulted Cole into the seat beside the man he had already come to worship. At twenty-six, Cole was no different than many of the eighty-man team taking part in this mission. Every one of them had known who Doolittle was well before they shook his hand, and now every one was honored to regard Doolittle as his commanding officer. Born in Dayton, Ohio, the home of the Wright brothers, Cole grew up in a setting that was a natural inspiration to a boy who saw the air service as his future. He had earned his wings less than a year before but had quickly showed a talent for piloting the larger B-25s, while so many others sought glamour in the seat of the fighters.

The training was mostly at Pensacola and consisted of repetitive efforts to take off in as short a distance as possible. Over time their skills increased, though even as Colonel Doolittle announced them ready for the mission, none of them had actually flown a B-25 bomber off the deck of an aircraft carrier.

In Japan, nothing the United States or her allies had yet accomplished in the South Pacific raised any real concern that Japan and her emperor had anything to fear. Their military, especially the Imperial Japanese Navy, was considered by the Japanese to be the most powerful in the world. And thus far, they were right.

Doolittle's mission was simple in design, if not potentially disastrous for the men who would take part. Sixteen B-25 Mitchell bombers would be ferried westward, ideally four hundred miles from the Japanese coast. The navy would provide a task force commanded by Admiral Bill Halsey onboard the USS *Enterprise*. A second carrier, the USS *Hornet*, would actually carry the bombers onboard for their launch. The carriers would be accompanied by a flotilla of smaller warships—escorts that would guard against Japanese interference. The mission Doolittle had been assigned was the stuff of pulp novels—food for headlines. But there could be none of that, at least not yet. Each of the men, Cole included, was made aware that secrecy was not only necessary, but that it would likely save their lives. They would fly over open ocean, a new experience for nearly all of them, seeking out a lengthy list of military and industrial targets in Tokyo and other cities. No one had an illusion that this mission would end the war or cripple Japan's war machine. It was, plain and simple, a gesture. The Japanese had proven themselves to the world and had shocked the American government by extending their dangerous hand all the way to Pearl Harbor. Doolittle's mission was symbolic at best, but the meaning would be clear: You reached out and damaged us. Now we will do the same to you.

The planes had been stripped of all non-essential weight and were packed with auxiliary fuel tanks, placed in nearly every nook available. Many of the naval officers on the *Hornet*, and many in Washington, were skeptical that these large bombers could actually become airborne by propelling themselves across the short stretch of the *Hornet*'s flight deck. Doolittle's men absorbed his own confidence and embraced his lessons, that with the right amount of training and practice, the mission could be accomplished. But Doolittle's confidence stopped there. He knew he could train his pilots in the art of the short-field takeoff, but Doolittle knew that taking off from a carrier was a one-way trip. The bombers were simply too large and too clumsy to land on the flight deck of any carrier. And so, once airborne, the bombers would disappear westward, the crews relying on the accuracy of their navigational instruments, to drop their bombloads on their designated targets in Japan. Then, they would continue on, attempting to reach airfields on the Chinese mainland, where they would be aided by supposedly friendly Chinese troops. To that end, arrangements had been made with Chinese military officials to transmit a homing beacon from a number of airfields as the bombers drew close, since most of the bombers would reach Chinese territory after dark.

But one more variable had been tossed into the mission. The Japanese were known to have a loose cordon of seagoing observers in an arc well out from the Japanese coast. Not all were warships, but more often fishing boats or small freighters equipped with electronics for communicating with Japan. Early that morning, one such boat had been located, seeming to be nothing more than a fishing trawler. But onboard the *Enterprise,* where Admiral Halsey absorbed the reports, there was more than mere concern. The task force still had one hundred fifty miles to go to reach the designated launch point, which would bring the B-25s within four hundred miles of Japan. Though he ordered the trawler sunk as rapidly as possible, Halsey had to assume that the Japanese command had been notified of the task force's presence. And even now, the Americans were within range of Japanese land-based bombers. Halsey made the decision to launch Doolittle's planes well short of where they were supposed to be. That added distance might doom every one of the sixteen planes, already tight on fuel, to a water landing. And even if they made it to China, the weather might not be any better in the difficult mountains inland from China's coast than it was at sea.

"Keep the altitude below two hundred. If the weather opens up a bit, we'll drop it lower. Between the wind and the waves, we should stay where we are." Doolittle spoke into the interphone now. "Navigator, I'm coming back." He glanced at Cole. "Take her, keep straight and low. Well, hell, you can do it."

Doolittle climbed out of the pilot's seat, slipped past Cole, who clamped his hands on the yoke. "Got her, sir."

He stared straight ahead, fog and rain and choppy seas. There was a thrill, always, to flying so low, whether over water or trees. But this time, there could be no playing, no weaving through obstacles. He thought of the fuel, the number stuck in his head. Eleven hundred and forty-one gallons. Well, less now. No more Jap ships, I hope. One anti-aircraft shell hits us, and we're nothing but a fireball. I guess that's the best way to go. Don't care much for the idea of drowning or sharks. Or ending up in a Jap prison.

Doolittle was back now, eased himself into his seat, and said,

"Hank says we're bucking a headwind, maybe twenty-five knots. That won't help a damn bit. We're getting shoved sideways a little too. He doesn't know how much. Next time, he's buying the beer."

Doolittle took the yoke and Cole tried to relax, saw a hint of sunlight through the gray clouds. "Clearing up, sir. Maybe."

"Yeah. Maybe."

Cole searched for words, a curiosity he had felt for weeks. "Was this your idea, sir?"

Doolittle said, "What if it was? You gonna toss me out?"

"No, sir, not what I meant. There's a lot of pieces to this puzzle. Just wondering."

"Well, a good many of those pieces were mine. But the idea came out of Washington, as amazing as that might sound. And it didn't come from the army. Admiral King's operations officer, Francis Low, Captain Low. Actually, they call him Froggie. Some. Not me. But he laid all this out for the admiral, and they took it from there. I always heard Admiral King was a pain, a tough cookie, and not in a nice way. But he tossed this to his people, who tossed it to me. So, if we end up eating rice for the next twenty years, blame Froggie."

Cole wasn't sure how much of that was serious, knew it didn't matter. He checked his watch: three hours flying time, and still nothing but ocean.

Doolittle said, "Don't be in a hurry, Lieutenant. We'll be over the Japanese coast soon enough, but we've got a whole hell of a lot more air to fill."

"Colonel, I guess we were briefed on this, but I'm still not sure I understand why, after our bombing run, we're not heading north-west? Russia's a whole lot closer. They're allies too, maybe just like the Chinese."

Doolittle didn't hesitate. "You're right, every detail, except one. Joe Stalin's got his hands full against the Germans. He helps us out, lets us land on his dirt? The Japs might not appreciate the gesture, and all of a sudden, Stalin's pissed off the Japs, and now he's got a two-front war. Those folks in Washington, nice suits and shiny shoes, they want to make nice with Papa Joe, or Uncle Joe, or whatever the hell they call him. I'd rather land there, for certain. But we're going to China."

They flew in silence for most of an hour, the sky opening up to a dusty blue flecked with fat white clouds. Beneath the plane, the swells rolled heavily toward them, the sharp winds still pushing them head-on.

Cole felt himself getting hungry, and said, "Sir, in my B-4, I've got some candy. Want some?"

"Thanks, Dick. No. I brought a couple ham sandwiches."

"Uh, well, yes, sir. Got those too. Chocolate bar sounds good about now."

Doolittle motioned approval with his hand, and Cole leaned down, pulled the cloth bag from behind his seat. He shuffled through, razor, shaving cream, and cotton balls, his father's pen, a pad of paper, matches and cigarettes, and most important of all, something to eat. He was suddenly embarrassed at the sheer volume of rations he had brought along. He tried to keep the contents from Doolittle's sharp eye, but heard now, "We could have added another two gallons of fuel with the crap you brought. Give me a chocolate bar."

Cole obeyed, shoved the bag out of the way, ripped the wrappers from both chocolate bars, and handed one to Doolittle. More silence followed, and more curiosity from Cole.

"Sir, you were a boxer, right? You ever meet Joe Louis?"

"He's twice my size, Lieutenant. I fought as a bantamweight. That was pretty good, actually. They'd put me up in front of all these pipsqueaks, and I'd rough 'em up. Had good fists, a strong gut. Course, I was a pipsqueak too. Just tougher."

"Not sure I could be a fighter. Things could get hurt."

Doolittle laughed. "They do."

Doolittle looked up, the clouds fewer now, crisp blue sky. He spoke into the interphone. "Sergeant Leonard. Can you see if anyone's still behind us?"

The voice came back: "Yes, sir. Lieutenant Hoover's bird is a couple of miles dead astern. He's been keeping his altitude with us."

Doolittle looked up at the sky, the clouds fewer still. "Wonder where everybody else is? I'm hoping they all made it off the ship."

"I'm sure they did, sir. They did what you taught 'em. Too bad we can't ring 'em up on the radio."

"You know better than that, Lieutenant. Radio silence means radio silence. Japs got ears too."

They sat quietly for a long minute and Cole couldn't hold his curiosity. "Sir, forgive me, but I might not have the chance to, you know, fly with you again. I just gotta ask. What's it feel like to have all those cameras in your face, to shake hands with all those big army hotshots, generals and stuff? What's it feel like to be famous?"

Doolittle sat back, raised a hand, pointed ahead, and Cole looked out that way, his heart a cold lump. Doolittle said, "You might find out for yourself, Lieutenant. That's Japan."

"I'd love a cloud or two, sir. Too much blue sky. Nowhere to hide out here."

Doolittle leaned forward, stared up. "Jap plane, three thousand. Heading out to sea. Probably chasing after our task force. He's ignoring us. Nice of him."

Cole hadn't thought much about the ships they had left behind. "One plane? They're sending one plane to take on our ships?"

Doolittle didn't laugh. "Don't count on it. But I heard all I need to know about Admiral Halsey. There are so many people, good people, officers, commanders, that you never pay attention to.

Others get a reputation, and people like serving with them. That's Halsey. That task force turned tail and headed away from here the second our last plane took off. *Haul Ass with Halsey*. That's what a bunch of those fellows told me."

The quiet returned, Doolittle leaning forward, then to the side, taking in as much of a view as the bomber would allow. He spoke into the interphone now, "Damn it all, Lieutenant. Looks to me like we missed Tokyo."

"Sir, it appears we're roughly thirty miles north of the city. I've recognized various landmarks. I'd suggest, sir, heading one eight zero."

Doolittle glanced at Cole. "He's the navigator."

Doolittle banked to the left, Cole, seeing a large lake in front of them, thought, Hell, if that's what you need to be a landmark, I oughta be a navigator too.

They kept low, no more than a hundred feet above whatever obstacle lay on the ground below them. Cole turned in every direction, thought, No anti-aircraft fire, no interference from Japanese fighters, no reception at all. Couldn't be any better than that.

The city spread out before them now, and Doolittle kept the plane as low as possible, houses and buildings now replacing the trees. Cole felt his insides grip tight, his eyes on every structure, but he glanced upward, and then said, with too much volume, "Sir! Jap fighters. Formation of three. Wait, there's six more, six more. Not more than a thousand feet."

Doolittle leaned forward and said, "Good eye, Lieutenant. Let's find out if they see us."

Doolittle banked the plane gently, still low to the structures below. Cole kept his eyes on the fighters, saw all nine mirror the bomber's movement. "Sir, they see us."

"Yep. They're setting up for a dive on us. Hang on. I'm boring into the city straightaway. They can't know just who we are, and they're not going to shoot up their own people."

Doolittle pushed the throttle forward, a stream of precious fuel goosing the engine, the RPMs increasing. Cole's gut tightened even more, the bomber skimming the rooftops, but held securely by Doolittle's calm.

"Looks like we lost 'em, sir. You were right."

Doolittle didn't respond, and Cole understood. Of course he was right.

Doolittle spoke into the interphone: "Bombardier, you awake?"

"Yes, sir."

"We're getting close, Fred. I'm climbing, leveling out at one-two-zero-zero. Open the bomb bay doors."

Cole felt the rumble, and then the hard rush of air through the bomb bay below him, as Doolittle pushed the plane farther up above the city. There was no sightseeing now, Cole scanning the instruments, the altimeter, Doolittle leveling the plane at twelve hundred feet.

"There's the Imperial Palace. Nobody jumps on that. Not a target. One more mile, there. That dense area. The building in the center is an armory. All yours, Bombardier."

Cole waited for it, the four red lights on the dash, all four bombs falling away. The plane seemed to flutter, rising quickly, two thousand pounds lighter. The reflection came across the windscreen now, the fiery blasts from the incendiary bombs, fire rising behind them. Through the interphone, Cole heard the excited voice of the bombardier. "Folks, that's what we call the Fourth of July!"

Doolittle said nothing, eyes straight ahead, and Cole jerked his head to one side, saw a puff of black smoke, then another. "Sir, they're shooting at us!"

Doolittle eased the yoke forward, losing altitude. "Of course they're shooting at us. That's what they're supposed to do." He spoke into the interphone. "Sergeant Leonard, man your gun. Nobody sneaks up on us. The AA fire is missing us by a mile, but we need to keep an eye out."

Leonard responded, "Sir, it's only ground fire. And . . ."

The blast erupted to one side, a hard chattering of shrapnel along the side of the plane. Leonard said, "Um, sir, that was a good bit less than a mile."

Doolittle jammed the throttle forward, dropped the nose, and was far too low and too quick now for any gunner. They skimmed over the city again, and Doolittle glanced at Cole. "Feel better?"

They crossed the Sea of Japan, and reached the Chinese coast by eight that evening, a journey that had already consumed twelve hours. For another agonizing hour, Doolittle and his navigator strained to hear the homing signal that was supposed to lead them to a safe landing at Chuchow, a signal they could not know that the Chinese had simply neglected to send. Doolittle was forced to risk the difficult terrain of the mountains and navigate through weather that was getting worse by the minute. With empty gas tanks, and a solid cloak of darkness settling over them, Doolittle had no choice but to order his men to bail out. Dick Cole found himself suspended by his parachute from the branches of a tree, only a few feet above the ground. As quietly as possible, he secured the chute and used it to make a hammock, where he slept through the night.

TWO

Yamamoto

"*T*his is Radio Tokyo. A large fleet of enemy bombers appeared over Tokyo this afternoon with much danger to non-military objectives and some damage to factories. The known death toll is between three and four thousand so far. No planes were reported shot down over Tokyo. Osaka was also bombed with great destruction. Tokyo reports several large fires burning.*"

Yamamoto glanced up at his chief of staff. "You have the other account?"

"Yes, sir. Several, actually. Here. Shall I read?"

"Read."

"*The army reports a small effort was made against our defenses by renegade American pilots. Nine planes were shot down by our skilled gunners. The cowardly raiders purposely avoided industrial and military targets and viciously dumped their incendiary devices on schools and hospitals.* There are a good many more, most of them falling in between the false and the ridiculous."

Yamamoto felt sick, worse now, tried to hide it from the others. He glanced toward the staff officers. "You are dismissed, gentlemen. Admiral Ugaki, please remain."

They obeyed, as they always did, silence and cigarette smoke, the wardroom hatch closing behind them.

"Are you all right, sir?"

Yamamoto felt a cold tightness in his chest, struggled to breathe. "No, I am not all right. They might as well have dropped their bombs upon me. My country, my invincible, invulnerable country has just been assaulted. I told the ministry, months ago, I told them this would happen, that just because we may win battles, we cannot assume it will always be so. Conquering Wake Island and the Philippines and Guam and Hanoi is not at all like conquering the United States of America. There are too many in the government of this *invincible* land who have never tasted a hint of defeat. Well, yesterday, there was defeat. And if bombs fall on Tokyo, they explain it all away with lies. They paint us all a portrait with a brush of beautiful miracles, bathing the Japanese people in our perfect specialness." He stopped, looked at Ugaki, saw sadness. "Sit, Matome. There are times when one needs a friend, someone to spit out the awful truth without offending the delicate. That radio report . . . I am certain that reporter did not speak officially for Radio Tokyo. More likely, that poor fellow saw an American plane fly past his own house, rattling his windows. You could hear the panic in his words, and before the government censors could find him, he found his radio transmitter. There will no doubt be punishment for his crime."

He fumbled with his collar, loosening the button at his neck, and paused for a deep breath.

Ugaki watched him, concern on the man's face. "Sir, you should retire to your quarters. There is no pressing duty now, and I can handle any matter. Allow me to serve you, sir."

Yamamoto didn't respond, couldn't avoid the cold blanket of despair he felt now. "The government is telling us that we shot down nine planes. Out of how many? Ten? Forty? How did they arrive here? What phantom island out there houses such bombers? Or did they come from carriers, something new the Americans have sent our way, a massive ship that might next send us their B-17s? We had no idea they were coming, no warning, *no warning*. We have wonderful defenses, marvelous anti-aircraft guns, paraded before our people with such pride. And so, it finally happens, and we are caught completely unaware. Bombers flying over our rooftops. And the army assures us that they shot down nine planes. Our gunners just happened to be awake and aware, pointing their loaded guns in the right direction. Our army's gunners are so efficient that they had no problem shooting down bombers flying past them in a blur, perhaps, what—two hundred miles per hour? I should like to find these gunners, put them aboard my ships. But of course, they are army, and the army does what it wishes, when it wishes. And they tell us what they wish us to hear. Perhaps they would show me just one of these wrecked bombers they gloriously shot from the sky."

Ugaki stood, a careful eye on Yamamoto. "Please, sir. Allow me to escort you."

Yamamoto nodded slowly, stood, felt unsteady, his hands out on the table in front of him. He fought for his breath, and said, "I am not well, Matome. I am wounded. I can describe it no other way. My country is injured, my emperor, all of our perfect world has been wounded. I predicted that the Americans would send us their bombers, but I never believed it would happen so soon. We have won every fight. Until now."

"Sir, this was hardly a fight. A raid, by a small squadron. Their damage was minimal, they accomplished nothing of importance. I spoke to several people in the ministry who all confirmed that it was no more than fifteen or sixteen aircraft, twin engine variety. They passed through Tokyo and the other cities and seemed headed west, toward China. That is no victory, sir. It is an attempt at mockery, and this time they were lucky. But I am convinced that what it will do is ignite a fire in our people, inspiring calls for revenge. It will serve us well, sir."

Yamamoto looked at him now, fought to stand straight. "You are wrong, Matome. Anyone in Japan who believes that is wrong. There will be consequences. Decisions have been made that will now be changed by what the Americans have done. Perhaps *my* decisions. What if they had assaulted the emperor, the palace? Or perhaps they did, and their bombardiers missed. What importance would their *insignificant raid* have had then?"

"Regardless, sir. This will push us forward, add energy to our planning. Even the naysayers will fall in line with your strategies. The Americans may have written their own epitaph, written by your hand. The emperor was untouched, and it will always be. He *is* Japan. Nothing else can matter."

"Such poetry from you, Admiral Ugaki. Write that in your diary. But I'm afraid your lyrics are wasted on me. I will resume our planning for the new operation. We will gather the staff very soon."

Yamamoto moved out from behind the long table, took another deep breath, and Ugaki was there quickly, one hand gently under his arm. Yamamoto eased himself toward the door, said, "Admiral Nagumo is scheduled to return in several days, yes?"

"Two days, sir."

"Yes, two days. I lose time, Matome."

He pulled gently away from Ugaki, moved into a wide passageway. Ugaki stayed back, stood in the wardroom door, and said, "When he arrives, we shall put the final details together. We have the approval of the Naval Ministry, and we shall move forward with great energy."

Yamamoto shook his head, steadying himself with one hand on the bulkhead. "Perhaps, Admiral. But today, the *energy* belongs to the Americans."

He tried to sleep, the enormous quarters around him feeling smaller, the bulkheads pressing inward, crushing him. He fought to take a breath, closed his eyes and thought of her. I need you so very much. You would comfort me, my perfect flower. He wasn't thinking of his wife, a sickly, cynical woman who seemed to delight in annoying him. And so, he kept away from her and from his children nearly grown, his presence simply not needed. But Chiyoko was the most important woman in his life, a geisha who had become something of a mentor to the younger girls she worked with. Yamamoto had tried to be discreet with his relationship, but he knew she was a poorly kept secret. After so many years, he had dared to bring her onboard his flagship, brief visits, and the whispering, what there might have been, had grown quiet. It was, after all, his business, and he was their commander. For the admirals and ministers above him, there would be silence as well. It was quite likely they carried indiscretions of their own.

He had not seen Chiyoko for several weeks now, an aching loneliness within each of them. She lived far to the north, close to Tokyo, and there was no simple way for her to travel, not now, not with the war. But the ailment he felt now was not about loneliness or something the doctors could treat. It was a sudden burst of crushing depression, a reaction to the assault by the American bombers. If Chiyoko could be there, he knew in some dark place that it might not matter, that she might make no difference at all.

For the first time in his life, he understood what failure felt like. It was nothing he had done, of course, no great mistake, nothing done by his staff. But it was Japan's failure, all of them. It is our weakness, he thought. We have so many great victories and they have come so easily. Admiral Nagumo will return home a hero yet again. He did nothing against Pearl Harbor except stand on the bridge of his flagship and worry, while young pilots dropped their bombs. Now he destroys British ships in the Indian Ocean, and I suspect that when the reports are complete, it will be the same. He stands tall and basks in glory while others, many others, do the work. And so, I must *rely* upon him again, even though I cannot.

He rolled over to one side, noticed the flowers for the first time. Omi, he thought. He smiled, thought, My orderly looks after me as much as my chief of staff. But flowers would not be for me. He expected *her* to come. No, not now, Omi. Save the flowers for a better time. We are at war. Does no one understand that?

No, they do not. And so, we have become lazy, arrogant. No enemy dares to touch us. And touch us they did. It was a message that few here will understand. Today, there is hand-wringing in the government, anger and shame from the defense forces, blatant lies from those gunners or their commanders who claim nine planes shot down. Their pride is injured, and so they create lies, as though that will hide their shame. But the people, the civilians, cannot be told what this truly means. Bombs fell on Japan. A few, minor destruction, to be sure. But the door has been opened. In time there will be a great many more bombs, and a great deal more destruction, and there will be dead and dying. I told them all, before our extraordinary victory at Pearl Harbor, that I could offer Japan six months, time enough for us to construct a strong defensive capability. That is what we must have, because the Americans will not just roll over. They will rebuild and resupply, and they will be angry. I had once believed they might be too reluctant, too timid for a war. I was so very wrong. I deluded myself. And now, the ministers and admirals and generals who believe that this shameful bombing raid is somehow insulting to Japanese pride, and that it means little else . . . *that* is delusion.

He sat up, the room spinning, and he clenched his fists, punching down on the bed. Why are you so weak? You must not show this to your staff, or to anyone. Not even to her. So cure this! You know what to do. The plans have been made, and the great young minds—Commander Genda, all the rest—they are behind you. They do not cower in some corner because the Americans have bombs.

He scanned his quarters, blinked through the dizziness.

And yet, you old fool, here you sit, encased in a mighty palace of steel, a ship that is a testament to obsolescence.

On February 12, Yamamoto had transferred his flag and his headquarters from the battleship *Nagato* to the mammoth dreadnought *Yamato*. The new ship, with eighteen-inch guns, was nearly three times the size of any other battleship afloat, seventy thousand tons carrying a massive girdle of steel around her hull to protect her against any kind of seaborne assault.

And he thought, We created this monster for what purpose? What can we do with this giant fortress of a ship? Will we chase the enemies of the emperor all over the world, like a cat after mice? Who would confront us? Who would dare to stand tall with fists raised?

He lay back against a soft pillow, steadied the swirling in his head. So, why are *you* here? You ridiculed them when they began to build this ship. They were fighting the *last* war, with weapons that will no longer defeat anyone. You know it is the airplane that will rule this war, and that the aircraft carriers are the future. And yet, here you sit. Or is this your *throne*, so that you may control the chess game from a fat battleship? Or perhaps you are afraid of the young minds and their planning. They take chances. They understand the need for risk. They *fly*. And what about you? You still surround yourself with steel and fat guns. Your navy has had so much glorious success, but now the Americans have slapped you in the face. Are you too old for risk? Are you afraid of being slapped? Perhaps that is the answer. Let the young men fight their war. They look to you for authority, for praise. Fine, grant them that. But do not try to fool them into believing you are the great hero from the past. They require my authority, and I suppose I must hold on to that, at least for a while. And so, I am so much happier in a great steel fortress. But do not pose the question, as they must be posing it to themselves. What war can you win from here?

THREE

Rochefort

14TH NAVAL DISTRICT, PEARL HARBOR, HAWAII—APRIL 20, 1942

He stepped down the short corridor, ignored the offices above and farther down, where Admiral Bloch housed his command and staff. Rochefort avoided those men whenever possible, since none of them had any need to know or understand just what was happening in the basement below. If he had any purpose to climb the stairs to the building's higher levels, it would only be to obey a request from his commanding officer, Admiral Bloch. That kind of request was rare.

Rochefort turned down into the long stairway, reached the bottom, and stared briefly at the heavy door, which resembled the door of a bank vault. He pulled hard, the door easing open, never locked now. To one side was a small desk, and a man rising abruptly, one hand on his sidearm.

"Oh, forgive me, sir."

"For what? You didn't shoot me. Did you want to?"

"Only if necessary, sir."

"Sit down, Chief. As long as that forty-five's loaded, you're doing your job. Anybody you don't know wanders in through that door, shoot *them*."

"Is that an order, sir?"

Rochefort didn't smile; nothing unusual in that. "I don't give orders. Just suggestions."

"Aye, sir."

Rochefort seemed to wince at every "sir." He moved past the man, his lone guard, the CPO they called Tex. The room was as it always had been, an icebox of stale air, as though an air conditioner had stuck on the coldest setting possible. The light was bright but still, small lamps sat on many of the desks, and only a few of the more than one hundred chairs were empty.

The great luxury for Rochefort was the enormous space Admiral Bloch had granted him: nearly five thousand square feet—the entire basement of Bloch's command center. If any of Rochefort's crew felt as though they were isolated and closed off from the rest of the world, it was by design. That was exactly how Rochefort wanted it to be.

They called it the Dungeon, every one of Rochefort's hundred or more crew accepting the name as completely accurate. There were few interruptions—and virtually no visitors—except those Rochefort approved, and any stranger below the rank of admiral had first to confront the potential menace that was Chief Petty Officer Tex Rorie.

The clutter on each desk reflected the work each man engaged in—the cryptanalysts, the linguists fluent in Japanese, radio and ship traffic analysts, and anyone else Joe Rochefort considered to be an asset. The odd relationships within the Dungeon belied most of what the men had been taught in their navy and marine training. Rochefort had no use for the formality of rank, and the crew consisted of seamen, petty officers, junior and even senior officers.

If anyone held too smugly to his seniority, insisting on the advantages of his higher rank, Rochefort was quick to sweep that away.

There were other characteristics of the Dungeon that some men accepted only grudgingly, while to others, Rochefort's command style offered them a perfect assignment, suited for both talent and personality. Most had specialized in language and radio skills, with a special focus on Japanese. Many were talented with tools as mundane as crossword puzzles, developing the kind of instincts and analytical abilities to stare at numbers or nonsensical collections of letters and somehow find hidden meaning. Some were expert in the crude hardware that sorted and organized massive amounts of data stored now on IBM punch cards, one part of the machinery of this strange and hidden laboratory, whose sole function was to determine just what the Japanese were going to do next.

Almost all were in some way a misfit, few of them with any resemblance to the navy's typical gunnery officer or engineer, those sailors and marines who spent most of their time at sea. Very few of those men would have appreciated the privilege of working long hours belowground in a dismal basement with a concrete floor and faulty air conditioner. As each man was recruited and accepted into the Dungeon, he was quick to understand that there were no set shifts, no eight-hour days. Rochefort himself might work thirty-six hours at a time or longer, his only break coming with a brief rest on a cot tucked in one corner near his desk. The twenty-four-hour workday became a normal routine, most of the men allowed by Rochefort to perform a full day's work followed by a day's rest or recreation. Many of the men let off steam in Honolulu, but the days of wide-open bars and the party atmosphere of Hotel Street had passed. Now the island was ordered into darkness each night, defense against anything the Japanese might try to do. And so, recreation was usually low-key, dinners and quiet parties, and rarely with anyone taking part who didn't already work within Rochefort's crew. If there was one requirement of all these men, it was that they keep their duty to themselves. Anything that took place in the Dungeon was top secret.

The room was almost always a fog of cigarette and cigar smoke, and of course, pungent and fruity pipe smoke, Rochefort's own vice of choice. There were no windows, of course, and to one side of the room was an enormous air vent that seemed to exist solely for decoration. With the scarcity of fresh air, the smoke became a thick layer of fog against the ceiling, but no one seemed to mind, nearly everyone making his own contribution.

As though to offset the dreariness of the long hours, the room was always shiveringly cold. This was not by choice, though many assumed it was a conspiracy by Rochefort himself. In fact, the air-conditioning in the Dungeon was simply faulty, and with no working air vent, the temperature dropped severely every night and stayed that way through most of the daylight hours.

Rochefort's personal style surprised any new man, especially the enlisted men. As Rochefort eased into his own desk, his shoes came off, replaced by bedroom slippers. Since he rarely wore a formal uniform anyway, it was not all that unusual to observe him slipping his arms into a dark red smoking jacket. He never seemed to acknowledge his unusual dress to anyone in the Dungeon. It was simply what he wore. The casual dress had quickly become contagious. Even the enlisted men were allowed dungarees, and none of the officers were expected to don neckties. The only man who still offered Rochefort the formal "aye aye, sir" was CPO Rorie. To everyone else, Rochefort insisted on a first-name basis, in all directions. Whether you were a twenty-year-old petty officer or a thirty-five-year-old lieutenant, that was an adjustment that took some time.

Rochefort wiped at his face, shivered, the smoking jacket not nearly as effective as it had been most of the day. He looked out at the men closest to him, one man's desk piled high with IBM cards, the man completely hidden behind his makeshift mountain. Beside him was another desk, the cards arranged neatly in narrow boxes, the officer studying a single card, making a note on another pad of paper, and sliding the card into the box. The cards were arranged according to each man's routine, and Rochefort would never dictate just how the job was to be done. But it was a study in contrast, two men accomplishing the same work with wildly different personal habits. Rochefort didn't care as long as they accomplished their goals—to discover just what the Japanese were planning to do next.

The door slid open slowly, and Rochefort's first instinct always was to be annoyed at the interruption. There was little time for anything else; CPO Rorie was at the doorway, inspecting the intruder. Rochefort could see past and was surprised to see daylight. He looked toward another of his officers, said, "What time is it?"

"0840, Joe."

"No kidding?"

Rorie backed away from the doorway, with a glance toward Rochefort. "Sir, Commander Layton is suggesting in the strongest terms that you accompany his aide here to CINCPAC."

Rochefort tilted his head, and Rorie stepped aside to allow Rochefort to examine the young man. Rochefort nodded slowly. "You're Ensign Holroyd, right?"

The young man seemed surprised Rochefort remembered his name. No one else was surprised at all. "Yes, sir. Commander Layton insists you accompany me . . ."

"I heard it already, Ensign. I assume Layton's got some coffee perked?"

The ensign's attention seemed to wander, eyes scanning the vast variety of work being done, and the odd variety of men doing it. Rochefort had no patience for the curious. "Eyes front, son. You bring a car?"

"Uh, certainly, sir."

"You old enough to drive?"

"Of course, sir."

"Layton say what he wants?"

Holroyd didn't seem to know how to respond, and Rochefort weighed the options: whether to follow the young man or kick him out. Rorie seemed to read his mind and picked up the usual routine. "Shall I shoot him, sir?"

Rochefort smiled for the first time, reacting to the sudden terror on the young man's face. He slipped the smoking jacket off, put his khaki jacket on, then his shoes, following the same pattern. "All right, squirt, let's go. But if Layton doesn't have coffee, you'll be finding some."

HEADQUARTERS, CINCPAC (COMMANDER IN CHIEF, PACIFIC), ADMIRAL CHESTER NIMITZ, PEARL HARBOR, HAWAII—APRIL 20, 1942

Commander Edwin Layton had been Rochefort's acquaintance, if not best friend, since the early 1920s, both men doing a lengthy stint in Japan as part of the navy's language study program. It was the entryway to what they did now, Rochefort a level below Layton, who answered directly to Admiral Nimitz. Both Layton and Rochefort had been assigned the discreet job of interpreting and deciphering Japanese military messages. Often Rochefort led the way, snippets of Japanese communication labored over by his crew, hoping to find a greater meaning than what the Japanese themselves might have intended. And there were the oddly specific messages, the language clear, but the meaning completely obtuse.

The complex labor involved in deciphering just what the Japanese were talking about was, of course, the very reason for Rochefort's Dungeon. But he was not alone. In Washington there were crews at work as well, and whether or not Rochefort ignored those people, they most definitely did not ignore him. A rivalry had built up, but there was nothing playful or sporting about it. The Washington group known as OP-20-G was supposed to work in coordination with Rochefort's group, known as HYPO, the navy's code for "H," which naturally meant Hawaii. As part of the routine, Rochefort would send interpretations and decryptions to his counterparts in Washington and, presumably, they would do the same for him. He knew it was his duty to play ball with them, even if they had demonstrated clearly that they had little interest in playing ball with him.

"You got coffee?"

"I got coffee, I got scotch, bourbon, and pineapple wine. Well, maybe the marines took the wine. They'll drink anything."

It was a common joke, Rochefort rarely drinking due to chronic belly problems he never seemed to overcome.

Layton looked past Rochefort and said, "That's all, Ensign. Forget everything you did for the last hour. You hear me?"

"Of course, sir."

Rochefort said, "Except that chief petty officer. Tex. Remember him. He hates people who talk too much."

"Absolutely, sir."

The ensign moved away, the door closing. Rochefort sat down and Layton said, "Jesus, Joe. You look like hell. Worse hell than usual. I was hoping you'd put on a tie. The admiral wants to see us both. He needs a confidence booster. Right now, I'm not sure what he'll think." Layton fumbled through a drawer, retrieved a black tie. "Here. Do it. It matters."

"I thought HYPO matters. We don't wear ties."

"Oh, for Chrissakes, Joe. Put on the damn tie. You want Admiral

Nimitz to take you seriously, at least try to look like you're in the navy."

Layton stood, moved out from behind his desk. Rochefort put on the tie and watched Layton straighten his ever-present glasses. "You still look like a bank clerk."

Layton laughed. "And you look like the guy who'd rob the bank. Let's go."

They moved down the corridor, past office clerks and their commanders gathered around typewriters, navigating through all the business of running the Pacific command. Rochefort had made this walk many times, and so far, his impression of Admiral Nimitz was a positive one. Nimitz had stepped into the unenviable role of the permanent replacement for Admiral Husband Kimmel, the man now being pilloried in every corner of the country as the scapegoat for the surprise attack on Pearl Harbor. When Kimmel was relieved, his immediate replacement had been the battleship fleet commander, Admiral William Pye. It was a strange irony to Rochefort that the navy would select a man to command the Pacific fleet, even temporarily, whose greatest experience was commanding the one part of that fleet that had been so crushed by the Japanese. Worse for Pye, once Nimitz took command, Nimitz took immediate steps to remove the battleship fleet out of Hawaii altogether. Whether Pye appreciated the lesson or Nimitz's logic, Nimitz and the rest of the navy understood just how badly they had been beaten by the Japanese, and that the battleship had become obsolete. Any war fought at sea was likely to be won by the airplanes and the carriers that brought them. As the navy's wounded battleships were gradually pulled from the mud at Pearl Harbor and hurried back into useful service, Pye was ordered to sail them out of Pearl Harbor altogether, adding to the undamaged fleet now assigned to anchor in the port of San Francisco. Nimitz seemed to understand the obvious: Keeping battleships at Pearl Harbor just made them targets.

Rochefort followed Layton, saw eyes glance his way, smiles directed at him, and thought, What's so damned important about a tie?

The marine guard was familiar, wore no expression, pulled open the door into the admiral's outer office. An officer stood, Lieutenant Kickliter, another of Nimitz's many aides. Layton acknowledged the man, who said, "Commander. He's expecting you."

Rochefort looked back toward the marine guard, who pretended not to be checking him over. He followed Layton past the lieutenant's desk and saw Kickliter back away, giving him an odd look as he scanned Rochefort up and down. Rochefort realized he hadn't bathed in more than two days, not unusual for him. Well, hell, he thought. I can't do everything right.

Nimitz was behind his desk and he hung up his telephone, sat back. He was a plainly handsome man, with sharp blue eyes that seemed to read everything in the room. There was nothing that showed Rochefort he had a sense of humor, which suited Rochefort just fine. It was something they mostly had in common.

Nimitz pointed toward a pair of chairs. "Have a seat, gentlemen." The wait was brief and Nimitz looked at Rochefort. "You're doing good work over there, so Commander Layton tells me."

"Thank you, sir. I'd prefer he didn't do that."

Layton squirmed in his chair, and Nimitz seemed surprised by the answer. "Commander, the first time I met you, right after my appointment here, was in your domain, your *Dungeon*. Not the most inviting place, and you weren't the most inviting host. But I'll overlook that anytime, if you can keep this command informed just what the hell is going on out there. You made a good call about the Japanese movements into the Indian Ocean, and you correctly forecasted their invasion of Rabaul."

"Thank you, Admiral, but we're not always right. I regret there have been serious lapses."

"If you mean Pearl, 7 December, you're right. But let that go,

Commander. This whole navy and half of Washington bears that guilt."

Not like I do, he thought. But it wasn't an argument to make with an admiral.

"Point is, Commander, you and Commander Layton need to keep doing what you're doing." He motioned toward Layton, who seemed to straighten in his chair. "He reports to me every day, and even if he doesn't announce the fact, I know that much of what he's telling me comes from you and your people. It isn't necessary for you to confirm that." Nimitz paused. "You know, I've asked Commander Layton just what kind of work is involved with decryption and all of that. He lost me in the first sentence. I'm not willing to let that go. So, Commander Rochefort, I would appreciate some attempt on your part to tell me what your people are doing. You've hit the nail on the head most of the time in figuring out where the Japs are going to be, what they're doing there, and how many ships it's taking them to do it. How do you figure it out? And don't worry. Nothing you tell me is going anywhere else. Admiral King has been sending me decodes and all that from his people in Washington, and much of it has turned out to be wrong. If you tell me to keep that to myself, I will. Surely they'll be right once in a while, but so far, my money's on you. But . . . if I'm going to take you seriously and commit naval forces against an enemy who doesn't seem to know how to lose, I would prefer to understand why I should trust you. In other words, Commander Rochefort, what the hell are you people doing over there that makes you so damn smart?"

Layton was looking at him with a broad smile, but there was no smile from Nimitz.

"Well, sir, there is an awful lot going on with my people. Nobody can do it all."

"Do *what* all, Commander? I'm just trying to understand why I should pay attention to what Commander Layton's telling me.

You have a dartboard over there? Dice? Fortune tellers with crystal balls?"

Rochefort knew he had no choice but a straightforward response. "Sir, we're currently working with the JN-25 code, what the Japanese have been using for a while now. That has allowed us the luxury of chipping away at the meaning of more and more of the encrypts. You mentioned Rabaul. After a great deal of effort, we have been able to determine that the Japanese call sign for Rabaul was RR. Similarly, Truk is PT, and Palau is PP. As these indicators are used, it provides us a reasonably clear picture of where the Japanese are focusing their attention. We are carefully watching for the MO designation, which we are convinced is Port Moresby. That is a likely target, since it sits in a strategic position for northeast Australia."

Nimitz seemed unconvinced. "How did you get PT to mean Truk?"

Rochefort hated this kind of question. He looked down, ignored Layton. "Sir, the Japanese have gone to great lengths to develop an effective and complicated code. They use a five-digit code that they encipher after it is placed into their typical code, and before it is actually transmitted. To encipher their message, they use columns of one hundred thousand mixed five-digit numbers arranged in a random pattern. When the message is to be sent in simple code, the sender selects a start point in the table, and subtracts that number from the table using successive code groups. When the message is received on the other end, he needs only to know the starting point in the enciphering column, reversing the process and adding the deciphering five-digit numbers from the table, so as to obtain the plain code. After that, it's simple for the receiver to translate the code."

Nimitz stared at him for a long moment, and Rochefort ignored the fresh smile on Layton's face. "Is that *all*, Commander? It's that . . . simple?"

"Well, Admiral, while a hundred thousand random numbers are certainly adequate for their purposes, the Japanese really only use a third or so of that number, and we have determined that they are using five-digit numbers that are mathematically divisible by three. That means they can check themselves for errors, since if a digit is received that does not divide by three, it is incorrect."

Nimitz leaned back in his chair. "You have how many men under your command?"

"One hundred four, sir."

"They all think like you do?"

Layton interrupted, "Admiral, no one thinks the way he does."

"No doubt. But you have a second-in-command over there? Somebody who could fill in if something should happen to you?"

It seemed an odd question, and Rochefort said, "Yes, sir, more or less. There is no strict chain of command, but the most senior officer is Commander Tom Dyer. He and I share much of our own workload. There are others of course, but most are extremely specialized."

Layton laughed. "And he knows all their names. Sir, Commander Dyer is the one I told you about. Has the sign over his work table. *You don't have to be crazy to work here—but it helps.*"

Nimitz had no smile, said, "I have two things to tell you, Commander. Commander Layton is under the strictest security regarding this information; thus, I'm certain you are unaware. Two days ago, sixteen B-25 Mitchell bombers were launched from the carrier *Hornet*. They made a lengthy one-way flight over Japan, where they made bombing runs over a variety of targets. The mission was commanded by Lieutenant Colonel Jimmie Doolittle, and by all accounts, he accomplished exactly what we intended. With one notable exception. The flight was a one-way mission only because the bombers could not return and land on the deck of a carrier. The plan was for the flight to take them safely across the Sea of Japan to designated friendly airfields in China. From what little we can determine, none of the aircraft survived, though many of their crews have reached friendly hands."

Rochefort felt a stab in his stomach. "Why was I not told of this, sir?"

"Commander, what you are told or not told is not for you to question. Secrecy was absolutely essential. You have more than a hundred men in your command. Are they locked away at night? I am telling you this now for one very good reason. The Japanese are winning this war. That is a fact. We have hit them occasionally, a wild goose chase through the Marshall Islands. But the engagements that matter, the ones that cost ships and planes and lives . . . we have very little to show for what they've done to us." He paused. "Commander Layton knows this, so I'll keep it brief. When I was assigned here, I flew into Pearl Harbor with a little bit of a fantasy of being met with brass bands and flags flying. What I saw sickened me. They were still pulling bodies out of the harbor. What I saw was defeat, gentlemen. We were whipped by a superior force, strategically and tactically. And Pearl was only the beginning. The British have been shoved all the way to Ceylon. The Australians are practically afraid to leave their own ports. That's why the Doolittle mission was so important. We had to strike back in any way we could, to let them know we're still alive out here. It will be extremely useful to know their reaction to the Doolittle mission. I would anticipate public outrage and private embarrassment. Your observation and listening posts are very likely to be inundated with a flood of broadcasts, as the Japs try to figure out what the hell happened to their perfect little world. They will talk about revenge, to be certain. They have been shamed and they react badly to that, wouldn't you agree, Commander?"

"I would think they would react in a very forceful way, sir."

"Count on it. We expect something dynamic, some action on their part so they can show the world that they're not going to be pushed around. Or some such nonsense. I am expecting your team to tell us what they're planning, where, when, and with how much force."

"We will work on it, sir. Right now, we're able to glean the clear meaning of roughly ten percent of what we intercept. With extra effort, we should push that number higher. Fifteen, even twenty percent, as long as they don't change their codes."

Nimitz stared at him. "Ten percent? What the hell are you talking about?"

Layton lowered his head. The message was clear. *You're on your own.*

"Well, sir, with the volume of material we're working with, with so much effort being made every day to handle the intercepts and transmissions we're receiving, I am quite satisfied that ten percent is an excellent result. Of course, until that number improves, the other ninety percent requires some intuition, which is where I focus much of my own time. Filling in the blanks, so to speak."

Nimitz still stared at him. "The longer you're at this, the greater your success rate, is that it?"

"Well, sir, our success rate depends much more on intuition. The labor provides us the ten or fifteen percent. I do my best to come up with the rest."

Nimitz glanced at Layton. "And that's how you came up with Rabaul and Truk and the rest?"

Rochefort shrugged. "Yes, sir." He paused. "Um, sir, if this Doolittle thing is going to stir up the Japs a bit, I had better get back to work. With your permission."

Nimitz looked at Layton now, said, "You're dismissed, both of you. And Commander Layton, make damn sure nothing bad happens to this man. I have a feeling there aren't too many birds like you two in the whole damn navy."

FOUR

Yamamoto

Commander Yasuji Watanabe was tall and thin, with a toothy grin even when no one else seemed to find anything humorous. On Yamamoto's staff, he was substantially more popular than Captain Kuroshima, the man who seemed never to bathe and who surrounded himself with a fog of cigarette smoke and a snowfall of ashes. That the two men should be close friends made no sense at all to Yamamoto, any more than it did to his chief of staff, Admiral Ugaki. But they worked well together, as much as they did apart. Kuroshima had tackled this new challenge from Yamamoto with the same fearless resolve that had driven him to create much of the planning for the assault on Pearl Harbor. Now he would pull together the new plan, still with aircraft and their carriers, and still to be protected by the might of Yamamoto's fleet. The new strategy would engulf the small pair of islands the Americans called Midway, a square mile of land that served one primary purpose: an airfield and a launch point for American aircraft that could patrol an area more than twelve hundred miles closer to the islands now in Japanese possession. And Midway would serve as a buffer, a front-line observation point against any Japanese movements toward Hawaii from the northwest. The argument against Japanese capture of the islands was that few in the Naval Ministry believed that once it was occupied, Midway could actually be held. If Midway was to become a staging area for strikes against Hawaii, it was logical to assume it could work the other way around. Another significant argument against any attempt to establish a base at Midway was the challenge for the Japanese in resupplying their forces there, so far from home. Any transport or supply ship would have to cross a great deal of empty ocean that was certainly patrolled by American submarines.

But Kuroshima's plan had the one champion whose voice mattered most. The plan had originated with Yamamoto, and it was Yamamoto who drove that point through the heart of the Naval Ministry. As had happened the year before, when Yamamoto's Pearl Harbor plan had run into a brick wall of opposition from his superiors, the force of his will and his unequaled popularity within the navy made him too powerful for those who opposed him. The attack on Pearl Harbor of course had finally been approved. Now his plans for Midway, and the specifics designed by Captain Kuroshima, had gone through the same theater, opponents making their arguments, offering far more logical alternatives, or simply lashing out at the flaws in any plan Yamamoto offered them.

There was an infuriating consistency to the Naval Ministry's regard for Yamamoto and his strategies, opponents who dismissed him with an odd contempt, as though the only man in their service who had actually won victories should be paid little respect at all. Throughout the inevitable debates, other plans were given great voice. There was insistence that the combined fleet focus their attacks on various islands, including Samoa and Fiji, which lay directly on the shipping route between the United States and Australia. Even more radically, some of the naval chiefs trumpeted plans for an invasion of Australia itself. The naval ministers and admirals seemed infected by the absurd belief that nothing could go wrong with any plan that had come from their own brilliant minds. Oddly, it was the army who drilled some logic into all the premature celebrations. If there was to be an invasion, especially of a land the size of Australia, there would be soldiers, not sailors, to carry the load. With that kind of veto power over most of the ideas being spouted by the Naval Ministry, eyes began to turn once more to Yamamoto. But the army had never been convinced that Yamamoto could serve their wishes any more than could the Naval Ministry. Yamamoto's entire plan revolved partly around the capture of Midway using the army's troops. That threw up a familiar obstacle that brought wrath down on him from the generals.

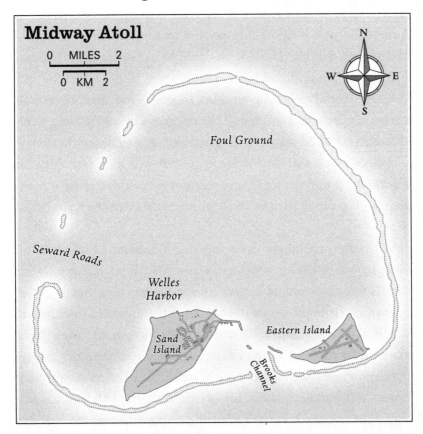

Midway Atoll

0 MILES 2

0 KM 2

N

W   E

S

Foul Ground

Seward Roads

Welles
Harbor

Sand
Island

Eastern Island

Brooks
Channel

Throughout the month of March, and well into April, Yamamoto found himself mired in yet another stalemate of ideas, the
sort of morass that had pushed him to threaten his resignation the
fall before. Then the threat had worked, and his plan for the attack
on Pearl Harbor had been given reluctant approval. Now it wasn't
completely necessary for him to go that far, though his own staff,
as frustrated as he was, had pushed him in that direction. But this
time, Yamamoto actually had support, though tepid, from some
of the ministers, who had full appreciation of Yamamoto's resolve.
Their objections to his new plan seemed to fade away under pressure from Yamamoto's own lobbying and that of his staff officers,
especially the jovial and persuasive Watanabe. Yamamoto kept
himself mostly in the background, and allowed Kuroshima and his
cigarettes to do much of the wrangling alongside Watanabe, a
contrast in personalities that proved extremely effective. Yamamoto knew that his staff officers could be as persuasive as he was,
and that no matter his absence, his presence would always be felt.
While he would never slap anyone's face with the obvious, they all
knew that there was risk for all the ministers in confronting a cel-
ebrated hero—the man who had succeeded in crushing the American fleet in Hawaii. In his favor as well was an odd confusion
among the ministry that Japan's military success had been so complete and so rapid, they weren't too sure just what they should do
next.

With the arguments dragging on, Yamamoto had revisited
thoughts of resigning, whether or not his entire staff went with
him. Rumors spread, of course, and as he expected, much of the
opposition from the ministry and naval chiefs seemed to crumble.
When Doolittle's sixteen American bombers made their fiery
mark on Japanese cities with such astonishing suddenness, the arguments from Yamamoto's most ardent opponents simply collapsed, and suddenly the army attached themselves to whatever
Yamamoto wanted. He despised the army, down to the lowliest

private, and looked with contempt upon anyone who slung a rifle over his shoulder and pretended that it made him a warrior. But the generals were the worst of all, the men who offered the navy nothing, no credit, no praise for the victories that Yamamoto and his ships had brought them. And, of course, the most powerful general was also the prime minister, Hideki Tojo, the strongman who truly ruled Japan, who pushed the emperor to do his bidding. Yet, suddenly, Yamamoto was their hero, as they sought to understand his new strategy that would win not only the navy's war, but their own.

If the Americans were to be prevented from sending planes over Japan, it would be necessary to eliminate the vehicles that brought them close enough to make war: their aircraft carriers. And that was the backbone of Yamamoto's planning for the capture of Midway. They would create a lure that the Americans could not resist, offering them a target they would have to engage with their carriers.

At Pearl Harbor, Japan's targets had been offered to them by default—the American battleships. That mission had been mostly successful, but to Yamamoto, the mission had been a failure; no matter how many battleships the Japanese planes sent to the bottom of the harbor, the American aircraft carriers had escaped altogether. They simply weren't there.

He sat in his quarters, restless, an unopened bottle of sake on the table beside him. It was yet another gift from some admirer, this time some nameless naval officer seeking some favor. That's what they do, he thought. Certainly, they should. Why not, after all? They have earned promotions, so many of them, while the generals have their meetings and waste their time instructing the newspapers how to lie to the people.

He stood, took a glance at the sake, and thought, No, give it to

Omi. He earns it, too. After all, he must clean up after *me*. He stepped out into the smell of grease and cleaning fluid, the crews doing their work every hour of the day to keep the flagship as gloriously shiny as possible. He stepped past a man carrying a soapy bucket, the man surprised and backing up, splashing gray water toward Yamamoto's feet. The man's eyes were wide, full of apology, and Yamamoto stepped over the spreading puddle, saying nothing. He moved out into the open air, and saw many more of the crew attending their duties. Beyond lay the city of Hiroshima, silhouetted by an orange sunset that bathed the land and the water around him.

He leaned his hands onto the rail, shook his head, and said in a low voice, "Yes, the Americans will bring more fire to this glorious place. Those B-25s were only once, a test, perhaps even a *game*. There will be many more very soon. We must stop them or this will end very quickly, very badly." He glanced around, shook his head. They do not need to see their commander in chief talking out loud to himself. Perhaps that is why I found approval at the ministry. They think I am mad. Perhaps all those fat men in the big chairs have become afraid of me. It is, after all, how we think in this country. The most powerful man is the man who scares you. I suppose that cannot hurt. But my strategy must be allowed to move forward yet again. I want no games, no ridiculous clashing of swords with the army and the Naval Ministry. They must understand what is so obvious. To win, we must *win*.

ONBOARD BATTLESHIP *YAMATO*, HIROSHIMA BAY—APRIL 23, 1942

"I should prefer, Admiral, if my men were granted some rest. They have earned every luxury by their skill in destroying the enemy. They have proven once and for all that our navy is invincible."

Yamamoto slumped in his chair, glanced at Nagumo, and wondered if the man was finally through making speeches. Nagumo seemed to slump as well, and Yamamoto thought, He looks so much older now. Perhaps he thinks the same of me. He struggled to say something positive, finally the words coming. "You did well with the fleet in the Indian Ocean. I am certain that you have destroyed the British will to fight us further. If there is an enemy now that we must point to, it is the Americans. And that is why there will be no rest. We are fighting a war, not playing in some kind of Olympic games. We do not take time to march in parades and polish each other's medals. And, Admiral Nagumo, despite what our newspapers say, or what you would have us believe, no one's navy is invincible. We have won victories. But do not assume it will always be that way."

Nagumo seemed chastened, but Yamamoto wasn't ready to let him go. He glanced to the side, the younger faces studying him, some of them watching Nagumo. Commander Genda caught his eye; the young flyer, the man who knew everything about the airplane and what kind of weapon it could be. He sat with the rest of the staff officers around the far end of the table, along with his chief of staff, Ugaki, and the junior men, Watanabe, and of course, the ever-present shroud of cigarette smoke that engulfed Kuroshima. Admiral Nagumo was flanked by two of his own aides, men who seemed to resent being summoned to the flagship on such short notice.

Yamamoto was already weary of the interview, knew that Nagumo would offer him little else. "I would point out to you, Admiral Nagumo, that there are many, including officers on this ship, who believe that the attack on the American navy at Pearl Harbor was a failure. Enormous mistakes were made."

Nagumo seemed to inflate, as though needing to defend his honor. His aides mimicked the move, obligated to defend him.

Nagumo said, "Sir, I cannot believe there would be such talk. The emperor himself offered his congratulations to the *Kido Butai*. And to me."

Yamamoto could feel weakness in Nagumo's voice, and thought, Protest all you want. You know it's true. "I don't refer, Admiral, to our decision not to engage the American force with an additional strike. I refer to our failure to discover the location of their aircraft carriers. Three carriers, at least, and not one dent in any of them. That error will come to haunt us. It haunts me now. Burying battleships into the mud of that harbor did nothing to win us this war. Do you disagree?"

Nagumo looked at the far end of the table, seemed to know he would get no support from Yamamoto's men. "Had we sunk their carriers, it would have been a better thing, yes."

Yamamoto stared at him, thought, Where is his fire? I have insulted his honor, and he sits there like some fat potato. But I have no choice. He is the senior admiral available, and he is the emperor's hero. "Well, Admiral, we shall sink those carriers now. Perhaps this time, our effort will be more precise, more logical, more . . . brilliant. Captain Kuroshima has developed much of the upcoming plan." He looked to the far end of the table. "Captain, summarize for Admiral Nagumo. Explain why his men do not have the luxury of a few weeks of recreation."

Kuroshima stood, boiling with smoky confidence, his hand sweeping away a pile of ash to the deck behind him. "Admiral Yamamoto, the plan that the Naval Ministry has approved and which I have been honored to assist with calls for an enormous flotilla of ships, the entire *Kido Butai*, as well as a great many more support vessels. This will include of course four attack carriers, which will carry the aircraft that will be in position to attack the American carriers as they present themselves. The flotilla will consist of four parts. Seeking out the American carriers is the highest priority.

"However, a second part of the flotilla will transport three thousand army troops for an amphibious landing on the island of Midway, to occupy and strengthen the airfield and other defensive facilities. Prior to the landings, the island's defenders will be decimated by aerial assault, eliminating any defensive capability by the Americans.

"A third part of this flotilla shall sail north toward the Bering Sea to destroy American defenses along the Aleutian Island chain and then occupy at least two islands for use as a staging area for airstrikes against American cities along their west coast.

"The fourth part of the armada will include this flagship and a formidable force of steel strength in the form of battleships and other combat vessels. In addition to all of this, there will be a fleet of submarines, sent forward to observe and possibly destroy any American effort that emerges from Hawaii. They will position themselves to act as a screen to prevent any surprise action by the Americans."

Yamamoto was dismayed. "Captain, I had hoped for a more detailed report, numbers of ships, locations, and so forth. I know you have such documents. Make them available to Admiral Nagumo at once." He wanted to stand, to address them with the kind of formality they deserved. But Nagumo's gloom seemed to drain strength from all of them. "There are many parts to this puzzle, gentlemen. We are relying on those things in which we excel, our pilots, our carriers, our submarines."

"Sir."

He did not expect to hear from Commander Genda. "Commander? You have something to add?"

Genda stood, full of the manic energy he brought to every encounter. "If we keep to the timetable as planned, intending to assault Midway and the American fleet by 3 or 4 June, I am concerned that our pilots are not adequately trained. There just isn't time to prepare them."

Nagumo said, "I would agree. We are moving too quickly."

Yamamoto sat back, thought, It's the first time those two have ever agreed on anything. "I note your observation, but I will not change our timetable. We will move quickly, because speed is essential. This entire operation relies on utmost secrecy, something you all remember from the Pearl Harbor operation. Now, there are American warships and submarines in places we can only predict. We will not wait. Commander Genda, you are a master at training fliers. I have confidence in you to do that with exceptional skill."

Across from him, one of Nagumo's aides said, "Forgive me, Admiral, but why don't we just bomb Hawaii again? If the American carriers are there, we might succeed where we did not before. And even if we ignore their ships, a bombing assault will certainly terrify them into believing we can do that at any time."

"You mean like they can do to us? You are forgiven for having been well out on the high seas when the American B-25s tore across our rooftops last week." Yamamoto was angry now, tried to control his breathing. "Perhaps, Commander, you are unaware that we did bomb Hawaii for a second time, on 4 March. Two long-range flying boats made the raid, and from the observers we have on Oahu, they succeeded in dropping their bombs in a grove of trees up on some desolate mountainside. I assure you all, the Americans have seen our bombs, just as we have now seen theirs. No one is terrified of bombs. No one is simply going to quit. We have a war to win. If that terrifies you, perhaps find work elsewhere."

He tried not to see the shock on the man's face, knew he had gone too far. There was awkward silence, the young commander forcing himself to hold his tongue. Yamamoto turned to Kuroshima again. "There is one crucial ingredient which must be emphasized to all the task force commands." He looked again at Nagumo. "If we reveal our hand too quickly, if the Americans are made aware that we are sailing to Midway with an enormous force, a force they cannot confront, they are likely to stay home, keep to the defensive position at Pearl Harbor. While that would allow us an easy capture of Midway, it would defeat our greater purpose here, which is to destroy their carrier fleet. Everyone must perform his duty precisely on schedule. Do you understand?"

Nagumo nodded. It was not the kind of energy Yamamoto was hoping to see. "You are dismissed. Admiral Ugaki, please remain."

He sat back, waited as the others filed out, Nagumo first, trailed by the aide who forced himself to hide his anger at Yamamoto's insult.

Ugaki slid closer, said, "Be careful, sir. That one, he's one of those young Turks, puts great faith in the blade."

"Perhaps he would do me a favor."

Ugaki seemed surprised, but he had heard these kinds of pronouncements before. "Sir, I am not at all pleased that Admiral Nagumo should be the commander of the *Kido Butai*. He is a man past his time, a man who smells of defeat." Ugaki paused. "I find I can never forgive him, sir. I have tried, all manner of exercise, explaining, justifying, trying to convince myself that he had no choice. But it is not to be."

Yamamoto looked at him. "Pearl Harbor?"

"Yes, sir. If he had listened to the pilots, to the warriors, there could have been another strike, the Americans could have been crippled even more. Or, if he had made some attempt to locate the carriers outside of Hawaii. Any first-year military academy cadet would know that in a disaster, the Americans would summon their carriers to return home. He could have waited two days, maybe three. He feared the American planes, when we know they had meager training, and that we had already destroyed most of their aircraft on the ground. Forgive me, sir, but his actions, or lack of actions, were outrageous. And so, we would not be engaged in a new plan, a far more difficult and complicated plan."

"It will work, Matome. And we have the approval of all those who claim to matter. My *superiors*."

"Do they really support this? Are they just reacting to the American bombs?"

"Does it matter? The plan will go ahead. However, if it will make you feel better, more confident, I shall put you in charge of war games next week. I will invite every senior officer who is available, and we shall demonstrate how the assault on Midway will be our greatest achievement. I keep hearing that our navy is invincible, a word that makes me very uncomfortable. But if I am right, if this plan is successful, then perhaps that description is true."

Ugaki seemed to accept Yamamoto's logic and said, "Thank you for your confidence, sir. I shall conduct the war games, as you ask. I must ask, sir, am I to make use of six carriers or four?"

"Four. I have approved the ministry's request to send the other two southward to take part in the assault on Port Moresby. In the next few days, they should sail into the Coral Sea."

As the remainder of Admiral Nagumo's force returned home from their extraordinary success in the Indian Ocean, the naval ministers continued to insist that no matter Yamamoto's overall plans for Midway, the ports in and around New Guinea and the Dutch East Indies were still of paramount importance. Rabaul, on the island of New Britain, had been secured, but the larger and more useful port of Port Moresby, on the southeastern peninsula of New Guinea, was still a formidable obstacle, defended by land and air forces of Australia. The Japanese had no reason to believe that there would be any real difficulty securing the capture of Port Moresby, which would hand the Japanese a base in easy striking range of northeast Australia. The only possible obstacle would be intervention by a force of American warships or carriers. So far, the Japanese had no knowledge that any Americans were there.

FIVE

Nimitz

The trip had worn him out, but there had been no other option. When Admiral King summoned you, you simply showed up. They had met in San Francisco, and of course, with King flying in from Washington, meeting Nimitz halfway, King would have the upper hand even more than usual. As Roosevelt's new chief of naval operations, Ernest King didn't need to offer anyone a compromise.

Nimitz had learned to work well with King, something many others found nearly impossible. King could be stern and unyielding, acerbic and belittling, but as time had passed, the man who had replaced Harold Stark had satisfied the president that he could more than handle the job. Nimitz had to agree.

Nimitz's mode of travel had been by flying boat, a plodding and bouncing ride, accented by brutal cold and a miserably uncomfortable seat. He sat at his desk now, flexed a sore tailbone, thought, King wouldn't have put up with that. He'd have ordered the air to warm up, the seat to absorb more of his fanny. He stood, fought through the fog from his lack of sleep, and moved to the window overlooking the submarine base. He searched through the formations of *fish*, but there were too many, too crowded, with some moving out of the harbor even now. A simpler time, he thought. Well, didn't think so then. But your sub command was a very long time ago. Thirty years? Well, that's depressing, I suppose. Best keep that to yourself. Best you can do for those fellows now is watch them head out to sea to hunt for the bad guys. I always thought being in charge was a good thing. Not so sure now.

He had come to Pearl to officially relieve Admiral Kimmel, a decision made in Washington that could have inspired something of a mutiny among Kimmel's diehard supporters in Hawaii. A great many naval officers, from Hawaii to D.C., were convinced that Kimmel had been given the bum's rush. The American people needed a scapegoat for the Pearl Harbor disaster, and he was the right man. Those were the shoes Nimitz stepped into, accepting the job with considerable hesitation. The pressure from his closest friends was relentless. Even his wife, Catherine, had kept reminding him that for years he had dreamed of receiving a significant command, and this was certainly that. But the nerves continued, Nimitz reminding his wife that a large part of the fleet he was now to command lay on the bottom of the sea. Or, at least, the floor of the harbor.

He still scanned the submarines, but there was little to tell them apart; that subtlety was done on purpose to keep their identity obscured from prying eyes.

It has to be one of them, he thought. Maybe . . . over there, moored with those other two. He shook his head. Or maybe not. Does it matter? It's not yours to captain. Not anymore.

It had been New Year's Eve, not quite four months ago. The

change of command was one of those particular ceremonies the navy excelled at. The official transfer of command away from Admiral Kimmel had taken place on the deck of the sub USS *Grayling*. The choice of the vessel had been Nimitz's, a salute to his own experience years before and his effort to boost morale in the service that few seemed to regard as essential. The *essential* ships were of course the battleships, and he could see the hulking black skeleton that was all that remained of the *Arizona*. Well, I suppose the Japanese agreed with that. He turned away from the window, thought, If we are to win, we have to learn how, all over again. The Japanese have figured it out. For all intents and purposes, they've been unstoppable, and we've been awful at adapting.

There was a short knock on the door, and a young voice said, "Sir, excuse me. Admiral Halsey is here."

Nimitz felt a small burst of energy, the usual response to a visit from Halsey. "Send him in, Lieutenant. And have Admiral Draemel join us here."

Halsey was there before the young aide could leave the office. He was a short man, with enormous eyebrows and a peculiar turn to his jaw that made it appear he was preparing for a fistfight. Nimitz had never asked, but he assumed fistfights might have been common in Halsey's youth. Now, Halsey had shown Nimitz that he was likely the finest combat commander in the fleet. Nimitz hoped that talent would become contagious.

"Have a seat, Bill."

Halsey sat slowly, betraying a stiffness he tried to hide. "Good to be back. My boys need a break, Admiral. The boats too. It's a hell of a long way to the South Pacific and back."

"You came in, what? Two days ago?"

"Three. I knew you were on the mainland meeting with Admiral King, so I had to hightail it back here, in case he fired your ass. I'm probably next in line, you know."

Nimitz absorbed the odd mix of enthusiasm, sarcasm, and disrespect. He let it go. "Bill, you need to turn right around and take your task force to New Guinea, the Coral Sea. You know that Admiral Fletcher is there now, with *Yorktown* and *Lexington,* and I'm afraid that's not enough. The Japs are pushing hard to capture Port Moresby, and we can't let them. The Australians are scared to death, and Doug MacArthur wants to make that place his major base of operations. The Japs could screw up everything, and it would give them a straight shot across our supply lines to the Aussies."

Halsey rubbed a rough finger over one eyebrow, the brow not obeying. "Sir, I know you want me down there in a week or less. But you know I can't turn the *Enterprise,* the *Hornet,* and the rest of the task force around in two days. *As soon as possible* is two weeks. If Fletcher's there now, he's got the people and the ships. Do we know what the Japs are bringing to the party?"

"Two carriers, possibly three. Their own task force. Transports, certainly, for the landing at Port Moresby."

Halsey nodded slowly, staring down. "You sure Fletcher's up to the job?"

"For crying out loud, Bill, you sound like Admiral King."

"No need for insults, sir. But look, Fletcher turned back from Wake Island, he's been slow on the move when we took our shots down in the Marshalls. A pretty stout number of senior officers say that he's a little timid, not aggressive enough."

"No officers say that here, Bill. Get that straight. Don't make me chew you out, for God's sake. Neither one of you won the war down there. Both of your forces chased ghosts and Japanese fishing boats. Yes, I know, you busted up some Jap ships at Kwajalein. Good job. But the Japs aren't crying in their tea about any of that. They wounded the *Saratoga* with one lonely submarine, and now she's out of action for another month or two until we get her repaired. We haven't done much damage to anything the Japs are sending against us."

"Jesus, Admiral, I'm sure glad you didn't chew me out. If you'll allow, I'll play the only card I have. We did haul Jimmie Doolittle close to Japan, and we came home to yell about it, all of us."

It was a sore point with Nimitz, and he weighed saying what he really thought. The door opened, and he saw the smiling face of Milo Draemel, his chief of staff. Draemel seemed to read Nimitz's mood, and said to Halsey, "Greetings, Admiral. Welcome back. They gave you a hell of a reception in the harbor. You'd have thought you won the war. More sailors in white than I've ever seen. Well deserved, certainly. You sent a good flock of Jap ships to the bottom at Kwajalein."

Halsey shrugged. "Tell that to your boss. I can't even get a hand-shake for the Doolittle mission."

Halsey was smiling, deflecting anyone's anger, but Halsey knew that Nimitz had objected to the operation, had considered it an enormous waste of time and resources. Nimitz had rolled the thought through his brain a dozen times, and did so again. If Halsey had not taken two carriers that far west, they would likely be in position right now near Port Moresby, instead of needing to return to Pearl Harbor. And while Doolittle's mission was still a closely guarded secret to the American public, he was already por-trayed as a hero among the army and navy brass. But Nimitz found it hard to pat anyone on the back for a mission that cost time and resources and yielded not much more than a handful of propa-ganda. Making people feel good was, to Nimitz, a distant second to sinking ships. His job was to push the Pacific fleet to move one step ahead of the Japanese, and to that end, the Doolittle Raid ac-complished nothing at all. Whether or not it was obvious to Wash-ington, Nimitz knew that out here the Japanese were a good bit ahead of the game.

Draemel was still occupying Halsey with backslapping humor, but Halsey looked at Nimitz now, no smiles. "I'll do the best I can, you know that. We'll push to the South Pacific with all we've got.

And if you tell me you've got full confidence in Frank Jack Fletcher, well, then so do I. How do we know what the Japs are sending our way?"

Nimitz glanced at Draemel. "Good intel, Bill. Go with it."

"If you say so. I'd just hate to see any more of this Jap foolishness in this harbor. I like you better than Kimmel. Hate to see you yanked out of here."

Halsey was smiling again, and Nimitz knew it was his parting shot, to leave on a pleasant note. But there was nothing Nimitz found pleasing about Halsey's words. "Dismissed, Bill. Put your people into motion, and head out when you can."

Halsey stood. "Aye aye, sir. I'll inform you when we're ready to go."

Halsey moved past Draemel and was quickly out the door.

Draemel sat slowly, and said, "You were a little tough on him. You all right?"

"He's the best we've got. But I can't go handing out roses every time we sink a Jap minesweeper." He paused, flexed his back again. He could feel the familiar curtain of depression settling over him, said, "I'm getting out of here for a while. Maybe toss some horseshoes. Join me?"

"Certainly. Again, Admiral, are you all right?"

Nimitz thought a moment. "Not sure, Milo. We've got people and ships scattered all over the Pacific, we still have wrecked ships in the harbor, and Commander Layton keeps giving me all kinds of itchy briefings from that oddball Rochefort and his Dungeon. The Japs aren't going to just sit tight and wait for us to figure out what they're planning to do, and they won't wait for us to build a bigger navy. Whether it's Australia or right here in our backyard, we had better prepare."

"For what?"

"If I knew that, I wouldn't be so worried. Listen, arrange for me to take a quick trip up to Midway. I haven't spent any time with either of those fellows in charge, Commander Simard and the other fellow, the marine."

"Lieutenant Colonel Harold Shannon. He heads up the Marine Sixth Battalion."

"All right, good. Set it up for day after tomorrow."

"I'll take care of it, and I'll let them know you're coming."

"No, you won't. Sometimes I prefer just dropping in."

Midway was little more than a gathering of large sand dunes and a small cluster of trees where dugouts and ammo dumps had been carefully hidden. The main island was in fact two: The first was Eastern Island, an obvious name for its position relative to the slightly larger Sand Island, the second of the pair. The spits of land were nearly surrounded by a thin ribbon of coral, which encased a lagoon, a natural barrier that kept Japanese submarines or anyone else just a bit farther away. Eastern Island had been fashioned with an airstrip, capable of launching anything the Americans had, including the B-17 bombers. Sand Island was equipped with the dugouts and storage facilities that housed the seaplanes, including the large PBYs.

Nimitz's visit was brief and indeed a surprise. Both the naval and marine commanders had wondered to themselves and each other just why he had dropped in. They had accompanied him as he inspected the various storage depots, the airstrip, and any other part of the defenses he seemed curious enough to ask about. Included in his tour was a handshake moment with many of the pilots stationed there, and a good many of the marines whose primary assignment was to shoot anyone who wandered up onto the sand who simply didn't belong there. Nimitz had seemed intensely curious about one particular point, a question asked of both senior commanders. Just what would it take to keep the Japanese out of Midway? The answer was entirely predictable, especially from the marine. They would do just fine with what they had. But more would always help.

As brief as the visit was, the impact on the base and its men was enormous. It was easy for anyone assigned to Midway to believe they had been sent to some kind of sandy purgatory, forgotten about completely. Nimitz had seen it in their faces, even the hard-boiled marines showing the strain of so little to do but exercise and train, and then do it all again. But Nimitz had given them a shot of morale, and if he left them wondering just why he had come, the truth was, he didn't really know. If it was simply for morale, he could accept that, and so would every man on Midway. To emphasize their importance, though, Nimitz went one step further. After he returned, he issued promotions for both Simard and Shannon. It was more than a gesture of respect for men doing good work. It was the recognition that if the Japanese came, these men and their commands would very likely be on the front line.

HQ, CINCPAC, PEARL HARBOR, HAWAII — MAY 6, 1942

"With profound regret but continued pride in my gallant troops I go to meet with the Japanese commander. Goodbye, Mr. President.

—Jonathan Wainwright, Lt. Gen."

Layton stood in front of him, beside Draemel, both men silent. Nimitz read the paper again, and said, "This came from . . . what? Radio intercept?"

Layton nodded, and said simply, "Yes."

Nimitz stared at the paper. "This has reached Washington by now, I assume. The president knows."

Draemel said, "Surely, by now."

"Either of you know him, General Wainwright?"

Both men answered together, "No, sir."

"I've never met him, but I've been following what's been going on out there. From the time I got here, I was afraid we didn't have the strength in the Philippines to hold off the Japs. I doubt he ever had a real shot at beating them back. His back was to the wall. The Japs had all the time in the world to mass against him."

Draemel said, "What do we take from this, sir?"

Nimitz let the anger out, just for a moment. "It means we've surrendered Corregidor. It means the Japs have beaten us to a pulp in the Philippines. It means more than ten thousand Americans and Filipinos are now Jap prisoners. It means we no longer have any control in the Philippines."

His voice had risen, a hint of emotion. Draemel said, "MacArthur's safe, at least."

Nimitz fought to control the fury that the name shoved through him. "Oh, yes. Doug is safe. Doug made sure of that. I'm not sure how any captain of any ship in this navy would do that. 'Hey, you fellows, stay with this sinking ship while I take off. See you around.' I guess the army does things differently."

He knew he had crossed a line, sat back, eyes closed, rubbed a hand on his aching forehead. Don't go shooting your mouth off about anyone in the army. You'll start a very stupid war. MacArthur's a hero to an enormous number of people. Just . . . not me.

Draemel and Layton were obviously waiting for his next move, for whatever he wanted them to do. He didn't look at them, but said, "Gentlemen, return to your offices. And, of course, keep this to yourselves. It will become public soon enough, but not from me." He waited as they slipped out of the office, and said under his breath, "I hope you survive this war, General Wainwright. You went down with your ship, and for that, I'll shake your hand. But the Japs are a lot tougher than I ever thought they'd be—than *anyone* thought they'd be."

He rose, moved slowly to the window, stared at his submarines for a long moment, and said aloud, "My God, this is an awful damn day."

HQ, CINCPAC, PEARL HARBOR, HAWAII — MAY 8, 1942

Layton had arrived on the minute, the briefing every morning promptly at 0755. Nimitz could see the concern on Layton's face, said, "Sit down, Commander. Give me the bad news."

Layton obeyed, sat beside Draemel, and seemed puzzled by Nimitz's words. "Did you know there was bad news, sir?"

"Then give me the good news. Tell me anything, Commander. I'm wondering if anyone knows what on earth is going on out there. The Coral Sea can't be so gigantic that two task forces can't seem to find each other. My fear is that the Japanese know where we are, while Admiral Fletcher doesn't have the first clue where they might be. That's what I'm going to hear from Washington, I promise you. Admiral King isn't all too thrilled I sent Fletcher out in command of this potential engagement. So far, all you've told me about Fletcher's messages are that he says he's doing fine, or maybe good, that he's shot down a Jap plane, or maybe not, that his pilots have jumped all over a Jap fleet, or maybe not. You get the picture, Commander? What am I supposed to think? What do I tell Washington? They're picking up some of this same confusion I am. Admiral King will want answers. And when it comes to radio traffic and figuring out what's happening, that's you. What does your friend over in the Dungeon have to say? He predicted there would be a scrap down there, he pinpointed Port Moresby as a Jap target. So far, he's been spot-on. But now, there's garble and confusion. Garble from Fletcher, garble from you. I need some answers."

He didn't like the expression he saw on Layton's face. "Sir, you know that we picked up Admiral Fletcher's report that his pilots sunk a Japanese carrier. He also sent reports that *Yorktown* has been damaged, and *Lexington* might have been hit even worse."

"I heard that two days ago. Fletcher called in that it wasn't too bad, that *Yorktown* was operational, just busted up a little, and there was some concern on *Lexington* about fire. So, what's new?"

There was a soft knock, and Nimitz motioned to Draemel, who moved to the door. Nimitz saw the slip of paper handed him and knew from the color that it had come from the listening posts.

Draemel glanced at Nimitz, didn't return to the chair, and handed the paper to Layton and said, "Your people are working, Commander."

Nimitz watched as Layton unfolded the paper, saw a look on Layton's face he never hoped to see.

Layton read briefly, seemed to stare at the words for a long moment. Nimitz felt the impatience, but he kept silent, thought, He'll tell me when he can. Layton put his hand on his leg, the paper still between his fingers. "Sir, the listening posts and our own radio traffic picked up the messages this morning that *Lexington* suffered a . . . fatal explosion. Admiral Fletcher ordered her to be scuttled by torpedo. She's gone, sir."

Nimitz leaned back in his chair, stared past Layton. "Good God. Are you certain?"

Layton nodded. "Quite so, yes, sir."

Draemel sat again, soft words. "How many lost?"

Layton looked at the paper. "Doesn't say, sir. They had time to get people off, so maybe only a few."

Nimitz leaned forward, his arms on the desk. "Keep this under your hat, Commander."

"Always, sir."

"Dismissed. Keep me posted as soon as you hear anything further."

"Absolutely, sir."

Layton stood, adjusted his glasses, then paused with an obvious show of emotion. He was out the door now, and Nimitz waited for it to close, then said to Draemel, "A week ago, Fletcher was all champagne and roses about the Coral Sea, saying that he was going down there to sweep the place clean. Maybe he had to talk like that. Halsey talks like that. Fletcher knows there are quite a few people around here who don't think he can carry the load. Now, there's not much for him to do but sail back into Pearl Harbor with his tail between his legs."

Draemel kept his eyes down, said, "Admiral Halsey is still hauling it that way. If there's a fight to be had, Halsey can add some real firepower. I suppose we should tell him what's happened."

"He'll find out soon enough. We have priorities. Fletcher knows he can't just sit around and wait down there with one wounded carrier and a handful of cruisers. We still don't know how many Jap carriers are involved, but I promise you, they're smelling blood in the water. Fletcher knows he has to light it up and get *Yorktown* out of there quick as he can. Halsey can be useful in another way. I want him to sail farther west, make sure he's within range of Jap observation planes. When he knows he's been spotted, definitely spotted, he can hightail it out of there, and head back here."

"Why, sir?"

"I want the Japs to believe our whole damn carrier force is lurking around New Guinea. That should slow them down from whatever plans they have for Port Moresby. And, if they have other plans anywhere else, this might encourage them to show their hands, thinking they have open seas everywhere else."

"That's a big risk, sir."

Nimitz didn't need doubts, not now, and not from his chief of staff. "We lost a carrier, Milo. With *Saratoga* on the west coast and *Wasp* still in the Atlantic, that only leaves us with three out here. We have to take risks. We're not in control of this thing."

He wanted to stand, gaze at his submarines, but there was no energy in his legs. He knew the familiar feeling, the depression moving in, like a slow-rolling wave. "I don't envy Fletcher. He'll have to prove himself now, and sometimes that's a challenge a man can't handle. He's not a misfit, he's not what Admiral King thinks, that he's timid. I know he's better than that. Maybe he's just . . . unlucky."

Nimitz forced himself to stand, and Draemel seemed to read him, said, "How about some target shooting, sir. You aced me pretty well the last time."

Nimitz considered the offer, then shook his head. "Not now, Milo. I ought to take up boxing. Get me one of those heavy bags they use. I need to punch something."

SIX

Yamamoto

The war games had begun on the first of the month, a promise Yamamoto had made to satisfy the doubts that still infected some members of his staff, and more important, those ranking commanders of the ships that would be the essential pieces of the attack force, both Admiral Nagumo's *Kido Butai* and many others.

He was sensitive to criticism from the summer before, when his planning for the assault on Pearl Harbor had also involved elaborate war games. But Yamamoto had taken no chances then, had stifled any dissent to that plan by serving as his own referee. It was the most convenient way he could imagine to expedite his planning, by demonstrating to every officer present that the plans would succeed. That was a certainty. He made sure the war games confirmed that.

Now, the referee was his chief of staff, Admiral Ugaki, and even if Yamamoto had no direct hand in the proceedings, it was clear that Ugaki would entertain very little dissent. The games would not be left to chance, no matter who might criticize the outcome. The moves would be decided by throws of the dice, but it became apparent that the fall of the dice had very little to do with the games' outcome.

The massive ship had never entertained so many officers of rank, most of the admirals not accustomed to rubbing shoulders with either their peers or their subordinates. The lowest ranks invited to the games were full captains, who were unaccustomed to being treated like ensigns. The *Yamato* had become one grand meeting place, where, when the games were not in session, the men drifted into groups large and small, where advice was offered, tales told, bragging rights established. The mood was festive, the men confident, and through it all, Ugaki managed the proceedings with what could only be called an iron hand. For Yamamoto, his job was simplest of all. He mostly stayed out of the way.

The wardroom was thick with smoke and white uniforms, mostly older men, only the most senior allowed to participate within the wardroom itself. The others, spread throughout the ship, would receive the results of the games on paper, or if they had the right friends, they might gain some insights others would not hear.

"The next exercise will commence. Your attention please."

Around Ugaki, the voices grew quiet, the men playing the roles of the tacticians leaning low over the table prepared for their next move.

"All right. Admiral Kioru, it is the Americans' move. Proceed."

Kioru was a small, thin, bald man with wire glasses who bore a stark resemblance to Prime Minister Tojo. "Yes, sir. I have launched an assault on the carriers of the empire, from land-based airstrips on one of the nearby islands."

There were low mumbles in the room, and Ugaki said, "For the purposes of the game, I will allow the existence of an American airfield where none now exists. Commander Okumiya, you may toss your dice."

Okumiya served as one of the officiators, had made every effort to appear unaffected by the weight of the brass around him. He threw the dice against one corner of the table, said, "Admiral, according to the regulations, the dice have shown that the Americans scored nine direct hits on our carriers. That would sink the carriers *Akagi* and *Kaga*."

The mumbling increased, and Ugaki held up his hands. "Quiet, please. It is of no concern. I would change that outcome. The number of hits is recorded as three. *Kaga* has been sunk. *Akagi* received only light damage."

The mumbles quieted, a nervous hush, and Ugaki said, "It is no matter. *Kaga* will return for a future exercise. We will now move on."

There were new voices now, low greetings, and Ugaki turned, saw Yamamoto standing quietly by the door, arms crossed. Yamamoto glanced around the room, studied what he could see of the table, gave a slight nod to his chief of staff, and said, "All is well, then."

Ugaki gave a bow his way, and Yamamoto smiled, then slipped back out through the door.

ONBOARD BATTLESHIP *YAMATO*, HASHIRAJIMA, JAPAN — MAY 8, 1942

He had granted a brief leave for Ugaki, a reward for five tedious days managing the war games. But the man was back early. Unusual.

"Were the birds not flying, Matome?"

"I did not go hunting this time, sir. I spent many hours at the shrine for my wife. She has been gone for two years now. I miss her very much. It is difficult to forget her."

"Don't try. Hold on to her, whether in a shrine or right here. You have been given a gift of great value, the love of a woman, the love *for* a woman. Never lose that."

"I would offer the same wisdom to you, sir. With all respect, of course."

"Wisdom accepted. I am hoping to see Chiyoko very soon. There is much happening, many things right here that require our attention. I had hoped you would remain on leave, take advantage of some time away, but I have to be honest. With events as they are, I'm glad you've returned."

"What has happened, sir?"

"In time, Matome. I have scheduled several of my aides to join us, as well as Commander Genda. All are involved in our planning for future operations. I would seek their input."

"Am I to officiate, sir?"

It was now their private joke, but Yamamoto wasn't laughing. "Go, have some refreshment. We meet in one hour."

Ugaki stared at him for a long moment. "You will wait. You will not confide in me. It is not good, is it, sir?"

"It is not horrible, Admiral. Go. Return in one hour."

They filed in with the kind of energy Yamamoto missed.

"Sit down, all of you." He looked to one corner of the room, his orderly, Omi, waiting for a command. "Omi, bring sake and those crackers I had last night. They are quite good. Perhaps tea, for those of us too young or too old to appreciate the effects of fine spirits."

He tried to smile at his own joke, saw curious faces watching him. "How young you are. And so very experienced. I was that

way, a very long time ago. I have been told that I am the sole surviving officer of the great battle against the Russians, the battle
that won a war." He held up his crippled hand. "The battle that
took away my fingers." He smiled, easing away anyone's discomfort. "It was the only success that day by the Russians. Somewhere
in the Japan Sea, two fingers float like small fish. I have long given
up having them returned."

The men smiled, a few chuckles, as though they weren't sure
what he was telling them. Omi entered now with a large tray, bot-
tles, and bowls, and Yamamoto kept silent, patient, Omi well aware
he was now an intrusion. The orderly left his cargo, then slipped
away silently, and Yamamoto said, "There are doubts still about
our Midway operation. I do not believe any of you attended the
war games. No matter. It was an exercise in silliness, designed
solely to entertain those who refuse to be entertained. You are
more important to me than preening peacocks, all those admirals
who have forgotten what is required to win a war." He paused. "I
have been told, by those above me, that to win a war you do not
have to crush your enemy. You must only make him want to quit.
Maybe. But that is not my concern. I have one job, and you have
one duty to me. Fight the next battle. It is better of course if you
win that battle. I am being told that as of this morning, we have
won a great battle to the south, in the Coral Sea."

The voices rose, the young men glancing at one another with
broad smiles. He saw Ugaki at the far end of the table.

"And, sir, you do not believe that."

He ignored Ugaki's comment, said, "I am told we sank two of
the American carriers, a battleship, numerous cruisers and destroyers." He ignored the positive comments, the men watching
him now for more cues. "I am also told that in tomorrow's edition
of the newspaper, they will publish an interview with someone
who claims to be an expert on aircraft carriers. He will tell the
Japanese people . . ." He looked down to a small piece of paper.

"The American losses suffered in the latest battle have shattered the American dream . . . and the loss of their aircraft carriers suggests the doomed collapse of the United States." Yamamoto stopped, scanned the room. "Does any one of you believe this nonsense? If you even hint to yourself of such blind optimism, I have a question for you. If we achieved such an overwhelming victory in the Coral Sea, why did Admiral Inouye withdraw all of his forces from that entire area? Why did he suddenly abandon all plans to attack and occupy Port Moresby? Those were his orders. That was his purpose in moving his fleet into those waters. It seems he changed his mind."

His voice had risen, and he looked at Ugaki now, a silent request to intervene. Ugaki understood, said, "Listen, all of you. Do not forget that we have swept the British away from Singapore all the way past Ceylon. For centuries, the British were thought to be the world's greatest sea power. But no more. Now it is Japan. But the Americans are angry. They want revenge for Pearl Harbor. It is up to our navy, and its fliers, it is up to you to pour our strength against whatever the Americans have to put up against us. None of us should believe that the Americans will simply read our headlines and pull in their claws. Your emperor has confidence, absolute faith in what you are capable of. Enjoy the sword he has given you. Use it well."

Yamamoto thought, Very well, Matome, give them something inspiring. Now, I will take it away. He poured himself a small cup of tea, took a sip, felt the steam soothing his face. "There is another reason why most of you are here. Even Admiral Inouye does not hide the dismal fact that we lost more than one hundred skilled pilots in the Coral Sea engagements. *One hundred.* But . . . he insists the Americans lost three times that many. He did not explain to me just how he knows that or what evidence he has. He can also produce no evidence of the destruction of the American ships that he so loudly cheers about. Does it make sense to any of you that if you had utterly defeated the enemy's ability to strike back at you, you wouldn't perhaps have one of your pilots take a few photographs? A sinking aircraft carrier is a marvel to behold, so I've heard. And why would you flee the area? Are you in such a hurry to return home to your glorious parades?"

He was shouting now, felt thunder in his chest, took a long breath, then another, tried to calm himself. Ugaki looked at him with concern, said to the others, "We are all certain that the Midway operation will move us forward to where we have planned. Either we will occupy and fortify Midway, thus setting the stage for an invasion of Hawaii, or the Americans will respond by sending their fleet to engage us. Either way, we are staring at victory. In time, the Americans will be driven out of the Pacific altogether, hiding behind fortresses on their West Coast."

Yamamoto ignored Ugaki's grand boasting, tried to stretch away the tightness in his chest. He held up a hand, quieting them. "I am told by the Naval Ministry that Chancellor Hitler himself sends us glorious congratulations for our victory in the Coral Sea. Yes, Hitler is watching all that we do on this side of the world. I am not comforted by that thought." He paused, the room silent. "I do not mean to crush you with a blanket of gloom. I have to know if you understand the magnitude of the Midway operation, just what we are attempting to do, and how we must respond to the Americans when they stand up to us. And they will. Admiral Nagumo is once more a man of many doubts, and doubts can be contagious, which is why I did not invite him here today."

Across from him, Commander Genda's eyes filled with the oddly disturbing fire. "So, Admiral, I now understand why *you* have decided to accompany us. But I have wondered, sir, why you would confine yourself to this great battleship, holding your position far to the stern of the *Kido Butai,* while the aircraft carriers carry the sword. You are not confident in Admiral Nagumo, and yet you command *Kido Butai* to lead the way."

Yamamoto raised a hand. "There will be no talk of that. None. We know why Nagumo is in command of *Kito Butai,* that he is the senior admiral in this service to me, and that he is a *great hero* of Pearl Harbor." He stopped, knew there was more sarcasm in the last words than he intended. "I am more interested in your opinions about specific parts of this operation. Commander Genda, can you avoid references to Admiral Nagumo?"

"Of course, sir. Admiral, I am concerned about the waste of resources in sending an occupying force to the Aleutian Islands."

Yamamoto was surprised, equally surprised to see nods from the others. Down the way, Commander Watanabe and Captain Kuroshima seemed surprised as well. They had designed the plan.

Kuroshima said, "Why, Commander?"

Genda paused a second, as though he might be on risky ground. "Sending a fleet of valuable ships to the north is a waste. We might be better served keeping them together with the main body. The power of surprise or the power of strength at Midway could only be helped by including those ships. The Aleutians will still be up there. Those islands will be ours for the taking any time we want."

Kuroshima lit another cigarette, tossed the match on the deck behind him, said, "We want them now. The Americans could make excellent use of those islands as a staging area for attacks on Japan. It is not a far distance from the western end of the islands and the northern part of Japan. And once we occupy the islands and establish a formidable base, we will open the door to assaults either by air or sea on the American west coast."

Yamamoto said, "Commander, one of the criticisms the ministry has had for the Midway occupation is that we are too far away to support a strong base there. Establishing that base in the Aleutians solves that problem. It is much closer to Midway than we are here. A well-protected supply depot can easily be constructed there."

Genda sat back, absorbing all he had heard, but Yamamoto

could see he wasn't satisfied. "Sir, the Americans will not simply stand aside and allow us to build great bases along the Alaskan coast, any more than they will stand aside and allow us to occupy and fortify Midway."

Yamamoto said, "That is our greatest hope, Commander. When the Americans come out to confront us, we will be waiting for them with far more force than they can bring. That is the point of the entire operation. I would have hoped this was plain to you."

Genda smiled, another rarity, and nodded sharply. He seemed to light up, the fire rolling again into his eyes, red on his face. "I understand, sir. Forgive me, Admiral, all of you. I have been focusing on training my pilots. I have not been a part of many strategy meetings. I am deeply concerned about the loss of so many skilled pilots in the Coral Sea. Every man lost costs us a great deal."

Yamamoto scanned the others, Watanabe raising a hand, Yamamoto nodding his way.

"Perhaps Commander Genda, indeed perhaps all of us, should take comfort in the certainty that this war cannot last very much longer. It should prove unnecessary to train great numbers of fresh pilots. Our carriers are greater in number, faster, better equipped. Our planes are far superior, and, Commander Genda, as a credit to you, our pilots are far superior as well. It is a formula for certain success."

Yamamoto winced, fought the need to correct that kind of thinking, and said, "What will happen if you are wrong? What if the Americans surprise us, if things do not go according to our careful plans?"

Genda spoke out now, loud and boisterous, surprising him. "*One touch of the armored gauntlet.* That is all it will take to achieve victory. My men shall be prepared, sir."

Yamamoto knew the old expression, pulled himself inside, wouldn't drain away their enthusiasm. "Enjoy your sake, all of you."

Yamamoto kept his eyes low, forced himself not to hear their boasts, their naked optimism. He saw Ugaki rise, go to the far door, pull it open a few inches. Yamamoto hadn't heard the knock, but saw the note now, Ugaki scanning the words. Yamamoto felt a twist in his stomach, could read his chief of staff well. Ugaki came around the table, most of the others caught up still in the good cheer. Yamamoto took the note, read its simple words, held up his hand, and spoke in a low voice. "Silence. We have just received word that there was an accident aboard battleship *Hyuga*, during a training mission. A breechblock in one of the turrets failed. There was considerable loss of life, including the entire turret crew and others nearby. I do not have the exact number here. We shall learn soon enough." He stood. "Continue here, gentlemen. I shall have my orderly bring more sake, if you wish. Admiral Ugaki will remain. Please, Matome. Hear their questions, their concerns. I will be in my cabin."

He moved quickly out the door, didn't need to hear *voices* just now. He reached his cabin, moved inside, was wrapped in the smell of flowers and a fresh pot of tea. It is Omi again, he thought. He moved to his bed, sat, loosened the buttons on the white coat, then stopped, frozen for a long moment. He tried to think of the captain of the *Hyuga*, the flagship of the Second Battleship Division. The name wouldn't come, and Yamamoto thought, Is he alive? How many men? Will she be able to sail? But the larger question punched him, the words he could never say to his staff. Why right now? *Why* must we have such an omen?

KURE HARBOR, JAPAN—MAY 14, 1942

He had waited for her on the train platform, his usual dress of civilian clothes and a disguise, no desire to attract anyone's attention. The doctors had told Chiyoko not to make the journey, that her illness was too severe. For nearly two months, a vicious bout of pleurisy had weakened her past the point even where the drugs could help.

He had no idea how serious her condition was, and had pushed her to come south on the train. The *Yamato* had sailed only a short distance north, the base at Kure designed for maintenance and repair. At Kure, Yamamoto had always allowed his officers the opportunity to visit with their families before any major campaign, and with more than two hundred ships to take part in the Midway operation, no one could argue whether this campaign was *major*.

As she stepped slowly from the train, he saw just how sick she was, and he carried her to the waiting car, no concern what anyone else might think of such a bold move. Once they reached the small hotel, he had carried her again, and now, seeing her for the first time alone, close, he was horrified by her appearance. The pleurisy that had stricken her lungs had drained her of weight and color. Her fragile weakness was as dismaying as her appearance. But he had insisted on this, the only time he would be able to see her before the next great campaign. Now, holding her gently as he lowered her into the warm bath, he felt a vast wave of guilt, afraid that his own selfishness might have killed her.

He stood, backed away from the tub, and dried his arms from the bathwater. "Are you comfortable? Is there anything I can do to help?"

She managed a smile. "Sit down, Iso. The water is very nice. Thank you for assisting me."

"I am so very sorry, Flower. I did not understand how ill you have been. I would have sent my own doctors. The navy has very good physicians."

"So do I. There is little they can do. Time will help. Seeing *you* will help." She coughed, a small chirping sound, but it curled her up, the pain on her face driving a knife through him.

"I am helpless, Chiyoko. What do I do?"

"Sit there and look at me like I am loved."

He lowered his head. "That much I can do. All day long. All night if you like."

She rolled her hands slowly through the water, and said, "I saw your friend Hori. A few days ago. I confided in him that you would be here. He would very much like to see you."

"I do not wish to leave you."

"Leave me. Tomorrow. There is a small fish house very close. I told him you would meet there at one o'clock."

He shook his head. "I am under your spell. Perhaps your control. Very well, I will meet him. He is a good friend, and right now I need one."

Admiral Teikichi Hori was indeed Yamamoto's closest friend, the two men sharing a background and a longevity in the navy that set them well apart from many of the admirals who claimed a higher rank. Both men were considered moderates or even liberals throughout the struggles for supremacy in both army and navy, just which faction would rise to the most prominent position, capturing the emperor's favor, while rising to positions in the Naval Ministry. The more radical factions were not content to negotiate or conference their way through any disagreement, and Yamamoto had been the target of assassination attempts more than once. But the difference between the two men had a devastating effect on Hori. Yamamoto was a hero, famous, so much so that even if his views were far more moderate than some of the young firebrands around him, he was revered. Hori did not command that kind of respect, and so, as the more radical elements gained power in the highest positions, Hori found himself on *inactive duty,* which meant that although officially he was still an admiral, there would be nothing to command, and nothing he could do about it.

Yamamoto ducked low, pushed gently through a beaded screen, looked around, removed his shoes. The bar itself was well lit, several chefs working behind it, but the rest of the place was dark and very discreet. He smiled, thought, She is always caring for me, even when she is not by my side.

He heard a voice to one side. "Ah, there is my accountant. Very punctual. As it should always be."

Yamamoto tried to hide the smile, searched the far corner, saw Hori motioning to him. He moved that way, eased himself down onto a pillow, and said, "Must you always draw attention? You can be so noisy."

Hori laughed. "But you are so very amusing. You dress like an accountant. Do you believe anyone would make a fuss over the magnificent admiral?" He paused. "Well, perhaps. So, you have graced me with your time. How is Chiyoko?"

"Frightening, my friend. She is very ill. Had I known, I would have left her alone, not forced her to travel."

"And she would be angry for weeks. She said pleurisy. Her lungs are aching terribly. It is good she is here with you."

"I am still not certain. There is so much happening, so many concerns, fear, uncertainty. And worst of all? Arrogance. It is a deadly thing. I want them all to question me, all of them. I am trying to teach the younger ones, the men who would be captains, to understand what we are doing, why we do it. Learn, don't just *accept*."

"What of Nagumo? Is he accepting?"

"Nagumo doesn't accept, and he doesn't ask questions. He just gripes."

Hori laughed again. "He always did."

Yamamoto felt his mood darkening, didn't want that, not now, not with his friend. "Things are changing, my friend. The Americans have changed. Early this year they were picking at us, like they were too frightened to make us angry. They attacked several islands where we have small bases, had meaningless success. Quick strikes, then run away. They have poor intelligence. They would strike with carrier aircraft, dozens of planes, on a target that had no meaning. They would sink a minelayer or some civilian merchant ship and scamper back home. I'm quite sure those pilots bragged about sinking a fleet of battleships."

"I know of this. Even the newspapers seemed to get it right."

"But it has changed. Coral Sea was very different. They came in force and they stayed. Both sides took losses, but it was *our* fleet that scampered away. No, my friend, they will send no more Doolittle Raids. That was a game, a circus act. They have become serious. And we must be as well. It is why we must put this plan into action in June and no later. We must not allow the Americans the time, or perhaps the good fortune, to gain confidence." He paused. "Those men who keep to their offices in the ministry, who haven't been to sea in years, those men are quick to spew out their doubts about our new campaign. But the men who will go to sea, who will command the guns, fly the planes, who will give their lives . . . they are accepting all of this, our planning, our strategy, with pure blind faith. Dying for the emperor is a fine, honorable thing. But I want them to know *why*. These men have too much faith in me. They believe that I cannot make mistakes. How did they learn that?"

Hori leaned closer. "You taught them, Iso."

Yamamoto let out a breath. "Then, my friend, who taught me?"

Hori looked down. "I've never seen you so *afraid*."

Yamamoto was surprised, but said nothing, and Hori said, "How many Americans have you seen in this war? How many of their guns have you faced?"

Yamamoto understood the question. "None. Not one. I have not seen an American since I was in their country."

"How about a German? Our *allies*. Met any of them?"

"What is your point?"

"You are going to sea, riding the waves in your great battleship, the brand-new *obsolete* battleship. What happens if you actually confront the Americans, perhaps a battleship of their own? Do you hate them? Will you rush to the kill? When your officers look to you, will you tell them to offer no quarter? Or, perhaps, Admiral, you will look at the Americans and think, You know, I *don't* hate them. So, perhaps, Iso, your fears and your doubts come from knowing that your plans might be flawed, that you might make mistakes because you don't hate your enemy."

"I have my duty. You are being ridiculous."

Hori looked at his face, a hard stare into his eyes. "I know something of your plans. I know this operation is incredibly complicated. Perhaps . . . badly complicated. Perhaps mistakes have already been made. And perhaps the Americans will make mistakes of their own. You know how often great campaigns are won by the side who makes the least mistakes. The only advice I can offer you . . . trust the right people. It might be Nagumo, it might be all those optimistic young men with fire in the veins."

"I will trust them before we ever reach our targets. If you know our plans then you will know that *Yamato* and her task force will keep back, several hundred miles, while the carriers do their work."

Hori stared at him. "It is not my place, Iso. But *that* might be the first real mistake I've seen you make."

SEVEN

Rochefort

He had followed events in the Coral Sea, snippets of radio and other coded reports that came through his own sources, as well as the communications that weren't really his to hear, the messages his crew could pick up that came straight to CINCPAC. It was a mixed blessing. Rochefort had already pinpointed, and reported to Layton, several important details of Japanese operations, the potential invasion of Port Moresby, the route they might take to get there, and the kinds of ships involved. He had followed most of the Japanese radio broadcasts as well, and from there had heard boastful reports of the death of the two American carriers, at a time when messages still came into Pearl from *Yorktown*. But word had come from Admiral Fletcher himself, confirming that *Lexington* had gone down. *Yorktown* was damaged but mobile, and for reasons not even Rochefort could grasp, the Japanese had taken no advantage of their success. Fletcher reported the sinking of one Japanese carrier, thus the most significant successes had been equal. But the Japanese had reacted by simply pulling away, leaving behind their ambitions toward Port Moresby for some other day. It was not hard to think of the fight in the Coral Sea as a victory for the Americans, or at least a draw, though of course Japanese public radio portrayed events in a very different way. Ultimately, as Nimitz kept his appraisal mostly to himself, it seemed that it was a fight that nobody had really won. Or lost. The sinking of *Lexington* had of course rocked CINCPAC, but within the Dungeon, the men had taken that news with a short pause in their labors, a few comments and curses toward the Japanese. There could be no handwringing. Their war had to be won in a very different way from the fliers and gunners on the ships so far away, those men who might absorb the loss of the *Lady Lex* as a personal tragedy. Very soon, Rochefort's men were back at work. There was simply too much to do.

"What the hell are you doing here?"

Layton offered a brief nod to CPO Lurie, then dragged a metal chair close to Rochefort's desk. "You invited me, remember? I think I'll sit down. Thank you."

"Sorry, Eddie. Busy here. Working our asses off, all of us. We're close to a number of things, and I'm trying to figure out what matters and what doesn't. I ran into a recipe for seaweed sauce, for crying out loud."

Layton smiled. "Save that. Might be good."

"Funny. A real Bob Hope." Rochefort glanced at the others, heads mostly down, buried deeply into the mounds of papers and IBM cards on their desks. "Is Nimitz paying attention? Is he going to take us seriously?"

Layton nodded. "I do. So he will. The only stumbling block you have is Washington. You don't answer to CINCPAC. Your chain of command goes through OP-G-20. And those fellows don't much like you."

Rochefort couldn't help the surge of anger, his voice rising. "Those fellows are almost always wrong, in every conclusion they've drawn. I'm doing my best to just ignore them. I thought they were there to support what we're doing, and in return, I'd do the same. To hell with them. They take our good info and toss it in the can, then come up with intel that might as well be pulled from *The New York Times* or some dime novel. It's idiotic."

Layton leaned back in the chair. "Easy, Joe. Just do your work. You've made a friend in Admiral Nimitz. You asked if he'll take you seriously . . . well, he thinks you're a lunatic, but anybody in this job has to have some of that."

Nearby, one of the men peered up over a pile of cards. "Damn right. Sir."

Layton nodded that way, then said to Rochefort, "Look, the report you gave the admiral a couple weeks ago was pretty much spot-on. That's what he needs to hear. You get things right, and he'll trust you to do it again."

"Which report was that? The four-point note?"

"Yep. You reported that the Jap action in the Indian Ocean had ended, that they were bringing their ships home. You said they weren't going to attack Australia, when half of Washington claimed they were. You predicted the occupation of Rabaul and their movements south of there, which ended up in the fight in the Coral Sea. And you predicted something to unfold in the central Pacific. So, you got the first three right. Now the admiral is waiting to see what number four means."

"I have an idea about that. I've told you about the location code they keep using. *AF*. So far, no one's come up with the meaning, not Washington, not Australia. Think about that bombing attack the Japs made on Oahu a couple months ago."

"Yeah, they busted up a few pineapple plants. Missed everything else."

"They refueled those flying boats out at French Frigate Shoals, probably from one of their tanker-subs."

Layton said, "The admiral is sending a couple of our own subs out there to keep an eye on that area, in case the Japs try something like that again."

"Sure, if he thinks that's a good thing to do. I don't have much to do with ordering ships around or worrying about bombers. But I do know this. When those Jap bombers took off, they talked about flying close to *AF*. There isn't a damn sandbar out that way, except for Midway. Listen, Eddie. I called you over here for an actual reason. The coded transmissions still take a while to decipher, but over the last couple of weeks there has been a tenfold increase in the times they mention *AF*. We know Hawaii is *AH*. The only other significant spot of land out here is Midway."

Layton lost the smile, leaned closer to him. "You think *AF* is Midway? So far, all the 'A' call signs have indicated Alaska, the Aleutians. That's always made sense."

Rochefort was losing patience, especially since he knew Layton should know better. "Eddie, Hawaii is *AH*. The *A* is for America. What I'm trying to pin down is if *AF* is Midway. The Japs are planning something major in the central Pacific. They already control everything from the Philippines east to Wake Island. What's left? Hawaii and Midway."

Layton looked down with a frown. "And the Aleutians. And the whole damn west coast of the U.S."

"Oh Christ, Eddie. Washington sent me a report yesterday—the results of their *expert analysis,* saying that the Japs intend to attack San Francisco. Never mind there isn't a Jap ship within five thousand miles of the place. What's next? Boise?"

"You're supposed to be handing those reports over to me, you know. I have to brief Admiral Nimitz on all pertinent intel."

Rochefort stared at him, then glanced out across the room, several faces looking back. He looked again to Layton, felt whatever good mood he had mustered now draining away. "They're wrong. Let me repeat, Eddie. They're wrong. I have a way of proving they're wrong, if the admiral will allow. Commander Holmes has come up with an idea that might just nail down where the Japs are intending to go."

"What kind of idea?"

"A good one. I'd let him tell you, but he's out for the rest of the day. Something about seeing his wife. That's why I sent mine away. As long as Fay's in California, I don't have to worry about her. Look, can you set up a briefing with Admiral Nimitz? This is hot, Eddie."

"I brief the admiral every morning at 0755. Be there tomorrow."

Rochefort glanced around, said aloud, "Listen up. The battery's dead in my damn alarm clock. Can somebody tell me when it's 0740?"

One man held up a wristwatch, then others as well.

He turned again to Layton. "I'll be there. Now get the hell out of here."

Layton stood. "One question, Joe. When was the last time you took a shower?"

Rochefort thought about that, couldn't recall. "Hell, I don't know. A while back."

"Well, take one now. Admiral Nimitz doesn't care for the smell of dead fish."

HQ, CINCPAC, PEARL HARBOR, HAWAII—MAY 15, 1942

"Sit down, both of you. You know Admiral Draemel, Captain McCormick. You made quite an impression on the captain, Mr. Rochefort."

Rochefort recalled the visit, one of those annoying VIP tours, as though they were a tourist attraction. Layton was usually the man responsible for setting those up, but had learned to keep the visits to a minimum. Neither Rochefort nor his crew had any need for eyes peering over their shoulders. But Captain McCormick had been far more agreeable, and far more necessary. It was hoped that Nimitz could be persuaded to visit the Dungeon, so he could see for himself the scale of sheer work being done under Rochefort's hand. But Nimitz couldn't find the time, and instead had sent Lynde McCormick, his war plans officer. Rochefort had no idea what McCormick had reported back to Nimitz, but had to assume, since Rochefort still had a job, that McCormick had been positively impressed. Rochefort knew, with his uncontrollable crankiness or the outright hostility he often launched toward much of the brass at Pearl Harbor, that he could never be sure if there would be repercussions that might come back to bite him. Most of the time, he just didn't care. He refused to worry about hurt feelings. He had work to do.

Nimitz wasted no time. "Commander Rochefort, Commander Layton tells me you have a plan to reveal the intention of the Japanese fleet. You have already identified much of that fleet, and their location, which is extremely helpful. It is obvious to me that they are planning some kind of major operation in the central Pacific. But there are a good many in Washington who think otherwise, who ignore the obvious."

Rochefort hated that word. "Sir, excuse me, but very little of what we're coming up with is *obvious*. If it was, we wouldn't be spending so much energy to nail down every tidbit of data."

Nimitz seemed annoyed with the response, but he measured Rochefort's words, and said, "All right, if you say so. *Obvious* would be helpful, but I understand you've only got so much to give us. So, what's this plan of yours?"

Rochefort took a breath, glanced at Layton, then the others, and saw McCormick nod toward him, a gesture of encouragement.

"Sir, I believe the Japanese have been using *AF* as a call sign for Midway."

Nimitz said, "I know better than to ask you why. Go on."

"I don't mind telling you, sir. One of my men, Lieutenant Commander Jasper Holmes, is an engineer by training. He is aware that Midway generates its fresh water from saltwater converters. Without that equipment, supplying Midway with fresh water becomes a logistical problem."

He saw impatience on Nimitz's face, thought, Maybe he knows that already. He paused, took a breath. All right, just spit it out. He looked at Layton, who seemed to have the same thought. *Get on with it.* "Communication between Pearl and Midway is by telephone cable, correct?"

Layton said, "Correct."

"Well, since that line of communication is immune from message interception, might we use the cable line to instruct the radio base there to broadcast an emergency message in clear language, that Midway has had a massive breakdown in its saltwater evaporators, so they would issue an urgent call for freshwater tankers? Or something similar."

Nimitz crossed his arms. "To what purpose?"

Rochefort hadn't expected skepticism. The plan seemed perfectly logical to him. He was irritated, but he knew better than to show that to Nimitz. "Sir, the Japanese will certainly monitor our signal, especially if it is sent in clear English. How they respond will tell us . . . something."

McCormick said, "Interesting plan, Admiral. It doesn't cost us anything, and if the Japs ignore it, Commander Rochefort's people can keep at the code business."

Rochefort was surprised to see a smile from Nimitz. "Nothing to lose. I like it. Commander, you still have to follow chain of command, so be sure you pass this idea along to Washington."

Rochefort sagged. "Certainly, sir."

"Doesn't mean you have to wait for permission. Whatever messages we send out over the wire are CINCPAC's business, not yours. So, keep at your work. Every detail counts. I admit, Commander, this might be the best idea I've heard in a while. And I'm curious to see how the Japs respond." Nimitz paused. "This could be interesting."

The order went to Midway by undersea cable, Captain Simard putting on a performance that was exactly as Rochefort and Nimitz had hoped. To anyone listening, it was obvious that Midway had a genuine problem, an emergency water shortage that would affect not only the sailors and marines stationed there, but anyone else who might come ashore.

THE DUNGEON, 14TH NAVAL DISTRICT, PEARL HARBOR, HAWAII—
    MAY 21, 1942

The chief stood abruptly, his usual response to anyone pulling open the heavy door.

Rochefort looked that way: a reflex. In the dim light, he saw the glasses first, then a smile, and said, "Oh Jesus. You've been promoted, right? You'll be insufferable."

Layton sat in his usual perch, and said, "No, but you might be."

"A pay raise? What the hell did I do?"

"Maybe nothing. Maybe everything."

"Knock it off, will you? I've got a room full of riddles without yours."

"Fine. Here it is. Admiral King sent a message to Admiral Nimitz. Your bosses in Washington at OP-G-20 have determined through their tireless code-breaking efforts that the Japanese are intending a major operation against Australia, Fiji, and New Caledonia. Admiral King only partially disagrees, and insists that the enemy's aim could also be Hawaii or the West Coast, possibly Alaska. In Admiral King's view, any talk of Midway is intended only as a ruse by the Japanese, to draw our attention away from their actual operation."

Rochefort felt sick to his stomach. "What the hell is wrong with those people? There is nothing at all in our intercepts or decryption to indicate any of that. What is Nimitz saying to this?"

Layton smiled. "The admiral responded by saying he is *unclear as to the meaning* of Admiral King's message. So, of course, it will take him some time to interpret that message."

"He's giving me some rope to hang myself."

Layton smiled again, removed his glasses, wiped at the lenses with a handkerchief.

Rochefort said, "Damn it all, you're stalling."

Layton replaced the glasses, still kept the smile, and said, "The clear uncoded message went out from Midway two days ago, stressing the urgency of their sudden water shortage."

"Nice of you to let me know."

"How many times have you told me how you don't want to hear anything about operations? Well, this is operations. Pay attention. This is your baby, Joe. The Japs responded to the emergency message this morning. They were issuing what can best be called warnings, bulletins about the severe water problem on an American base. That message seems to have gone out to a substantial number of ships. Then, we received a radio intercept that two Japanese freighters are ordered to bring their own saltwater converters to handle the water problem on . . . *AF*."

Layton stopped, seemed to shake, a nervous smile, and held out his hand.

Across the room from Rochefort, several men were standing, offering Rochefort and many of the others a hearty salute, ac-

knowledging the men whose work had solved the riddle. Rochefort accepted Layton's handshake and looked at all the others, their
ragged clothes, drawn faces, and tired eyes.

Layton said, "The admiral has been informed, of course, and
he's beaming about it. If you were in his office, he'd slap you on
the ass. Well, maybe not. But you should inform Washington, I
guess. And Australia."

Rochefort sat back in the chair. "They'll find out soon enough.
We did the work. Let's enjoy it, at least for a day or two." He took
a breath, felt the cold air around him, and suddenly felt very, very
good. He stood, all eyes on him. "Congratulations, all of you. I
am happy to confirm that any messages we can decode or intercept that contain *AF* . . . those bastards are talking about Midway."

EIGHT

Nimitz

The letter from General Emmons had annoyed him, but he wouldn't just stew about it at his desk. He did what he usually did: trotted his frustrations down the stairway, pushing through the steel door outside, and headed toward the churned-up sandpit where he kept his set of horseshoes. But today he couldn't concentrate at all, and so his accuracy suffered; nothing about his game he could feel good about. He kept the man's face in his head, the one man on Oahu he didn't want to fight a war with. General Delos Emmons was the army's new commanding officer in Hawaii. He had assumed command in late December, several days before Nimitz. Emmons replaced General Walter Short, who, like Admiral Kimmel, had been summarily removed as punishment for their perceived roles in the disastrous events of December 7.

Nimitz knew very little about Emmons, except that now, from the letter that had crossed his desk, he understood that Delos Emmons had very little use for cryptanalysis or code breaking. It sounded to Nimitz as though if Emmons couldn't see it or touch it, it didn't exist. The doubts that Emmons tried to aim toward the work being done by Layton and Rochefort had little effect on Nimitz. But it was infuriating to Nimitz that the army would take such a very different view of the potential for a serious engagement with the Japanese. Emmons insisted that Nimitz should focus the navy's energies on what the Japanese could do, not what they *intended* to do. Implied in that of course was the potential for another attack on Pearl Harbor.

He walked through the loose earth, kicked up the dusty mix of lava and sand, stopped, staring toward the nondescript office building that housed his headquarters. Don't go back, he thought, not yet. They can do without me for another ten minutes.

He turned toward the horseshoe pit again, fought the shaking in his hands, the anger boiling up inside him, anger he would never show his subordinates. But he couldn't erase the tone of Emmons's letter, the high-handed scolding. He stood with his hands on his hips, stared toward the harbor. How can so many intelligence offices have so many interpretations of the same information?

Emmons and the army had been clear that they at least expected an attack on San Francisco, while Douglas MacArthur, headquartered now in Australia, anticipated a renewed assault on New Guinea. The British continued to insist that the Japanese were not yet through in the Indian Ocean. Nimitz smiled, breaking through his gloom. It's all because I took their bombers from them.

It was Nimitz's prerogative—that if he felt there was danger in any one area of his command, he could employ the army's large bombers, the fleet of B-17s. That was precisely what he had done, sending many of them off to the airfield on Midway. No one outside of his own command was amused.

I have faith, he thought. I have to. No one can say anything with perfect certainty, but these cryptanalysis boys seem to have the best handle on just what the enemy is planning to do. But Emmons is making the same mistake the rest of them made in December. It's all about studying how many battleships or airplanes the Japanese have to offer, as though that will tell us how to be prepared. Ridiculous, stupidly ridiculous.

He stepped into the pit again, picked up one of the horseshoes, stood back behind the closest steel stake. He stared across at the other stake, aimed, let it fly. The horseshoe sailed six feet past, and Nimitz dropped his hands. Not today, he thought. That was the worst shot of the year. These people have got you wound like a spring. He looked again toward his headquarters building, wondered if anyone there was watching him. Well, he thought, today they saw me make a fool out of myself. Nobody misses a stake by that much. He let out a breath. And nobody plans a war based on how many guns the enemy has or might have. What I care about is just what they're going to do with them. We had plenty of guns on December 7, all locked away nice and neat. We had as many planes as the Japanese did, all lined up on the airstrips. That shoots big holes in your thinking, General Emmons.

He started back toward his office, thought, No one learns lessons, and Emmons is just one more in the line. No, you can't tell him that. That's not the kind of thing the War Department will want to hear, that the army and navy can't play nice in Hawaii. All I can do is what I believe is the right thing to do. Plan according to what we know. We're outgunned, certainly. So we need surprise, guile. From everything I can figure out, our intel is better than theirs, or if it's not, they haven't shown their hand. I think maybe it's time to bring that oddball up from his Dungeon again and let him tell the rest of us just what *he* knows.

Nimitz stepped into the building, moved past the offices, could always tell when the staffs saw him first, suddenly acting like they were intently busy. He didn't mind that, had always thought it was far better than if any junior clerk had his feet up on his desk.

He climbed the steps to the second floor, saw his chief of staff and two other men, junior officers. They snapped to attention, and Draemel said, "Good game today, sir?"

"Rotten game. Almost tossed one through your window. Listen. Contact the army's top brass, plus the top four admirals here. Have them all meet here in my office at 0800 tomorrow. Order Commander Rochefort to attend, and tell him to be fully prepared to inform all of us just where we stand, what we know, and what we don't."

He saw a smile on Draemel's face. "What?"

"Coffee and doughnuts?"

Nimitz didn't expect the question. "Just coffee. Nobody gets fat on my watch."

HQ, CINCPAC, PEARL HARBOR, HAWAII—MAY 25, 1942

They sat or stood in a semicircle, the captains behind, the four admirals plus Milo Draemel seated to one side of Nimitz's desk. To the far side were the two army officers, the first General Robert Richardson, who by chance was visiting Hawaii on behalf of Chief of Staff George Marshall. The other army officer was of course General Emmons. Nimitz knew when he issued the invitation that if the information gleaned through HYPO proved wrong, Emmons wouldn't miss the opportunity to rub sand in what he thought might be the navy's wound. Nimitz had to swallow the irritating fact that Emmons still held to the belief that if the Japanese were not aiming for San Francisco, all of their energy would likely be directed straight at Hawaii. Midway wasn't even in the army's equation. Nor did anyone in Washington seem to appreciate what HYPO had put together.

As he began to fidget himself, Nimitz realized just what kind of bind he was in. Rochefort would be there to reveal the intel that had been gathered and interpreted, spelling out where the Japanese would strike, and how. But Nimitz did not want Rochefort revealing just how he got that information. HYPO was a deep secret, and Nimitz had protected Rochefort and his team by hinting to prying eyes around Hawaii that the intel they were relying on actually came from spies on the ground in Japan. So far, that seemed to deflect any digging from the army or anyone else.

He glanced at his watch, saw others doing the same, and heard an audible sigh from General Emmons. Nimitz fought to keep calm, to keep silent, but the pulsing impatience of the men around him made that increasingly difficult.

Emmons turned to him. "Were we to meet at 0800? I have a full calendar today, Admiral."

Nimitz tried his best to seem nonchalant about the time, pushing toward 0830. "We all do, General. Please, just be patient. Commander Rochefort has his reasons, I'm certain."

Nimitz stared at the face on his watch, avoided the glares from men not accustomed to waiting on a subordinate. You had better have a good reason for this, Commander, he thought. You've put my butt in a sling. How long are we supposed to wait?

A knock on the office door answered the question. Nimitz was dismayed by Rochefort's appearance, a disheveled mess, his khaki uniform wrinkled, his tie loose and yanked to one side. Rochefort froze, looked around the room, and Nimitz saw what seemed to be fear. Nimitz didn't break a smile, kept an icy glare. "Nice of you to join us, Commander."

Rochefort still examined the room, the gathering of brass. "Thank you, sir. There is a reason for my late arrival. My crew and I were working all night to assemble . . . this."

He handed a sheaf of papers to Nimitz. Nimitz tried to keep the ice in his eyes, but something in Rochefort's attitude made him more interested than angry. "Tell us about it, Commander."

"Uh, sir, it's all right there."

"I'm not reading this like it's a classroom, Commander. What have you learned?"

Rochefort looked exhausted, but Nimitz wanted him to commit to his own efforts, stand behind what his men had been accomplishing. Otherwise, nothing Rochefort said would carry any weight beyond mere speculation.

Rochefort ignored the papers on Nimitz's desk, said, "We have intercepted a number of messages dated 20 May, as though the Japanese are making final preparations for a large-scale operation. There are several references to the Aleutians, which we have seen before. Now that we have determined that their call sign *AF* is Midway, many of the subsequent messages make much more sense. For example, we picked up the phrase *invasion of AF*. We have deciphered specific orders to various ships from their main fleet, their *Kido Butai*. That means the enemy will be bringing four carriers only, since they have previously dispatched two toward the South Pacific."

Nimitz ignored the others, stared hard at Rochefort. "Only four carriers?"

"Yes, sir. They have a fifth light carrier which we cannot precisely locate, but we believe it is being ordered north, as part of their attack fleet on the Aleutians."

"Go on."

"We have identified the locations of Carrier Divisions One and Two, as well as transport ships preparing to sail from Saipan. The orders we have intercepted are very specific. We are certain that the carriers will approach Midway from the northwest, accompanied by a significant number of cruisers and destroyers, with at least two battleships and accompanying service ships. The transports are most certainly carrying an invasion force to Midway. We have previously determined that the northbound fleet is also ferrying troops that are being sent to invade and occupy at least two of the islands in the western Aleutians." Rochefort paused. "This is as close to a complete order of battle as we can determine at this time. We have only just yesterday deciphered the phrase *koryaku butai*. It means 'invasion force.' That's what they're sending toward Midway." He paused, looked at Nimitz. "We will continue to work on more details, sir."

To one side, General Emmons said, "I have always believed, Commander, that if it sounds too good to be true, it probably is. So, since you have a crystal ball, just when is all this to take place? Do you have a date and time? Should we set our watches?"

Nimitz bristled at the general's sarcasm, but he knew that Rochefort was under Nimitz's own orders not to reveal his methods for deciphering any of this kind of information. He kept his eyes on Rochefort, who seemed to fight off the urge to spit on Emmons.

Rochefort said, "We are making every effort, through every hour of the day, to determine that very information, sir. We've directly interpreted phrases such as *forthcoming campaign, occupation force,* even something as mundane as *refueling hoses.* It's all part of the puzzle, assembling the meaning from so many separate parts. But, General, while it is not my duty to be concerned with operations and tactics, I understand the value of knowing not just *how* but *when* the enemy will strike." He looked at Nimitz again. "We're doing all we can, sir."

Nimitz wanted to say something positive, a verbal pat on the back, but he knew that many in the room had no idea just what HYPO did, or that it even existed. For now, it was a secret Nimitz intended to keep. He glanced at Marshall's man, General Richardson. Surely he's getting briefings in Washington from OP-G-20. And if Rochefort is right, most of what Richardson is being given is flat-out wrong. But Emmons . . . he has a right to be testy. He's got to be terrified of another Pearl Harbor attack. I just wish he understood how to predict one. I hope I do.

Nimitz said, "Commander, have you sent this information to Washington?"

Rochefort offered a predictable frown. "This morning, sir."

Nimitz knew that would satisfy Richardson, whether or not Rochefort had little faith in what Washington would do with the information. But there was no need to ask him now.

Beside Emmons, General Richardson said, "Commander, are you aware who you're up against, who we're all up against? Admiral Yamamoto is a genius, a man who can create elaborate plans, and change them in a way even to befuddle his own superiors."

Rochefort shook his head, a risky move. "General, I met Admiral Yamamoto on two occasions when I was in Japan. With all due respect, sir, I do not consider him to be a genius. He is definitely a strong-willed character, but what you describe as befuddling his superiors? That sounds an awful lot to me like insubordination. I certainly don't fear him, sir, because I think he is prone to carelessness, and it is my job to find carelessness so that you may take advantage of it."

Nimitz smiled for the first time, hid the smile with his hand.

Rochefort glanced out toward the window, faced Nimitz again, who saw an odd look he hadn't seen before.

"Something bothering you, Commander?"

"Sorry, sir. From my . . . office, I have no view of the harbor. I was curious how the salvage work was coming on the *Arizona*. I see the main mast is still upright."

Beside Nimitz, Draemel said, "Why are you so interested?"

Rochefort took a breath. "She was my ship, sir. I served on her a few years after the Great War. Engineering watch officer. It was 1924, to be exact. She meant a great deal to all of us."

Nimitz was surprised, but he couldn't let the briefing get sidetracked. "Questions, feel free, gentlemen. Don't hesitate. We all have work to do."

The inquiries came now, the men pouring out their doubts, not only on the details as Rochefort had presented them, but toward Rochefort himself, prying digs into just how he could know so many details that were completely unknown to most of them. Rochefort fought them off, all the while with an eye on Nimitz, as though confirming that he was still on solid ground. There were more arguments as well, the army officers sticking to the gospel as it came out of the War Department, claiming that the Japanese surely had far more grandiose plans than sending an enormous fleet to capture an isolated and indefensible atoll like Midway. Nimitz let them speak, heard all the usual preaching about the vulnerability of the West Coast, the ripe targets of San Francisco or Seattle, as well as the potential disasters that might certainly fall far across the South Pacific, and the vulnerability of Australia that seemed to inspire so much concern from Douglas MacArthur.

Then came more attacks on Rochefort, mostly from the army again. Their sneering arrogance was becoming too much even for Nimitz, and he saw a crack in Rochefort's veneer of patience. After a long harangue by Emmons, Rochefort said, "Sirs, I have presented to you what I know. I assume you gathered here because it mattered to you what the Japanese were planning to do. Intelligence is not science. Nor is it tactics. It cannot manufacture battleships and airplanes, it cannot train airmen, nor can it produce artillery shells, bombs, or torpedoes. I have done the best I can to provide you with an accurate assessment of what is about to happen. That's my job." He paused. "I'm good at my job."

HQ, CINCPAC, PEARL HARBOR, HAWAII—MAY 26, 1942

Nimitz had watched the carrier slide into the harbor, another out behind it. Like everyone who saw her, the sight of the *Enterprise* inspired something beyond mere pride. To Nimitz she was a beautiful beast, a mammoth ship of war, dwarfing the piers and smaller ships who stood aside, greeting her with a sea of men in white. Behind came the *Hornet,* another massive prize of the U.S. fleet, whose most notable claim thus far was having launched Jimmy Doolittle's sixteen bombers on their one-way flight across Japan. But like the men on the *Enterprise,* the *Hornet's* crew sensed that the return to Pearl Harbor was no maintenance call, and that new orders might be coming, if not known already by the men at the top.

Nimitz waited eagerly, knowing that once the carriers were moored, the task force's commander, Admiral Halsey, would report to him as quickly as possible. Nimitz smiled when he thought of Halsey, knew that if anyone was eager for new combat orders it would be him.

"Sir, Admiral Halsey has arrived."

Nimitz stood, no need to call Halsey into the office. He'd come anyway.

He saw Halsey now, and Nimitz stared with a dull shock. "Good God, Bill. Are you okay? What happened?"

"Sir, I stopped by to pay my respects, and to officially inform you that Task Force 16 has docked as ordered. We are already preparing for whatever mission you order."

There was no energy in Halsey's words, and Nimitz could clearly see why. Halsey seemed to accept the inevitable. There was no hiding what Nimitz could detect so clearly. "It's a skin ailment, sir. 'Dermatitis,' they call it. Frankly, sir, it hurts like hell. The doctor has ordered me to the fleet hospital for treatment. I don't mind telling you, sir, I feel like crap."

"I agree with the doctor, Bill. Get over there right away. I need you too badly, and you're in no shape to command anything."

"Sir, I strongly recommend that you assign Admiral Spruance in my place. Ray has my complete confidence. He should have yours."

"He does. Don't worry about that. I've already asked him to be my chief of staff when Milo ships out. I need somebody to do what he's told, and Admiral Spruance has never been a firecracker."

Halsey was shifting on his feet, in obvious pain. "I assume you're talking about me. No argument here. I feel like a bunch of fire-crackers were stuffed into my uniform when they went off. Damnedest thing I've ever gone through."

"Dismissed, Bill. To the hospital, now."

Halsey didn't hesitate, hobbled out in obvious discomfort. Nim-itz went to the window, stared at the two carriers, all the support ships that had come in with her. Task Force 17 will be here—probably tomorrow, he thought. Fletcher on the *Yorktown*. The whole harbor gave Halsey a hero's welcome, and I'm not sure if that will be repeated. I can't order a celebration. But he left with two carriers and he's coming home with one. And everybody here will know about it. Plus, Fletcher says *Yorktown*'s pretty beat up, needs a hell of a lot of repair. This is not the time for that. I need them all.

He had a sudden thought and wasn't sure how he should feel about it. With Halsey out of action, the senior admiral in com-mand of the task forces will be Fletcher. I suppose Spruance is fine with that. He doesn't have much choice. But I'm going to hear something out of Washington, for sure. Admiral King doesn't like Fletcher one bit, doesn't trust him, especially after the Coral Sea, losing *Lexington*. King's not the kind of man who will listen to *rea-sons*. That lack of confidence could be deadly to Fletcher, espe-cially if King's right. I don't think he is, but I've got no choice regardless. It was Halsey who told me that the best kind of leader learns to butt out of operations. I hope he's right.

He stared down, his eyes wandering over his precious subma-rines, scolded himself. Have faith, Admiral. They know what to do, and Fletcher and Spruance will support each other. God, I hope so.

HQ, CINCPAC, PEARL HARBOR, HAWAII—MAY 27, 1942

The briefing with Commander Layton had been routine, Layton explaining yet another variety of esoteric code-breaking details that drove Nimitz's eyes into a soft glaze.

"Sir, this is pretty exciting. We're working with the enemy's JN-25B cipher, which they haven't changed in an unusual length of time. That has been very helpful, allowing us a far greater period to analyze their signals and their date-time groups."

The last few words had Nimitz's attention. "What date-time groups?"

Layton seemed to light up. "Well, sir, making allowances for a garble check, Commander Rochefort's people, specifically Lieutenant Finnegan, determined that the enemy was using a twelve-by-thirty-one substitution cipher. The thirty-one kana of the first row were A, I, U, E, O, KA, KI, et cetera. The second row . . ."

"Commander, get to the point. I don't need a lesson in cryptanalysis."

Layton seemed disappointed, but reenergized himself. "Sir, yesterday, Commander Rochefort translated an order instructing two destroyer groups to embark from Saipan tomorrow, 28 May, and proceed at eleven knots for a 1 June rendezvous with transport ships that, presumably, they are to escort. They are to arrive at 1900 hours 6 June."

"You mean the attack will commence 6 June?"

"Oh, no, sir."

Nimitz fought the blossoming confusion in his brain. He looked down. "Continue, Commander."

"Sir, those destroyers will be escorting the occupation force that will arrive at . . . AF. Midway, sir. Those forces will arrive after the Japanese have completed their contact with Midway."

Nimitz stared at him now, saw the cheerful smile that meant Layton had a serious piece of news. "Spit it out, Commander."

"Sir, Commander Rochefort and his team have determined with certainty that the Japanese will be within airstrike distance from *AF*, um, Midway that is, on 3 or 4 June. The discrepancy has much to do with the Japanese, their logistics, weather conditions, and so forth. If they could get there on the third, they would. My estimate is the fourth. Joe . . . Commander Rochefort agrees."

Nimitz felt a stir in his stomach, picked up a sheet of paper on his desk. "This arrived by special courier this morning. It's a cable from OP-20-G, instructing me to anticipate the Japanese to commence their Midway operation on 15 June. Are you aware of this? It seems Washington disagrees with you?"

Layton's cheerfulness vanished. "It is apparent, sir, that what OP-20-G has done is to hijack Commander Rochefort's information and misinterpret it. There is nothing new about that, sir."

"Why would those boys in Washington go so far out on a limb they didn't build?"

"There is what I can only describe as . . . conflict between HYPO and OP-20-G. But sir . . . if we listen to Washington, we'll all end up as Japanese POWs. Begging your pardon, sir."

"I won't disagree with you. All right, Commander, are you sure about Rochefort's calculations?"

Layton seemed surprised at the question. "Of course, sir. Adding up the speeds ordered for the carrier divisions, plus the corresponding speeds sent to their cruisers, their disembarkation from their ports, the distance involved . . ."

"For crying out loud, Commander."

Layton took a breath. "Sir, the enemy will reach Midway on 3 or 4 June."

"And you are certain?"

"Sir, Commander Rochefort and I are both certain. There is no doubt."

Nimitz was shocked yet again, watched from his office as the *York-town* maneuvered into the harbor trailing a wide smear of oil in her wake. The sailors had turned out on the other moored ships, as they had for Halsey's Task Force 16, but there were fewer bands now and, as Nimitz had guessed, there were fewer reasons to celebrate.

He stared through binoculars, could see some of the damage the carrier had suffered, and had already directed she be put immediately into dry dock. He watched for several minutes, but knew the process would take far longer. It wasn't something he needed to observe, at least not until the carrier was high and dry. For now, he would play some horseshoes.

DRY DOCK, PEARL HARBOR, HAWAII—MAY 27, 1942

He had been given long rubber boots and climbed down the same ladder to the base of the dry dock alongside the workmen who were already attacking the damage to the carrier. Many were civilians, some not recognizing him at all, and those who did were impressed that the admiral of the fleet would get his feet dirty. What none of them knew was that Admiral Nimitz had once been a junior engineer.

He had heard the dismal predictions—that work on the *York-town* might require ninety days. What Nimitz could see now was that a good bit of work above the water line had begun at sea. The flight deck had been repaired enough to be usable, with much of the superficial damage whisked away.

He had a guide, of course, the ship's skipper, Captain Elliott Buckmaster, along with several engineering officers who spoke in enormous detail, explaining the necessity of patching the damaged hull, the slow process of cutting steel and welding, the interior swarmed over by pipe fitters and tooling specialists. As the tour continued, Nimitz became impatient with the men who seemed resigned to a lengthy repair, who seemed to have no appreciation for just why this ship had to be seaworthy. As the tour lengthened beyond his patience, his response made it clear to them all that their dire predictions, their need for perfection in the workmanship both in and out, could wait for later.

"*Yorktown* must be ready to sail in three days."

On May 28, Admiral Halsey's Task Force 16, now commanded by Admiral Raymond Spruance, slipped out of Pearl Harbor, the carriers *Enterprise* and *Hornet* embraced by the support ships, the cruisers and destroyers who would supply anti-aircraft and anti-submarine protection. Two days later, the patched and bandaged *Yorktown* and her escorts, Task Force 17, led by the combat fleet's commander Frank Jack Fletcher, sailed out as well. To the workers around dry dock, handshakes and backslaps were many, but there was no one with more pride in the work of those men than the admiral who watched from his office above the submarine base.

PART TWO

"Small errors cause big trouble."

    —Admiral Matome Ugaki, chief of staff, IJN

"On the morning of the 29th, we leave for battle . . .
Not that I'm expecting very much of it."

    —Admiral Isoroku Yamamoto, letter to Chiyoko Kawai

"This is fun!"

    —Lieutenant Mitsuo Fuchida, early morning, June 4, 1942

NINE

Baker

He kept his hands free, letting the student do what he could to bring the biplane in without any help. It was, after all, the purpose of the lesson, the young pilot having only three training flights under his belt. For Baker, it was closer to three hundred, but so far most of those had come like this one today, by occupying the back seat of the F3F trainer.

He loved the biplane, the open-air cockpit, the power you could feel in your face as the plane ripped through the air. But the plane now was for training the newer men, and Baker had become accustomed to staring into the back of a pilot's head, what almost passed for being able to read the young man's mind. Most of them handled the nervousness of landing without any problems, but there were others who simply came apart, the pressures of flying affecting those men in a very different way. If Baker couldn't predict the student pilot's fears, at least he had his own set of controls to take charge of the plane if he had to.

He knew this young man was more nervous than most, had seen it even before they had climbed in, the man's hands shaking as he worked the controls for takeoff. Baker spoke into the interphone, and reached forward to tap the young man on the shoulder.

"Come on, Ensign. Deep breaths. You're in control. There's no reason to be jumpy about it. She'll fly herself. You know that. She's a tough old bird, but she'll take care of you if you let her. Take her down now, nice and easy. It's a big fat landing strip."

The pilot said nothing, and Baker could feel the plane wobble side to side, the pilot fighting to keep control of the plane and control of himself. The ground was coming up quickly now, too quickly, and Baker grabbed his stick, eased it back, still talking to the pilot.

"Back off, slow throttle. You're too hot. Pull her up. You're okay, just do it. Go around again if you need to."

The response came now in a sharp yell, cutting through Baker's earphones. "I can't. Oh God! What do I do?"

"Get your hands off the controls. Hands back, keep 'em clear. I've got her."

He took over, pulled the nose up, slowing the plane, lowered the landing gear, what he had waited for the pilot to do. The plane drifted across the end of the runway, and Baker let it drop, a screeching jolt as it impacted, one low bounce, normal for him, even Baker letting out a breath of relief. He taxied the plane toward the tarmac, a crowd watching him, one instructor and a dozen students.

"I'm sorry, sir. I just couldn't do it. I don't wanna go up again."

"Kid, it's okay. Washing out isn't something to be ashamed of. No, forget I said that. I don't like the words. You can just *call it a day*. That's all. You'll be fine doing something just as important as this, maybe more. Some officers just aren't cut out for flying. It happens. It happens a lot. I'll not say anything to those boys, unless you do. But we can't just ignore this. There's paperwork we have to do. You understand, right?"

"Aye, sir."

He could hear the telltale quiver in the young man's voice, shook his head. How the hell does a boy sign up for this and fall flat on his face? And he's already an officer, if only an ensign, right out of Annapolis. They come here believing all those stories about glory, the Red Baron, Jimmy Doolittle. Yeah, and getting the girls. That's a lesson I learned quick in Hawaii. There's probably eight girls on Oahu for every five thousand guys. I think the admirals have those appointments all tied up. Can't be too different here.

He climbed up and out, the pilot already on the ground, several others coming forward, questions from all of them, the students gathering around, reacting to the look of utter despair on the young man's face. Baker moved away without hearing the chatter, moved toward the other instructor, Dick Howard, a tall lean man from somewhere in the Dakotas. Baker saw the look that said exactly what he already knew. Yep, another one. Howard moved with him now, toward the coffeepot he knew was waiting.

Howard said, "I could see his waggle. Fighting with himself. Hate that. Looked like he might do a barrel roll and dump you out. I don't know about this, Perk. We've been ordered to put these guys in a flight suit and do it fast. Every one that washes out is like an infection that could spread. What is it with these guys? That Grumman's solid as a rock. How are they supposed to climb in the seat of an F4F-4, put her down on a carrier deck? I've trained a hundred sailors to short land on a bouncing deck, but here they're on solid ground with room to spare. How many more are coming? Do we know?"

Baker shrugged. "As many as they send us. Every damn one of them wants to be a fighter pilot too. That's where the glamour is.

Damned Hollywood nonsense. Somebody in Pensacola needs to start telling these guys we need them to fly torpedo bombers or PBYs. I know there's a good bunch being trained for dive bombers. Not much glamour there, but that might be the best weapon we've got."

Howard said, "Just keep at it, Perk. The more guys who make it through, well, that's more we'll have to send up against the Japs. I gotta say, though, I didn't expect to see that most of these young squirts aren't all that young. Most of these guys are academy graduates, and half of 'em are older than me. The rest just have something to prove, I guess."

Baker smiled, glanced at Howard. "Kinda like us. We're all here because we saw too many flashy Hollywood movies, Douglas Fairbanks or somebody with a white scarf flapping around his neck."

They reached the coffeepot, two cups filled, and Howard said, "Hey, you hear about Butch O'Hare?"

Baker said, "I've heard rumors."

"Well, it's confirmed. The navy's announced it. He took down five Japs all by himself, somewhere down in the South Pacific. He's officially been named an ace. Commander Thach says he's in for a big-time medal, maybe the Navy Cross or even a Medal of Honor. I thought we'd be real well off with him on our wingtips, but damn it all, O'Hare's already on his way stateside. The president wants his face on posters, wants him shaking hands with rich guys, selling them war bonds."

Baker said, "I guess the better you are at this, the less they want you fighting Japs. That doesn't make a hell of a lot of sense."

Baker drank from the coffee cup, the brew curling his face. "Jesus, this stuff's been boiling all morning. I'm looking forward to getting back to a fine big carrier with a full-blown gedunk stand. That coffee's always better than this crap. Look, I guess none of this makes sense. They bring us here to train hotshot academy boys who think they want to fly, and they ship out the best pilots we've got. You know all those posters you see, where the Japs in their thick glasses are grinning ear to ear? Christ, now I know why."

Percy Baker had grown up in Galveston, Texas, where he spent far more time fishing Galveston Bay than worrying about schoolbooks. As a boy, his dream was to become a professional fisherman, to be paid to do the one thing he enjoyed more than any other. But that opportunity never came, no one foolish enough to pay a boy to do what he clearly would do for free. His second dream had come from all those hours along the bay watching the naval airplanes sail past, mostly trainers that often seemed to skim the water itself. By the time he was fourteen, he had decided that if he couldn't make a living with a fishing rod, he would learn to fly. To a boy in his teens, there was nothing unreasonable about either dream. But a rude shock hit him when he visited a naval recruiting office in Houston. It was the late 1930s, and with no war, and no certainty that the United States would ever be part of one, the opportunity to become a naval aviator could only come by being part of a select pool of applicants who had attended the Naval Academy at Annapolis. But Baker had too many hours with a fishing pole, resulting in mediocre grades, never an asset for acceptance to a military academy. His father worked for Union Carbide in Texas City, his mother in a local bakery. Both were hardworking people who supported their son's dream. But they had no clout at all with any local politician, much less a Texas senator, that magic ingredient that Baker would need to open those doors.

In 1939, by the time Perk Baker was twenty, he faced the reality of life that it was time to find a job that actually gave him a salary, most likely following his father to Carbide, one of the largest employers in the area. Both of Baker's dreams had begun to fade away when another trip past the Post Office in downtown Houston put him in front of a poster that froze him in his shoes. The navy was touting a new opportunity for any young man willing to do the work. It was the Naval Aviation Cadet Program. All that was required was attendance at boot camp, plus an eight-month course of preflight study. Successful graduation meant a commission as ensign in the naval reserve, and, best of all, the opportunity to train as a pilot. To Baker, this was no terrifying commitment; it was his doorway to the perfect career.

He had spent most of a year in Pensacola, first as a trainee, and then, after rising through those ranks with skills that rivaled those of most of the instructors, he found himself in the back seat of the biplane, staring at the helmets of the newer men. From Pensacola, he had been assigned to Barbers Point Naval Air Station in Hawaii. For a young man so enamored of the beaches and ocean of southeast Texas, Hawaii was every bit the paradise the recruitment officers claimed it was. But the navy had its own processes, and very soon, he was returned to Pensacola, where flying instructors were desperately needed. It was there, while dealing with washed-out recruits, that he learned of the attack on Pearl Harbor. The urgency for trained pilots increased, of course, and Baker returned again to Hawaii, then back to San Diego. He was beginning to get used to over-water flying in the massive PBYs, the flying boats that seemed as though they could circle the globe on a single tank of fuel.

In San Diego, the two-seat biplane had given way to the single-seat Brewster Buffalo, known technically as the F2A-1. But the Brewster had flaws, too many for the instructors, who could only watch their pilots from the ground. Crack-ups were more common, even if the pilots themselves appraised the Buffalo as a great deal of fun to fly. Fun wasn't in the navy's equation, and to the grateful relief of the squadron commanders, word came that a new monoplane was on its way. She was the Wildcat, officially the Grumman F4F-4, a brand-new bird said to be the equal of the Japanese Zero. That cheerleading had come from far up the ranks, which was typical. No veteran pilot that Baker knew had any expectations that the Wildcat was nearly as effective a fighter as the brass said. Many of those men had already been into combat against the Zeroes, either around the South Pacific islands or the Coral Sea. None of the pilots who had confronted the Zero wanted to show respect for such an enemy. But they couldn't help it.

It was an odd bit of fortune for Baker that besides the attack on Pearl Harbor, he had missed every other major engagement of the war. During the early hit-and-run campaigns in the South Pacific islands, he had been assigned to Bremerton, Washington, once more to train fledgling pilots. During the fight in the Coral Sea, he had been in San Diego. It was never about injury or some other problem. Baker was beginning to wonder if he was simply unlucky.

BARBERS POINT NAVAL AIR STATION, OAHU, HAWAII—MAY 28, 1942

"Welcome back, Shorty."

"Hey, I'm an officer, you know."

Bassett saluted him. "Okay. Shorty, *sir*. And I'm an officer too, so watch your mouth."

Baker measured Bassett, as he always did. Two inches taller, at most, he thought. But the nickname had stuck, as they always seemed to do. "You know, I'm still growing. I'll catch you yet. Plus, I fit better in a plane. You'll be chewing on your kneecaps."

"You stopped growing when you were four. That's why you're a runt. Hey, come on, you need to see this, if you haven't already."

They walked out through the hangar, and Baker saw a monoplane shutting down, the prop jerking to a halt, the pilot jumping down. He gave a quick acknowledgment to both of them, then disappeared into the hangar. The flight crews were out around the plane now, doing their routines, and Bassett said, "That's Price. Probably has to go to the john. Come on, take a closer look. You seen one of these new birds?"

"What the hell are they doing to the wings?"

Bassett laughed. "Just watch. They fold 'em straight up, close to the fuselage. Makes it a hell of a lot easier to stack them together on a carrier."

Baker moved out closer to the plane, the mechanics giving him a knowing smirk. Baker said, "How quick can you spread the wings out again?"

One man, grease on every part of his shirt, said, "Quicker than you can mount up. Promise you that, sir."

Bassett tugged at Baker's shirt now, both men backing away from the plane. Bassett whispered, "I make it a habit never to piss off a mechanic. But keep an eye on these clowns when they do the fold-ups. The F4F-4 is designed for that, but the designers forgot about the flaps. It's easy for the mechanics to damage them, and none of us need that."

"How do you know so much?"

Bassett laughed, pulled Baker along with him. "They're called *briefings*. Now that you're here, you should drop in to one."

Baker was annoyed at his friend's humor. "You know damn well I just got back from San Diego. Training another bunch of kids who needed wet-nursing. I'm happy to be at Pearl just to see a carrier again. I was supposed to be on *Saratoga,* and the Japs busted her open. Then they had me going with Commander Thach on *Lexington*. Well, I ain't talking about that. Now we're supposed to be on *Yorktown,* and she's sitting over there in dry dock. What the hell? I must be cursed or something. I may never see a damn Jap."

"I don't know, Perk. Something's going on, for sure. I saw it myself. You're right about dry dock. The *Yorktown*'s getting a real overhaul, and fast. I heard they want us back at sea as quick as possible. Some kinda stink's in the wind. Must be two thousand guys over there working her over, and it's been twenty-four hours a day. I heard that Admiral Nimitz told 'em she ain't gotta be beautiful, she's just gotta float."

"Damn, you know way too much. Somebody's gonna make *you* an admiral. I just hope they don't forget to fix up the gedunk stand."

Bassett slapped his shoulder, said, "Listen, in case you didn't get word, we've got a briefing at 1700, Commander Thach. He'll answer your questions whether you ask 'em or not. I'm just happy to be flying with him. You should be too."

"I been waiting for it since the Japs came in here. But the navy keeps tossing me out again. Hope I can stay this time. And I reported to Commander Thach when I got off the PBY this morning. He mentioned the briefing." Baker looked at his watch. "Oh, hell, that's ten minutes from now. I still ain't figured out this Hawaii time zone crap."

"Me either. But I can read a watch. We should show up early. Make a good impression."

They moved quickly into the single-story concrete building, followed by several other pilots, many of those strangers. Baker found a chair, the others sitting as well, as the room filled up with even more men Baker had never seen before. He wasn't alone with his curiosity, several of the men he knew with puzzled looks.

The door opened on the far end of the room, quieting the men.

Lieutenant Commander Jimmie Thach was the squadron leader most men sought out, the kind of respect that came from skill in the air and his skill at managing the men around him. Thach was several years older than both Baker and Bassett, and was a graduate of the Naval Academy. And from what Baker had already heard, Thach's men would get the first allotment of the new F4F-4 fighters, a testament to the respect he was receiving above him as well.

Thach stood with his hands behind him, and said, "If you're

wondering why there are so many of us, I'll answer that. My VF-3 squadron, the dozen or so of you who know me well, has been enhanced by the addition of VF-42. That was the navy's decision, and I don't argue. There are twenty-seven of us now, and I haven't flown alongside more than ten of you. We need to fix that, and fast." He stopped, studied the faces, his eyes settling on those few he knew well. "I have put a request in to Admiral Halsey that we be given adequate supplies of gasoline, oil, and mechanics so that we may do practice runs throughout the day. I have been told that Admiral Halsey is not fit for combat. He has been replaced temporarily by Admiral Fletcher, who will join us onboard *Yorktown*. Admiral Fletcher has agreed to my request. Starting at 0600 tomorrow, we will begin short-run takeoff and landing drills. If you want to fly with me, show me that you can."

Beside Baker, Bassett said, "Commander, can you tell us what it is we're preparing for?"

"Lieutenant, all I know is what they tell me. Captain Buckmaster has told me himself that *Yorktown* will be seaworthy as of 30 May. And we will go to sea on that date. Obviously, somebody over there at fleet HQ is all fired up for something, and I have no idea what it is. Don't really care. My job is to get you ready for anything they want us to do. You new boys, and you boys from VF-42, pay attention to the veterans. If I hear anybody treating this like a rivalry, I'll kick your ass. Commander Lovelace here is my executive officer, and he'll be watching every one of you. And you veterans, you watch all that noise you like to make. I was taught by a good man, Commander Art Radford, that the best pilot makes his noise with his airplane, not his mouth. I expect all of you to practice that."

Thach stood motionless, his hands still behind his back, then made a quick nod to the side, toward his executive officer, who stood, moved back, and turned an easel toward the men, revealing the drawing of a fighter plane. Baker could see the meatballs on the plane's wings and fuselage, knew it was a Japanese Zero.

Lovelace pulled a pencil out of his pocket, used it as a pointer. "I'm hoping that all of you know what this is. If you don't learn now, and you don't know what to do about it, you'll be dead in your first encounter." He paused, seemed to wait for a reaction, any one of the men spouting off about his own expertise. But the room stayed silent, and Lovelace nodded and said, "All right. Pay attention. You've all seen the new Grumman we've been given, the F4F-4. Fine machine. In many ways it's a better machine than the Zero. In many ways it isn't. Our firsthand observations, plus our intelligence sources, tell us some details about the Zero. She is incredibly agile. She has a top speed over three hundred miles per hour, and she climbs like a bird. She has what appears to be a pair of twenty-millimeter cannon in her nose, with four fifty-caliber machine guns in the wings." There were a few mumbles, none of them boastful. "That's the bad news. The good news is that she's a tinder box. Unlike your Wildcat, the Zero doesn't seem to have a self-sealing fuel tank. With the right piece of luck from you, or maybe a good aim, the Zero goes up like the Fourth of July. But you've got to get on her tail first. She gets on yours, and the only thing protecting you is that steel plate behind your seat. And if you're lucky, a soft landing in the ocean." He paused. "Questions?"

To one side of Baker, one of the new men raised his hand.

Lovelace said, "This isn't third grade. Speak up."

"Uh, sir, you mentioned the steel plate. Do all the Wildcats have them?"

"Yep. They add a good bit of weight to your plane, but they'll save your life in a dogfight. Best bet, though, is not to get into a dogfight in the first place. The Zero is pretty unforgiving, and don't any of you assume that the Jap pilots don't measure up. Those of us who've faced off with them have a lot of respect for those fellows. You underestimate them, you'll go down and fast."

Another new man spoke up now. "Sir, what do you do to shake them off your tail? A loop?"

Lovelace looked at Thach with a smile, said, "Jimmie, this is a question for you."

Thach stood, took his time. "When they put me in command of VF-3, the policy was to fly in three-bird formations. I hated that, and I told them why. A pilot would have to spend all his time making sure he didn't bump into one of the others. I was surprised as hell when some big brass agreed with me. So, in this squadron we fly in pairs, side by side, slightly above or below your wingman. There's a reason for this. A Jap gets on your tail, don't waste your time with all that razzle-dazzle crap. Both of you turn toward each other, passing close by, then level out and make ready to do it again. The enemy will either follow you, or he'll go after your wingman. Either way, one of you will have a chance to nail him either broadside or from the tail. It might sound complicated, but we're gonna practice that starting tomorrow. A lot."

Lovelace stood again. "What Jimmie's not telling you new boys is that the navy has acknowledged that this maneuver has a name." He scanned the men, searching for a familiar face. "Perk, tell the new fellows here what it's called."

Baker smiled. "It's called the Thach Weave. And, sir, I for one am happy to try it out."

ONBOARD USS *YORKTOWN*, AT SEA—MAY 30, 1942

The grumbling had been relentless, complaints about the handling of the new Wildcats. The F4F-4 was heavier than its predecessor, and though it could match the speed of the Zero, it was not at all as maneuverable. The weight came in part from the addition of two more fifty-caliber machine guns in the wings, increasing the armament there from four to six guns. Though navy brass assumed the pilots would welcome the increase in firepower, all of Thach's pilots knew that if you couldn't gain the upper hand against your enemy, no added firepower would accomplish anything. And from what the men knew of the Zero, maneuverability mattered far more than bullets.

With the drills at Barbers Point complete, the planes made their way to the carrier, landing in quick succession. Baker watched the flight crews carefully as his Wildcat had its wings tucked in, paying close attention to the handling of the flaps. So far, only Commander Thach had jumped on a flight crew for their carelessness, the kind of mishap that could bring down a plane without the pilot knowing why.

The fighters were gathered at the stern of the carrier, and for the first time, Baker began to pay closer attention to just what other kinds of planes the *Yorktown* was carrying. The fighters were the only single-seaters. Both the torpedo bombers and the dive bombers had a back seat that faced to the rear, the pilot supported by a gunner, most operating thirty-caliber single-barrel machine guns. The gunner served more than one purpose. With his view to the rear, he could alert the pilot if there was a problem on the plane's tail, while also being able to swivel his seat to face forward to his own radio and his own set of controls, should the pilot be wounded or killed.

There was another distinction for the bomber and torpedo crews that Baker found surprising. The pilots were almost all officers, as they were in Thach's fighter squadron. But the gunners were enlisted men. No one bothered to explain why to Baker, and he knew better than to ask. The navy did things the way the navy did things.

The practice continued, constant takeoffs and landings from the carrier's flight deck. Each time Baker went up, he scanned the sea around them, saw no sign of land, and only a scattering of support ships, cruisers, and destroyers. No one had yet told any of Thach's men just where they were going, or what they were supposed to be doing.

It was late in the afternoon, and only a few more of the squadron's planes were still airborne. Baker went through his routine now, lowered the plane's landing gear, a tedious, hand-cranking maneuver that required concentration to keep the pilot from breaking his arm. He looked to the side, the ship's island, and saw the green landing light. The Wildcat eased down to less than a hundred feet above the flight deck, passed by the island, made a large looping circle out beyond the ship's stern. He settled the plane in a shallow approach, the flight deck coming up to meet him, his tailhook hanging low now. He could see the arrestor wires across the flight deck, couldn't avoid the cold punch of nerves. Careful, Percy. Don't screw it up, not now.

To one side was the landing signal officer, holding his two paddles high, then giving the cut signal, Baker switching the engine to idle, the plane dropping gently to the deck. He waited for the hard yank, the tail hook catching the second arrestor wire, and the plane pulled to a stop. He smiled to himself, said aloud, "You've never missed one yet. No time to start now."

He taxied quickly to the designated tarmac area, behind the large safety net, the flight crews ready there to do their jobs. Baker shut the engine down, looked toward the island. He could see the photographer, the ship's official tattletale, the man with one job: Photograph anyone who screwed up. Baker wouldn't give him the pleasure.

More planes were coming in now, Thach and the last few, veterans and a pair of the new men. Baker stayed on deck and watched Thach land perfectly, which was no surprise. The Wildcat moved up behind Baker's, the engine shut down, the deck crews quickly folding the wings, maneuvering Thach's plane in close beside Baker's. Another plane came in now, Commander Lovelace, taxiing straight along the deck and moving behind the safety net as well.

Thach said to Baker, "Lieutenant, I'm heading down for a sandwich. Tell Commander Lovelace I'll be waiting for him. He owes me a Coca-Cola."

"Aye, sir. I'll do it."

Baker thought about going below himself, a Coca-Cola suddenly very appealing. Beside him, another pilot said, "What the hell? He's too hot. *Dammit.*"

Baker turned, saw the next plane impacting on its landing gear, then bouncing up high, too high, over the top of the net. The plane dropped hard now, the prop still spinning, the plane coming down directly on top of another. The chaos was complete, shattered metal and glass, men staring in shock, then moving forward, scrambling over debris to reach the pilots. The errant plane was quickly silent, the engine choked off by the metal from below. Baker moved forward with the others, eyes on the cockpits, a spray of blood . . . Lovelace's blood, on what remained of the bottom glass. He felt sick, was shoved aside, the deckhands doing their jobs, but it was a job no one had expected, an accident none of them had seen before. Hands went to the wings of the top plane, rolling it to one side, off the horrible mess of the cockpit below. The plane was clear now, shoved aside, the pilot still strapped inside, his face staring with the same horror that filled them all. Baker looked at him, the man's eyes now on the wreckage he had caused, Lovelace's bloody corpse now raised slowly, carefully, a stretcher brought up close. There were corpsmen as well, hovering, bending low over the body, but there was nothing for them to do.

Baker stared at the young pilot whose error had done this, felt a violent rage toward the man, the words in his head, Too young, too stupid to be flying. But the rage passed into sadness, grief for one of their own, a man that Thach would miss. *Thach.*

He heard the voice now, Thach coming back on deck, a sharp shout toward the wrecked planes.

"What the hell happened? Who's hit? Oh Jesus. Who is it?"

Baker looked at Thach, said, "It's Commander Lovelace, sir. He never had a chance, never knew what hit him."

The words sounded ridiculous, asinine, but Baker didn't know what else to say. Thach stood frozen, then uttered low words. "My best friend. Holy Jesus."

Thach moved forward, away from Baker, the deck officer there, holding him up.

"Nothing you can do, Commander. The corpsmen will take him downstairs. Your pilot is still in his plane. Won't climb out. Looks like shock. They're tending to him. Best go back inside, Commander. We'll do what we have to do."

There was a softness in the man's voice, something Baker had never heard before, the gruff and profane man showing Thach some heart.

Thach kept his eyes on the wreckage, said, "That's Howell."

Baker said, "Yep. First week on the job. Somebody like me okayed him for his wings. Too soon. He came in way too hot, bounced too high."

Thach said, "Never seen a fatality on a flight deck. Smashed-up equipment, sure, all the damn time. But this was Lovelace." He glanced at Baker. "We lost two today, Perk. Howell will never fly again. He'll never get this out of his head. And Lovelace . . ."

He looked at Baker again, a hard sadness, red eyes. "My best friend. Jesus God. And there's gonna be more of this. I can feel it, I can see it in the captain's eyes, the admiral. They're not telling us anything, and that tells us everything we need to know. Just be ready to die."

TEN

Ackroyd

"**G**et that damned wire out this way. Uncoil it now! Move it! You want Japs licking your ears? Let's go!"

The marines around him knew Ackroyd was serious, that the duty had been ordered from the top, which on Midway was Lieutenant Colonel Harold Shannon. But the marines always knew that although the officers might issue the orders, the gunnery sergeants were the authority. Even Colonel Shannon seemed to understand that.

Shannon and his immediate superior on the island, naval captain Cyril Simard, had taken Admiral Nimitz's visit to heart, immediately beefing up Midway's defenses, from dugouts in the tall sand dunes to machine gun and mortar placements in the patches of woods. Whether the marines needed any added incentive to do their jobs, Admiral Nimitz had taken no chances, penning a letter to the two commanders that reached Midway on May 20. The letter had a simple message: The Japanese are coming. There were no real details, none of the code-breaking specifics that Nimitz would soon receive from Layton and Rochefort. But none of that was required. When the orders came down, the marines went to work, manufacturing crudely designed anti-personnel mines, digging the defensive dugouts just a little deeper, reinforcing the makeshift sand caves with timbers and camouflaging brush.

Gunnery Sergeant Doug Ackroyd had already become a legend, one of the old-timers, serving in the Corps even longer than his commanding officer, Colonel Simard, who had fought the Germans in the Great War. Ackroyd's experience had come first in 1918, Belleau Wood, France, a rugged and bloody fight that, by all accounts, kept the Germans out of Paris. Then, Ackroyd was a green teenager, terrified of every loud noise. Now, he was over forty, with no patience for the stupidity of youth. The marines around him were almost all young, most of them inexperienced. Officially, they were the 6th Marine Defense Battalion, stationed on Midway as a security and defense force for the naval operations there. If the officers understood that they really weren't much of a force against the Japanese, it was the older veterans, the men like Gunny Ackroyd, who had been handed the job to change that. Out here, they had one task: Keep the Japanese off Midway. If there were doubts about that, it was only because none of them knew just how many Japanese might be coming.

He glimpsed to one side, saw the officer trudging up the hill of soft sand, out of breath, the man pointing out to one side.

"Sergeant, we've got more wire, finally. That ferry ship brought it in last night."

Ackroyd acknowledged Major Hommel with a casual salute, could see heavy sweat on the man's face, soaking his shirt.

Ackroyd said, "What kind of wire, sir?"

Hommel seemed flustered, a nervous wreck. "Barbed wire, Sergeant. String it out where it will do the most good. More's coming. I'll get you enough to ring this whole island. Now be quick about it!"

Hommel moved off, stumbling back down the soft sand hill. Beside Ackroyd, another man moved up, another of the older veterans, Bill Yon.

"He bring us any new orders, Gunny?"

"Those rolls of barbed wire coming off that truck. There's more coming. Get the men to work, keep spreading the stuff out."

Yon stared at the growing heap of wire coils. "Good Lord. How much of that stuff do we need?"

Ackroyd stood with his hands on his hips, flexed his shoulders, felt the sweat running down the middle of his back. "Enough to keep the Japs from grabbing us in the tenders. Do it. It'll make him happy."

"You mean Major Hommel?"

"*Barbed Wire Bob.* That's all I've ever heard him called, no matter where he's been. Loves barbed wire more than ordnance. He keeps the barbed wire companies in business. All right, move it. Get it unrolled and stake it up, or bunch it, whichever works best."

"You think the Japs are coming?"

"Hell, yes, the Japs are coming. Last night, Colonel Shannon showed several of us another letter he just got from Admiral Nimitz. Came in yesterday. That's why we're out here sweating up a storm. They got word from somewhere that the Japs are on their way, should hit us within a few days. I don't need to know any more than that. Neither do you."

"Gunny! Another ship's coming in. Maybe supplies."

Ackroyd followed the voice to a half dozen men struggling with rolls of wire. He saw the ship now, beyond the tallest dunes, and yelled out to the cluster of men, "Use gloves, you idiots." He studied the ship, and said to Yon, "Light cruiser. She's probably not sticking around. I hope she brought some decent cigars."

Yon said, "She's offloading something. Should we check it out?"

Ackroyd felt the peculiar itch in the back of his head when he heard a stupid question. "You a longshoreman now? Let the sailors handle it. It's their job. Jesus."

"Sorry. I'll work on the wire. Holy cow, there's a bunch more coils of the stuff coming off that truck back by the trees. Christ, Gunny, you're right. *Barbed Wire Bob.*"

Ackroyd stood alone now, stepped slowly to the top of the dune, studied the ship. It would suit me if they offloaded all those damn anti-aircraft guns they're carrying. What we've got here is junk. A cruiser's got no use for all that many anyhow. They should share.

It had been too many years since Ackroyd had aimed his rifle at the enemy, and then in some scorpion-infested hole in Panama he had tried to forget. Like most of the men who scurried around him now, he had gone through the rigorous, some said vicious, training at Parris Island in South Carolina. He was one of the first classes of men to pass through a place that had become infamous for its brutal conditions, and even now, he quizzed his men silently, tested their stamina with jobs that Parris Island would have tested before him. None of that made Ackroyd beloved, but for the men who saw gray hair at his temples, the mass of sharp muscles inside a tight T-shirt, their respect, combined with a touch of fear, meant that even the officers paid attention when he spoke.

Ackroyd looked back toward the flat stretch of beach, the men laboring with the wire. Wire, he thought. Here's how the enemy beats stupid-ass wire. He sends one man in first with a thick vest, he dies on the wire, or just falls on it, and every other son of a bitch steps right over him. There's your great barbed wire defense. Saw too much of that in France. That idiot major would rather have that stuff spread all over this beach than a half dozen machine guns. Dumb ass.

He heard a new sound now, looked again toward the cruiser.

There were trucks headed his way, blowing through the soft sand, moving down on the flat stretch of beach. His own men were scrambling to get out of the way, the truck drivers showing no respect for anyone in their way. Ackroyd felt the familiar heat in his face, rolled up the sleeves on his shirt, showing the round tightness of his biceps, always a good effect. The trucks stopped just below him, men bailing out by the dozen. He stepped deliberately through the heavy sand, saw a few of the men with bare chests and tattoos, most with bandoliers of thirty-caliber ammo draped on their shoulders. There were BARs and machine guns, pockets stuffed with grenades, every man with at least three or four knives in his belt. One man turned, looking past him, pulled a knife from his boot, zipped the knife just past Ackroyd, a light thump, perfect throw into a palm tree. Around the man, there was laughter, a backslap.

Ackroyd's blood was in full boil now, and he stepped forward, preparing to eliminate a fair number of teeth.

"Who the hell do you think you are?"

The laughter stopped, and one man stepped forward. "Lieutenant Keith Turner. Unless you're an officer, I expect a salute."

Behind him, the laughter erupted again. Ackroyd wasn't impressed, and said, "Prove it. Where're your bars?"

The men made new sounds now, a chorus of boos. The lieutenant flipped up the collar on his sweat-soaked shirt, revealing a silver bar. Ackroyd responded with a weak salute, returned by Turner.

"You didn't answer the question, sir. I'm Gunnery Sergeant Doug Ackroyd. We're working on this beach, so either pitch in or get the hell out of the way. With all due respect."

Ackroyd expected a squad of MPs to suddenly appear to nail him for insubordination, but no one in this crowd looked anything like an MP. Instead, he saw a smile.

"You oughta think about joining us, Gunny. I like your moxie. We're Company C, Carlson's Raiders. Company D is positioning on Eastern Island. Admiral Nimitz sent us up here to . . . help out."

The name meant something, Ackroyd rolling around the memories, recalling the 2nd Raider Battalion. He didn't know this lieutenant, or Major Carlson, but knew plenty about the work these men had done in China, fighting the Japanese alongside the Chinese Communists.

"Welcome to heaven, Lieutenant. I'll say it again. We've got orders to spread all the barbed wire in the world, plus add to the dugouts and machine gun and mortar batteries. If you feel like helping, we could use it. If you don't, sir, please get the hell out of the way."

Turner put his hands on his hips. "Not much you're afraid of, is there, Gunny? Looks like you've been a marine longer than most of us have been alive. Fair enough. I'll cut you slack." Turner glanced behind him. "Lieutenant Throneson, if you please."

The man stepped through the crowd, appearing no different than the marines around him, except his size. He was nearly a foot shorter than Ackroyd, and skinny as a rail.

Turner said, "Gunny, we will see to ourselves, make our camp up in those trees, if it's all right with you. Your colonel has already approved our position here. But I'm guessing he'd defer to you. You should know that Harold . . . Lieutenant Throneson fought in the Spanish Civil War. Several of us, actually. He's good at one thing, and it ain't got nothing to do with dames." The laughter came again, even Throneson smiling, obviously used to it. "You said you needed help. How about this? The lieutenant here is our demo officer. He gets a kick out of blowing stuff up. Including Japs."

Throneson said, "You have any dynamite in this place? Maybe some flashlight batteries?"

Ackroyd was curious, realized there were a half dozen of his own men now gathered behind him. "Aye, sir. Plenty, far as I know. What the hell do you want with that stuff? Um . . . sir."

"I make anti-personnel ordnance, Gunny. You know. Bombs."

MIDWAY, EASTERN ISLAND — MAY 31, 1942

He stood close to the runway, watched the torpedo bombers taking off, sluggish and loud, flying past him with none of the thunder that inspired confidence. Across the way, men moved out onto the runway, quick work, cleaning any debris, brush, or shreds of old timber, anything kicked up by the planes. Ackroyd ignored them, heard an odd noise, saw an albatross, what everyone on the island knew as the Midway gooney birds. It flew past him, then turned, the soft rhythm of its wings slowly flapping, and landing a few feet away from him. The birds were large, and for the most part, tame. And though graceful in the air, they were comically clumsy in the sand. Most of the marines and sailors considered them to be a mascot.

Ackroyd watched the bird, and wondered if it was one of those he had begun to confide in. "What the hell do you want? I got nothing to eat. I'll come back later with some chow. I know you're not too picky. Stale bread seems to work just fine. So, you born here? Well, sure. Where the hell else would you be from? Sand Island has to be like Europe to you. I'm from Alabama. Everywhere's Paris compared to that. I bet you can fly faster than those damn Vindicators. If those damn torpedo planes went any slower, they'd go backwards. We need to figure out how to strap a bomb to your belly. You'd be cheaper to operate."

Despite his crust, Ackroyd could never be cruel to a gooney bird. He kept it from the men of course, his growling image serving him well in any tough situation, whether a fistfight or a disagreeable order. But he talked often to the gooneys, fed them what he could, spending discreet minutes on some secluded stretch of sand, wondering if the ridiculous-looking bird actually understood him, or, like now, if it was in fact the same bird as so many times before. The thought made him smile. Maybe he's actually my *friend*. Don't really need one. But don't really have one either.

A louder noise came now, far down the runway, the first of a formation of much larger planes coming in, touching down in line, the hard rumble of their four engines.

He spoke to the bird now. "Well, I'll be damned. Those are B-17s. Wonder if they're staying here for our benefit, or they got lost trying to find Hawaii. If they stay here, well, Gooney old bird, you're out of a job. They'll carry the bombs."

With a steady flow of ships coming in from Hawaii, the armament and sustenance supplies on Midway continued to increase and improve. Admiral Nimitz had made good on his word that Midway would be beefed up as much as could be positioned in the limited area. The armament included additional aircraft, including army B-17 and B-26 bombers, more modern dive bombers, fighters, and a handful of fresh torpedo planes, as well as a dozen or more twenty-millimeter and three-inch anti-aircraft guns. A happy surprise even to the veterans like Sergeant Ackroyd were the five tanks that rolled ashore off the ferry *Kittyhawk*.

For all the armament now filling the space on the atoll, Ackroyd was drawn still to the dangerous oddballs of Carlson's Raiders. The suggestions of Lieutenant Throneson were well received, the marines assembling all manner of nasty anti-personnel devices, more than a thousand of them placed strategically along the waterfront. If the Japanese attempted an amphibious landing, it would be costly.

As he watched the bombers land on the tight runway, Ackroyd felt an unexpected emotion, a surge of enthusiasm that finally the marines, *his* marines, would confront their enemy. It had been a very long time, and the memories—the bad memories—had faded. He ignored that, and thought instead of the kids who worked for him, the kids who were officers. I had my time, he thought. Now it's theirs.

He looked out to sea, soft swells, empty ocean. All right. We're ready. If we have to do this, let's do this.

ELEVEN

Yamamoto

He was furious.

"What do you mean they turned back? It was not a difficult mission. It was not particularly dangerous. Those pilots were experienced, tested. Who made such a decision to bring them home?"

Ugaki shifted in his chair. "It could not be helped, sir. The Americans . . . well, sir, it seems that the Americans beat us to the punch."

"I'm not interested in *clever repartee*, Admiral. If there are good reasons for failure, I would like to know what they are. I am weary of bad omens."

It was called Operation K, one more attempt for Japanese long-range bombers to overfly the island of Oahu. But this was no weak effort at a symbolic bombing run. The two Kawanishi flying boats were to journey directly around Pearl Harbor, making careful note of just how much of the American fleet was anchored there, and if possible, observing if any of the ships were making ready to set sail or if they were simply gathered up like a flock of defensive birds. All along, Yamamoto's thinking had rested on the assumption that the Americans had no intention of pouring out of Pearl Harbor to engage a far superior Japanese navy. They would have to be drawn out, convinced it was the necessary thing to do. How that would happen would depend on the success of the assault directly on Midway, with possibly some notion that the Americans would respond to the Japanese invasion and occupation of the islands in the Aleutians. Either way, Yamamoto insisted on knowing just what kind of force he would face. The two Kawanishi bombers were to provide him that intelligence.

The mission for the two flying boats involved a lengthy flight, too lengthy for their fuel capacity. Several hundred miles from Hawaii lay a small spit of land and sandbars known as French Frigate Shoals. Operation K provided for two fuel-carrying submarines to lay in wait off the Shoals, as the flying boats would land. The planes would then take on adequate fuel to reach Hawaii and return to the Shoals, where they would refuel again for their trip home, the island of Jaluit. The plan seemed almost too simple, and assuming the planes overflew Oahu at a high altitude, they could perform their mission virtually undetected.

On May 31, the plan went into operation, but the fuel-laden subs reached French Frigate Shoals only to find an American destroyer escorting a seaplane tender, both ships at anchor. Waiting overnight, in the hope that the Americans would move on, the subs then observed that instead of a barren spit of sand, the Shoals had become a small American base for submarine and amphibious operations, almost exactly what the Japanese had intended to do.

With no hope of accomplishing their refueling mission, the submarines had no choice but to slip away, while the flying boats returned to their bases. Operation K had simply collapsed.

"Did no one think that the Americans also have flying boats? Did no one think that French Frigate Shoals might also be an important position on American maps?"

Ugaki had absorbed most of Yamamoto's anger, playing the role that Yamamoto required him to play. But Yamamoto knew there was no blame to be laid at the feet of his chief of staff. Nor could he fault the men seated around the wardroom, his staff, the senior officers of his flagship.

"I will not accept what some among you insist, that we are a force guided by fate, by omens and curses. We are guided by strategy and wisdom. If it is not my own, it is yours, all of you. It is why you are here. But there cannot be failure."

Ugaki scanned the others, and said, "What would any of you have done to avoid this?"

Kuroshima spoke up, animated, waving his lit cigarette. "We should have sent at least one light cruiser to accompany the submarines. The Americans would not have stood up to that. They would have scampered back to their mothers at Pearl Harbor."

Ugaki said, "Yes, they would have scampered back to Pearl Harbor with all manner of details about why. There would be no secrecy. Possibly our entire operation would have been exposed. And who would bear that responsibility?"

Yamamoto let Ugaki have his moment, the others now hesitant to speak up. In the silence, Yamamoto thought, No one accepts responsibility, so they all share it. Which means nothing at all. Of course not. No one answers for our blunders but me. "Admiral Ugaki, it is time to move past this. I am more concerned about the raw stupidity now sweeping across Japan. Whatever foolishness might happen out here, so far from home, we can control. We have great guns and skilled pilots, the greatest weapons of war in the world. If we err, we have the tools to fix our mistakes. But I cannot tell those useless fools in the ministry how to do their jobs."

His words seemed welcome, especially if they meant no more haranguing from his chief of staff. Across from him, Kuroshima said, "Sir, I admit that I was shocked by the lack of discretion for this mission. For the Pearl Harbor operation, we maintained perfect silence well after the fleet left Japan. This week, there were parades. Fishermen saluted us, then ran home to tell their wives or anyone else how many great warships they saw. Why was there no effort made for secrecy?"

Yamamoto hated the question, but not as much as he hated the answer. "Because we have become arrogant. We will not lose because we *cannot* lose." He paused. "I have been well acquainted with Naval Minister Shimada. He is my friend, and I trust him, more than I trust any one of those cackling birds around him. On Navy Day, less than one week ago, he stood up at the Diet and announced our complete plans for the Midway Operation. Anyone there could run out and tell the nearest newspaperman what he heard. But worse, Shimada felt it necessary to enlighten our government and our emperor with the prizes we have gained in all our victories. Do you know that our navy has sunk eight battleships? Or six aircraft carriers, fifty submarines, fifteen cruisers? Magnificent success. And pure fiction. He must believe the emperor is a five-year-old who swallows every tall tale. These are the people who are leading us through this war."

His gloom was self-inflicted now. "Go. There is much to do. As of right now, the order will go out across the entire fleet that we will now maintain complete radio silence. If we are to know what Admiral Nagumo's aircraft carriers are doing, we must intercept even the faintest of transmissions from his pilots, and nothing else. The same is true of course for the Midway invasion force. We must also keep a tight ear on our phones for any transmission from the Americans. Go now, stay close to the ship's operations."

They stood, and Yamamoto pointed to Watanabe. "Remain, please."

The others filed out, a last glimpse back from Ugaki. Yamamoto waved him away, and saw now Watanabe's puzzled expression. Yamamoto reached behind him into a cabinet, retrieved a small box and a large flat board, a chess set.

"They would be jealous, you know. You are the only one who can sometimes beat me. I must correct that situation. Sit down, Commander."

Watanabe obeyed him, pulled his chair up close across the table. "I am nervous about this, Admiral."

"Chess? Or Midway?"

"Midway, sir. We are nearly six hundred miles astern of Admiral Nagumo's flagship, from all four of the aircraft carriers. I do not see how we can offer any assistance, should they be attacked."

"They will not be attacked, Commander. The Americans are a flock of scared birds, clustered in the banyan tree. They will not fly unless we make them fly. They will not attack us unless we attack them. They know how strong we are. The American is many things, but he is not a complete fool. It is up to us to convince him to leave his tree, to accept that he must make battle, no matter the odds. Then, we have him."

"Sir, still . . . I just don't know how we can be of use if we are hundreds of miles astern of the fight."

Yamamoto had heard this argument at the ministry, from men he did not respect. He did not need to hear it from a man he did. "Commander, this ship is one piece of a navy that is superior to every such force in the world. But the battleships have played little role, their crews sitting in port hearing only of the great successes of the carriers and their escorts. These crews have grown restless, they want their share of the honor. So, now? Look around you. Now they are at sea. Now they are part of a great operation, a task force to support the destruction of the American fleet. Once we have destroyed that fleet, a great many targets await us. Hawaii perhaps. The American west coast. Some have suggested the Panama Canal. The big guns on this ship can destroy any target they find. The crew and the officers take great pride in that. They know their place is at the head of the parade. This time, I merely had to allow them to come along for the ride."

Watanabe tilted his head slightly. "Admiral, you don't believe any of that. You know that without the carriers, we are a toothless force." He seemed to awaken, sat bolt upright. "Forgive me, sir. I am out of my station to say such things."

"Yes, you are. We will not speak of this again. Here, you have the white pieces. Make your move."

"As you wish, sir. But I do not believe my mind will be on the game."

"I am glad you distract yourself with such doubts. This time, and from now on, I shall defeat you. I am certain of it. I will show you, as I have shown so many others. I never lose."

He felt the fog before he reached the deck, the wet cold that seemed to melt a soft sheen onto every metal surface. He moved outside, but the wind met him, a hard chill, unexpected. His aide was there, a raincoat in hand, and Yamamoto thought of rejecting him, unseemly for the admiral to protect his perfect white uniform from a little rain. But he rethought his position, the rain blowing harder now, and he stepped back inside the passageway, and said to the aide, "Some nights it is best not to take a stroll. You may leave me."

The man bowed, backed away, and Yamamoto moved along the

passageway toward the bridge of the massive ship. He knew at least two of his staff would be there, working alongside the ship's captain and the ship's senior staff. He climbed the final ladder, another passageway, a guard at the bridge, stiffening, then pulling open the hatch. Faces turned toward him, but not many, most staying focused on their work. He understood now, the splatter of rain against the glass of the bridge, dense fog beyond. The men stared, some issuing orders into sound tubes, delivering commands to the radio room for the shortwave messages to be issued to each part of Yamamoto's task force. The shortwaves were barely effective, but they had to be used, so that the signals were weak, far too weak to reach Nagumo's fleet six hundred miles ahead, and weaker still to be picked up by any American listening station. The orders seemed urgent, pure concentration on the faces of the officers. Yamamoto felt suddenly out of place, saw Ugaki looking back at him, answering Yamamoto's silent gesture. *Come.* Yamamoto led him into the passageway now, and Ugaki said, "Worst night I've ever seen, sir. Dense fog, rain. No sign that it will end any time soon. The weather systems in this part of the ocean move from west to east, so we're traveling with it. There isn't much else we can do. We've got the ships maintaining submarine alert, a zigzag pattern as much as possible. All the lead ships are trailing signal buoys to keep the task force together. But even that is dangerous, sir. A collision is not out of the question."

Yamamoto weighed the words, was not happy to see Ugaki this upset. "Relax, Admiral. If we cannot see, neither can the enemy. I do not imagine a submarine would be enjoying this weather either. If Nagumo is enduring this, all the better. He will know that the Americans cannot see him any more than we can. Think of it as a vast smoke screen, and every second we draw closer to our goal. Blindness is our ally."

"I am still concerned about enemy submarines. One lucky boat, spotting us even in the fog—it could be deadly. If not for us, for one of the aircraft carriers. And there is no way we can communicate with Admiral Nagumo."

"We can, Matome. But we will not. Be very clear. There will be absolute radio silence. The only sounds I wish to hear are victory celebrations."

He could see that Ugaki was troubled. "What is it? Speak your mind."

"I still wish you would consider pushing this invasion force past Midway and on to Hawaii. The damage to the enemy could be much greater."

Yamamoto shook his head. "You would have me alter our carefully designed plan at this hour?"

"No, of course not. My apologies, sir."

"If all goes as we design it, you will have your Hawaii. There will be little left of the American fleet to defend it."

There was good reason for Yamamoto's confidence. As part of the vast plan, nineteen submarines were sent eastward, intending to string a line of both observation and destruction through the waters that separated Hawaii and Midway. If and when the Americans ventured out of Pearl Harbor, the submarines would certainly make contact. Even if no torpedoes were launched, they would be in position to monitor exactly which American ships were moving, at what speed and which direction. If, along the way, the subs could sink an American aircraft carrier, all the better.

The submarines were to be in place by June 2, the same day that Yamamoto's three task forces pushed through the miserable weather toward Midway. What Yamamoto could not know, primarily because of his own order for radio silence, was that the submarines had dawdled before leaving Japan, and continued to dawdle along the way. By June 2, instead of nineteen submarines lying across the presumed path of the American fleet, there was only one. The others would be at least two days late.

SEVEN HUNDRED MILES WEST OF MIDWAY—JUNE 3, 1942

She was an American Navy PBY, one of the massive flying boats whose range made her perfect as a long-distance scout.

This day, she was piloted by Naval Ensign Jewell Reid, an experienced pilot who had endured the boredom of these kinds of reconnaissance flights for days. But this one was different. As he neared the outer limits of his plane's range, Reid spotted what seemed to be tiny dots on the horizon, growing larger as he closed the distance. At 9:05 A.M., Reid had determined exactly what he was seeing, and radioed his report to the control center at Midway. Maneuvering close enough to identify individual ships, Reid made a report, followed by his detailed description of the eleven ships in the task force. Though Reid did not know exactly what his sighting represented, that this was only those ships designated by Yamamoto to attack and occupy the island itself, Reid's report was as succinct as anyone on Midway needed to hear: *Sighted main body.*

In minutes, Reid's report reached the hand of Admiral Nimitz at Pearl Harbor. Those with Nimitz saw something rare. The admiral offered a beaming smile. He knew, as did many of the others with him, that despite the doubters in Washington, Joe Rochefort was right.

TWELVE

Ackroyd

"Forgive me, sir. I don't follow Hollywood stuff and all. Who is he?"

Shannon smiled. "That's why I like you, Gunny. You don't get distracted. He's John Ford, a big-time Hollywood director. Admiral Nimitz gave him permission to do some filming out here. He's got his camera full and if he can get some shots of the Japanese, he might make us all famous. But we need to keep him alive and safe. Put him up in one of the radio shacks or hangars on Eastern Island. He can do his filming, but if the Japs show up, I don't want to find his shot-up carcass. Pick somebody you think can handle this. I'm putting his butt in your hands."

Ackroyd groaned, tried to keep it to himself.

Shannon said, "Look, Sergeant, just send somebody to babysit him. It doesn't have to be you. If this show starts the way Nimitz's people keep telling us, I'd rather have you out front manning those machine guns. I still think there's a good chance the Japs are gonna hit us across the beaches. Just keep your men down in those slit trenches."

Ackroyd felt some relief, knew immediately who he'd send up with the celebrity. "I'll take care of it, sir. Gunnery Sergeant Yon gets all gooey about movie stars. Carries a picture of Rita Hayworth in his pocket."

"Fine, if you say so. Tell Yon not to be a pain in the ass. Ford's come here to do some serious work, so there will be no sucking up. He's not out here looking for the next Clark Gable."

"I'll pass that along, Colonel. And don't worry about me. I'm gonna ease over toward the Carlson Raider boys. They're carrying enough firepower for a whole regiment. And none of them will be hiding behind sandbags."

Shannon drank from a coffee cup. "I guess it's a good thing Admiral Nimitz sent them up here. But we need discipline, everybody working together. The Japs are coming, sure as hell. I don't want any stray dogs screwing things up."

"Sir, that's a pack of dogs I don't mind sticking to. Rough bunch, for sure. But rougher on the Japs."

"I hope you're right." He drank from the cup again. "How much longer you planning on being here, Sergeant?"

Ackroyd had fielded this same question for years, hid the real answer even from himself. But his reputation was solid, and Ackroyd knew exactly what Shannon wanted to hear. "I guess I'll retire when somebody like you tells me I gotta leave. I figure, I stay in shape, follow orders, well, most of 'em, if I don't bust up too many of my men, or don't slug any young and stupid lieutenants, you'll let me stay. Besides, right now, sir, you and I both know we need veterans out here, not little boys with pop guns. The Japs ain't playing. Well, hell, sir, you know that."

Shannon laughed. "Happy to have you, Gunny. Now, see to this Hollywood fellow. He's not a fighter, so make damn sure you keep him safe. That's a headline I don't want to see, *Hollywood Bigshot Killed Because of Careless Marines.*"

Besides the unexpected glamour surrounding the arrival of a Hollywood celebrity, Admiral Nimitz had added considerably to both defensive and offensive power on Midway. The deployment of barbed wire was now legendary, the dugouts deeper than ever, and machine gun nests and anti-personnel mines were distributed liberally across every shoreline. To the base's meager aircraft squadrons, the army had sent a total of nineteen B-17 bombers, the largest offensive aircraft in the American arsenal. To that, the navy and marines had added an additional nineteen dive bombers, to be protected by seven more fighter planes. The addition of so many aircraft had of course improved morale, though the experienced pilots were aware that their newly assembled air force was mostly composed of obsolete planes, which could prove horribly inferior to their Japanese counterparts. But not even Midway's two commanding officers, Simard and Shannon, had any reason to be choosy. It was all that Nimitz could send them.

With the increase in weaponry, both for air and ground combat, Midway had become a fortress, what seemed to some to be an odd contradiction for what was little more than a gathering of sand dunes, coral reefs, and gooney birds. No one could completely escape the feeling that they just might be birds themselves, sitting ducks, outnumbered and outgunned by their enemy. But many of the marines had taken a cue from the odd bunch of misfits, Carlson's Raiders, and their confidence level had soared. If the Japanese were coming in through the shallow reefs, they would have to face every weapon in the American arsenal, from barbed wire to bayonets to machine guns. The question was: Just when are they coming?

THIRTEEN

Nagumo

"I am here, sir. They will not confine me to any bed. I shall not
let you down."

Nagumo studied Genda's pained face, the ragged cough, the
weakness in his steps. "Commander, your presence is always welcome. But your survival is essential. Your condition is not your
fault. You should return to your bed. Your illness is not to be taken
lightly."

Genda dropped his head, let out a breath. "It is merely pneumo-
nia. Your surgeon has done fine work. I am fit for duty."

Nagumo had his own reports from his surgeon, but he wouldn't
argue with Genda. He respected him as the most capable officer
on the carrier for guiding and training the pilots. But the training
was complete, and the missions were now deadly serious. Nagumo

studied him still, Genda's condition bringing up Nagumo's own feelings of weariness, the nagging curtain of depression.

"Certainly you know that Commander Fuchida is ill as well. Appendicitis. Perhaps this is one more in a very long trail of bad omens."

Genda moved to a chair, and without a pause to ask permission, sat painfully. "Admiral Yamamoto does not believe in omens, sir. Neither do I. If we are prepared, if we act decisively, we make our own *omens*. I am sorry for Commander Fuchida. Who will lead the mission to Midway?"

Nagumo had only one other choice in mind, so he said, "Lieutenant Tomonaga, the flight officer on the *Hiryu*. You know him, of course?"

"I know him well, yes. A very good pilot. A good leader. Though I would perhaps respect most of the choices you would make."

Nagumo said nothing for a long moment, then smiled. "You are perhaps the only man in the navy who would say such a thing to me. Well, perhaps Admiral Kusaka. He is an excellent chief of staff." He paused. "I am an old man, Commander. I suffer from the rapid judgments of younger men. I am still disrespected for my decisions at Pearl Harbor, perhaps even by you. I am told now that this entire Midway operation could have been avoided if I had ordered Midway to be struck on our voyage away from Hawaii. How exactly do I respond to that? Wars are not fought in hindsight. There is no perfect solution to every encounter."

Genda looked at him, the pain in the young man's face slipping away. "So, there is no perfect solution to this operation, then? Admiral Yamamoto would not wish to hear such doubts. He has crafted this operation with great care."

Nagumo heard the anger in Genda's words. "I am aware of Admiral Yamamoto's planning, his talent for details. In war, events shift, conditions change. He has left me with no flexibility, he has issued orders that are to be followed no matter how events may change. And now he sits on his great battleship hundreds of miles away, and I cannot speak to him. His radio silence has crippled us before we even contact the enemy." Nagumo reached for a cup of tea, felt the cold, called out, "Ensign Kito, a pot of tea. Anything for you, Commander?"

Genda shook his head weakly, and Nagumo felt a nervous concern. "I wish nothing to happen to you out here, Commander. You are too valuable to this navy, to our emperor."

Genda managed a smile. "You need not exaggerate, sir. Perhaps I am valuable to Admiral Yamamoto. Is that a problem for you?"

Nagumo knew to tread lightly, but could not keep up the façade. "Amazing impudence. There was a time when I would have arrested you. Never mind, Commander. I do not fear your influence out here, and I am certain that you do not fear mine. Perhaps this is why Admiral Yamamoto has silenced us all. There can be no loud voices, because no one argues with the great Yamamoto."

He knew he had gone too far, studied Genda's expression, saw what seemed to be pained disgust. But he ignored the young man's expression, continued. "Commander, I have no fear of confiding in you, shouting at you, if the need arose. By the time you could betray my indiscretion, this campaign and my role in it will have concluded. Not even Yamamoto can change that."

"If you wish to shout at me, sir, then please do."

"No shouting, Commander. Just a tired man's frustrations. Admiral Yamamoto has divided us into four task forces. One of those is around us now. *Kido Butai* is powerful, and an extraordinary weapon, one that you yourself have helped create. Four aircraft carriers with the power of hundreds of every type of offensive aircraft. Marvelous." He stopped, the young ensign delivering the pot of tea, then pouring into two small china cups. "Thank you, young man. Leave us." He waited for the ensign to leave the wardroom, then said, "The second task force will occupy Midway, with my aircraft assisting, an invasion force of considerable power. That is supposed to be another of Yamamoto's *good plans*. The third task force is even now plowing its way toward Alaska. I have heard the explanations for the value of such an operation. It is pure foolishness. Why do we not combine those forces with our own, especially since they have sailed away with a pair of light aircraft carriers, a dozen destroyers and cruisers, and four battleships? *Four.* Sailing to nowhere." He expected a rise out of Genda, but didn't get one. "So, perhaps you agree, Commander. No matter. We are overruled. And of course, the fourth task force, a fleet of our finest warships, led by battleship *Yamato,* the most powerful ship in the world, lying so many miles astern of us, waiting for . . . what? The admiral knows that if we locate and confront the Americans, the mighty power of his armada will take a full day to get here. So, why are they even out there? If Yamamoto was in Japan, he could monitor our signals. But he is six hundred miles away, in the middle of the Pacific Ocean, sitting in dead silence. Per his orders of course." He drank from the teacup, stared away for a long moment. Genda sat in silence, and Nagumo said, "How old are you, Commander?"

"Thirty-seven, sir. Is that important?"

Nagumo laughed. "To you, I suppose. We have something in common, you and I. We missed the great days, the marvelous victories. I don't mean Pearl Harbor, or the Indian Ocean. I mean Tsushima, destroying the Russian fleet. I was too young, just eighteen, not yet trained. I heard it all, though. The newspapers roared their victory cries. A wonderful time for our nation, for our emperor. And that is why we have no choice but to obey Admiral Yamamoto. He is a veteran of that fight. I do not say *hero,* as some do. His fingers were shot off. I do not recall if he actually sank a Russian ship with a crippled hand. Quite a painting that would make, yes?" He smiled. "There, you see? Radio silence is a blessing and a curse. You must endure my insults to your hero. And I must carry out my mission in one way, a narrow alley, from which there can be no curve. Do you believe that is how wars should be fought?"

Genda was wholly uncomfortable now, but a loud knock distracted Nagumo, the door opening slowly, the face of Kusaka.

"Admiral, might I join you? Our orders have been carried out, and the ships are all in line as required. The carriers are maintaining their H formation, and will do so until conditions change. If you wish, sir, I can have the aides bring us dinner in here. We have red bean soup and rice cake, with seaweed. Oh, greetings, Commander Genda. I hope you are feeling better."

Nagumo shook his head and thought, I wondered if he would even notice Genda's presence. Of course, Genda is Yamamoto's man, not mine.

"No dinner yet, Admiral. Join us, yes. Commander Genda and I have been discussing chain of command, how some of us have a more . . . lax approach than others."

Kusaka seemed defensive, and Nagumo knew he was protective of his admiral. "Is there some problem, Commander Genda?" The words came in a rush.

Genda seemed to weaken, and Nagumo thought they had done enough. But Genda looked at him with the odd fiery stare that so many seemed to fear. "If you cannot be guided by Admiral Yamamoto, sir, then what is your intention? What will you do if the orders are yours alone?"

Nagumo was surprised by the question. "Why, Commander, for now, I can only do what I've been told. Our aircraft are in range, our pilots are prepared. It is time to bomb Midway."

FOURTEEN

Ackroyd

The night had passed quickly, many of the men relaxing just enough for a few hours of sleep. There was little worry the Japanese would come ashore at night, and no worries at all that they would send bombers whose bombardiers, it was assumed, were no more accurate in the dark than the Americans. With the first hint of dawn, the tension returned, increasing by the minute. As the darkness would finally give way to a cloudless sky, they all knew that yet again, the chances of a Japanese attack by sea or air would certainly increase. The one advantage they had now was that they would likely see it coming.

Ackroyd walked just inside the massive cordon of barbed wire, stared out into the dark surf, and caught the first glimpse of white froth. He shared the nervousness of his men, though none of them spoke of it, no one offering up the mindless boast, begging the enemy to start the fight. They can come anytime, he thought.

There are probably subs out there, dropping off commandos, frog-
men, or whatever they call them. *Rice men?* Hell, whatever.

He said in a loud whisper, "Alert! Eyes forward. Keep your hands
free to set off those charges. Keep the ammo boxes clear, no sand
clogging up the works. Those bastards could show up at any time,
and they're sneaky sonsabitches. You won't see them until they hit
the wire."

No one questioned just how he knew that, the men long ago
accepting what he told them as gospel. The sounds around him
were muffled, no one wanting him to add to their nervousness. He
caught a spark of light down the beach a few yards, moved that
way quickly, and couldn't hold the whisper, his anger cutting
through the cool air.

"You kill that cigarette or I'll toss you out front of this wire.
Nobody turns stupid out here, not today. Sure as hell, there's a Jap
sub out there, maybe five hundred yards off this beach, and his
three-inch gun just swung on your position, you damned idiot. It'll
be full daylight in a half hour. Plenty of time to get your ass shot
off."

In the faint light, he wasn't sure who it was, knew the man
wouldn't speak up. They all heard me, he thought. And they'll all
pay attention. This isn't about torpedoes and dive bombers and
B-17s. This is about one Jap with his finger on the trigger, and you
in his sights.

He turned and faced the water. Or maybe they're aiming at me.
Well? You out there? The longer we have to wait, the less sharp
we'll be, so let's go.

There was only silence now, broken by the soft hiss of surf
washing up on the beach. Hotshot Hollywood guy, he thought.
Just wonderful. Comes out here to take pictures of the blood. He's
over there in some pile of sandbags, thinking he knows what's
going to happen, making sure his camera's all focused, or what-

ever the hell those guys do. Well, Mr. Hollywood, if the Japs are really coming, we'll do our best to give you a show.

He heard a siren, jerked his head that way, stared at Eastern Island. He waited for it, the siren coming again, and now voices close by, "Hey, Gunny. What's that for?"

"They're calling the pilots. I don't think this is any damn drill."

In short minutes, the new sounds came rolling toward them, the hard rumble of engines on the Eastern Island runway. He kept his eyes that way, tried to ignore the butterflies unrolling in his stomach. The planes didn't delay, a parade of aircraft climbing skyward, straight over his position. He tried to count, ten, four more, big ones, twenty, twenty-six. Those are the bombers, most of 'em anyway. They musta found something to aim at. Hit 'em before they have time to hit us. There's a good plan.

They flew over in one screaming roar, increasing altitude, arcing away slowly, moving far out to sea. He estimated the direction, west, no, maybe northwest. Jesus, it's gotta be the whole bunch of 'em now. There's the B-17s. Holy crap. What a racket. He fought the urge to shield his ears, knowing the men would see that. Just take it, he thought.

There was a new sound now, higher pitched, more planes going airborne, and he watched, clenching both fists. Yep, that's the fighters. They're faster, they'll catch up, like babies chasing mama. Damn, I'd like to be up there, looking over all of it. And then some Jap would shoot my wings off. Nope. Better off right here.

Ackroyd had rarely thought of flying, didn't have the eyes for it, but he spoke to the pilots every chance he got. He had made something of a nuisance of himself, but his age carried weight, and so they took the time to respond to his curiosity, so many questions. He had heard so much meaningless bravado, young, inexperienced fliers, whose only success in the air had come from shooting at target sleeves or dropping bombs on piles of lumber in Pensacola.

But this was different, very different. He watched them climb higher, some of the squadrons coming together in ragged formations. They're green, he thought, like so many of these clowns right here. How do you learn not to die? Some won't.

Around him, curiosity took hold, and the voices were coming up toward him:

"What's up, Gunny?"

"Where they going?"

"They leaving us behind?"

He still watched them, barely able to see individual planes now, enjoyed and dreaded the moment. But he had no patience for stupid questions. "When they tell me, I'll tell you. Now shut the hell up, and keep your eyes on the water."

"Gunnery Sergeant!"

He turned, saw the familiar stumbling figure of Major Hommel. "Right here, sir. Even the Japs know that now."

Hommel was oblivious to Ackroyd's sarcasm, Ackroyd always grateful for that. "Sergeant, alert your men. The radar station reports the enemy is approaching from the northwest, ninety miles out and closing."

"What kind of enemy, sir?"

"Bombers, for sure. They should be here in twenty-five or thirty minutes. Pull your men down tight. Our fighters are doing what they can to hold 'em off, but we need escorts for our own bombers. Captain Simard is scrambling around over on Eastern Island, pulling together whatever pilots and planes are left. Oh God. This is it, I suppose. I have to get back to the dugout. Colonel Shannon will be needing me. I need to find Lieutenant McGee. Do your best, Sergeant. God be with you."

"And you, sir."

Hommel was quickly gone, kicking through sand as he scampered away.

The men were silent now, and down the way, a young lieutenant, Perkins, passing the word. Good, he thought. Tell 'em all. Heads down, nobody sightsees.

He spoke aloud now, no reason for quiet. "You heard the major. Stay below those sandbags, keep down in your trenches. Nobody gets their head blown off because he has to peek. We've got enough anti-aircraft pieces on this island to blow 'em all out of the sky. We still don't know if there's gonna be an amphibious landing, so do your jobs. None of you is good enough to shoot down a Jap plane with your forty-five."

He stepped back, higher on the dune, stared out to the northwest. Our planes must have passed those bastards on the way out. You bomb mine, I'll bomb yours. I guess that's how we fight wars nowadays. He looked back toward the larger dunes, could see the anti-aircraft batteries. Well, we ain't got a whole hell of a lot of planes left over there. So, I guess it's up to the AA batteries. Shoot straight, boys.

He knelt low in the slit trench, watched the PT boats moving slowly through the lagoon. Targets, he thought. Guess they know what the hell they're doing. If it was me, I'd be headed out to sea at full bore. More room to maneuver. I'd kinda like bigger guns too.

The sounds came now, faint, increasing, and Ackroyd scanned the skies to the west. Holy crap, there they are. A pot load of 'em. He called out, loud, no need for discretion. "Keep your heads down. Let the AA boys do what they do best."

Behind him, the anti-aircraft guns began firing, streaks of fire toward the formations of bombers. Ackroyd pulled the straps on his helmet, clamping it hard on his head, his eyes on the V formations high above. The puffs of smoke blossomed around the planes, flak from the AA guns, and almost immediately, one of the planes burst into flames, falling loosely from the formation. Ackroyd felt his hands shaking, watched the plane coming close, fiery impact back in the dunes. He wanted to shout, cheer, but there were too many planes still coming. High above, he caught the streaking fighters, unsure if they were . . . Another bomber fell now, a fighter on its tail. Yes! It's ours. *Our* fighter. We're there too. Let's go, do it. Another plane came down now, tumbling black smoke. It impacted in the lagoon, close to one of the PT boats, and Ackroyd disobeyed his own order, peered up and over the sand-bags, saw the PT boat move close, men in the water. Well, he thought. Seems they *do* know what the hell they're doing. Check him out, boys. Maybe secrets to be found. Maybe he's just a stupid unlucky Jap whose number was up.

The fighters high above the formations seemed completely sep-arate from the action below them, weaving their patterns, ignor-ing the bombers. He stared, but had no idea what he saw, and had no explanation for what was happening. The V formations were nearly overhead now, and he saw something new, the bombers un-leashing their best weapon. To one side, voices called out, the men seeing what he saw now. Black dots fell closer, spreading out all back behind them, the first one impacting, then more, thunder and smoke, a great fiery blast, too loud, too much fire. Ackroyd ducked low into the sand, and thought, *Fuel tanks.* Jesus. Bastards made a good shot. More impacts erupted closer behind them, a direct hit on an AA battery, but many more came down just in soft sand, harmless blasts, except for the terrified gooney birds scram-bling to escape.

A new sound came now, men shouting, fear and wonder, the next wave, Japanese dive bombers seeming to fall from the sky, the awful shriek, the bombs released at the last second, more targets hit and more missed, heavy blasts, shrapnel, small buildings lev-eled, more anti-aircraft guns disabled.

As the bombers pulled away, Ackroyd stood, a hard shout, curs-ing, realized he had his forty-five in his hand. He couldn't hold his fury, aimed at the last of the planes. But he heard a voice now, the young lieutenant. "Let it go, Gunny. Waste of ammo. You know that. They might think they just softened us up for the amphibious attack. Eyes on the water."

Around him the men joined in, standing, a last glimpse of the bombers as they re-formed into the Vs. But now there was one last horror none of them knew to expect.

From high above, Japanese fighters, mostly Zeroes, whipped through the skies close overhead, chattering machine gun fire, thumps of cannon, the fighters strafing any target, any building or structure missed by the bombers. The fighters dodged their way through the anti-aircraft fire, almost no effect from the aim of men who had never drilled on a target this fast. Ackroyd cursed loudly, called out, "Shoot them, aim better for Chrissakes! You're shooting behind them!"

He felt a hand on his shirt, turned in a rage, and saw Perkins, the baby-faced lieutenant, with a hard glare Ackroyd had never seen.

"Down in the trench, Gunny. Now!"

Ackroyd said nothing, settled down in the slit trench, and heard one of the enemy fighters coming close, barely airborne. He pulled his helmet down again, curling up, the men alongside him doing the same, streams of machine gun fire ripping the sand just behind him, just outside the trench. He looked for Perkins, saw only the man's hand draped over the edge of the trench, a stream of blood falling from the man's fingers, soaking in the damp sand. Ackroyd pulled himself to his knees, then others—a corpsman there now— tearing open the lieutenant's shirt. The corpsman looked at Ackroyd, no words, but another plane roared past, unleashing machine gun fire farther down the line. The corpsman ducked low, his face down beside the chest of Perkins, then he raised up with a grim stare at Ackroyd, and shook his head.

He didn't know Perkins except as a ninety-day wonder, a green officer who read his orders from an instruction manual. There were no thoughts, no words that would help any of the rest of his men. Ackroyd sat back down, ignored those few men still up, staring at the bloody mess that had been their lieutenant. Gradually they settled back into the trench, faces turning toward the barbed wire, the open surf. And then it was quiet. Within minutes the Zeroes had peeled away, joining their bombers on their return flight home.

MIDWAY, SAND ISLAND—JUNE 4, 1942, 7:30 A.M.

The *All-Clear* had been sounded, the men emerging from the dugouts and trenches, and more men appearing from the huts and other structures that had been spared the destruction from the bombs. More Japanese planes had gone down across the span of Midway, but there had been American fighters coming down as well, those who did all they could to hold the Japanese away. In the end, the Japanese planes were superior, their pilots with more training and more experience. It was a painful lesson that no one knew how to address.

Ackroyd kept his men close to the protection, knew better than to believe that an enemy this capable wouldn't suddenly return. The danger was still there that the bombing raid might only have been the preliminary to an amphibious assault. All along the coils of barbed wire, the marines warily manned their anti-personnel devices, hunkered in behind their machine guns.

He walked to the top of a tall sand dune, saw the billowing black smoke from the destruction of the fuel tanks, more smoke from a variety of wrecked buildings, the infirmary, the brig, machine shops, and PBY hangars. He stared over toward Eastern Island, and spotted more smoke there, but not as much. Of course, he thought. Why wreck the runway if you think you're gonna use it? Son of a bitch. That's the point, ain't it? They'll be back. Boatloads of 'em.

He heard new sounds, reflex dropping him down, but this was

different, the engines familiar. He heard cheering along the waterfront, but he held it in; he wouldn't feel any kind of celebration, not yet. The planes banked overhead, making their approach to Eastern Island, and they were coming in low and slow, some trailing smoke, some with ripped metal and shattered windscreens. But he couldn't see more than that, didn't know where they had been or what kind of enemy they had found. The sound alone told the tale, but he saw it too. There weren't as many planes, not close to what took off that morning. Beside him, his corporal climbed up from his sandy trench.

"Jesus. Half of 'em. Where'd the rest go? They fly to Hawaii maybe?"

Ackroyd felt the energy drain away, and said, "Hawaii's a million miles away. If they ain't here, they're in the ocean."

There was nothing else he could say, no cheerleading to his men, no empty optimism. He knew what he was seeing, even if no one else would. The skies emptied, the last of the planes coming down onto Eastern Island. He looked around his positions, the smoke drifting past, but the men were still prepared, machine gun nests and most of the anti-aircraft batteries. And somewhere down the beach, Carlson's Raiders were still eager to meet the Japs face to face. But something's wrong, he thought. Something happened that wasn't in the cards. He couldn't say it to his men, couldn't do anything to take away their grit, their courage, their expectations of destroying their enemy. But he knew inside that so far, there was only one answer. The Japs came here, and our boys went out there, and maybe we found their carriers. But those pilots, *our* pilots, a hell of a lot of them didn't come back.

FIFTEEN

Nagumo

The Japanese had nothing that resembled the enormous asset of American radar, and so it was the Japanese destroyers that would form the outermost ring of the protective belt around the vulnerable aircraft carriers. The destroyers performed other functions as well, serving as the task force's guard dogs. In the event of any intrusion from an enemy, the ships could throw up a curtain of anti-aircraft fire, and living up to their very names, their speed and depth charges made them the most deadly weapon against a submarine attack.

Nagumo had been on the bridge of the *Akagi*, a cramped and uncomfortable space, but like the others around him, he saw the tracers suddenly erupting from the distant cordon of destroyers. The American planes from their base at Midway had now appeared. The first bursts of tracer fire had gone skyward far out on the perimeter of the task force, but they served as signal enough to the three dozen Zeroes, the Combat Air Patrol for the four Japanese carriers. The CAP served as the airborne lookouts, cruising and circling high above their ships. The alert had been given to all four carriers, and when the Americans closed in toward their targets, the Zeroes dove through the first wave of the American formations, punching great holes, sending the lumbering torpedo planes into the sea. The American dive bombers fared little better, and their fighter escorts, Midway's outdated F4F-3s, were quickly outmaneuvered and outfought by the Zeroes. With their protective shield of fighter escorts fully occupied in their own struggle for survival, the slower and clumsier American attack planes were mostly chewed up by Japanese anti-aircraft fire, as well as the relentless assault from the Zeroes. Though many of the American attackers survived long enough to release their bombs, the results were dismal. None of the bombs found their target with enough effectiveness to cause any real damage. Even the B-17s, dropping their deadly payloads from altitudes too high for the Zeroes to intercept, found no success at all, not a single bomb impacting on a target.

ONBOARD CARRIER *AKAGI*, AT SEA—JUNE 4, 1942, 7:15 A.M.

Nagumo huddled on the small bridge, staring hard into the binoculars. Already there were cheers, the crew of the carrier reacting to the intense drama of what they had just experienced. Beside him, the ship's captain, Aoki, said, "They have gone, Admiral. We have driven them away."

Nagumo lowered the glasses, felt a rush of joy—something new. "You are not quite correct, Captain. We drove them out of the sky. We *crushed* them. But most were not sent away. They are in the ocean around us. There is wreckage even now, still afloat. Very soon, what remains of their airplanes will disappear into the heart of the sea. If there are survivors, bring them out of the water. We may learn something. If none survived, our victory is complete."

Behind him, his chief of staff, Admiral Kusaka, said, "Sir, many planes on the horizon, through those cloud banks."

Nagumo spun around, couldn't avoid another hard bout of nervousness. "Where? Have they come again?"

"Better than that, sir. They are ours." He stared through the glasses, all the men straining to see, and Kusaka said, "It is Lieutenant Tomonaga. He is coming in now, to *Hiryu*."

"With how many?"

"I am trying to see, sir. The clouds make it difficult, and there are many. A great many."

Nagumo gave up counting on his own. "That is not a bad thing, my friend."

"Yes, Admiral. They are splitting formations, moving onto each carrier." Kusaka paused. "There are gaps, sir. Not all have returned."

"Measure our losses against our victory, Admiral. How many Americans did we send into the water?"

Kusaka smiled. "Many more, sir."

"Admiral Nagumo!"

Nagumo turned to one of the carrier's officers, with another man wearing radio earphones, straining to hear.

"What is it?"

The officer waited, the radioman staring hard to the deck, a pad and pencil on his knee. The paper went up to the officer.

"Sir, shortwave from the *Hiryu*. It sounds like a message has come from Lieutenant Tomonaga. He says . . . no, he insists, that Midway must be struck again."

Nagumo felt a familiar depression, the sudden need to save the world from a problem he did not invent. "Admiral Kusaka, come with me. Send for Commander Genda if he is able. No delay."

He led his chief of staff to the compact wardroom, sat heavily, ignoring the open door, one part of his brain shrugging it off: What does it matter who might hear us?

Kusaka sat across from him. He knew his commander well, and kept silent. He would speak only if it was necessary. Nagumo heard a noise in the passageway, then a guard led Genda in, one hand under Genda's arm. Nagumo pointed to a chair, and Kusaka moved to help as well. Genda seemed annoyed at the attention.

"I am well. Do not coddle me, please."

After a long moment, Nagumo said to Kusaka, "I need your serenity, my friend. Every devotion you have to Buddhism would be of great help to me now."

Kusaka seemed concerned. "Sir, I cannot offer you my devotion to the Buddha as a tonic. Any more than Commander Genda can tell you how to fly a plane."

Nagumo looked down at his hands, saw the age, and tried to clench stiff fingers. "No, I suppose not. You know our mission. We were to destroy the defenses on Midway, and immediately invade the island, occupying it and establishing our base there. By doing so, we would draw the Americans out of their safe harbor and convince them they must rescue their base on Midway with reckless haste." He stopped, could hear the incoming aircraft from the Midway mission, a slow procession as the planes landed on the flight deck. "Commander Genda, if Lieutenant Tomonaga told you that one bombing mission on Midway was not adequate, that there had to be a second, how would you react?"

Genda seemed to understand the real question. "I would send a second mission."

"I am not ordered to do any such thing, do you understand that? Admiral Yamamoto drew out very specific assignments. The transports are prepared to land an occupation force on Midway, no matter what Lieutenant Tomonaga says. What do you say to that, Commander? It is well known that Admiral Yamamoto counts on your every word. No matter what I do, he will seek an explanation from *you*. He will listen to *you*. Certainly not to me."

"Sir, I will not respond to that. I do not know how Admiral Yamamoto regards my views. If Lieutenant Tomonaga insists on a second bombing mission, it is only because the first was inadequate to prepare our occupation of the island."

Nagumo nodded, still studied his gnarled hands. "Admiral Kusaka, prepare the planes for a second mission. There must be no delay. We cannot give the Americans time to regroup, and I suspect we have severely damaged their airborne capability, so we shall have a much easier time of it in the sky."

On Admiral Nagumo's orders, the returning planes from the first assault on Midway were held aloft, while the additional squadrons onboard the carriers were equipped with land bombs for a second attack on the atoll. Though the planes from the first assault were greatly in need of both fuel and ordnance, they would simply have to wait until space was available on the flight decks. The process was slow going, those fighters and bombers allowed to land on the carriers adding to what seemed to be a traffic jam. As a precaution against any unexpected intrusions by any more American attack planes, Nagumo gave the prudent order, the four carriers combined would launch more than thirty Zeroes as a Combat Air Patrol to circle overhead, even before many of the Midway attack planes had been brought home and lowered to the hangar decks below, taking them out of the way. As Nagumo's orders to switch the bombers to land-based weapons continued, many of the planes from the first assault, including their commander, Tomonaga, could only circle their carriers, low on fuel, until space was available.

Earlier that morning, Nagumo had taken the appropriate step of sending out reconnaissance patrols, precisely designed flight patterns that resembled spokes of a wheel. Knowing that any enemy would be coming from Midway or perhaps points south toward Hawaii, Nagumo was comfortable that the pattern laid out had covered those possibilities. Now, it would be up to the sharp eyes of those pilots; if they were as vigilant as their commanders hoped, any surprise presence of American ships would be observed before the Americans could make any offensive move of their own. Of course, as Nagumo knew, there was no reason to believe that the Americans had any ships anywhere outside of Pearl Harbor.

"How long will this take? Can we not move any faster?"

The flight officer saluted him, obviously surprised that his admiral should suddenly appear on the flight deck. "Sir, we are reequipping the bombers with their necessary land-based bombs. I understand the mission has changed. We will again do great damage to Midway."

"Your mission is to equip and refuel the bombers and their fighter escorts. I do not wish to hear speculation from a deck officer. How much longer?"

"An hour, sir. Possibly more." The man glanced skyward, the drone of engines still overhead. "Sir, we must retrieve our squadrons as soon as possible. Their fuel supply is extremely low. We should not wait to pull men from the sea, and sacrifice their aircraft." He paused, looked down. "Forgive me, Admiral. I shall push the men hard. We shall be prepared on your orders."

"Inform me when the bombers are prepared to launch."

Nagumo turned without speaking, several of the ship's senior officers forming an escort. He moved back into the ship's island, hands behind his back, an aching frustration in every step. "Leave me now. I am safely indoors. That is what you insist upon, yes? We must prevent a great wind from tossing me over the side?"

The men made their bows, and moved off to the various posts.

Nagumo stood still for a long moment, and thought, So, what do I do now? My observers are observing, my patrols are patrolling, my bombers are preparing to bomb. This is why men choose to be pilots, I suppose. They do not sit around and wonder what their airplanes are doing. They believe they have control. They are wrong. Right now, many of those pilots are circling overhead, waiting for me to decide if I will clear the deck by launching another mission to Midway, or clear the deck by sweeping the bombers to the hangar deck below. Either way, I cannot order the flight deck cleared and have it happen in a flash. I can only sit back and pretend to be patient, while others do their jobs.

He thought of going to the bridge, that dismal place fit for no more than a handful of men, while more likely a dozen or more stuffed themselves inside. It is a great honor to be the flagship, so they say. I wonder what this ship's captain thinks of that? He must do his job with a dozen flag officers underfoot. He moved through the passageway, and thought of his quarters, the only place on the ship where he could find some comfort. He knew that Yamamoto often had *her* there, without shame and without discretion. A woman on a ship, he thought. A *geisha*. He accepts no dishonor, he shows no embarrassment. It used to be that a man found honor in his own victory. Now honor is old-fashioned. Victory comes from staffs and decisions, victory comes from the strength of great fleets, ships and planes, and not from the hearts of men. And I cannot change that. Am I so naïve that I would try? Or am I just old?

He looked at his watch, 0800.

"Sir!"

He turned, was surprised to see the ship's executive officer, Ryso. "Is there a problem, Commander?"

"Sir, we have received a message from search craft number four, from cruiser *Tone*. He reports contact with American ships. Here, sir."

Nagumo took the paper, and read, *"Sight what appears to be ten enemy surface units, in position bearing ten degrees distance 240 miles from Midway. Course 150 degrees, speed over 20 knots."*

He felt suddenly sick. "Where is Admiral Kusaka?"

"On the bridge, sir."

"The captain as well?"

"Yes, sir, and Navigator Miura."

"Summon Commander Genda to the bridge. I will go there now. Go!"

The man rushed away, and Nagumo swirled a myriad of thoughts through his mind, one bursting through: *Midway.* That infernal place can wait. If that report is accurate, the American ships have somehow eluded our watch. If he is wrong? Did he spot a fleet of fishing boats? This is maddening. Did our submarines not prevent this kind of surprise? None of that matters now. We must re-equip the bombers with torpedoes, and we must prepare the Zeroes to escort them. We must do it *right now.* He thought of the flight deck officer: *an hour.* So, how long to re-equip the planes yet again? Torpedoes, not bombs. Another hour? We must retrieve the Zeroes, refuel, reload their guns. And what other surprises might there be? If we have reconnaissance planes, so does the enemy.

He climbed to the bridge, the depressingly small room with glass on three sides, noticed the ship's captain, Aoki, bowing to him. Nagumo had no itch for pleasantries, and said, "Ten surface ships. What kind of ships? Don't you think it would be good to know that? Are any of them carriers? I want more information. Contact that observer now."

More men entered the area: another radioman, the ship's navigator, the executive officer, Kusaka's aide. The noise level expanded now, a cacophony of chatter on the ship's intercom, men with maps on a small table, Genda leaning low, drawing a line on a map, Kusaka scanning the report on a piece of paper.

The noise level continued to increase, the bridge cramped, overheated, and Nagumo backed into the bulkhead to one side, his head churning with thoughts, ideas, puzzles, and solutions.

They are coming, he thought. But why are they here? This was not the plan. Now, certainly, they have found us, and they are moving closer to launching their planes. But, no, at 150 degrees, they are parallel, moving perhaps toward Midway. Reinforcements? If they are merely adding strength to their forces at Midway, could this be why Tomonaga insisted we strike Midway again? How long does it take to remove planes from the flight deck, bringing up another squadron? How long does it take to change the bombers from torpedoes to land bombs, and then, do it all again? And all of this because of a report from one man who may or may not be right. Ten American ships? There could be thirty, with aircraft carriers. So, they are divided? Where are the rest? Is this why Yamamoto stays away, so he does not have to answer questions like this?

One of the crew was seated on a small bench, and Nagumo motioned to him, *move*. The young man obeyed, Nagumo sitting. He had no strength in his legs, his breaths coming in short painful gasps. He curled his arms around his chest, fought for calm, trying not to see all that was happening around him. How much is confusion, he thought, or precision, how much do these men know that I do not. They would never tell me that, and I can never admit it. Perhaps this is why Yamamoto stays back, so far away. There, he cannot fail and he cannot make grave errors. There, he does not worry how many men he will send to their deaths by making poor decisions.

Nagumo realized Kusaka was watching him, and his chief of staff moved closer, saying, "Sir, there are many questions. We do not believe the American ships are where they are reported to be. We have sent a message to the observer to make a more careful assessment of the ships he has sighted. I must say, sir, that if there are ten warships, even in a location somewhat different than what we are told, those ships would not be out here without purpose. They would be escorting at least one carrier."

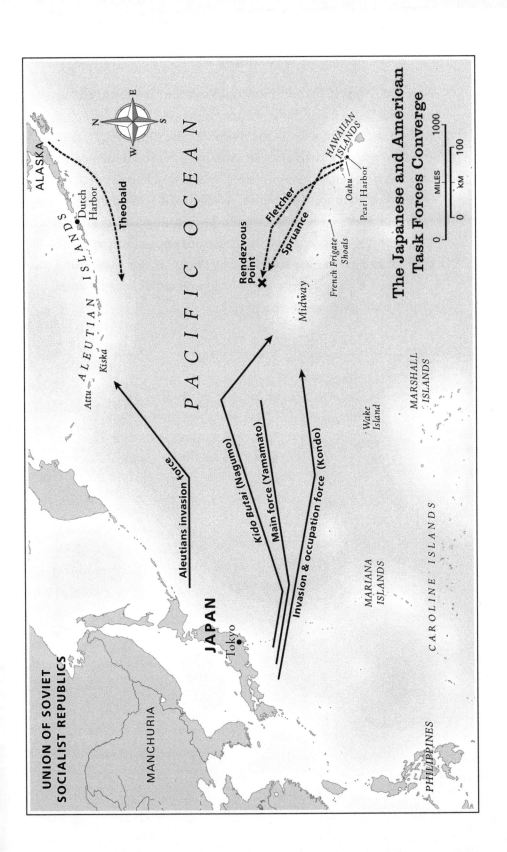

The Japanese and American Task Forces Converge

Nagumo shook his head. "How can we know? If we launch our fighters and they find nothing, we are vulnerable."

Kusaka stared at him for a long moment. "Sir, nothing is certain. The flight crews are hard at work switching out the ordnance on the planes. If the enemy is out there, we will find him."

Nagumo tried to feel some spirit, to offer a show of optimism to his chief of staff. He nodded slowly, looked down at the deck. "Then, perhaps, my friend, we shall have our opportunity after all. If their planes come, we shall destroy them. If our planes find those ships, we shall destroy *them*. I suppose either way, Admiral Yamamoto will once again be a hero."

SIXTEEN

Baker

He was lost again. The ladder was unfamiliar, steam lines running alongside an open hatch to nowhere, a bulkhead opened up for repair. He peered through the openings, tools and fittings, the workers somewhere else on the ship, still doing the most important tasks to put *Yorktown* back together. It was early for the repairmen yet, those men with the luxury of sleeping past 0500, while the pilots and their crews had been awake since before 0300.

This had happened to Baker at least once a day, the immensity of the carrier still strange even to many who had served on her for several weeks. At least, he thought, I haven't wandered into anymore dead ends. Embarrassing as hell. Maybe not as bad as stumbling into the bridge. I thought that marine guard was gonna take my head off. I knew I shoulda gone to bed instead of watching that damn movie. I'm still asleep.

It was common for the senior officers to use the hangar deck as

an enormous movie theater. For most of the men, it was a welcome distraction, though the selection of films had become amaz-
ingly monotonous. How many times have we gotta watch Shirley
Temple, he thought. But I did. And now I've got fog in my brain. I
need a shot of the doc's carrot juice. Supposed to be miracle tonic,
sharpen the eyes. Thach swears by it. Or maybe swears *at* it. All I
know is I'm done with Shirley Temple. At least for a week or two.
A little Myrna Loy would be nice. A grown-up. Garbo too. He
began to feel more confident in just where he was, passing a handful of engineering hatches, Yep, he thought, this is it. I'll be fine
now. He turned to the right, confronted yet another dead end,
nothing but masses of pipes and steam fittings.

"Can I help you, sir?"

He sagged, turned, and saw the marine, the man seeming to
understand that officers were usually idiots.

"I've gotten turned around, Sergeant. I'm a pilot, VF-3. Can you
direct me to the briefing rooms?"

The marine showed no expression; he had clearly done this before. "This way, sir. Second ladder, up two decks. You'll be there."

"Thank you, Sergeant." How the hell does he know that, he
thought. Maybe they drill it into them, just to make morons out of
the pilots. He climbed the first ladder, then stopped as he caught
smells. Familiar. *Chocolate. Cigarettes.*

He climbed the second ladder, suddenly found himself facing
the gedunk stand. My lucky day, he thought. At least from here I
can find my quarters. And the briefing room.

Even at this hour there was a short line at the stand, and Baker
was suddenly thirsty. As he waited his turn, he saw familiar faces
now, more of the pilots, some from the torpedo squadron, VT-3.
Men nodded their acknowledgments, most of them showing the
same level of fatigue Baker felt, men whose night's sleep had lasted
barely past midnight. It was his turn and he put a dime on the
counter.

"Seven-up."

The bottle was cold, the sweet liquid just as he hoped, a long flood of fizz down his throat that watered his eyes. He tossed the bottle into a waste can, moved through the group, then heard a voice aimed at him.

"Hey, Perk. Briefing in an hour. I heard Thach is pissed. Don't be late. I'm heading for some breakfast. Come along?"

"Right with you, Eddie." He saw that Bassett was already in his flight suit, knew he was running behind. "In a minute. I'll suit up, meet you there."

He scrambled to his quarters, pulled on the flight gear, did his usual check. The arm pocket held the wax pencils, the tool for following his course on the plastic-coated chart that stayed mostly on his knee. His chest pockets housed his small flashlight, a small bottle of sinus pills that could double as pep pills, and a tube of Vaseline. He stopped at that, looked at the yellow grease in the tube; he had never been sure exactly what to do with it. But it was assigned as part of his gear, and he knew better than to argue. In his pants pockets were two wool rags, one for wiping pencil lines off the chart, the other to wipe fog off his windscreen, should that be necessary. He also carried a second flashlight, and no one had to explain why. It was the one piece of equipment that could save your life in a water landing, no less than your life preserver. He donned his helmet, tightened the straps, then reversed the process and clamped the helmet under one arm. He glanced into the small mirror, long a part of his routine, then said aloud, "I need food."

He moved quickly down the passageway, climbed another ladder, and was bathed in the smell the newer pilots dreamed about and that the veterans had learned to dread. It was steak. A steak-and-egg breakfast meant a mission, and out here in the middle of the Pacific, it had to be serious.

He slid into the mess area, surrounded by pilots, some from Thach's command, others from the torpedo and bombing squadrons. The chatter was typical, dotted with comments about their own commanders, somebody always stirring the pot. As the room filled, the tension seemed to build as the men attacked their breakfast with the kind of energy that comes from nerves.

Baker spotted Bassett, moved that way and sat across from him. Both men had come aboard *Yorktown* at the same time, both men earning their commander's respect for more than merely teaching student fliers. Baker watched the mess orderly, the man slapping down plates of steak and eggs in front of both of them. Bassett said, "Don't get excited. It's still powdered eggs."

Baker stuffed a bite of juicy meat in his mouth. "How do you know that?"

"Up on the hangar deck, a wire pen. Full of powdered chickens."

The groans came from around them, and now another of Thach's men, Brassfield, said, "Yeah, that's where they keep the powdered cows for these steaks. Hey, it could be worse. They coulda given us CPO dogs."

Baker thought of the canned hot dogs most of the enlisted men were eating and looked at his steak; he had barely tasted it. Bassett seemed to read him, and said, "Take nothing for granted, Perk. You'll be glad you had this meal in a few hours. But if I was those other fellows, and had me a gunner sitting behind me, protecting my ass, I'd want him fed real good. I'd give him the whole damn powdered chicken."

More laughter, but Baker saw the look in Bassett's eyes, and knew that not everything was funny. The fighter pilots flew alone, one-seaters, and the only man who protected your backside was in another plane. The relationship between bomber and torpedo pilots and their gunners was very different and very special, something Baker knew he'd never experience. It remained a mystery to him why the pilots were all officers, while their gunners were always enlisted men. Not sure just who the most important guy is in that pair, he thought. Maybe if it's two officers, they end up arguing about which way they should go.

Down the table, another of Thach's men called out. "Hey, anybody know what's got the commander all pissed off?"

"Who said I was pissed off?"

The voice surprised them all, and Baker turned toward Thach, saw the unmistakable look of a man pissed off. No one responded, and Thach said, "Briefing in twenty minutes. Be on time. *Right* on time."

There was an unusual urgency to Thach's words, and whether or not he was angry about anything, Baker knew that Thach was rarely a stickler about his briefings.

The men were finishing their breakfasts, the orderlies clearing away the plates. Bassett said, "I was gonna get me a damn shower. They said we could have fresh water both ways this morning."

Baker didn't believe him; he was too used to the *saltwater wash, freshwater rinse* routine.

One of the others said, "Yeah, I heard that too. Showers and steak. Jesus, it's like we're being pumped up for something special."

Baker had a sudden thought, and couldn't keep it quiet. "We're going up. I bet it's the Japs."

No one disputed his words, and there was a brief quiet moment. Across the room, Thach's new executive officer, Bill Leonard, said, "Let's go. Briefing room. Right now."

He saw the gathering, a handful of familiar faces, the pilots of Thach's team. They filed into the briefing room, chairs set out in rows, each man knowing his own place. Thach sat up front, beside him his executive officer, Leonard. Baker watched Thach carefully, knew him well enough to know Thach had been up all night.

Thach stood. "Quiet. There are some things you need to know.

On 1 June I was briefed by *Yorktown*'s air officer, Commander Arnold. Until then I had no idea what our mission was. Until now, neither do you. So, here it is. *Yorktown* is the centerpiece of Task Force 17. Task Force 16 is centered around *Enterprise* and *Hornet*. So far we've been considered the reserve, ready to help where needed. That's changing. Early this morning the Japs attacked the island of Midway, and from first reports to Admiral Fletcher, they shot up the marine and navy base pretty good. This morning, planes from Midway located at least a portion of the Japanese main body, and attacked with torpedo bombers, dive bombers, and army B-17s. The pilots claimed they destroyed every ship in the Japanese fleet. You know how that goes. My guess is nobody hit a damn thing. So, it's up to us. Knock hell out of the Japs before they do the same to us." He put one hand on the chair beside him and took a deep breath. "For the past three days, all of you have drilled and practiced in every part of our flight operations, except one. You can't practice Japs shooting at you. So, what do we do, how do we perform when we actually face the Japs? I have been meeting regularly with the other two squadron commanders, the torpedo bombers, Commander Massey, and the Dauntless dive bombers, Commander Leslie. We have determined that my command shall put its primary focus on protecting the torpedo bombers. As you know, with the weight of their torpedo, the Devastators are as slow as mules and will fly at a lower altitude, less than twenty-five hundred feet, to conserve fuel. We will maintain an altitude to the rear at five thousand feet, assuming a lazy S course so we don't run past them. Questions?"

Bassett said, "Some of us are wondering, sir. What's wrong?"

Thach stared at him for a long moment. "All through this, I believed I would have most of my squadron, at least sixteen to twenty Wildcats. Then I was told I would have eight, the remainder staying here as the CAP for *Yorktown*. This morning, I learned it would only be six. *Six* of us to hold the enemy off the bombers. I've pushed back against Commander Arnold, pushed him to go to the top, all the way to the admiral if he had to. It didn't work. They're more concerned about having the Japs down our throat right here. I would have thought the Japs should be more afraid of us, but I guess . . . well, I'm just a pilot. Admirals make decisions. I fly planes. With me will be Baker, Macomber, Bassett, Dibb, and Cheek. The rest will serve as CAP, or be held in reserve as needed. No bitching. This is no picnic, and we're not out to play around out there. If you're assigned to stick to the ship, there's a damn good reason. If the Japs get this far, you could be the final line, the last protection this boat has." He paused. "Something I've wanted to say. You all know that your aircraft is an offensive weapon. Your job, always, has been to go get the bastards. This time it might be different. With the new machine guns, you are down to twenty seconds of full-bore firing until you run out. *Twenty seconds.* It's easy to forget that in the middle of a scrap. Avoid dogfights with the damn Zeroes. Accept that their advantage is maneuverability. Don't try to climb after them. They'll knock you out of the sky sure as hell. If you think I'm blowing sawdust at you . . . I'm just trying to keep you alive, so you can do your job, and today, your job is to keep somebody *else* alive. So, take this seriously. If you're up against the enemy, close quarters, don't be afraid to use your prop to cut him up." The men mumbled now and Thach raised a hand. "Enough. I hope none of us get into that position, but it can happen. If you're out of ammo, your prop is the only other weapon you've got. However, if any of you think about ramming your plane straight into the enemy, well, that's up to you. It's a hell of a way to get a medal. I'd rather come back in one piece. My wife would appreciate that. Now, go rest up. We'll have wind indications and directional instructions up on deck. When it's time to go, you'll hear it."

Just after 7:00 A.M., the first flight was launched from *Enterprise* and *Hornet,* the two carriers of Task Force 16. As Admiral Fletcher waited anxiously on *Yorktown's* bridge, Admiral Spruance, onboard *Enterprise,* had put the first wave of attacks into motion. The directional finders, the various spotters, the estimates from the planes now returning to Midway, placed the Japanese fleet in an area within range of the American carrier planes. But errors and confusion swept through much of the operation. *Enterprise* and *Hornet* launched their torpedo planes at different times, intending the varying speeds of the different planes to overlap so that the squadrons would reach the enemy as one coordinated force. But the pilots had almost no experience working alongside other squadrons, and there was confusion about which compass heading would lead them to the Japanese fleet. The instructions to the fighter escorts were a jumble, leaving some to believe they were to escort the torpedo carriers, while others flew closer to the dive bombers. To add to the confusion, heavy cloud layers kept the fighter escorts from keeping their sights on the planes they were assigned to protect. Unlike the Japanese, whose skill in carrier operations was unequaled, the Americans had very little practice at this kind of warfare. The result was that some of the bombers reached the enemy fleet in roundabout paths that consumed most of their fuel, while others, particularly the squadron from the *Hornet,* led by Commander Stanhope Ring, flew so far beyond their intended targets, they either had to ditch in the sea or struggle to locate Midway itself before they exhausted their fuel supply. Eventually, Ring's mistaken efforts would earn his mission the satirical label the *Flight to Nowhere.* But there was no humor for the men in their planes who watched their gauges, their engines draining their fuel, still with no idea where the Japanese might be.

By the time the torpedo planes sighted their target, most had no protection from their fighters at all. The fighters had either lost sight of their charges, or had mistakenly bunched up to protect other squadrons, leaving their own completely vulnerable. At 0915, Commander John Waldron, of Torpedo Squadron 8, led his Devastators directly toward what he could see to be a substantial number of Japanese ships. Waldron's instincts were in direct contrast to Ring's, who had insisted on going the other way. Even without fighter cover, Waldron signaled to his fifteen torpedo bombers to begin their attack. Aiming first toward the carrier *Akagi*, Waldron's men were set upon by close to forty Zeroes. The results were predictable. All fifteen torpedo planes were shot down into the sea. The lone survivor, Ensign George Gay, shielded himself from Japanese searchers beneath his life raft. He would be in the water for a full day before he was rescued.

The disaster that befell Torpedo Squadron 8 was made more agonizing by the reports later received that their fighter escort, commanded by Lieutenant Jim Gray, still circled the area some twenty thousand feet above the water, unable to see what lay below. With his gas gauges running low, Gray had no choice but to return to his carrier.

As word filtered back to Task Force 16 that the mission had produced more casualties than successes, Admiral Spruance deferred to his superior, Admiral Frank Jack Fletcher, to make the next move. Fletcher had intended to hold back *Yorktown*'s planes as a reserve, but one observation made the decision for him. Spruance had observed a Japanese scout plane, very far and very high, but instead of a hasty retreat, the plane had lingered. The Americans understood now that they had been spotted as well. There were two choices: withdraw at top speed, putting distance between the task forces and the Japanese fleet, or launch the planes from *Yorktown*, to accompany whatever force remained from Task Force 16. Fletcher gave the order. *Launch the planes.*

ONBOARD USS *YORKTOWN*, AT SEA—JUNE 4, 1942, 8:40 A.M.

"Pilots. Man your planes."

Baker ran through the passageway, up onto the flight deck, searched through the confusion. To one side, a dozen Devastators were warming up, each one bearing its primary weapon, a Mark 13 torpedo nearly as long as the plane, what those men called their "pickle." The weight of the torpedo was enough of an encumbrance that the Devastators barely cleared the end of the flight decks. Worse, Baker had heard the bitching from the pilots and their gunners. The Mark 13 was, for all intents and purposes, a piece of junk. Despite insistence from the navy's ordnance department, the men who had tested the weapon could testify that more often than not, the Mark 13 simply failed to explode. None of that was helped by the torpedoes' slow speed, which produced angry grousing among the men that any mission against the Japanese was a complete waste of time. Baker knew from too many conversations with those men that many called this kind of mission by another name: suicide.

Nearby, the dive bombers were being pulled into position behind the Devastators, their crews going over every moving part, ordnance men checking the bombs beneath their bellies. Some of the Dauntlesses would carry a single five-hundred-pound bomb, with the addition of two one-hundred-pound incendiary bombs beneath the wings, while others carried only a single thousand-pound bomb. Like the Devastators, the load was enough to produce butterflies in the pilots, and ensure that the fighter escorts would have to slow their own speed so as not to outrun the men they were supposed to protect.

Baker counted the Dauntlesses—seventeen. The number was of no comfort, the men whose lives might depend on nothing but six of Thach's fighters. The pilots poured out across the deck now, the fighter pilots holding back, with no place yet for them to go.

The pilots and back-seat gunners of the other planes were gathering alongside their machines, offering silent salutes, handshakes, and pats on the back. Then, with a signal from the flight officer, they climbed up and into their bombers.

Baker couldn't avoid a burst of confusion, saw the other four pilots, then Thach. He searched for the Wildcats, then heard Thach's familiar voice. "The Wildcats are coming up on the elevator now. The dive bombers will go off first, since they have to climb. The torpedo planes will go off second. Once they're clear of the deck, we'll follow."

Alongside the island, Baker saw Thach's other pilots, the men who would be left behind. There were no cheers, no smiles, none of the usual well-wishing. Damn, they're pissed off, he thought. Guess I would be too. It wasn't Thach's idea to leave them behind, that's for sure. How the hell are we supposed to protect thirty damn bombers, flying at two different altitudes?

He saw the Wildcats now, the tractors pulling them off the elevator platforms, the crews tackling the job of opening the wings. Careful, he thought. They've done this for a little while now, but, damn, I don't need to lose any piece of my wings.

Out on the flight deck, the first of the Dauntlesses roared off with a gut-churning rumble, the deck beneath Baker's feet vibrating. There was no pause as the next took off right behind, then the third. Within minutes, twelve more were up and away, and almost immediately the torpedo bombers followed. Baker felt himself shivering, watched as the last of the Devastators flew off, the fighters now pulled into line. There was an odd silence now, the drone of the last bomber fading as the planes climbed away. He saw more Wildcats coming up on the platforms, eight, ten. He felt a jolt and thought, Somebody changed their minds, thank God.

Thach called out, *"Let's go."*

Baker moved to his plane, every part familiar, every quirk well known. He watched Thach, followed his lead, all six men up and into their seats. The crews were there, last checks on the planes, and Baker saw the other planes, silent, no one aboard. Of course, he thought. They're for the CAP, the reserve. In case we don't . . . well, in case we screw up. Fine. Let's don't screw up. You guys can go eat another steak.

Baker waited for it, then saw the next command from the flight officer, the signal to fire up, the engine coming to life, small coughs of blue smoke, then the familiar growl he loved to hear.

Thach led the way, moved his Wildcat slowly out onto the flight deck, the flight officer giving the signal, Thach throttling the engine hard, holding the brakes, then letting go. The Wildcat surged forward and was airborne before it reached the end of the runway—Thach's talent. Bassett was next, following the same routine, and was quickly airborne. It was Baker now, and he eased the plane to the center of the runway. He took a long breath, but there could be no delay, the others close behind him. He pushed the throttle forward, felt the noise and power surrounding him, the plane's engine engulfing him, his feet hard on the brakes, the plane quivering, demanding to be released. He glanced at his watch, 0905, then said aloud, answering the hard roar of the engine and Thach's command, *"Let's go."*

They formed up in a loose formation of pairs, keeping far below the twenty-thousand-feet altitude Baker was accustomed to. Even then, it was difficult to maintain visual contact with the torpedo planes, while high above them, the Dauntless dive bombers followed their own navigational course. Whether the fighter escorts could maintain any contact with the dive bombers might depend on sheer luck.

They had been away from the carrier for no more than ten minutes and Thach let out a yelp on his radio. Baker saw why. In the sea below them, a bomb detonated, and a few seconds later, another. Thach waved to them all, a silent message, *up*. Baker glanced that way, but there was nothing to see. He understood now; he had seen this before, an electrical malfunction in the Dauntlesses. As the pilot triggered the mechanism to arm the bomb, the malfunction also caused the bomb to release. For anyone beneath them, the malfunction could be something of an adventure. Baker sat back in his seat and thought, Maybe we should ease back a ways. But, sure as hell, Commander Leslie will fix the problem. I wonder if those two unarmed planes will turn back? I wouldn't. They've still got their smaller bombs, and a rear gunner. Keep at it, show your buddies you're still with 'em. Maybe that's easy for me to say.

He eyed the torpedo planes below, passing through a thick wall of cumulus clouds. He followed Thach's lead, began a lazy S maneuver, the other four Wildcats doing the same. He knew only what Thach had told them: that the Wildcats cruised at nearly forty knots faster than the lumbering torpedo planes. Losing them would be simple if they didn't pay close attention.

His mind drifted through all the usual thoughts when he was airborne, but there was a difference now, the tightness in his stomach, the tightness in his hands on the yoke. His eyes scoured the sky, but there was still no sign of the Dauntlesses, no sign of anything else. He glanced at the gas gauge, no issues there, pulled out his navigational chart, laid it on his knee. He could see Thach clearly, and Bassett to his left. He checked his compass, scribbled on his chart pad, and confirmed his heading. All right, Perk. Just stay awake, and there won't be a problem.

The drone of the plane's engine was its own comfort, but the navigation was every bit as important. He ran his own numbers, knew that the other five would do the same. If any one of them had a problem with their course, a quick order on Thach's radio or a hand signal would put them all to work, recalculating one more time. The phrase came to him, as it always came to him.

Can Dead Men Vote Twice.

He practiced the exercise yet again, if for no other reason than to pass the time. *Compass plus Deviation equals Magnetic plus Variation equals True course.*

Okay, he thought. My memory's intact. And I can still see them, and there's at least a few of the torpedo planes down there. We gotta be close. But close to what?

He saw the first ships now, off to one side a mammoth aircraft carrier in a hard turn to starboard. His heart jumped in his chest, and he focused on the other ships, a stream of anti-aircraft fire rising, but not at them. Through the clouds he caught glimpses of planes, a dozen or more torpedo bombers, and more coming in low from another direction. The air seemed to bristle with so many insects—planes circling far in the distance, some barely off the water. There was more anti-aircraft fire, and more planes swirling above the ships, much faster, slicing through the formations. He held tight to the yoke, watched Thach, and waited for the hand signal, either down or up. He saw their own torpedo bombers again, clearing the low clouds, and saw them lining up, preparing their run. He wanted to cheer, do anything to help them, but the Zeroes had found them, cutting through the formation, one bomber quickly in flames, tumbling into the water below. Now more went down, one launching its torpedo in panic, far too distant to be effective. Baker's eyes went in every direction, seeing fire and streaks of red, small explosions, more bombers going down, bloody splashes underneath him. He caught a signal from Thach, missed its meaning, but felt it now, a thunderous vibration, a punch cracking his windscreen, another punch from behind, a sharp thump into the steel behind his back. The Zero passed him now, close, wingtips nearly touching, the Zero peeling away. He shouted into his radio, saw the hole, the radio completely wrecked, leaving no way to talk to anyone else. The Zero turned again with a hard tilt of its wings, but Baker lost it, saw more Zeroes coming around them, gathering, rolling through the Wildcats, faster, quicker. Baker peeled off with nowhere else to go, no bombers to protect, the Zeroes now rolling past from every direction. He lined up on one, fired a burst, a useless miss, cursed and dropped low, closer to the water. There was smoke in the air and fiery splashes. He jumped the plane higher, a few feet, banked hard to the left, now spotted the Zero he hadn't seen going past him. He jerked the plane back to the right, caught a quick glimpse of the Zero's tail and fired another burst. He saw smoke, blessed fire, the Zero engulfed, then nosing down into the sea. He shouted again, *"Got you, you bastard."* But there was no one to hear. More Zeroes dropped down and swept around them. He pulled the Wildcat up, gentle tug on the yoke, knew it was dangerous, slowing him down. But the Zeroes close by missed their opportunity, only now seeming to look his way. He had gained altitude, more room to maneuver, and saw his own planes executing the familiar weaving motion, and he knew it was Thach, his perfect defense. The Wildcat fired into the flank of the Zero, the plane igniting like a torch. There were more fights in every direction, the torpedo planes now moving over the outer ring of Japanese destroyers, absorbing a curtain of anti-aircraft fire. He looked up, a Wildcat coming across his nose, very close, and saw now, it was Bassett. Baker began the weave maneuver, but it was too late, the Zero within a few yards of Bassett's tail. The cannon fire erupted from the Zero's nose, the Wildcat coming apart, tumbling hard into the water. The shock paralyzed Baker, but he fought to hold it in, control the raw fury, the urge to shoot everything he had at nothing at all.

He saw more dogfights, and remembered Thach's words: *no dogfights.* But the Zeroes had done their good work on the torpedo bombers, the same as it was all morning, as it was in every direction, all through the fleet. The attacks from all three American carriers never seemed to end, but as the Japanese knew now, never seemed to accomplish anything. And as the Americans were learn-

ing, if the attacks weren't crushed by the Zeroes, it was the anti-
aircraft fire that made the slow plodding bombers with their slow
and heavy torpedoes nearly useless against the Japanese defenses.

Off in the distance, the fighting continued, bombers and Wildcats struck down by swarms of the Japanese weapons, some of the
tail gunners from the American planes striking back as well. The
Wildcats did all they could to hold the Zeroes away, but there were
too many, and the Japanese pilots had the skills.

With most of the threats to the big ships swept aside, the Zeroes
focused their attention on the Wildcats, though from what Baker
could see, far beyond the fleet, most of the remaining American
planes had simply vanished, the survivors returning home. He
kept his Wildcat low, closer to the water, so it would be more difficult for the Zeroes to engage him, but still they tried. With the
torpedo planes nowhere to be seen, the Zeroes aimed for those
few Wildcats that still tried to do their job. It was a test of equals,
but they weren't equal. And through it all, Thach and his men had
to believe they had failed, that the Japanese were simply too good,
too vicious, that we had a great deal to learn about airplanes. The
fights stayed low, some very close to the water, more of the Zeroes
coming down from their perches, no one to tell them what might
still be high above, where the dive bombers waited their turn.

Far above the fighting, the Dauntlesses rolled into position,
banking hard, rolling over, preparing to make their bombing runs.
With the Zeroes so far below, occupied in so many chaotic fights
with the Wildcats, the dive bombers found there was nothing in
their way.

SEVENTEEN

Nagumo

The Americans had come yet again, a fourth attack from torpedo bombers and the Dauntlesses, some protected by the Wildcat fighters. By now the Japanese had measured their enemy well, the four aircraft carriers finally understanding that the American torpedoes were slow, that a sharp turn away, even by the largest ships, could escape the path of that weapon. As each attack approached, the effort by the American torpedo planes grew to feel tragic, even Nagumo recognizing the futility of their meager skills, planes that were too slow and cumbersome, that were easy targets for the Zeroes and the anti-aircraft fire from so many ships. The first waves of dive bombers had shown more ability, and seemed to be better airplanes. But too often their bombing technique had been to approach their targets at a shallow dive, nothing like the near-vertical attack of the Japanese planes. Coming in at a flatter trajectory meant that the American Dauntlesses made themselves a far easier target for the swarms of Zeroes, as well as the shipboard anti-aircraft batteries. To add to the disadvantage for the Americans, each of the four carrier captains knew his craft well, maneuvering his ship in sharp sweeping turns, avoiding every attempt by the Americans to actually make a strike. It had been the same all morning, even for the mighty B-17s, whose high-altitude bombing allowed the Japanese carriers the time to simply maneuver out of the way. For the cruisers and battleships, it was the same, good men at the helm, ships that responded with agility to the moves required to evade their attackers.

Through it all, Nagumo weighed the statistics, the numbers of American planes, and just where they had come from. It was a certainty, based on the reports from his own attacking craft, that the Americans didn't have nearly as many aircraft on Midway as what he was seeing now in the air around his carriers. Whether or not his own scouts had located American carriers somewhere within range, in fact, here were their aircraft. He found no comfort in that thought.

"Sir! Another message. The observer from *Tone* scout number four now claims that the American ships he is observing are a mix of destroyers and cruisers, with an additional two cruisers twenty miles distant from the first group. This surely indicates a second task force, sir."

Nagumo rubbed a hand on his face, looked out through the glass. "That *indicates* nothing."

Aoki seemed frustrated with Nagumo. "Sir . . ."

Kusaka put a hand on Aoki's arm, quieting him. "Leave us, Captain. Perhaps only a moment."

Aoki made a curt bow, and did as he was told. Kusaka sat across from Nagumo, motioned to the door, the silent order for the other aides to leave. The door closed, leaving silence in the wardroom, and after a moment, Kusaka said, "Sir, something must happen. We must not merely sit here and await what move the Americans will make. Their attacks have been deliberate and well planned, regardless of the flaws in how they fight. If they come again, they must be destroyed again. If those ships are escorting carriers, *they* must be destroyed. We shall find their carriers, and they will be destroyed as well. That is, after all, our mission, our purpose for being here. We have already knocked dozens of their attack planes from the sky. We must retrieve Lieutenant Tomonaga's fliers before their fuel is exhausted. There seems to be a pause in the American attacks, and we must take advantage. The carriers can resume their windward courses, allowing the planes to land. The bombers are having their ordnance changed from land bombs to armor-piercing even now. The torpedo planes will take a little longer, but we can change them over as well. Sir, we must issue orders. What should we do? We must not lose Tomonaga's men, and we must clear the flight decks of all four carriers, so that we might make the next move. Do we spot the bombers belowdeck and make way for our second assault on Midway, or do we send off the bombers to destroy the American ships? This is the decision you must make."

Nagumo looked at him, blinked, then again. "I know what my duty is. If we send the strike planes out to attack the American ships, we will do so without adequate fighter cover. Too many of the Zeroes are in need of fuel and ammunition. Is that correct?"

Kusaka nodded. "Completely correct, sir. But the bomber pilots would gladly sacrifice themselves to American fighters for the opportunity to assault an American carrier."

Nagumo crossed his hands at his waist. "What carrier is that, my friend? I have heard no confirmation from our *scouts* that the Americans are sailing past with anything other than cruisers."

There was a sharp knock on the wardroom door. Kusaka hesitated, but Nagumo motioned weakly. "Yes, enter."

It was Captain Aoki, and he glanced at Kusaka, then said, "Admiral, we have received another report from the *Kone's* scout. He now says there is a single carrier astern of the American task force. We have no way to confirm this, of course, but I believe this requires us to act decisively."

Nagumo nodded. "Thank you, Captain. I shall consider it. Continue to switch the bomb types as rapidly as possible. We cannot attack that carrier without torpedoes or armor-piercing bombs."

Aoki's voice grew higher in obvious frustration. "Of course, I know that, sir. Why do we wait? We can launch an attack with only a part of our forces."

Nagumo looked at him. "Part? No, we must launch the attack with our entire attack force. It has always been that way, and it shall be right now. Return to your bridge, Captain."

Aoki gave his crisp short bow, the door closing. Nagumo heard voices in the passageway, an argument, then another knock.

Nagumo said, "Can they do nothing for themselves?" He responded again, "Yes, enter."

He saw one of Aoki's aides, a paper in the man's hand, and Aoki standing just behind him.

"Sir, we have received a shortwave message from Admiral Yamaguchi. He says that a portion of his attack group on carrier *Hiryu* has been armed and is prepared to fly to seek out the American task force. He says that carrier *Soryu* is also ready. Admiral Yamaguchi implores you, sir, to order the assault to begin."

Nagumo was losing patience. "Tell Admiral Yamaguchi that a partial attack is no attack at all. We would be bait for the American sharks. They have capable fighters and would tear us to shreds without our own fighter escorts. I do not wish to explain this again." He ran out of breath, looked at Kusaka. "Admiral Yamaguchi is a good man, certainly. Like so many out here, he is Admiral Yamamoto's man, chosen for his loyalty to the admiral. But he is young. Just because he commands Carrier Division Two does not mean he may use their weaponry in violation of our doctrine. Must we tell him that?"

"I will communicate what must be said, sir."

More voices in the passageway, and Nagumo looked up with weary eyes. A young lieutenant stared at the two admirals, made a deep bow, and said, "Sirs, the destroyers have begun to report. The American planes are coming again."

ONBOARD CARRIER *AKAGI*, AT SEA—JUNE 4, 1942, 9:40 A.M.

"This is *glorious*."

Nagumo ignored the man beside him, did not respond to the man's gloating pride. Behind him, across the ship's narrow bridge came another voice, from one of his officers.

"Another one down. Another. The fighters are performing as we hoped."

Nagumo couldn't be heard through the clamor of excitement around him, but said in a low voice, "We did not hope. We demand. They are obedient to their training."

"They are, sir. Always."

He was surprised to see Genda, the young man supporting himself against the bulkhead. Around them, the fighting swirled with fiery intensity, the Zeroes sliding back and forth through formations of torpedo bombers. The ship lurched hard to port, a surprise, and Nagumo's hands smacked on the glass.

"Enemy torpedo launch. We are clearing the path." A half minute passed, the cheering halted, heavy silence on the bridge. Nagumo couldn't help the butterflies, felt himself breathing heavily, but the voice came again, from the helm. "All clear. Torpedo missed to starboard."

Genda said, "I am impressed with your carriers, Admiral. You fly your ships as we fly our planes. One weapon complements the other."

Nagumo started to respond, when he felt another lurch of the ship, executing the same maneuver.

"*Torpedo to starboard.*" A pause again. "It is destroyed. Machine gun fire from battery three."

Genda laughed through a cough. "I didn't know you could shoot a torpedo with a machine gun."

Beyond Genda, Kusaka said, "If it moves slowly enough, Commander, anything can be killed with machine gun fire."

Genda coughed again. "I must echo your crew's enthusiasm, sir. This is a glorious show. But for the smoke, we could see an entire flight wing annihilated."

"Sir, observers report . . . dive bombers coming in high from the east."

"Sir, destroyer *Hito* reports dive bombers high above from the south."

There was another silent moment, and Nagumo felt the familiar stirring sickness inside. "Alert all CAP planes. The other Zeroes. Prepare to destroy the enemy as before. They will level their dives as the others have done. Notify all ships to ready their batteries."

Genda said, "Sir, there are no CAP planes to intercept them. Many of Lieutenant Tomonaga's fighters have made their landing and require refueling. The others . . . they are nearly all out here . . . I can see them. They are at low altitude." Genda raised his binoculars, stared hard at those planes within range. Nagumo looked at him, knew that Genda would know exactly what was happening.

"What does this mean, Commander?"

Genda lowered the glasses, kept his stare through the glass. "Sir, the fight with the torpedo bombers brought our CAP down too low to respond to the planes coming from above. There was not enough discipline in our pilots. They saw easy prey, and they pounced. But they left their position in the air high above. We must hope for the anti-aircraft batteries."

Nagumo thought, I do not understand. The fighters must still prevail. They can climb to meet the enemy. He looked out the southerly window, could see the American bombers now, falling in close formation, the gunners on every ship in the area opening up. But this time they did not flatten out their dive, and Nagumo could see the angle, nearly vertical, the voice in his mind . . . as it should be done.

Captain Aoki stared out that way as well, and said, "They are diving on *Kaga*. Perhaps we are spared."

Nagumo watched as the first plane dropped the black speck from its belly, and said, "Perhaps we are not."

The smoke rose immediately, more planes dropping their loads, impacting on the great ship. At forty-two thousand tons, *Kaga* was by far the largest of the four Japanese carriers, and so she was the most tempting target for men who had never made such an attack.

The bombing squadrons from *Enterprise* reached the Japanese fleet minutes ahead of the flight from *Yorktown*. Lieutenant Commander Wade McClusky's *Enterprise* squadron met their targets by dividing, intending to attack each of the two carriers closest, *Kaga* and Admiral Nagumo's flagship, *Akagi*. But as had been the case all morning, confusion played another part, and both wings of McClusky's Dauntlesses initially took aim at the same target, *Kaga*. Yet there was one significant difference. Unlike so much previous futility for the Americans, McClusky's bombers hit their target, and within short minutes, the massive carrier was engulfed in smoke and fire.

But not all of McClusky's bombers followed him to the most obvious target. Three more of the Dauntlesses, led by Lieutenant Dick Best, put their sights on the next ship in line.

ONBOARD CARRIER *AKAGI*, AT SEA—JUNE 4, 1942, 9:55 A.M.

The bridge crew stared out toward *Kaga*, but there was nothing to see. The smoke spread out in an enormous black screen, columns boiling up skyward, the enormous ship spilling out its own death.

"What do we do, sir?"

The question was infuriating, and Nagumo looked for the source, saw Captain Aoki with his hands out. "You fight, Captain. Or are you unable? There are planes on the flight deck, prepared for attack, yes?"

Kusaka intervened now, and said, "Sir, there were only a few aircraft spotted on deck, Zeroes mostly, with the bombers on the hangar deck, as you had ordered. As you can see, the destroyers are moving into place, and will pick up survivors from *Kaga*. For now, it is all we can do."

"Here they come. Dive bombers."

Nagumo saw the young man staring up and did the same, followed tracers of the anti-aircraft fire. Through an opening in the clouds he saw three specks, now rolling over, wings straightening, aiming nearly straight down, aiming at *him*.

From both ends of the ship, the anti-aircraft batteries came to life, but it was a weak gesture, many of the other ships still focused on the chaos around *Kaga*. Nagumo stared at them as they dropped closer, losing altitude, and expected to see the blessed Zeroes, their saviors, or at least a distraction to draw the Americans away. But the American planes began to level out now, then began to pull out of their dive, one at a time, each one already laying its small black egg, the bombs on course to *Akagi*.

The first bomb impacted directly on the flight deck, punching a hole through to the hangar deck, where the bomb detonated. Nagumo felt the jolt, the deck beneath his feet rising, tilting, the ship suddenly lurching to one side. The next two bombs were near misses, but damaging just as well, enormous plumes of water rising far above the island, the ship rolling again. Now the fire came, pushing out through the hole in the deck, spraying out the sides of the hangar deck. More explosions came now, torpedoes and bombs scattered about the hangar deck. The men around Nagumo began to scream and shout in a horrible chorus of confusion, some men doing their jobs, some simply in full panic.

Nagumo felt hands on his shoulder, had no strength to resist, and heard Kusaka. "Sir. We must leave. *Sir*. Please. *Now*."

"Perhaps I should remain."

"We need you, sir. *Now*."

From the helm, the navigator, Miura, said, "Sir, I have no control of the helm. The rudders have been damaged."

Aoki was there now, his face close to Nagumo. "Admiral, my damage control officer, Commander Dobashi, says there is no extinguishing the fires. There is no hose pressure, no working valves. I have attempted to shut down engines, but no one responds from the engine room. We must assume the worst. Sir, we have lost all the aircraft spotted on deck and below. Our ordnance is igniting as we speak. Admiral, the enemy will not allow us to survive."

Kusaka leaned close, as though none of the others should hear him. "Sir, *Akagi* can no longer serve as your flagship. We must move your flag to one of the cruisers. They are moving close even now."

Nagumo stared out the bridge window at the growing fire on the flight deck, the wood strips peeling back, igniting one by one. A Zero was parked to one side, bursting into flames, more of the deck feeding the fires.

I must remain, he thought. How can I leave? After a long moment, he said, "Perhaps it is not yet time."

Kusaka moved himself into Nagumo's dreamlike stare, and said, "Admiral, you are commander in chief of the First Carrier Striking Force, as well as this ship. It is your duty to carry on the battle."

Nagumo tried to focus, to emerge from this astonishing nightmare. He stared at Kusaka for a long moment, no words coming, slowly nodded his head.

EIGHTEEN

Baker

The Zeroes left him for a brief minute, Baker climbing into a heavy cloud, the only safe place. He emerged from the far side, no Zeroes in sight, cursed himself to do his job. He eased the nose of the plane downward, searched frantically for any of the torpedo bombers still airborne, trying to see whether or not they were still attempting to send their torpedoes toward the massive carrier. His hands gripped the yoke, and he felt the shaking inside his hands, his chest. He tried to shove it away, knew it was fear, plain and simple, the terror of watching for and escaping the Zeroes, of feeling the slugs impacting the steel behind him. Easy, Perk, he thought. His mind took him to the briefing from this morning, plus so much chatter from the pilots, the dismal news that the Devastators had all the maneuverability of great fat mules, the Japanese Zeroes barely facing a challenge in shooting them down. Even the tail gunners, the planes' only defensive weapon, could barely touch the twisting, diving Zeroes as they pumped the torpedo bombers with machine gun and cannon fire. How did those poor bastards feel? How did they even climb into their planes? You've got nothing to bitch about. Dammit, you know what Thach would say: *Do your job*.

He searched the sky around him, saw nothing close by, the Zeroes still pursuing the last of the torpedo bombers. Stop sightseeing. *Do your job, damn it all*. He rolled the Wildcat into a steep dive, his eyes on a pair of Zeroes pursuing the only Devastator he could see. Another Wildcat joined the chase, too far to identify, but his focus was on the first Zero, the plane seeming to ignore him, oblivious to his presence. It seemed too easy, his dive taking him closer to the Zero, the pilot busy lining up on the Devastator. *Now*. Baker poured out machine gun fire, a full three seconds, the Zero dropping suddenly with heavy smoke. He dove with it, but there was no need, the plane tumbling, coming apart, spinning into the sea. Baker yelped, then made a mark on the knee pad, a lesson from Thach, keep track of how many you nail. It could come in handy one day. That's two, he thought. Holy crap. Now, where's that other one . . . he saw the fireball, the Zero going down below another Wildcat, the plane in a steep dive straight into the water. The Wildcat wagged his wings, and Baker responded the same way, then made a sharp turn, watched the lone Devastator moving out away from all the targets below. His mind spoke to the Devastator's pilot: You've made it so far, sport. I hope like hell you hit something. But right now, just keep going. We'll do the best we can to keep these bastards occupied. He pulled the Wildcat into a climb, pushed into more clouds, a thicker layer, then out, then up into another. He was clear now, had a good view of the water, and he forced his hands to uncurl off the yoke, a brief release, flexed them, his fingers painfully stiff. He fought for calm, gripped the yoke again, but there was nothing calm about anything he had to do. He made a wide turn, and searched for any of the torpedo bombers who might still be attacking the Japanese ships. Must be late for them, he thought. By now . . . Christ, and look at all those ships. It looks like nothing got in. They're untouched, no smoke, nothing. A crappy end to a crappy mission. I hope more of the Devastators got away.

He thought of Bassett, felt a hard tug in his gut. I guess there's no chance he survived. Hope he didn't feel it. *Stop that.* Jesus. Pay attention or someone will be breathing down your neck. But wait . . . who knocked down that Zero? Too far away to see. My money's on Thach, for sure.

Baker's altitude had increased to nearly ten thousand feet, taking advantage of the pause in the fight. He scanned the sky above him, clear and blue, slight wisps of clouds, and now he saw the Zero in level flight, as though patrolling the sea below. Baker dipped his nose, adding speed, banked through a cloud, emerged from the other side, the Zero barely a hundred yards in front of him. The advantage was all to Baker, dropping quickly to the Zero's tail. He saw the meatballs, fat red circles on the plane's wings, the Zero cruising at level altitude and making no attempt to maneuver, less than a hundred feet below him. Baker's heart began to race, his usual reaction, and he thought, That Jap's used the clouds just like I did, but he has no idea I'm here.

Baker pushed forward on the yoke, fingers on the buttons that would fire whatever remained of his ammunition. He had a sudden scare, wasn't sure just how much of his ammo he had shot away. He wanted to test the guns, a single shot, as brief as possible, but knew better, wouldn't give the Zero any hint of where he was. He gripped the yoke with cold fingers, pushed the Wildcat over into a shallow dive, rocked the plane to one side and drew up directly behind the Zero. The plane still made no attempt to escape him, no defensive maneuvers at all. Baker slid his fingers onto the firing buttons, and now he felt the fire from behind, cracking his windscreen, hard thumps into the steel behind him. He breathed oil, coughed, pushed hard on the yoke, dove off to the right, caught a glimpse of the Zero behind him, realized now there was more than one. The word drilled him, a lesson from Thach, from so much experience. *Bait.* The Zero had been a dangling lure, jiggling with shiny beauty, waiting for the fish to bite. And Baker had bit.

He rolled over hard, then back again, the Zeroes boxing him in. The fear turned now to terror, and a brief thought for Bassett flashed in his mind. Shot out of the sky, and now me. *Damn. You stupid ass.*

He saw red streaks zipping past his windscreen and rolled again to the right, dropped down, increasing speed, the only maneuver he had. He heard a rumble and caught the reflection in his windscreen, a flash of light. He banked that way, saw one Zero tumbling into fiery pieces as it fluttered toward the sea. He saw a Wildcat now, maneuvering in behind the second Zero. The Zero peeled off, dove straight away, the pilot with no more belly for the fight. Baker eased the Wildcat back to the right, the other one catching up to him, close beside him, and he spotted the face of Thach. *Bless you, you wonderful son of a bitch.*

Thach tapped his earphones, the signal to use the radio, but Baker shook his head, made a slashing motion across his neck. Thach understood, motioned for him to return to the enemy ships. Baker followed Thach's lead, realized now he had no idea where the ships were, or how many of the torpedo planes might have survived. He followed Thach down through the clouds, scanned the ocean below him. The fuel gauge wasn't a problem, not yet, but the fights with the Zeroes had been costly. He searched again, dropped his plane clear of the clouds, a broad blue carpet beneath him. And now he saw the smoke, great black plumes rising in the distance, two enormous ships in obvious distress. He felt a child's excitement, wanted to fly that way and get a closer look. *What happened . . .* but Thach peeled off the other way, and Baker knew he'd better follow. In the distance, he saw Zeroes again, like so many flies around yet another of the great carriers, circling as though wanting to land. His heart was racing again, nervous hands gripping the yoke. He strained to see, searching the sky above him, all around, but the Zeroes seemed uninterested in this small group of Wildcats.

Thach led him as close as they dared go, the anti-aircraft fire from a handful of destroyers rising up in a spider web of red and pink tracers. But their aim was elsewhere, the Wildcats ignored, the gunners seemed far more interested in a very different prey. Baker saw them now, single specks from high above, flashes of sunlight reflected on the wings. The Dauntlesses dropped toward the carrier in a seventy-degree dive, and Baker aimed the nose of his plane that way, ready to add any support he could give. The first Dauntless pulled up and away, leaving behind the one weapon they had that seemed to work. The first bomb impacted directly on the carrier, nearly dead center, buried beneath the flight deck, igniting quickly in a massive blast, ripping huge pieces of steel upward. Baker was closer now, inside the ring of anti-aircraft fire, still hoping to give aid to any of the bombers in trouble. Thach was just ahead and below him, the other three Wildcats gathering together as well, but the targets were few and distant, with no interest in a duel with the fighters. Thach led them in a soft sweeping circle, all eyes on the Zeroes, but the Zeroes seemed helpless to throw any effective fire against the dive bombers. The Dauntlesses came in a full dive, far faster than the Zeroes could reach, and when the bombs were released, the impact seemed to shock even the Japanese pilots, their own ships, their *nests*, igniting into fiery wrecks. Baker stared at the scene below, the astounding destruction of the big ship, and the Dauntlesses that were destroying it. Baker aimed for a lone Zero, the only job he had now, but saw three more bombers dive in toward another of the carriers, then pull away, one bomb detonating deep in the ship's core, the carrier seeming to erupt like a bursting volcano. Baker kept his eyes frozen to the ship, but there was little to see but the dense smoke and flames.

He focused again on the Zeroes, saw another distant target, but Thach was beside him now, a waggle of the wings. As the dive bombers gathered together, plotting their own course back to *Yorktown*, Thach led his fighters back to their protective formation above them. For the Dauntlesses, fuel was low, increasing the need to escape from any more assaults by the Zeroes. It was the same for Baker and the others, their ammunition gone, or nearly so. For now, for the bombers who had found their targets, the men who had come into the Japanese fleet from several directions, who had surprised the observers, the gunners, and the deadly CAPs to drop their bombs nearly uncontested, for all those men who came mostly from *Enterprise* and *Yorktown*, it was time to go home.

JUNE 4, 1942, 11:20 A.M.

He counted the bullet holes, eight in the tail, seven more in his left wing, thought, I'm glad as hell I didn't know this up top. He looked again at his hands. For Chrissakes, stop shaking. Thach was there now, stepping away from his plane.

Baker said, "They busted my oil line. Might not have made it. Smelled it, but didn't know how bad it was."

Thach seemed to rub away a headache, and said, "Don't worry about it. They shot away my oil line and put a slug right into my gas tank. I guess we're both lucky."

Baker ran his fingers over the bullet holes. "Maybe we all are. I saw Bassett go down . . . Oh Christ."

"Yeah, I know. I saw him too. Nothing we could have done. I don't know about Sheedy. I thought he was in formation with us, but he disappeared. He might have had to break off and go to *Enterprise,* especially if he was leaking oil. I'll have the captain send a shortwave message over to check it out. Not much else we can do."

"Did we lose the Devastators?"

"Not sure. Most of 'em. Saw that myself. Most of the Dauntlesses made it back. They're circling overhead, lining up for landing."

"Guess they'll all get medals. Never seen a carrier blown to hell before. Not one. Christ, three of 'em." He pointed to the *Yorktown*'s island. "Somebody on the bridge has to be pretty damn happy about that."

They watched as the first of Commander Leslie's dive bombers tailhooked in, was tractored to one end of the carrier quickly, making room for the next plane. As the noise died down, Thach said, "I guess there were three carriers. Nobody told me what the targets were. Hope to God there's not another three out there with another flock of those bastard Zeroes."

Baker waited for the next bomber, saw a plane trailing a flutter of loose metal, a dozen or more bullet holes. "Guess we're not the only ones who had a fight."

Thach said, "I'm headed up the ladder to report to Admiral Fletcher. Come with me. He'll want to know what both of us saw. Nobody's believing scout planes anymore. After that, we'll meet in the briefing room. I'll gather everybody, talk about this, in case we have to go up again." He paused. "And find out who's still with us." They started into the island, the first ladder upward, and Thach stopped, said, "Never woulda thought it."

"What?"

"Those Zeroes. Best plane I ever saw. The pilots too. They know what the hell they're doing, and we need to pay attention to that. God knows what else they'll send at us."

NINETEEN

Yamaguchi

He stared through the binoculars, two enormous columns of smoke filling the sky, erasing the horizon. The third carrier was obviously dying, but without the flames, the ship settling low, dead in the water. The radio signals came still, but weak, meaningless chatter, panic from men who knew their ships were going down.

They didn't listen to me, he thought. Now we are facing defeat. He turned, shouted to an aide, "Alert the watches. Alert all gun stations. The Americans will know they have missed us. They will return."

It was an order he didn't need to give, but for the single moment, there was nothing else to do. He had pushed *Hiryu* farther from the combat, slipping away, if that were possible, from the sight of the American fighters and dive bombers. His Zeroes, his CAP, still flew overhead, and around *Hiryu* his protective belt of destroyers moved with him, all of them adding distance from the chaos around the devastated ships.

"Sir, Admiral Nagumo has successfully evacuated his command from *Akagi*, and has established his command from cruiser *Nagara*. He is issuing orders by signal and by shortwave. One moment, please, sir." The man focused on his earphones. "Sir, *Nagara* reports messages will be coming through in a few minutes."

Yamaguchi stepped back from the glass, lowered the binoculars, ignored the radio operator, said aloud, "So now our commanding admiral will guide us once more with his wisdom." He looked at the others on the bridge, a handful of officers and the men manning the various instruments. "Well, here is a *suggestion* for our Admiral Nagumo that requires very little discussion. Send this. *Leave a single destroyer to protect the injured carriers. Send all other ships in direction of* Hiryu, *to strengthen our attack on the Americans.* Send that now." He saw faces watching him, a pair of officers nodding their heads in agreement. "So, I am not too impudent, then? Do I disrespect our commander, especially after so much *success*? Or perhaps I would have preferred they listen to *this* command, when I told them how to attack the enemy, that we should not wait and dither and agonize over our decisions. We had dozens of aircraft prepared to fly this morning, and we waited, because our admiral was not satisfied that we were ready. So, now we will agonize over the death of three of our carriers. Does he agonize with us? Or does he await his fate when he stands before Admiral Yamamoto and the emperor?"

He turned to the glass again, anger in his hands, no need for binoculars, the smoke now more than ten miles behind.

"Add more distance. Make the Americans work to find us. And then we shall have time to prepare. And while Admiral Nagumo bides his time and makes decisions that affect no one, we shall take up the gauntlet."

"Sir. Signal from Cruiser Division 8. It must be coming from Admiral Nagumo."

"What's the signal, Ensign?"

"*Attack the enemy carriers.*"

Yamaguchi lowered his head, and thought, Four hours too late.

He stared out toward the distant smoke, thought, I begged him. I did everything but shout in his face, and if he were here, I would have done *that*. We found the enemy, and no matter if we have a single bomber, we *must* attack them. And from Admiral Nagumo, I get caution and scolding. No doubt he feels I am too young, too inexperienced to understand how we attack our enemies. Perhaps now I will show him how *I* would do it.

Tamon Yamaguchi had earned his position well, without the curse of youth that others, particularly Admiral Nagumo, seemed to condemn him for. Yamaguchi was fifty-nine, had served the navy with enormous distinction as far back as the Great War. After the war, he had traveled to the United States, had been educated at Princeton University, and like his supreme commander, Yamamoto, Yamaguchi had spent a number of years in the United States, learning customs and culture that would serve him well in the *next* war. He had spent much time commanding task forces along the coast of China, had supervised air strikes within that country that earned him even more of a reputation as a ruthless and effective leader. But his greatest achievement thus far was his participation in the attack on Pearl Harbor, commanding two of the aircraft carriers that took part, *Soryu* and *Hiryu,* the same carriers he commanded now, as second in command of *Kido Butai.*

Impatient, with a short fuse for incompetence, he had supervised the training of his pilots with ruthless efficiency. Thus far, in actions all across the Pacific, that training had been extremely effective. What Yamaguchi hoped for, more than any single accolade, was a show of respect from those above him. Yamamoto had offered him that without hesitation. Admiral Nagumo seemed instead to dismiss him for it.

The planes had been spotted on deck, and Yamaguchi understood that whatever boasting he aimed now at Admiral Nagumo carried very little weight. With so much attrition from the morning's fighting, the dive bombers available for any mission now totaled barely eighteen planes, along with only six Zeroes as a protective shield. It wasn't that these planes required more time to prepare, as Nagumo had insisted earlier that morning. For now, it was all that *Hiryu* had left to send.

Overhead, more Zeroes had gathered, some of them orphans from the other three devastated carriers. But they had been airborne throughout most of the American assault, and had acquitted themselves extremely well against whatever weapons the Americans had sent against them. But Yamaguchi could do nothing with those planes except watch them patrol overhead. Like those few planes still below on his hangar deck, they had too little fuel to go anywhere else.

He was tired of binoculars, tired of watching burning ships, tired of the indecisiveness of his superior. He thought of Yamamoto, off in some perch hundreds of miles away. *He should have chosen me to command the Kido Butai.* He knew that Nagumo was meek, old, and worn out. *So they offer me a plum, a token command, a carrier division. Two ships in my command, and one of those is destroyed. And still, everything I do, I answer first to Nagumo. So, what kind of answer do we have now?* He thought again of Yamamoto. *I should be honored by his faith in me. Of course, no matter what has happened, that will not change. But still . . . he is so very far away. Would we have fought the Americans differently if he had been on Akagi's bridge? I have to believe* it so. But, so far away . . . I wonder if he even shoots battleship *Yamato*'s massive guns, just for something to do?

He knew Yamamoto's chief of staff, Admiral Ugaki, very well, both men attending the Naval Academy together. Both men were popular with their subordinates, though few believed the two men were equal in age, Yamaguchi wearing a soft round face, giving him a much more youthful appearance than his friend. It was that youthfulness that stripped him of respect from some of his superiors, primarily Nagumo.

He thought of Yamamoto again, the meetings and conferences, the young men who energized the campaign, Genda and Watanabe, and so many more. No, do not insult them, do not dismiss Admiral Yamamoto or his staff for errors. The errors are out here, where we face the enemy. The plan has been good, but the command has not. And yet, despite what we have lost, we have not yet lost this fight.

"Sir, the bombers are spotted, and warmed up. The Zeroes will follow, as ordered. Lieutenant Fukai insists he can rearm and refuel the torpedo planes within the hour."

"How many torpedo planes?"

The man hesitated. "Ten, sir."

Yamaguchi moved across the bridge, stared down at the planes, the whirling props, pilots waiting for the signal, *his* signal. "What do we know of the American positions? The latest reports?"

He looked toward the officer, the man with a telephone in his hand, a line to the flight deck. "Sir, the last report was the scout plane from cruiser *Chikuma*. We have provided the compass heading to the flight leaders. The scout reports there is at least one carrier. We will find them, sir."

"I am pleased by your confidence, Lieutenant. But if we do *not* find them, there is no reason to return home."

American bombers find
and attack Japanese aircraft carriers.
Only *Hiryu* escapes.

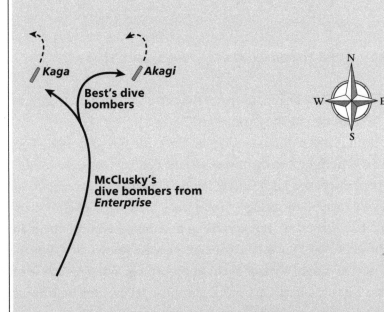
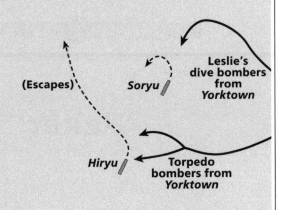

TWENTY

Baker

"The CAP is staying up, for now. Are you absolutely sure we hit two of the Jap carriers?"

Thach glanced at Baker. "We hit *three,* for sure, Admiral. They were still upright, but there was a lot of fire."

Fletcher cocked his head, seeming to know he was being heard by every man on the bridge. "You sure? Three? That's better than I could have expected. But according to Admiral Nimitz, there are supposed to be four total. Not sure how he knows that, but the PBY scouts caught sight of them this morning. What pisses me off is that I haven't heard a word from those fellows for four hours. With what *they* saw, and what you're saying, we're still chasing one Jap carrier. Only one. That feels a hell of a lot better." Fletcher paused. "And you're sure you saw three damaged?"

"Absolutely, sir. Two were on fire, one seemed to be dead in the water, putting out some smoke."

Fletcher looked toward the *Yorktown*'s skipper, Captain Buckmaster, then to another man Baker didn't know. Fletcher said, "Lieutenant Biard, it seems you and your people were right. *How* you were right is a question I can't answer. Admiral Nimitz put you out here to advise, but he wouldn't tell me just what you were advising. You're supposed to be analyzing Jap intel, but I haven't seen anything of that. And, so you know, my own people have done just fine without Pearl Harbor's intel, as we can plainly see right now."

Baker had no idea who the lieutenant was, saw a smirking smile, Biard obviously with no affection for the admiral. Fletcher looked at Thach again.

"This is one of those *crypto* fellows, Commander. Reads tea leaves for some of Admiral Nimitz's people. He doesn't like me any more than you pilots do. All that black-shoe brown-shoe business. Can't say I've had much use for intel officers or you fellows either. You're an arrogant bunch, too cocksure for my taste. But I've never seen a pilot yet who could stand five minutes in an engine room." Fletcher paused, hands on his hips. "So, did either of you see any stray PBYs out there? I'd like to give one of those jokers an ass chewing for leaving us in the dark."

Baker started to speak, hesitated, caught a nod from Thach, *go ahead*. "Sir, our PBYs are no match for the Japanese Zero. If any of those scouts were suddenly facing the enemy, he'd have very little chance. It's possible they're all down."

Fletcher seemed to back up, his anger defused. "You could be right, Lieutenant. Well, I'll send word over to Task Force 16, see if Admiral Spruance has heard anything more." He paused. "Here's a pat on the back, Commander. You and your boys did a hell of a job. How many you shoot down—I mean, by yourself?"

Thach seemed to dread the question. "I believe . . . three, sir."

Fletcher looked at Baker now. "You?"

"Two, sir."

"I knew it. I damn well knew it. All this talk about Jap Zeroes. But those bastards can't keep up with us. That's a compliment, both of you. Remember that the next time anybody tells you your black-shoe admiral has a stick up his ass."

"Admiral Fletcher."

Baker saw a young lieutenant, perfect white uniform, a paper in his hands. He made a great show of handing it off to Fletcher, as though the piece of paper was his particular kingdom.

Fletcher read, deadly serious now, said aloud, "Radio Electrician Bennett reports bogies forty-five miles out, inbound. Thirty to forty planes." He looked at Thach. "Can you get airborne, Commander? You've got fifteen minutes."

Baker felt his stomach knot up, and Thach said, "No, sir. We just landed, and we've no fuel or ammo. The CAP is still in place, though. They'll do a fine job, sir."

Fletcher moved over to the open terrace of the flag bridge. "I guess they'll have to."

The announcement went out over the loudspeakers, the crew rolling into action in a way that was very different from the routine of sending planes into the air. To avoid the potential for fire, fuel lines were purged, filled with inert gas. All watertight doors were locked down, and any excess gasoline tanks were simply shoved overboard.

For the dive bombers of Commander Leslie's squadron, not yet completely down on the flight deck, orders were issued for them to maintain altitude, and, despite low fuel supplies, to add their machine guns to the CAP of Wildcats. But the defensive wall wouldn't simply stay in place. With the crucial asset of radar, something the Japanese didn't have, the CAP could act more like an offensive weapon, moving out away from *Yorktown* to meet the assault before it ever reached the ship itself.

They met some twenty-five miles from *Yorktown,* most of the

Japanese pilots stunned by the surprise appearance of so many American fighters. The cost of that surprise was deadly, mostly for the Japanese, several of their bombers knocked down, while their protective shield of Zeroes quickly became scattered throughout the area, the fighters seeking their own survival as much as protecting the dive bombers. Yet through it all, a handful of Japanese bombers slipped past the American fighters, while others, pursued by the Americans, pushed the entire melee toward *Yorktown,* decreasing the distance until the deck crew and bridge officers could see that fight for themselves.

They watched from the flight deck, Baker aching for the crew to put his plane together, prepare for a quick takeoff. But it was not to be, the gas lines empty, and no time to replace his wrecked radio.

He stood with the others, Thach, Cheek, a number of the pilots from other squadrons. The fighting they could see rolled over the distant destroyers like daredevils in a flying circus, a display of spins and arcing circles, pursuit and escape, smoke and bursts of fire, wrecked aircraft diving into the sea. There were cheers around him, but Baker knew they weren't sure just who it was hitting the water, who had the upper hand, and who was dying.

"Let's go. Clear the deck." The voice came from the deck officer, a thick and unpleasant man name Fogle. "Inside, gentlemen. Commander Thach, the bridge wants VF-3 to gather up in your ready room. The deck crews will see to your aircraft."

Thach obeyed, leading Baker and the others inside. They moved quickly to the windowless room, the air of frustration already building. The gripes came now: "Damn it all. We're gonna miss out . . ."

Thach shouted, "*Shut up.* Nobody needs to get busted up by shrapnel out there. A stray machine gun bullet can do as much to you as a Zero. So knock it off."

The room grew silent, Baker focusing on a heavy thump in the distance, then another, many more. Baker said, "What the hell was that?"

Thach kept his voice low. "Five-inch guns. Anti-aircraft fire from our destroyers and cruisers."

The sounds seemed closer now, not as heavy, and Thach said, "One-point-ones. That means less than five miles. All of you, brace yourself. Hold on to something. They're coming. Most likely dive bombers."

Baker wasn't sure what he meant, saw the others kneel down, some curled up in the corner. He sat down on the deck, gripped the chair, still wasn't sure why.

The first big thunder came now, a sharp vibration in the bulk-heads, bouncing them all off the deck beneath them. Now came the second impact, louder, more intense, and voices shouting out-side, men moving past the ready room at a sprint.

One of the pilots called out, to Thach, to anyone else. "What the hell's going on? I think we're hit."

Now there was a third thump, the ship rocking fore and aft, and more men rushing past, men in fire suits, axes, and sledgeham-mers. Thach stood up now, the men ready to follow him out.

"*No.* Stay here. We'll be in the way. Those fellows, damage con-trol, they know what they're doing. You don't. I'll get info and bring it back here. Anybody leaves this room without me telling you to, I'll kick your ass."

"Jesus, Commander, what if we're going down?"

Thach turned to the man. "You see any water? You hear any-body yell *abandon ship*? I'll be back, once I can find out what's going on."

He was gone now, rumbles of cursing came from the pilots, but Baker knew Thach was right. There was nothing they knew how to do. I know one thing, he thought. We're right below the island.

If this room was suddenly full of water, you could bet your ass we're sinking.

The damage was extensive, but the fires were mostly extinguished due to the good work of the fire crews. Baker could see it for himself now, the flight deck a shambles of wood and steel, one gaping hole nearly dead center by the island. There was other damage as well, another hole punched in the island itself, shattered gun emplacements, and out toward the bow, another pile of wreckage, what had been the forward elevator. He saw the worst of it now, men covered in sheets, at least five bodies nearby, and another dozen tended to by corpsmen. He wanted to help, add anything he could, but knew better, so he kept back as those men did their jobs. Repair crews were already at work, laying timbers over the blasted openings, doing what they could to smooth out the flight deck, to make *Yorktown* useful again.

The deck officer was shouting at Thach now, and said, "The captain says we're able to push her up to sixteen knots. That should be enough headwind to get you in the air. There's no more fuel in the lines, so you'll have to make do with whatever's in the aircraft right now. Not sure how much we were able to put into the tanks before we had to shut down. You should have eight aircraft with twenty gallons or more, but I can't promise. They've got the flight deck cleaned off for you to use most of the runway. I'd advise that."

Thach turned, a hard look at Baker and the others around him. "Jones, Baker, Langston, Leonard, Dibb, Lasser, Henry. You're with me. The rest of you, no bitching. If we can fuel up the rest of the aircraft, you'll all have a chance to get your asses shot off. You seven, climb aboard, let's get warmed up. At sixteen knots, we'll have just enough headwind to get airborne. Maybe. You get wet, there's a nice destroyer off the port bow to pick you up."

Baker said, "Sir, where are the Japs? We chasing them?"

The loudspeaker cut through Thach's response.

"Now hear this. All hands. Radar reports incoming bogies at thirty-three miles. Incoming, at two eight zero degrees."

Thach moved toward his plane with a glance back at Baker. "Answer your question? The party's coming this way."

Baker rolled clear of the flight deck, felt the sickening dip toward the water, the engine straining to pull him airborne. He held tight to the yoke, no time yet to crank up the landing gear. The plane finally seemed to catch the air, began to rise, and he gripped the handle, hand-cranked the gear, counted, the routine, until he reached thirty turns, the landing gear now secure. With the gear up, the plane picked up speed, and he glanced around now, saw Thach far to the front, the others falling into formation. But there was no time for altitude, the radio in Thach's ear passed out to the rest of them, the message simple and direct: The bogies were right in front of them.

Baker saw them now, low and slow, and realized they were torpedo bombers. But slow had a different meaning to the Japanese, these planes nothing like the lumbering Devastators that had made such easy prey.

Nearby, the fighters divided into smaller formations, then no formations at all, and Baker climbed as far as he dared, circled around, saw streaks of fire from one of the gunners on the bombers, and now a Zero whistling past him from far above. Baker kept one eye on the Zero, put his sights first on the bomber, larger than he had seen before, with fat red discs on the tail and wings. He closed the distance quickly, fired the machine guns, and saw tracers rip up along the fuselage, into the cockpit. The bomber dropped, circling into a spin, and Baker focused on the Zero now, saw it banking, heading for one of Thach's other pilots. Baker pushed that way, couldn't close the gap, the Zero suddenly bursting into flames, another of Thach's men cutting across. Well, hell, I'd have had him, he thought. You damn hog, whoever you are.

He leveled out, no more than a thousand feet above the water, searching for another target, and realized he was passing over the destroyer escorts, could see *Yorktown* dead ahead. The torpedo planes were much fewer now, Thach's men slicing them up, but now there was a loud curse on the radio, and Baker searched anxiously. Why? What happened? He saw Thach move past him in a slight dive, saw the Japanese bomber now, diving as well. Thach's guns ripped the plane, the bomber tumbling into a spin, but the plane's torpedo had released, the pilot's last act. Baker dived low, a clear view of the torpedo's trail, fired a burst, tried to ignite the *pickle*, but nothing happened. He pulled up, helpless, watched the torpedo slam hard into *Yorktown*'s port side. Another blast erupted beneath the waterline now, a second torpedo impacting very close to the first. Baker felt each blast low in his gut, horror and sickness, then furious anger. But there was no time to stare, nothing he could do. He pulled up, banked away from *Yorktown* and the antiaircraft fire from the carrier and her escorts now blanketing the few remaining bombers. He made a wide arc, searched for any kind of target, saw others doing the same, but the bombers had either gone down, or without their heavy payloads, had turned away, much faster, skimming above the water to safety. Above him, Thach was in a duel with a Zero, but the Japanese pilot had the better of it, raced away. A thought punched through Baker's brain. Where the hell are they going? I hope somebody's paying attention to that. It looks to me like 280 degrees, maybe more north. I wish we had the fuel to chase them.

He banked around, knew Thach would offer the signal for the planes to line up for their return home. But he saw smoke from the carrier, a great deal of smoke, and swung past *Yorktown*'s bow, staring for a long second, straight down the flight deck. He understood now there would be no landing, the calls of the radio already spitting out instructions in his ear, the compass heading that would take them the few miles to *Hornet* and *Enterprise*. He didn't want to leave her, not yet, but his view of the flight deck told the story. *Yorktown* was listing, and no other explanation was needed for the men in the air. The slope to the deck passed twenty-five degrees, and if she took on much more water, she would pass her balance point and roll the rest of the way, trapping most of her twenty-five-hundred-man crew.

TWENTY-ONE

Yamaguchi

The scout planes from the American carriers continued to fly, spread out across the smoky sky near the wounded Japanese ships, and then farther out, seeking some hint of the remaining Japanese fleet and its lone carrier. At 2:45 P.M., word was received by the radio rooms on both *Hornet* and *Enterprise* and passed along to the bridge of the wounded *Yorktown*. It was the best news they could hear: A fourth Japanese carrier had been found. She was barely seventy-five miles from *Yorktown,* and in one more stroke of raw good fortune for the American dive bombers, she was actually closing the distance. For the planes launched to confront her, it would be a short flight.

ONBOARD CARRIER *HIRYU,* AT SEA—JUNE 4, 1942, 3:00 P.M.

"Are you quite certain, Commander?"

The man seemed hesitant, almost afraid. "Yes, sir. The bombers are nearly all shot down. Lieutenant Hashimoto has returned from the fight, and reports that there are two American carriers destroyed. One is burning, the other was struck by torpedoes and is dead in the water. But for our pilots, the engagement with the Americans was costly."

Yamaguchi felt his face redden. "I believe it was more costly for the Americans. How many of Hashimoto's pilots have returned? I must know."

"He is on his way to the bridge, sir."

The pilot was there now, still in his flight suit, the look of a man who had not slept in days. He saluted, and said, "Admiral Yamaguchi, I regret that my mission was both successful and a great failure. I have lost most of the men under my command. None of the other bombers survived, and the fighter protection was brought down as well. However, I observed a torpedo strike on the American carrier, and I believe she is now dead in the water."

"What of the other carriers?"

"I did not see more than the one we destroyed."

Yamaguchi paced slowly in the confined area, the others standing aside. "The dive bombers reported success in striking a carrier, saying it was aflame. Did you see that?"

"No, sir, just the one we torpedoed. If I can speak to the bomber pilots, perhaps we can . . ."

"No, you may not speak to them. They did not survive. But I must believe we have struck two carriers, possibly with fatal blows. The Americans must surely believe that by killing three of our great ships, they have won the day. They are wrong. We will still prevail. Lieutenant, are you prepared to lead another torpedo attack? I believe we are very close to the remaining American task force, and what is no doubt their only remaining carrier. If that one is destroyed, they will be completely vulnerable to the guns of our largest ships." He paused, thought, Perhaps this is what Admiral Yamamoto has been expecting all along. This will be his great moment after all."

Hashimoto seemed to sag, but put a surge of energy into his response. "I am ready as always, sir. For your command, for the emperor."

Yamaguchi studied the man. "How many missions have you flown today?"

"This will be my third, sir."

Yamaguchi knew that was extreme, could see it in the man's face. "Do your best, Lieutenant. Gather the pilots down below the island. I want the planes to be prepared to begin the mission at 1630."

Hashimoto saluted again, moved out and down the ladder. Across the narrow bridge, the ship's captain, Kaku, said, "Sir, three missions in one day is difficult enough. Facing a deadly foe . . . we could be sending these men to certain death. I do not believe the Americans are so exhausted that they cannot put up a good fight. Their torpedo bombers have been wiped out. But from all we can tell, they did not lose as many fighters and dive bombers as we did. They will draw on their reserves."

"Do I appear to you to need such mundane theories, Captain? It is war. We kill, they kill. It matters little who got the most sleep or who is counting planes." He looked toward a junior officer, seated nearby. "Give me the sound tube."

The man obeyed, the sound tube now in Yamaguchi's hand. He shouted, "Who is this?"

The voice on the other end sounded annoyed. "Ensign Gajo here. Sir, is this Admiral Yamaguchi? Indeed?"

"If I pull your tongue up through this tube, you'll be able to answer that. So, be silent and listen. I want to know precisely how many fighters, bombers, and torpedo bombers we can launch by 1630."

There was infuriating silence on the other end, but finally, an older voice, an officer with more confidence than arrogance. "Admiral, this is Commander Agawa. By the time you request, we can spot our entire force, five bombers, five torpedo planes, and six Zeroes. But the Zeroes . . . we must hold those close overhead, to protect the ship."

Now the silence belonged to Yamaguchi. "We have no more?"

"Sir, I apologize. It is *all* we have. We had expected the return of many more planes from the flight launched earlier. We were prepared with fuel and armament. But as you know, sir, there were very few. I will also say, Admiral, that the pilots are in a bad way. They have done wonderful work today, but I have men here falling asleep on their feet. And they have not eaten since breakfast. Sir, what would you have me do?"

Yamaguchi stared out through the glass of the narrow bridge, felt a suffocating gloom. Is this how Nagumo makes his decisions? He waits for no other alternative, then chooses the easy path? No, I will not simply give up.

"Commander, spot the planes for takeoff at 1800 hours. That will give the men ninety minutes more to nap or perhaps to eat. It can cause little harm to delay our attack until dusk. The surprise will be that much greater."

ONBOARD CARRIER *HIRYU*, AT SEA—JUNE 4, 1942, 5:00 P.M.

Most of the pilots had eaten at least some rice, something to put in their stomachs. Many, including Hashimoto, had ignored food for the opportunity to grab a bit of sleep. On the bridge, Yamaguchi paced nervously, the words driving his every step. *We will catch them at dusk. They will not see us.* We have so little, but we have surprise, and that will make the difference. If they have but one carrier, this could be an easy struggle. We send them to the bottom, and their planes will have nowhere to go. He broke his thoughts and looked toward one of the bridge officers, a man as argumentative as he was.

"Commander, how do we know the Americans had three carriers in their force?"

He was surprised by the man's hesitation.

"The pilots told us. Or the scouts, cruiser *Tone*'s scout was most helpful."

Yamaguchi snapped, "*Tone*'s scout gave us bad information, then good, then bad again. He was not where he should have been this morning, and he simply got lucky. If I should ever confront that man, I should toss him into the sea. So, now, tell me again. How do we know how many carriers the Americans have?"

The officer lowered his head. "Events will prove that we have been correct, sir. It is up to God."

Yamaguchi stared at the man. "Is this the same God that is worshipped by the Americans?"

The officer fell silent, and Yamaguchi knew there was no answer to his question. We believe we have destroyed two of their carriers, he thought. Surely they believe they have destroyed three of ours. So, it is mathematics. And the skill of our few pilots. And let us not forget *luck*.

From outside the bridge, one of the lookout posts called out, a man with his binoculars. "Sir! Enemy dive bombers!"

Yamaguchi pushed past the other officers, all clamoring to see. "Where?"

The man held the glasses to his eyes, pointed nearly straight up. "Directly overhead."

The Japanese were wrong in the assessment of American carrier losses. While *Yorktown* continued to suffer from the bomb and torpedo strikes, neither *Enterprise* nor *Hornet* had been located or attacked at all. By five o'clock, twenty-four dive bombers had been launched from the deck of the *Enterprise,* including fourteen whose home had been *Yorktown.* Behind them by another half hour would be more than a dozen planes from *Hornet.* Keeping their altitude close to twenty thousand feet, the bombers arced their way around the Japanese carrier and her escorts until they could approach from the west, straight out of the setting sun. The surprised Zeroes offered a gallant fight, several of the bombers knocked down, but the weakness of the Japanese gauntlet was fatal for *Hiryu.* Despite the agility of the carrier, sweeping curves to avoid the bombing strikes, four five-hundred-pound bombs struck the carrier directly, burrowing through her flight deck, setting off the chains of violent destruction. As the darkness settled over the scene, the American planes returned to their carrier, while *Hiryu* continued to burn, the fires emerging from belowdecks to hangar and flight decks. For the Japanese, there would be no more concern for any kind of air assault against the Americans. Other than a small handful of Zeroes from *Hiryu*'s CAP, the Japanese had no planes left. As for the Zeroes, they had lost their homes. There was nothing left but to fly into the sea.

ONBOARD CARRIER *HIRYU,* AT SEA—JUNE 5, 1942, 2:30 A.M.

The fires had spread to nearly every deck, including the engine rooms and other passageways below the water line. The heat in the steel trapped men in compartments who couldn't escape without burning themselves to death. And so they would burn to death simply by waiting, or suffocating as the flames consumed their air.

"Sir, we are listing past fifteen degrees. That will not change. We are taking on water well below deck." The captain paused. "Sir, it is time to abandon ship. For the crew, there is no other chance to survive."

Yamaguchi could feel the heat boiling up around him, heard screams and the hard crack of fire surging over more of the ship.

"Send a message to Admiral Nagumo. I am ordering the crew to abandon ship. The destroyers are prepared to pull them from the sea."

He put one hand on the bulkhead, withdrew it quickly, too hot to touch. "We must leave the bridge. Where is a safe place?"

One of the officers, burns on his uniform, saluted with an injured hand. "Admiral, the flight deck. Port side, forward. The fire has not yet reached there."

He looked at Kaku. "Order the crew to that place. They can reach the water with lines and nets. The rescue ships will be able to see them by their silhouettes. Go. Summon the crew." He stopped, unable to ask the obvious. *How much of a crew do we have?*

The officers moved quickly from the bridge, and Yamaguchi waited, a last look aft, the flames now boiling up over half the flight deck. The heat was suffocating now, and he moved out quickly, down the ladder, following his officers to the flight deck. He felt the heat through his shoes, did as the others were doing all around him, and made a quick run to the last place on the ship the fires had not yet touched.

He was surprised by how many men waited for him, several hundred, more joining them. They crowded close, no place left to go, the lines now lowering the men to the water. Yamaguchi saw the destroyers moving close, nodded to himself, yes, save them. No one else needs to die, not from so many good men.

Kaku called out to his men, "This war is still to be fought. You must lead the way."

He seemed to choke up, the words fading, and Yamaguchi raised his voice as loud as he could. "I admire you, all of you. You have fought the great battle of the war. None of you bears responsibility for the loss of this ship. It is my blame that the enemy bested *Soryu* and *Hiryu*. I command you, all of you, to abandon ship, and to continue your fight, continue your service to Japan and to the emperor." The energy in his voice had faded, emotion and exhaustion, the words coming in a low voice. "I shall remain with my ship."

One of the officers moved close, and said, "Sir, they are lowering your standard, and the national flag. I swear to you, sir, we shall keep them safe."

There was a sudden burst of music, a surprise, most of the ship's band off to one side, playing the Japanese national anthem. He wanted to speak to them again, offer them something more, but there was no more to give. Beside him, Kaku said, "Admiral, I shall remain here with you. Many others would join us. I have ordered them away."

Yamaguchi nodded. "No one need die with us. Japan needs good officers still."

Through the crowded deck, an officer pushed his way close, and said, "Sir, there is a considerable amount of money in the ship's safe. Should I attempt to retrieve it?"

Yamaguchi shook his head, managed a smile. "The captain and I shall require money for our first meal in hell."

The crowd was thinning now, the crew nearly off the ship. Yamaguchi watched the officers now, lowering themselves. Beside him, Kaku said, "The fires. They are coming up behind us."

Yamaguchi said, "That will be a slow death. Did you give my order?"

"Yes, sir. Once the men have been pulled out of the water. The duty will be carried out by destroyer *Makigumo*. Six torpedoes."

Yamaguchi nodded slowly. "Their captain is a good man. It will be done efficiently."

"Yes, sir. Only when the last of my men has been pulled from the sea."

Yamaguchi glanced at his watch, the dial lit by the fires growing around him. It was nearly four-thirty. He watched the destroyer now, saw her suddenly moving away, then coming about, her bow now aiming directly at *Hiryu*.

Yamaguchi pointed, a hint of daylight breaking in the east, while below, the torpedoes came.

TWENTY-TWO

Buckmaster

Even before the final, and potentially fatal, torpedo strikes, Admiral Fletcher had moved off the ship, transferring his command to the heavy cruiser *Astoria*. Buckmaster had chewed on that for a long minute, but Fletcher's reasoning, in the end, made perfect sense.

"I can't fight a war from a dead ship."

For Captain Buckmaster and the men on the bridge, the words burned deep, but Buckmaster knew that Fletcher was hurting as much for *Yorktown* as he was for every man lost in the air missions. But Fletcher's command went far beyond the painfully stricken carrier. To remove himself to some place where he could exercise control was the right thing to do. And Buckmaster knew that was Fletcher's way.

For now, Buckmaster's way was to do whatever he could to save his ship, and with Fletcher gone, he had absolute control. If anything could be done to save the carrier, it would be up to him to find the way.

He had taken command of *Yorktown* early the year before, and had gathered a considerable amount of respect from the many pilots assigned to the ship for the many months he had held that command. Buckmaster's background was unusual, both to his pilots, and to the black-shoe officers he served with. Unlike so many of the flag officers throughout the navy, Buckmaster was both a graduate of the Naval Academy, as well as a brown-shoe aviator. He had earned his flight wings in 1936, at the age of forty-seven, nearly twice as old as most of the young men who trained alongside him. For two years after, he had been assigned a variety of flight duties, from command of training squadrons to managing aircraft ordnance.

There had been talk among his officers that the black-shoe Admiral Fletcher would rub Buckmaster the wrong way, but since Fletcher's arrival on *Yorktown,* it had never been like that. If there had been friction at all, it had been through the confusion and chaos of the Coral Sea battles, but neither man held a grudge against the other. The only man who seemed convinced that Fletcher had been woefully inept had been Admiral Ernest King in Washington. Neither Admiral Nimitz nor Captain Buckmaster shared that view. Fletcher's responsibility in command of the entire Midway fleet, Task Forces 16 and 17, had earned respect even from the most prejudiced officers, no matter what color their shoes.

With *Yorktown* in extreme peril, listing now past twenty-six degrees to port, Admiral Fletcher's decision to transfer his flag to the *Astoria* made perfect sense. Communication was sketchy at best, the carrier's radar systems knocked out, radios now woefully unreliable. Buckmaster had his hands completely full of the extraordinary labor now ongoing to keep *Yorktown* afloat, while at the same time incurring as few casualties as possible. It was no stretch to believe that the Japanese were watching every move being made on the wounded ship, most likely through the periscope of a submarine.

He stared out to the flight deck, the repair crews struggling to complete the task of patching the enormous hole caused by what had surely been a five-hundred-pound bomb. He gripped a handle on the bulkhead, the only way to stay upright, felt an odd queasiness, looking so completely downhill, as though the crew at work might suddenly slide off the ship into the sea.

He punched that out of his brain, looked back toward his executive officer, Dixie Kiefer. "Tell me about radar."

"Commander Firestone says we should have it operational in an hour, maybe two." He paused. "Maybe three."

Buckmaster looked out again to the deck, the hole being patched now with sheets of steel supported by wooden timbers. "Nice to have you up here, Dixie."

"Thank you, sir. I guess the forty-yard rule doesn't really matter now. We'll sink or swim together."

It was custom that the skipper and his XO would remain forty yards apart during combat conditions, ensuring that at least one of them should survive a well-placed explosion.

"Not sure I agree, Dixie. If this isn't combat conditions, I don't know what the hell that could be. We're lucky to be afloat. I'd appreciate you not using that word again."

Kiefer thought a brief moment. "Sink."

"That's the word. Listen, how about opening the gedunk stand, everything free. Give the men something to eat, even if it's junk. Give them some energy."

"Already did, sir. It helped. Some."

To one side, a young ensign, manning a radio phone said, "Sir, Commander Aldrich reports that the torpedo hits cut the power to the pumps. He is unable to move any more water to the starboard side to correct the list."

There was silence around him, and Buckmaster asked himself the same question he knew every other man was wanting to say. What the hell do we do now?

Aldrich was the damage control officer, had shown a wide streak of genius in how he had handled the first bomb strikes. Fires had been extinguished, even in areas where incendiary devices were stored, a cure for a vulnerability that might have destroyed the ship in one blow. Instead of waiting for the inevitable eruption, Aldrich had flooded the ship's magazine with seawater, eliminating the danger from the fire. Now, though, the torpedo strikes had caused very different problems, severing power and water lines, shutting down boilers in the engine compartments, and rendering the ship essentially dead in the water. Dead, except for the terrifying list, every man on the ship aware that should *Yorktown* lose much more stability, she would most definitely roll over.

Don't think about it, he thought. Well, hell, of course you're thinking about it. There are twenty-five hundred men out there looking your way for answers, a plan. Something. If the pumps are gone . . . the boilers. We can't move enough to escape a torpedo or dive bomber. I know Fletcher is keeping an eye on us, and sure as hell, they've sent a dozen CAP planes way the hell above us.

Behind him, a man fell, a sharp cry, the man rolling downhill into Buckmaster's legs. "I'm sorry, sir. I slipped. My hand slipped."

Buckmaster anchored his feet against the bulkhead, pulled the man to his feet, others helping as well. "It's all right, Ensign. None of us are standing upright. Any word from Task Force 16?"

The young man returned to his radio receiver, shook his head. "No, sir."

Toward one end of the bridge, an officer emerged from his

small cubby. "I can tell you what the Japs are saying, if you're interested."

"Mr. Biard, I'm always interested in what the Japs are saying. But I've got a ship in serious jeopardy right now. Unless their planes are about to show up one more time, I don't care much what they're doing or saying. And if we can get the radar up and running, I won't need you to tell me."

"Well, sir, at least you didn't cuss me out. Don't know what I did to Fletcher to get him so pissy at me."

"*Admiral* Fletcher, Lieutenant. That's one reason right there. You show respect, or you don't show up at all. Start now. Give me something useful about the Japs, or get off my bridge."

"My apologies, sir. When you work at HYPO, pretty much nobody pays any attention to respect or rank. We just do our jobs. So, well, the Japs think they sunk two carriers. We sunk three, and the fourth one is running like hell trying to get away from us. They are chatting about coming after our fleet, a nighttime attack. But nobody's made a decision."

"How the hell do you know . . . ? Never mind. Admiral Fletcher never understood what it is that you do, or why you're here in the first place. He didn't believe half of what you told him. That rubbed off on me. I know about the fourth carrier, and there's a boatload of aircraft going after her. Now go back to work. If this ship capsizes, won't much matter what the Japs think."

He regretted saying the word "capsize," knew eyes were on him. He glanced up at Kiefer, the others, then looked again out the window of the bridge and couldn't avoid staring down at the sloping deck, the edge of the portside flight deck barely above the surface of the water. "Get me Commander Aldrich."

A few seconds passed, then the phone was in his hand.

"How much more can you do?"

"*We can't straighten her out, sir. The intercom and interphone lines*

are cut fore and aft. We're leaking oil, which means potential for fire.
We've got a total of six aircraft onboard, which right now are worthless."
Aldrich paused. *"Awaiting your instructions, Captain."*

Buckmaster handed the receiver to the young ensign. He turned again toward the flight deck, said, "Tell Commander Aldrich to stand by for my order, and instruct him to carry it out with all speed. Issue the order ship-wide, all hands, either by signal flag, intercom, or messenger. No delays."

Kiefer moved close, said in a low voice, "What order, sir?"

Buckmaster looked down, eyes again on the lapping sea as it brushed up on the far side of the flight deck. Not any worse, he thought, not yet. Thank God. The thought struck him. What did God have to do with this? All right, if You're listening, I got a favor to ask. There's close to twenty-five hundred men on this ship. Get 'em off safely.

Kiefer said quietly, "Sir?"

Buckmaster turned to him, put a hand on his shoulder. He looked to the others, then down at the deck sloping beneath his feet. He fought the tears, but lost the battle. "Mr. Kiefer, order abandon ship."

It was orderly, the men lining up along the starboard side, high above the water. Ropes had been dropped, life rafts tossed down. The motor boats were mostly useless, no power to operate the cranes, but the men seemed to ignore this one additional problem. Buckmaster watched the ropes, the men like so many ants, dropping slowly along a string, couldn't avoid the rows of shoes, discarded in neat formations along the edge of the deck, toes all pointing out. They'll regret that, he thought. No good for swimming, but they'll wish they had something on their feet later on.

But it wasn't all neatness and good order. Men slipped, dropping the sixty feet into the water, others scrambling to help those who were weak swimmers. For those who questioned why the men didn't simply wade off the port-side flight deck, Buckmaster had no need to explain to anyone else that if the ship suddenly capsized, every man there would be buried. At least on the starboard side, they would be away from the roll. He didn't ask if anyone agreed. It was simply the order.

As the men slid down the ropes, there were injuries as well, the oil gradually soaking or splashing upward, adding a new hazard, the ropes too slippery to hold a grip. The oil brought greater problems, the enormous leaks on the port side gradually spreading around both ends of the ship, coating the water as the men tried to make their way toward the waiting rescue boats from the nearby destroyers. Men became sick, helped only by others with the strength to ignore the awful stink.

In time, nearly twenty-three hundred men found sanctuary on the smaller ships, including Admiral Fletcher's new home, the cruiser *Astoria*. The destroyers, the smallest vessels in the task force, faced the immediate problem of housing and feeding more men than those ships could provide for. Immediately, Fletcher ordered ships to be sent from Pearl Harbor, with the specific task of ferrying most of *Yorktown*'s crew back to Hawaii.

As the ship emptied, men came from well belowdecks, fighting to climb the sloping and oily ladders with the wounded, some in pairs hauling stretchers, some by themselves. The flight deck and hangar deck had become dangerous places, men sliding along, risking a hard spill into the oil. But still they reached the ropes, the wounded lowered as gently as possible.

In the water below, emotions were mixed, some men grateful to be alive, offering prayers, some crying, some gasping for air as they struggled with the oil. But others were giddy, joking to one another as though by surviving this one horror, they might never have to experience anything like it again, and so adding an air of lightness to the entire scene. Some questioned why they had left their ship, as though the captain had turned cowardly, a nasty rumor that was shouted down as quickly as it emerged. Even from the surface of the water on the starboard side, it was very clear that *Yorktown* might not survive another hour, much less another day.

"Time's up, Dixie."

Kiefer was breathing heavily, had climbed the sloping ladder in a grim effort to reach the bridge. "I know, sir. I think it's done. Just a few officers on the hangar deck, waiting their turn."

Buckmaster had put his XO in command of the *abandon ship* order, knew that Kiefer would handle the job exactly as he would. "Okay, Dixie. Head down there. It's your turn. Somebody's gotta make sure the officers keep it orderly. You know how ridiculous they can get."

Kiefer smiled at the poor joke, nodded. "I'm going, sir. Just make sure you're behind me. Don't make me have to come up here and drag you to the ropes. I'll bring the marines if I have to."

Buckmaster tried to keep the smile, but there was pain in Kiefer's eyes. "I'm not staying up here, like some martinet from the sixteenth century. But I'll not leave until I know I'm last to go. Nobody gets left behind." He paused. "We've done all we can."

"Aye, sir."

Kiefer started for the ladder, slipped slightly, fought for control. Buckmaster expected some joke, one more goofy stab at humor, the kinship between the two that had never changed. But Kiefer held himself against the rails of the ladder, didn't look back, and now was gone.

Buckmaster turned toward the glass, nothing new to see, stepped out onto the port side wing, open air, a warm sun, and the stench of oil. He waited a long minute, then crossed over, through the bridge, to the starboard wing, studied all the commotion below, the streams of men moving down the ropes. He saw the last few officers dropping down, some with perfect elegance, some tumbling head over heels into the water. This should be funny, a joke on all of them. There will be teasing from some. Not from me.

He saw Kiefer now, the man glancing up toward him, a subtle wave of his hand. Kiefer swung over the side, holding a rope, but his grip wasn't there, either because of the oil or the burns, and Buckmaster saw the man's feet, then upright, the man bouncing sideways off the ship's hull, a long plunge to the water below. Buckmaster gripped the railing, wanted to call out, warn some-one, the last few men still bobbing in the water. But he saw Kiefer now, the man floating on the surface on his back, another wave of his hand. Buckmaster let out a breath, shook his head, thought, I know him too well. Probably broke half the bones in his body, and he's got that stupid-assed grin.

He knew he was stalling. Men in the water were watching him, some pointing, others calling out. I have to know, he thought. No-body gets lost here. Nobody's left behind because I'm in a big damn hurry. I need to take a look.

He moved back inside, climbed down the interior ladder, passed through the radio room, the small office where the HYPO man, Biard, did his work. I wonder if there's a HYPO kind of guy over in Tokyo, figuring out what kind of mess we're in out here. Intel's a bunch of odd ducks, for sure.

He reached the starboard catwalk, struggled to keep his bal-ance, one hand holding the rail. He glanced down at the water, a long drop, saw the dangling ropes. God, I'm next, he thought. He reached the anti-aircraft guns, the eerie silence of the ship's best defense. They didn't help much, he thought. That's nobody's fault.

The tour continued, through his own quarters, officers' country, every major station he could reach. Below, the lack of power meant darkness, and he realized his flashlight was gone, discarded or simply lost. He took a breath, started down, felt his way, another ladder, down farther, couldn't avoid the sickening smells, kicked something soft, felt more of them now, bodies, a scattered heap of men cut to pieces by one of the blasts. He pushed himself to keep going, thought of dragging them up to the hangar deck, maybe finding a way to get them off the ship. But there were too many, the smell overpowering. He fought the sickness, the sadness, the terror of the darkness, struggled to keep all of it away. He moved a step at a time through the lifeless darkness, moving from memory, stepping past shattered steel bulkheads and now more bodies. After a long minute, he put energy into his voice.

"Anybody? This is the captain. *Anybody down here?*"

He repeated the call down another passageway, down one more ladder, felt a sudden rush of wind in his face. He stopped, listened, knew it was a bulkhead giving way, water filling a compartment far below. Or *just* below. He heard water rushing into a compartment, smelled the sea and the oil, called out again. No response, and he knew now that anyone down this far would already have climbed up, and if they didn't, they couldn't. No, even the wounded were brought out. These men . . . there are no wounded. No more, he thought. You've done your job.

He turned, retraced his steps, strained for any daylight, stepped over and through the bodies again. He turned, a new direction, heard the water again, crew quarters, mechanics stations. He thought of the engine rooms, shut down, flooded. If anybody's down there, he's already gone. Maybe they got out. Maybe soon I'll find out.

He saw daylight, the hangar deck, stepped out, the port side sloping down well into the water. The sickness came again, but it wasn't from the smell of bodies, of death, but from the death of his ship. He shouted aloud, angry at himself. *"Salvage her for Chrissakes."* We did it once, he thought. Fletcher knows it can be done. Nimitz too.

He scanned the hangar deck, tried to measure how badly she had continued to list. The oil made any footing treacherous, and he stopped, winded, looked again toward the hatchways that went below. How many men? I couldn't go everywhere. Some got blown right into the sea. How many pilots did we lose? I'll learn that soon enough too.

He called out again, a gesture of futility. *"Anybody? This is the captain."*

He eased himself toward the stern, eyed the water below him, washing up inside the hangar deck. The tugs will come, he thought, and we'll get you back to Pearl. I can't leave you out here.

He reached the stern, the water just a few feet below him, and he climbed up and over the railing, grabbed a waiting line, saw the raft, a handful of men who saw him. Beyond, the destroyer waited, more rafts, and he stopped, looked back over the rail, the flight deck, hangar deck below, water and oil and the death of so many of his men. Then he turned to the line again, lowered himself hand by hand, and dropped into the water.

ONBOARD JAPANESE SUBMARINE I-168, AT SEA—JUNE 6, 1942, 1:30 P.M.

The order had come while he was still off the coast of Midway. His gesture had been futile, launching a half dozen of his small artillery rounds from his deck gun, all the while wondering why none of the larger ships were joining him. He had heard nothing of the catastrophe to the carriers, the communication devices too unreliable. All he knew was that he was one part of an enormous whole, and Midway was still their intended mission.

But finally there had been an updated message, a surprise that he knew better than to question. The order was simple and direct. There was a wounded American aircraft carrier. He was provided with the coordinates, the estimated distance, and the goal. Sink her.

He was Lieutenant Commander Yahachi Tanabe, and this was his ship, the submarine that had spent days slipping around the American fleet before he had tossed shells onto the beach at Midway. But with radio silence, and his own caution, there was still no one to report to, no way to bring Admiral Nagumo's great warships within range of the carrier he saw now, the so many delicious targets around her.

He could see that the American carrier was severely injured, and had watched the towing operation, an obvious struggle to move a carrier that was riding low in the water and listing to one side. It was just a matter of drawing closer, a mile or less, to ensure the accuracy of his torpedoes.

For most of the morning, he had approached gingerly, could see the screen of destroyers around the wounded carrier, and knew that any carelessness would bring them close enough to sink him. He lowered the periscope again, stood back and looked to his navigation station.

"Distance to target."

"Six thousand yards, Captain."

"We will continue to approach with caution. There will be silence, do you understand? Surely, the Americans are listening closely, guarding their precious carrier."

Another hour passed, the periscope coming up no more than once every thirty minutes, his extreme caution not to attract the attention of an American destroyer lookout. He wiped sweat from his face, then raised the periscope one more time.

The carrier seemed to be a hulking giant, and he jumped back, said in a whisper, "Distance. We are too close. Navigator, what is the distance?"

"Six hundred yards, sir."

"*That is too close.* The torpedoes will not arm, and we will never leave here alive. Reverse course, move us away. Turn to starboard. We must pass once more beneath the destroyer screen."

They stared upward, the habit of men who sail so often beneath the enemy. But he stared only at the periscope, waiting for the right time to bring it up again. Now he glanced up with his officers, knew the destroyers were close, perhaps straight on top of them, and there could be no sound.

The whisper came from his listening station. "Captain. There is no longer any indication that the Americans are listening for us."

"What? Are you certain?"

"Yes, sir. Their detection equipment has gone silent. Perhaps they have all gone to lunch."

The others laughed quietly, but Tanabe gave a sharp wave of his hand. "Silence. There might be a reason. Perhaps they have different equipment. We are moving through the destroyer screen again. It cannot be so easy."

Tanabe waited, the agony of not knowing. He reached slowly for the periscope and brought it up. "Range."

"Thirteen hundred yards, Captain."

"Yes. I agree. And she has turned. The carrier has turned. She has become a gift for the emperor. She is full broadside."

ONBOARD USS *YORKTOWN*, AT SEA—JUNE 6, 1942, 1:30 P.M.

Buckmaster's hopes for a salvage and towing operation had been answered, Admiral Nimitz authorizing a tug to sail from Pearl Harbor to bring *Yorktown* home.

For now, the destroyer USS *Vireo* was doing the best she could, barely making headway as she pulled *Yorktown* and the weight of the water the carrier held inside. But Buckmaster had done more than arrange rescue for his ship. Some one hundred fifty men had returned to the carrier with their skipper to do as much as possible to make her seaworthy. Fires were extinguished, bulkheads sealed, as much excess weight as possible cut away, from steel plating to anti-aircraft guns, anything that could assist the carrier in righting itself. For now, it had seemed to work, *Yorktown*'s list straightening from near thirty degrees to twenty.

To assist in the variety of engineering and electrical problems, the destroyer USS *Hammann* had lashed itself alongside, providing electrical power and serving as an immediate rest and food stop for the men who labored through the tedious work on *Yorktown*.

"Sound taps."

The bugler obeyed, the piercing sadness of the simple tune hovering over them all. The music ended, the bodies of thirty-five men sliding into the water, no one speaking. Buckmaster stood silently for a long moment, then said aloud, "You are dismissed. Return to your stations. Let's get this ship home."

Kiefer kept his position behind him, stepped forward now, and Buckmaster said quietly, "Never done a burial at sea before. Don't care for it."

"Sir, at least they were able to identify most of them. The doc pulled fingerprints off all but ten."

Buckmaster wanted to ask about the ten, knew he wouldn't like the answer. He turned to the bow, the steel cable attached to the destroyer that was towing *Yorktown* with all the strength her engines could manage.

"I think we'll do this, Dixie. I knew that Admiral Nimitz would come through. He's not going to just give away a carrier. And sure as hell, not this carrier."

"I think you're right, Skipper. She seems to be pretty seaworthy. We just need to get that tug out here to kick her in the tail."

Buckmaster stared out to sea, past the *Hammann,* to the screen of destroyers. "Don't see this too much out here. The water's like glass. Couldn't ask for a prettier day. It'll help us move a little faster. We're making what—three knots?"

"That may be optimistic, sir. Two, at best."

"I'll stay optimistic."

Buckmaster saw one of the engineers jogging toward him, the man's shirt stained in grease. "What is it, Chief?"

"Sir, the portside five-inch gun has been cut loose. We're set to jettison her on your order—good God, what the hell is that?"

Buckmaster followed the man's stare, out past the destroyer, saw the foaming white trails. The men down on *Hammann* were pointing as well, the still slick water showing the sight all too clear. There was a mad scramble on the destroyer's deck, some of the workers on *Yorktown* seeing it as well. But there was nowhere to go. Buckmaster clenched his fists, said with a shout, *"Hang on. Torpedoes."*

The impact thundered all down along the flank of the carrier, the *Hammann* igniting amidship, the deck beneath Buckmaster's feet trembling, dropping him painfully to one knee. The chief was down beside him, hugging the deck, Kiefer on his hands and knees.

Buckmaster stared at the fires rising up from *Hammann* and said, "Come on! Those people need help."

He reached the railing, saw men frantically disarming the depth charges on the ship's stern, others diving into the water.

Kiefer said, "Why don't they abandon ship? Get the hell away from the fire?"

The chief was there now, said, "She's near cut in half, sir. She's going down quick. But they've got to disarm the depth charges.

They'll ignite if the ship goes down. It'll damn near kill every man in the water. Go, you bastards, go."

Kiefer said, "Go . . . ?"

Buckmaster felt the chief's anxiousness. "Get them disarmed. Come on."

The fire pushed the men on the carrier away from the rail, but Buckmaster fought the heat, stayed close, saw *Hammann* beginning to go down. The torpedo had ripped her into two large pieces, both settling down low in the water. More of the destroyer's crew began to swim, frantic strokes to get farther away from their ship. But the men doing the good work of disarming the depth charges had run out of time, and the eruptions came now, the depth charges going off piecemeal, then together, great fountains of water, thunderous concussions underwater that rattled *Yorktown* once more. Buckmaster tried to keep tight to the railing, but the fire from the shattered destroyer was too great, the heat overwhelming. He backed away, his last look, saw bodies on the water, men obliterated, burned, or caught by the crushing shock. Bodies came up, some floating, some pieces of men, some calling out in the sheer agony of their wounds, while others simply disappeared, taken down by the ripped pieces of their ship.

Buckmaster saw two of the other destroyers moving quickly, coming closer, the others farther out, launching depth charges of their own, attacking the Japanese sub. Bastard, he thought. Jap bastard. What the hell did this get you? We're helpless, we were all helpless. Wound a wounded ship. That's not war. It's murder.

Beside him, the chief tugged at his sleeve. "Begging your pardon, sir, but we need to think about what's happening right here. We took two heavy hits, plus whatever damage from *Hammann* blowing up."

Buckmaster stepped farther from the rail, turned, scanned the flight deck, a mess of timbers and scrap iron, men scrambling to toss it into the sea.

"Thank you, Chief. Dixie, he's correct." He stopped, both men watching him. "No ship captain should ever have to do this. None, ever. And I'm doing it twice. Dixie, prepare to order abandon ship."

ONBOARD DESTROYER USS *BALCH*, AT SEA — JUNE 7, 1942, 5:00 A.M.

The destroyers had set up as a ring around *Yorktown*, less for pro-tection than for the kind of solemn ceremony that sailors under-stand all too well.

Buckmaster felt relief that his ship had made it for one more day, one more piece of life for the inevitable end. The torpedo at-tack had offered one strange and unexpected benefit, bringing in enough water to help right the ship even further, by several more degrees. But no one held the optimism now that she would sur-vive, no matter the tow ships, no matter the engineers. For now, there was no immediate threat of capsizing, but clear to all, *York-town* was settling deep, drifting slowly downward.

He stood on the bridge of the destroyer, had watched at first with his binoculars, but with the first bit of daylight, they weren't necessary. The sounds came now, great spits of air as enormous bubbles trapped inside the ship released, one more exhale as the ship died, another ton of water invading, taking her deeper still.

He had the thought, every ship captain's nightmare, that going down with your ship was the proper thing to do, even if you knew it wasn't. They'll want me to serve somewhere. Would you cap-tain a carrier again? That's a hard one, and not up to me. And no matter what anybody says, I'm still captain of this one. Always will be. Maybe that's a curse, feeding somebody's superstition. He lost one, he'll lose another. But Nimitz doesn't believe that. I'd bet my life on it. But . . . do I?

The noises continued—the gasping, groaning cries from *York-town*. Around her he could see the ring of destroyers fully visible, their flags at half-mast. There were new sounds, and he put the glasses to his eyes, was suddenly sick, watching as *Yorktown* slowly rolled over to her port side, a gaping hole showing now on her starboard bilge.

Behind Buckmaster, the *Balch's* captain said, "Hands uncovered. *Attention.*"

Buckmaster lowered the glasses, obeyed the command from a man two ranks his junior. He heard tears now, a surprise, but they triggered his own, and he kept his salute in place, took himself away from everyone else, put himself once more on the bridge of his Great Lady. And then, she was gone.

PART THREE

"Our reconnaissance of the enemy was incomplete."

—ADMIRAL MATOME UGAKI, CHIEF OF STAFF

"There is no use talking about might-have-beens now."

—COMMANDER MINORU GENDA

TWENTY-THREE

Ackroyd

All throughout the afternoon of June 4, the anticipation had been agonizing, everyone on Midway certain that the bombing runs from that morning would be repeated. But the day had been long and beautiful, thick white clouds and a perfect blue sky, and by late afternoon, the men had begun to loosen, despite the shouted admonitions from Ackroyd and anyone else in authority. The only real excitement had come from the unnerving appearance of a squadron of dive bombers, twelve planes, which every anti-aircraft gunner was certain were Japanese. Once the cascade of fire had died down, the men on the ground realized the planes were in fact American, one of them crash-landing in the lagoon, the other eleven finding the strip on Eastern Island with virtually empty gas tanks. They were the remnants of Commander Stanhope Ring's ill-fated effort to find the Japanese carriers without actually knowing where those carriers were, the men relying on Ring's intuition, which turned out to be exactly wrong. Ring himself had already returned to *Hornet*, none of the pilots sure just why. What they did know was that Midway had been considerably closer to them than their carrier, a safe haven that kept them from dropping into the sea. Yet even then, the best estimates from the pilots were that the Japanese fleet was a hundred miles or more away, probably to the northwest. For men anticipating a sudden assault from hordes of Japanese, that news was a welcome relief. If there was to be a second attack, it wasn't likely to come in sudden surprise. And, for the men on Midway, who had no idea where their own fleet was, the pilots from Ring's squadron at least reassured them that within a hundred fifty miles, the Americans seemed to be prepared for whatever the Japanese were planning to do. After a short time on the ground, the crews of the eleven functioning planes gave their farewells, and once they were refueled, they left Midway for the shorter journey directly back to their carrier.

The rest of the afternoon on the fourth had been spent tuning gun sights and testing ammunition, all in an effort to work off the nerve-twisting guilt of how close any one of them might have come to shooting an American plane out of the sky. The officers and gunnery sergeants seemed to find new ways of expressing their disgust, many of them inventing new swear words on the spot. No one wanted to answer questions at any kind of inquiry to explain why they had killed one of their own.

As the afternoon passed, more friendly activity livened up the skies, particularly a number of B-17s that were sent back to Hawaii, more bombers than the commanders felt were needed. No one wanted to accept the risk that they might be trapped on the ground in the event of a new Japanese bombardment. Later in the afternoon, more B-17s appeared, landing after their unsuccessful attempts to locate the fourth Japanese carrier, some of those searching as well for a rumored fifth carrier. As they landed, Ackroyd and his men absorbed the scene, even Ackroyd enjoying the extraordinary roar of the four-engine beasts touching down in splashes of sandy smoke, taxiing quickly to make way for the next plane in line. But anticipation gave way to disappointment, the pilots whose bravado was always loud and long, as one after another they returned to Midway with nothing to show for it.

As the sun went down, the anticipation of another Japanese attack built again, Ackroyd doing what he always did, cursing his men into perfection, whether they needed it or not. With the darkness, the men around Ackroyd tried to offer one mighty exhale that, at least for now, there would be no bombing runs, no invasion. The one disturbing problem was the fuel tanks on the island that had been ignited by Japanese bombs. A day later they continued to burn, in effect a perfect lighthouse for any enemy planes. For reasons no one understood, the Japanese never came. But still, no one believed the single bombing run from the Japanese was all there would be. In the darkness, every snap of a twig brought the same tense response that had nearly wiped out the bomber squadron. Ackroyd knew that there was no cure for men with itchy fingers. The best they could do was keep low, keep watch on the shoreline, and, for some, try to get some sleep.

MIDWAY ISLAND—JUNE 5, 1942, 1:20 A.M.

The first shell came in a low-line arc, burrowing into the dense sand close to the water's edge, a thumping blast that startled the guards and woke the men. More fire came now, a half dozen shells altogether, most impacting harmlessly into the lagoon.

Ackroyd crawled along the edge of the barbed wire cordon and saw the officers emerging from their bunkers, all questions, no one with answers. The men in their sand trenches laid low, waiting for the next round, still no one certain where the fire had come from or how many more there might be.

"Keep your damn heads down!"

It was an unnecessary order, no one curious enough to stick

their head up in the darkness just to see a red streak passing close overhead. Ackroyd dropped down into his own foxhole, one end of the trench dug by a handful of Carlson's Raiders, men who had spent the day sleeping as much as preparing for a fight.

To one side, one of the lieutenants said, "Anybody see anything? Where's it coming from?"

"The water, sir. Small gun. Most likely a sub. A destroyer would have done a hell of a lot more damage. He's done skedaddled by now, before we find the range. Kinda like shooting a duck before he flies off."

Ackroyd didn't know the voice, assumed from the level of wise-ass it was one of Carlson's men. Ackroyd peered up over the edge of the sand, heard a new sound, the voice of Major Hommel, who called out, *"Searchlight! Now!"*

The light suddenly blasted over the heads of the men, and Ackroyd did what they all did, staring seaward, trying to catch a glimpse of who the enemy might be, and if it was a single sub or a whole fleet.

Nothing. He kept his eyes in the lighted area, the light moving slowly to one side, then back. More lights joined in, one on Eastern Island, sweeping over and past the airstrip.

"There he is! Sub, two o'clock."

Ackroyd was too low in the sand, knew the observers behind him had the height. But the heavy guns cut in now, orders from someone he couldn't hear. The arc of shelling went the opposite way now, a cascade of fire that drove the men downward.

"Cease fire!"

"He's gone. Submerged. Kill the light. Save it."

Ackroyd asked the question in his mind, but heard the same words nearby.

"What the hell's a Jap sub doing here? There's gotta be more than one."

To one side, from one of his own men in the trenches, came a loud voice of youth. "Hey! Keep the damn searchlight on."

Ackroyd climbed up from the shallow hole, crawled that way, still wary of incoming fire.

"You jackasses need a night-light? You heard the major. The bastard's gone. Probably just came up for a look, thought he'd play games with us. Maybe he figured we'd all be asleep. He won't be back. We got nothing here for him to send a torpedo at. First squad, get some sleep. Second squad, guard duty. Two hours. I'll send my gooney bird over there to make sure you don't fall asleep. He makes a good fink."

"You sure they won't be back, Gunny? Why'd they shell us?"

Ackroyd stared into the dark trench, knew the voice, and pegged it as one of the newest recruits. "Can you swim?"

"Sure."

"Tell you what, moron. He comes back, you can go out there and ask him."

MIDWAY ISLAND—JUNE 5, 1942, 2:30 P.M.

"Sub! Periscope!"

"Yeah, I see it. At the edge of the lagoon!"

Ackroyd sat up straight in his hole, saw men pointing the way, stood now, saw one of the lieutenants with an oversized pair of binoculars. More of the men began to repeat the call, rifles coming up, Ackroyd moving quickly to one of his machine gun positions. Behind him, beside one of the bunkers, Major Hommel called out, *"Hold your fire!* That's no sub. Holy hell. It looks like maybe a life raft."

Other officers appeared now, one with a radio, and Ackroyd saw the response, watched one of the PT boats maneuvering close to the odd sight. The men around Ackroyd still weren't convinced, rifles and machine guns prepared to do combat with whatever might be easing into the lagoon. The PT boat blocked the view now, and men called out with the stupidity of eagerness, *"Get out of the way. You're blocking my shot."*

Ackroyd moved toward the man, slapped the back of his helmet. "He's how far away, jackass? You think a PT boat can't handle it? The major said it was a life raft. That means either he's one of ours, which means he's rescued, or it's one of theirs, which means he's a prisoner. Put down your damn rifles, every one of you. None of you can shoot that far anyway."

He ignored the groans, and thought, They're disappointed. It's like they wanted to get shelled again. I'll take the life raft. Wonder who's in it? Somebody alive, I hope.

The two men had paddled their life raft for nearly ten miles, guided only by the column of black smoke still rising from Midway's bombed fuel tanks. They came from the *Hornet,* one more pair, a pilot and his gunner whose bomber had gone down for lack of fuel. As they reached the coral at the edge of the lagoon, the exhausted men left their yellow raft behind, grateful to be on solid ground, whether or not that *ground* was coral. But the sight of something new from the observers along the beach spread a wave of panicked excitement through the men, who had already endured the shelling from a brave, or perhaps foolish, submarine. As calm returned to the beach, Ackroyd watched the activity at the PT boat, the two men strapped onto stretchers, hauled quickly to the medical bunker.

"How do we know they're one of ours?"

"Could be spies."

Ackroyd returned to his permanent state of annoyance. "You see the raft on the boat? It's yellow. Jap rafts are black."

"Hey, Gunny, how the hell do you know that?"

He shook his head, watched as the men disappeared into an ambulance. "When you join the navy, they give you all kinds of information, like how to identify the enemy."

Hands went up now.

"Hey, Gunny, I got that book."

"Me too."

He turned, looked at the faces, most of them avoiding his eyes. "Just one time, I wish you idiots would stop going out of your way to be numbskulls. When you get around to it, try reading. But I can tell you something you won't find in that book. Those fellows in that raft . . . they're two lucky sons of bitches."

TWENTY-FOUR

Yamamoto

ONBOARD BATTLESHIP *YAMATO*, AT SEA—JUNE 4, 1942

There was no more need for radio silence. From that morning, Yamamoto had been able to pick up radio signals from a number of aircraft, some of the typical chatter among pilots, but the most alarming talk came through the radios of the scout planes, reporting the presence of the American ships. Yamamoto had no idea if Nagumo was listening to this talk as well, or more important, whether he was acting on it. The greatest surprise had come from the reports of the scout plane from cruiser *Tone,* who had first reported the presence of American ships, ships that, according to the plans designed by Yamamoto, should never have been there at all. Yet with all this unexpected information, Yamamoto held tightly to his order that there would be no radio transmissions going out to Nagumo's fleet, or anyone else close enough to hear them. If Nagumo couldn't hear his own scout planes, so be it. Yamamoto wouldn't break his own order. The noise from the transmissions from *Kido Butai* might continue, but Yamamoto would not reveal his own fleet's presence to the Americans in some clumsy chatter with Nagumo. There had to be faith in the plan, the very reason Nagumo had been chosen to lead *Kido Butai* into battle. As skeptical of the operation as Nagumo might have been, he would certainly follow orders. And if he was not reacting correctly to events as they now seemed to be developing, the blame would fall on Nagumo.

It was one more case of Japanese doctrine that Yamamoto knew so well. The plan had been designed, was being carried out, and would conclude as it was designed to conclude. Despite Yamamoto's long-standing objections to such an inflexible mindset, for this operation he had been swallowed up completely by the philosophy that his plans had to be perfect, because they were his plans. That the Americans would appear, and then attack prematurely, was not only a surprise; it was unacceptable.

For more than three hours after dawn, the reports were filtered through *Yamato*'s radio system that the Americans had attacked repeatedly, with virtually no success. For once, those reports carried no exaggeration. They were completely accurate. Yamamoto had been delighted to learn that the American torpedo bombers had suffered devastating losses, shot out of the sky by his fighter planes and *Kido Butai*'s anti-aircraft fire. He had absorbed that news with a special satisfaction, since his own torpedo bombers had caused most of the wreckage in Pearl Harbor. For the first time there could be a direct comparison between the identical types of weapons of both countries. Obviously, at least for now, the Japanese torpedo bombers had proven their superiority.

By 10:30 that morning, that smug confidence gave way to shock. Nagumo had now broken the order for radio silence, reporting that three of the fleet's carriers, *Kaga, Soryu,* and *Akagi,* had absorbed serious strikes from American dive bombers. The communication lines were now open, Yamamoto forced to confirm what he had refused to believe, that the Americans had suddenly prevailed in a fight they certainly should have lost.

Onboard Battleship *Yamato*, at sea—June 4, 1942, 8:00 p.m.

"How is Commander Genda? Is he safe?"

He knew the question would raise eyebrows, singling out one man among so many who had suffered through the morning's attacks. Yamamoto didn't care. Genda was too important to Japanese airpower, and to Yamamoto himself. Ships could be repaired. Men like Genda were impossible to replace.

Ugaki checked a long pad of paper. "He is listed here among the other senior officers, sir. He succeeded in transferring from *Akagi* to the cruiser *Nagara*, along with Admiral Nagumo's staff and most of the senior officers. I am not aware if he has been injured."

Yamamoto let out a breath, ignored the responses from his staff. He thought of Ugaki's words. "*Most?* Did they not all obey Nagumo's order to leave *Akagi?*"

Ugaki seemed to pause, then said, "There were some who could not . . . There were casualties, sir. The dead and badly wounded could not be removed."

Yamamoto felt foolish now, one more emotion piled upon the gnawing depression he had felt all morning. He forced a positive response, knew better than to question protocol when it came to the casualties. After all, he thought, I wasn't there. "I am grateful for those who gave so much. Too many will not return."

Ugaki glanced at the others, Watanabe returning the look, both men with concern for Yamamoto's dark mood and the ongoing stomach ailment he had suffered through since leaving Japan. Yamamoto tried to focus on a dozen questions rolling through his brain, knew they were all watching him. "At what time did we hear the planes?"

Watanabe said, "Sir? Which planes?"

Yamamoto seemed to burst to life now, a long flash of anger. "The *scouts*, the planes who radioed they had seen the Americans. The planes that Admiral Nagumo seems to have ignored. The planes that were responsible for allowing the enemy to penetrate our perfect shield, our CAPs, our anti-aircraft batteries. *Those* planes. We heard their radios from this far away. Did not Nagumo hear them as well? Is he deaf? Does he have faulty equipment?"

Ugaki kept his voice low, his attempt to calm Yamamoto. "It was 0730 this morning. Certainly, Admiral Nagumo heard his own scouting reports. The American torpedo bombers did not cause damage of any kind, and were eliminated entirely. Admiral Nagumo most certainly ordered his anti-aircraft screens to make ready, and we know he launched his CAP planes. It was a most effective defense."

Yamamoto was angry now, knew that his chief of staff was patronizing him. "The American attacks were a complete surprise. Do not spout the propaganda that will soon come from our newspapers, all that noise about our greatness in battle. We crushed the American torpedo planes because they are inferior weapons. But you conveniently ignore their dive bombers, their fighter planes. We must learn more details." He looked around the wardroom, the faces dropping, avoiding his eyes. "You all know what I know. No American should be alive today, no part of their fleet should be afloat. Victory was assured. It was perfect, a perfect plan. Now . . . you tell me the carriers, our magnificent warriors, might have been destroyed? Is someone delusional, ignoring the facts? Is Nagumo giving up, tossing his command away by accepting an easy path to defeat? I have instructed him to continue to fight, but even through the radio, I hear defeat in his voice. It is now dark, and the American aircraft are safely tucked away, comfortable in their floating shelters. They cannot strike back at us if they cannot see us. They have won this day, they are arrogant now, and they believe they are invincible. That is when we must strike. Nagumo will not order it, so I shall. It is time for the great fight, the all-out assault. We have the steel, we have the guns, and we shall make the Americans pay for their so-called success." He paused, was out of breath, his hands shaking, his stomach a swirl of fire. Ugaki sat down beside him.

"I agree, sir, that *Kido Butai* can attempt the nighttime assault. But it will require a full day for us to make a rendezvous with the other parts of the fleet. We are simply too far away. And of course, we do not precisely know where the American fleet has gone. One report said they are headed west, this way."

"Yes, I heard that. I hope it is true. An act of suicidal arrogance. They would sail into a perfect trap, and we should destroy them."

Ugaki put a hand on Yamamoto's arm, a rare gesture. "There are other observation planes, our long-range bombers from Wake Island, who have reported the Americans to be withdrawing, sailing east, increasing their distance from the burning carriers. Those reports seem more realistic, less like optimistic rumor."

Yamamoto pounded a fist on the table. "There will be no talk of burning carriers. We have good crews, men who know their jobs, who will sacrifice everything to save their ships. A fire is merely a fire. It can be extinguished by men who will do their jobs. I will not believe that the Americans have inflicted so much damage without our returning it threefold."

There was silence in the wardroom for a long minute, Yamamoto leaning low in his chair, trying to relax the hard pounding in his chest. He kept his gaze low, and said, "I heard them all morning, all the chatter among pilots, the radio signals from the observers. Nagumo should have heard even more. If he did not, or if he ignored them, then he has no place on a flagship."

The others stared at him, motionless. It was the first time he had spoken out so negatively about Nagumo. But there was no reason for discretion, not anymore. Ugaki seemed to gauge Yamamoto's every action, and said, "We can certainly pursue the American fleet, knowing we can destroy them quite easily. The first problem of course is just where to find them. By the time our observers locate them they could be supported by long-range bombers from Hawaii, or perhaps by a dozen more ships as well. We do not have confirmation as to how many carriers they can still bring to the fight. One was destroyed, certainly, but it is unclear if a second suffered serious damage. Those carriers, no matter if it's one or two, or five, carry aircraft that can destroy any fleet we send after them."

Ugaki stopped, seemed to measure Yamamoto's response, then continued, "Sir, there is still the option of assaulting and invading Midway. The Americans might not be expecting that at all. They would react when it was too late for them. That is, sir, the original plan, and it is still quite valid. If we occupy Midway, the Americans will have to come again, and we can have a much larger force waiting for them. If their carriers are put out of action, the rest of their fleet would be annihilated."

Watanabe spoke up. "Sir, we could easily reduce Midway to rubble with several of the largest ships from Admiral Kondo's invasion force. Then we could make a landing there virtually unopposed."

Yamamoto glanced at Ugaki, and said, "Unopposed except for American airplanes. Such optimism from you all. Such dreams. You predict that the Americans would make the same error twice, when they did not make it at all. Foolishness, all of you." He continued, "Matome, you claim we will destroy the American carriers as though it has already been done. The only destruction I am certain of, the only destruction that matters is what they have done to us. Even in your *optimism* you confirm that there is at least one aircraft carrier afloat and undamaged. Assuming it remains within supporting distance of Midway, we have no aircraft to counter them. Any amphibious assault would be cut to ribbons."

Yamamoto looked at Watanabe, managed a smile. "Did you

learn, Commander, when you were a cadet at the Naval Academy, that it is almost always futile to attack land targets from seagoing vessels?"

Watanabe seemed chastened. "Yes, sir, I did. Forgive me. I am just seeking some means of rallying this operation, finding success."

Yamamoto rolled the words in his brain, held up both hands, as though holding them off. "I do not require *rallying*, gentlemen. And I am not interested in *analysis*. No amount of discussion or any other jabber can rescue us from what has happened. But I will entertain no talk of our defeat or our failure. One part of our strength has been pushed back. We have a great deal more." He paused. "It requires no further conversation to make one very specific conclusion, one decision. Admiral Nagumo is relieved of the command of *Kido Butai*. Admiral Kondo will be named in his place. Further orders will pass through Kondo exclusively."

Ugaki seemed suddenly elated. It was no surprise to Yamamoto. Ugaki despised Nagumo. "I will carry out your order, sir."

"Immediately."

"Aye, sir. Immediately."

ONBOARD BATTLESHIP *YAMATO*, AT SEA—JUNE 4, 1942, 10:00 P.M.

He walked slowly along the catwalk, the passageway that led toward his quarters.

So, he thought, Nagumo is relieved, so what will he do now? Does he go shouting through the Naval Ministry that he has been unjustly treated, that I have stripped him of his honor? No, I do not believe he is capable of shouting, no matter how much he feels abused. He will *gloom* his way through life, mine and everyone else's. I have no patience for that, the sickness of failure. I will certainly have questions for him: How, why, when? And *if*. How many *ifs* are there? What did he do wrong, where did he fail? Perhaps he doesn't know, even now. And there will be no answers beyond what he will offer to save himself, or to save his honor.

He stared out to sea, a thick film of fog approaching from the north, blacking out the stars. We are so far away from it all, from the disasters they describe to me. My flagship, the magnificent, beloved *Akagi*, and so much more: my fleet, my good pilots and good officers. And that is my fault. There will be questions about all of it from so many, from the Naval Ministry and Prime Minister Tojo. They will insist I tell them how it became so . . . *bad*. Is it truly as bad as it seems? How could the Americans suddenly become so proficient at carrier assaults? Our fighter planes are the best in the world, and they lie in pieces at the bottom of the ocean. Along with our pilots. And that is the worst part of this. The Americans surely can manufacture pilots as they manufacture automobiles or washing machines. If we lose an airplane, we will make another. If they lose one, they will make ten. And that is why we will not win this war. But, Admiral Yamamoto, you must keep such predictions to yourself. Perhaps today's disasters are not as *disastrous* as Nagumo reports.

But of course they are. *Soryu* and *Kaga* have died painful deaths, both now on the bottom of the sea. How many men went with them? Now *Akagi* has been abandoned, and Nagumo gave that order, and then led the way. Would he order such a thing if there was hope?

He stared into the fog, the air thickening, a damp mist in his face. So many reports, and not all of them from Nagumo. There are others, he thought, many others, many reports, and none of them positive. Our newspapers will write of our great victory. That is all they know how to do. So, what will the Americans say? *The New York Times? The samurai has been given a bloody wound by the claws of the eagle.* They are entitled to their lyricism, I suppose. But no matter what any newspaper says, we will fight back. We have to. After all, there is no other way.

Why does that not lift my spirits?

He turned away from his quarters, having a need to see the young faces and the energy they brought to any problem. My staff, he thought, they work so hard for me. Loyalty is a valuable thing, and they are loyal. Sometimes they just don't accept what is real. I need to know how real today was, how bad, or if Nagumo is spouting gloom for no other reason than he is gloom itself. The Americans cannot be that good. They *cannot*. Are we that bad? Or just careless? Impossible.

He reached the wardroom, saw the usual fog of cigarette smoke, and saw Watanabe with a stack of papers, always the papers. Ugaki never smoked, not since the death of his wife, but around Kuroshima, the one-man furnace, it seemed not to matter. Ugaki could never escape the chimney, and Yamamoto valued Kuroshima too much to order him to change anything he did, no matter how many cigarettes he smoked or how few baths he took.

Yamamoto waited, and saw papers shuffled, radio dispatches held by younger aides, all of them standing at attention, waiting for him. "Is there more from the carriers?"

Watanabe said, "As you know from the reports, sir, two have gone down, *Soryu* and *Kaga*. *Akagi* continues to burn, and has been abandoned. *Hiryu* seems to have separated from the rest, though we have heard nothing from her in a while." He paused. "Sir, did you not receive the report from Admiral Nagumo?"

"I receive a great many reports from him. What now?"

"Uh, sir, the admiral has sent word that *Hiryu* appears to be burning as well. She was attacked some two hours ago by American dive bombers."

There was silence, Yamamoto feeling a twist in his chest. "So, there is at least one more American carrier out there."

Ugaki said, "Likely two, sir. There were more than two dozen bombers, with support fighters. That would suggest a second carrier. It seems, sir, that *Hiryu* did not have a chance. It was likely the only ship targeted by the Americans."

Yamamoto felt the familiar sickness in his stomach. "The aides will leave us."

The young men obeyed, the senior staff now seated around the table.

Yamamoto said, "How can we still make the fight? I am not yet prepared to claim defeat."

Watanabe said, "Oh, we can yet prevail, sir. Admiral Nagumo's last report was that we had sunk at least two American carriers. I say it makes little difference, sir. There is no indication that the Americans have a great battle fleet anywhere close. Recall, sir, we destroyed most of the battleships in Pearl Harbor, and our observers in Hawaii have long reported that their remaining battleships have sailed east. Most of what they can bring now is heavy cruisers. If we can bring enough force against their carriers, and they are destroyed, the rest of their fleet is an easy target. They can have little left to bring to the fight."

"Commander, I am never of the opinion that the Americans do not have enough for the fight. If they do not have it today, they will have it next week and next month."

Beside Watanabe, Kuroshima said, "With all respect, sir, I am more concerned with what they have today. I agree with Commander Watanabe. This operation is about today, taking Midway, destroying what they send to stop us. Am I correct, sir? We have opportunity still. I would choose not to be so concerned about what comes later. Crushing the enemy may very well guide us through a future we would enjoy."

Yamamoto nodded, looked down, and said, with no enthusiasm, "Certainly. So, I want to know more about today. What do you propose? Thus far I have heard nothing to give me *enjoyment*."

Watanabe smiled, seemed to appreciate Kuroshima's odd optimism, and said, "We are awaiting any new radio signals regarding the precise location of our Midway invasion force. As for *Hiryu*, it is something of a concern that we have not heard a report directly from Admiral Yamaguchi, but certainly he will remain on *Hiryu* until the last possible moment."

Ugaki said, "Commander, I have known Admiral Yamaguchi for many years. He is my friend. I can assure you, he will not abandon his ship. I understand his nature, his honor. If *Hiryu* is gone, so then is my friend."

There was a silent pause, Yamamoto picturing the fiery Yamaguchi, irreverent, a thorn in the side of every superior officer he had, including, certainly, Nagumo. It hardly matters, he thought. There may be nothing left for him to command.

Kuroshima spoke up now, with more energy than anyone else in the room. "Sir, we have heard communication from many of the ship captains among *Kido Butai*, and there is a growing enthusiasm for a night strike on the American fleet, a ship-to-ship battle that we cannot lose. We must pursue them with all speed, and at the same time, we must surround Midway, using our big guns to crush any resistance there, with a plan of using the airstrip to ferry in planes from Wake Island and elsewhere. It has been discussed, and it must be our best alternative."

Yamamoto wiped a hand over his face. That's what I said about this plan two months ago.

An aide appeared, the usual polite *excuse me,* and Yamamoto ignored him. But he heard the whispering, the man speaking to Watanabe, and he knew there would be another dreaded message, more talk of disaster. Or perhaps not. His brain tried to pump some optimism into him, a glimmer of hope for good news. He looked at the aide, saw the paper in Watanabe's hand, and said, "What is it, Commander?"

Watanabe passed it to Ugaki, who glanced at the writing, then handed it to Yamamoto.

He read, then slowly read again. "Admiral Nagumo reports that *Akagi* is without hope. *Hiryu* is burning badly as well."

Yamamoto forced himself into silence, felt a cold knife cutting through his stomach. "It cannot be true. I will not believe we could lose them all."

Kuroshima spoke out, with too much volume. "It is certainly a *lie*. It is at the very least exaggeration. Nagumo shows his poor spirit. This is why he has been relieved. Would he simply abandon *Akagi*? We know he has leapt off the ship like some kind of wharf rat, carrying away his flag, leaving his crew behind."

Ugaki said quietly, as though countering Kuroshima's temper, "Enough of that, Captain. We do not know all that has happened. We must rely on Admiral Nagumo, even in his shame. Admiral Kondo's occupation force is still a good deal away from *Kido Butai* for him to assume command immediately. I suggest you not allow yourself to offer such insults at a superior officer. Admiral Nagumo can still be of some use to the fleet."

He turned to Yamamoto. "We know the fate of our other carriers. If *Hiryu* is truly dying, the only alternative left to us is to unite the entire fleet and sail east, engaging the Americans in the great battle. I would like to believe that we may still depend on *Akagi*. The fire may not be a mortal injury. Often, the smoke disguises only a minor problem."

Watanabe said, "But even Admiral Nagumo admits he has no additional aircraft. It will take time to ferry the aircraft from Wake Island. For now we must rely only on our artillery. *Akagi* cannot be of assistance."

Kuroshima said, "What of the northern fleet, the Alaska task force? There are two smaller carriers accompanying, and their aircraft can be of enormous assistance."

Ugaki said, "They are several days away from us. We must assume that in less than a week this fight will be decided. No, we must continue the Aleutian Island operation. I am confident of success." He looked at Yamamoto now. "Sir, I will not believe that Admiral Yamaguchi has been defeated in any fight. We may still have use of her flight deck, perhaps in a day or two. My friend will fight to the end."

Yamamoto said nothing, but thought, How many airplanes are required for a fight to the end? How many artillery shells? He leaned forward, his arms on the table. "I want to know when you hear from Yamaguchi, from *Hiryu*, the instant the message is received. I do not wish to assume the worst, but this has been a day of worsts. Have the radio room search vigorously for a signal from the carrier. Press Nagumo for some information. Even if he sulks, he must know something."

Kuroshima was agitated again, waving his cigarette in a manic display. "We must take *Akagi* into tow, lead her back to Japan. We cannot leave her floating alone, a prize for the Americans. Can you see them humiliate us? They would display her as some kind of floating museum in San Francisco or the Potomac River. It would shame us for all time. I have to believe that it is only fire, and no further damage. From the reports, she still floats high in the water. We must see to her, sir. She has served us all well, Admiral, especially you."

Ugaki tried to keep his control. "Captain Kuroshima, your concern for our honor . . . is honor itself. But from what I am reading here, *Akagi* might be afloat, but she is dead in the water, consumed by flames, and she has been abandoned by nearly all of her crew."

Yamamoto saw a new dose of outrage on Kuroshima's face, held up his hand, silencing him. "Remember, I was captain of *Akagi*, years ago. No one has a greater affection for such a vessel as I do. Yes, she served me well. She served us all and she served the emperor. So, it is with regret . . . heartfelt regret, that I honor the wishes of those who know her condition, who are observing her now. I agree with you, Captain, that we cannot allow *Akagi* to be commandeered by the Americans. Thus, in her condition, there is no alternative. She must be scuttled."

Yamamoto could feel their eyes on him, no one speaking, even Kuroshima silent. He assembled his words, kept his emotions away, would not show them weakness, not now, not when so much depended on their loyalty.

"I am prepared to honor the request of those in command of *Kido Butai,* who, even now, are observing *Akagi's* fate. I will now order the sinking of the ship. And I will apologize to the emperor for sinking his ship by our own torpedoes."

ONBOARD BATTLESHIP *YAMATO,* AT SEA—JUNE 5, 1942, 1:00 A.M.

He sat in his quarters, had left the staff to their arguments and their optimism.

The great all-out nighttime assault had been canceled. The few remaining scout planes launched from the cruisers had found nothing to confirm that the Americans were sailing westward, into the teeth of a vise grip by the Japanese fleet. That grip was weaker than even Yamamoto had hoped, since Admiral Kondo's battle-ships were too far south to chance a rendezvous with any blunder-ing American captains. They could come still, he thought. They could sail close enough to allow our bombers from Wake Island to reach them. It is a hope. It is possible.

He poured from a teapot, still felt the shaking in his hands and the turmoil in his gut unending.

You are deluding yourself, Iso. The Americans will not be so foolish. Do they not know where Wake is? Not even the most thick-headed American admiral would sail his fleet so close to the finest bombers in the world. No, they have done their good work, and they will wait and fight another day. And we will be weaker for it.

Yamamoto had finally received word of *Hiryu*'s imminent death, fires consuming her, with her crew helpless to stand in the way. He thought of Yamaguchi. He will go down with her. For men like him, there is no other way. How different are my commanders? Nagumo leaves his burning ship to ride a boat launch to safety. Yamaguchi will drown in the waves. And Ugaki will mourn him. As it should be.

How many more will die like that, with the cloak of honor, as though suicide makes them more loyal to the emperor? Yamaguchi loved his ship more than the people he answered to. Of course he would stay with *Hiryu* rather than explain his way to honor. And Nagumo considered that as well. It is his nature to search for the most miserable outcome. So he will wait for the sword to come down, as though it is already done. For so many of them, so many of *us*, failure is to be punished, and the perfect punishment is *hara-kiri*. But I have never believed that, and never will. This failure is mine, not Nagumo's, not anyone else's. In command you accept responsibility, and if you choose to die by your own hand, you cast responsibility away. How simple. People will speak of you with sadness instead of scorn. Failure deserves scorn, and so it shall be. If any of them comes to me, to ask my blessing on their suicide, I will slap them in the face. There's your honor.

He stood, pulled a fat book off his shelf, containing photographs and charts, the details of his great ships. He thumbed through and stopped at the photo of *Hiryu*: magnificent, a grand fighting beast. *Kaga* was even larger, and she was already gone in what Nagumo had described as a deep explosion. *Soryu, Akagi,* scuttled or nearly so. He studied the photo of *Hiryu*. What have we done wrong, what have we engineered so poorly that our great ships ignite like torches? The engineers will know, they will make excuses, and if the war goes on, they will build more ships. And planes, surely. He let out a breath. And the men to fly them? I will call on Commander Genda. He will know what is needed and how the training must go. We shall fill the skies once more. He suddenly felt like crying. Did we not fill the skies already? And now the skies are empty.

He slid the book back on his shelf, noticed the seal on the cover—*Top Secret*—and thought, There is little danger that anyone will benefit from these pictures, not anymore. He stared blankly at the bookcase, had no energy for anything else except one thought: *Four carriers.* We sent two more to the South Pacific. If they had been here, how much difference would it have made? Would we have prevailed? Or would we have lost *six* carriers? And with that . . . the war.

There was a knock, and he sat again, in no mood for conversation. "What is it?"

The door opened a crack and he saw Watanabe.

"Sir, Admiral Kondo's cruiser divisions have reported that they will be unable to reach Midway by dawn. They fear they will be vulnerable to American aircraft after sunrise. I do not agree. But I need your authorization to order them to proceed to Midway. I believe the Admiral's battleships can join them in short time, and we can continue the attacks there."

"Why is Kondo changing his plan? I ordered him to drive toward the American carrier fleet, possibly for a nighttime assault."

Watanabe paused, seemed suddenly uncomfortable. "Sir, there was no opportunity for a nighttime assault. There is no sign of the Americans. They have, it seems, turned eastward, out of our range. But sir, that is why I suggest an all-out assault on Midway with the biggest guns in the fleet, an enormous combined assault."

"To what end, Commander? We have no carriers, no planes, and the Americans would wait for just such a move." He let out a breath. Ruling out a nighttime assault meant he was out of options. "A month ago, Midway was our bait, to lure the Americans to their death. Now, it is theirs. I know they are waiting for such a move. I know their planes will be armed and fueled and the radios ready to report what we're going to do. I do not wish to see their dive bombers destroy our great battleships."

"Sir, please. Victory is still in our hands. If we can find their carriers . . ."

"How will we do that? They are much more certain to find *us*." He felt the fury now, a crushing blow to his spirit. He thought of the return to Japan, and the utter humiliation from so much failure. No, he thought, I cannot allow my officers to push us into a greater failure. It is time for all of us to accept the truth. "No, Commander. It is too late now. Too much fighting causes all-out defeat. We must accept our defeat as it is now, and not add to our disaster. You will issue orders to Admiral Kondo and the other fleet commanders, to set course westward, to rendezvous with us here."

Watanabe lowered his head, and said, "I will do as you order, sir. What will our mission be then?"

"There will be no mission, Commander. It is time to return to Japan."

TWENTY-FIVE

Ackroyd

MIDWAY ISLAND—JUNE 6, 1942, 11:00 A.M.

"Really, sir? Me?"

The colonel stared without changing expression, and Ackroyd knew the meaning. Yep, he thought. Me.

Shannon smiled now, and said, "Look, Gunny, this isn't punishment. We know there isn't going to be much action now. Admiral Spruance has been pretty definite that we kicked the Japs in the teeth. We're not likely to get a bombing strike, because they haven't got any planes to bomb us with. But this fellow Ford could do all of us a lot of good. I told you a few days ago, he's a real hotshot, a wheel in Hollywood. Those people are watching everything we do, and they're rich enough to buy war bonds. That makes Washington happy. You're one of the most, well, let's say colorful non-coms out here. He wants salty, you can give him salty."

"How salty?"

Shannon laughed. "He's putting stuff on film. Don't get too carried away. Your mama might see it."

"Sir, my mama makes *me* blush. But I understand. Where is he now?"

"Up on that sand hill, behind the bunkers. He's supposed to set up his crew for some interviews."

The word made Ackroyd cringe.

Shannon seemed to know that. "Just go. Talk to 'em. Show 'em around."

Ackroyd saluted. "Aye, sir." He stepped out of the bunker, the island all around him a hive of activity. Much of it was defensive, the appropriate precaution given the bombing assaults. But the stress level had dropped considerably, the trigger fingers not as tight.

He stepped along a hardened pathway and climbed the hill, the tallest on the island. To one side the gas tanks still smoldered, dense black smoke, the wind thankfully blowing the opposite way. He stopped, scanned the island, and saw his anti-aircraft guns, his machine guns, and the absurd rolls of barbed wire spread nearly completely around the island. I guess that filmmaker guy thinks this is pretty, he thought, like something on a postcard or something. Hell if I know why.

He crested the hill and saw a handful of gooney birds. He looked for his pal among them, the distinctive black dot on its beak. But none of them were familiar, none of them seeming to recognize him. He saw the cameras now, three civilians manning the equipment, with one man clearly in charge. Another surprise: The man had a white bandage on his arm. He'd been wounded. Ackroyd moved that way and thought, Just call me your babysitter, but oh God, don't tell me the wound is serious. He remembered Shannon's words . . . *careless marine.*

"Excuse me, sirs, I'm Gunnery Sergeant Doug Ackroyd. Colonel Shannon has ordered . . . has *requested* that I escort you around some of the installation, give you a little more of a closer look. How's the arm, sir?"

The man held up his arm, as though a badge of honor. "I don't suppose they give Purple Hearts to civilians. No, it's a big scratch, Sergeant, that's all. Those officers back in Pearl Harbor who told me to stay out of the way, well, it seems they knew what they were talking about."

"Glad to hear you're all right, sir. The corpsmen here and the doc are some of the best." He had run out of conversation, and said, "The Japs seem to be leaving us alone for a while, so we can be a little more accommodating to you fellas. The colonel also told me you might just wanna talk to me. Not sure why."

The senior man came toward him, hand extended. "Pleased to meet you, Sergeant. So far, I can't say we had much hospitality, Japanese style. But I appreciate your effort, and Colonel Shannon's. I'm John Ford, these are my helpers. I have to say, you're a good bit older than most around here, more gray hair than I expected. Don't mean that as an insult, truly."

"That's okay, sir. I just gave you a speech that's the longest I ever said without swearing. I give a lot more insults than anyone can give me."

Ford waved behind him, pointed at Ackroyd, an obvious signal to begin filming. Ackroyd dropped his head, thought now of Colonel Shannon. Do it right, Gunny.

"What exactly do you expect from me, sir?"

"Well, first, we want to know about you, show the face of a longtime marine, your impression of all this, that sort of thing. I would have thought a man your age would be an officer."

"Doesn't always work like that. I'm not cut out that way. I talk too much and cuss too much, and the men like me just like I am, especially when I cuss at *them*. I figure I'm about done though.

Twenty-five years. That's a whole lifetime to most of these idiots."
He thought suddenly of Shannon's admonitions. "Wait, excuse
me, but am I not supposed to call 'em that?"

Ford laughed. "For what we're doing, this film, maybe not. But
I understand. It's the same in Hollywood. So, Sergeant, you have
any questions about why we're here?"

Ackroyd thought a moment. "Aye, sir. One. Why are you here?"

Ford laughed again. "Sergeant, I'm working with the OSS, the
Office of Strategic Services. I'm the head of the photographic
unit. They picked me, I suppose, because I've shot a lot of movies.
I know a little about film."

"Like what?"

Ford turned to the camera operator. "Make sure you get this.
Every bit." He turned back to Ackroyd now. "I make movies people want to watch. That's not always easy. Out here, I'm making
what they call a documentary, life on an isolated military base,
navy and marines working together, all of that. I didn't expect to
be filming a Japanese attack. But people will especially want to
know about that. We got some pretty gritty stuff, most of it by
luck. But it's good film."

"What the hell makes *good film*?"

Ford crossed his arms, laughed again. "You have no idea who I
am, or what I've done, do you?"

Ackroyd was embarrassed now, and said, "Not really."

Ford rubbed his hands together. "Excellent. Too often people
are trying to be my pal, thinking maybe I'll put them in a movie,
or they want me to introduce them to some big-time star. So,
here's a little of what I've done, Sergeant. I directed quite a few silent films, and then, well, things have been pretty good for me. I've
won a couple of Oscars, one a few years ago for *The Informer,* a
couple years ago for *The Grapes of Wrath.* There's a lot more I
could tell you, but I think you get the idea."

"You made a movie about grapes?"

He saw a hint of frustration on Ford's face, the cameraman behind him stifling a laugh. "Yeah, it was all about grapes. All right, Sergeant, why don't you tell me something about you, and what happened here."

"Well, Mr. Ford, I don't have much to say about me. I'm from nowhere in Alabama. We didn't have a movie theater, or maybe I'd have seen some of your stuff. The Marine Corps's been my whole life. I got no wife, not even a girlfriend lately. Didn't never meet anybody who mattered to me more than the corps. I fought in the Great War, and it kinda looks like this new war might blow up the same way. There's idiots out there in those sand trenches here who think this is fun, an adventure. They get a kick out of shooting guns but not one of 'em has seen a real close-up human target. I have." He stopped, but then the words kept coming. "I killed a man with a knife. Belleau Wood. Cut his throat. Not sure I want to do that again. Not sure I can." He stopped, saw the three men staring at him. "Sorry. You don't need to hear any of that. Well, Midway . . . I guess you can say that we're the front lines out here. Couple days ago, the Japs tested us, tried to blow us to hell, wondered how we'd fight back. We did, and they left. They ain't been back. They left a few men behind, and they took a few of us to hell with 'em. Now, I guess the next thing the generals and admirals have to figure out is how to push west, kick those bastards off the next island, maybe Wake and Guam, then the one after that. Mr. Ford, those are sons of bitches, and somebody needs to kill every one of them before they can kill us. I will say this though, sir. Anybody takes them for granted, thinks that just because we're big and tough and have good weapons, that we'll have to win this scrap. Well, sir, from what we're hearing, the navy's done a hell of a good job for all of us. The Jap fleet is hightailing it back to Japan, and there are a lot fewer of those big ships than when they got here."

Ford said, "I know that, Sergeant. I came out here to film you good men, to explore what makes the navy and the marines so good at what they do."

"Forgive me, Mr. Ford. But if those Jap ships had won their fight, about now all of that barbed wire you see down there would be wrapped around the lot of us. I take nothing away from those ships out there, and our pilots. But, sir, there's no doubt in my mind that we're standing here having our pleasant conversation because we got lucky."

TWENTY-SIX

Baker

ONBOARD USS *HORNET*, AT SEA—JUNE 7, 1942

"Why? Damn it all, why?"

Thach seemed more tolerant of this kind of question than usual, and Baker knew that with the loss of *Yorktown*, they all were feeling wounded. Thach said, "Because, Mr. Cheek, there's such a thing as the Combat Air Patrol. You've heard of it, I'm pretty sure. They need us up there making sure the Japs don't try to do to this tub what they did to *Yorktown*. That make sense to you?"

Baker knew they were all in full sulk, and Baker hadn't been able to shake that since he had landed on *Hornet*, which was, for now, his new home. He also knew he had nothing to say about orders, anyone's orders. This was, after all, a new command, and Thach had to answer to new people, and make a good show of it.

Cheek backed down, carrying the same respect for Thach as

Baker and the rest of the pilots. "I just thought . . . seeing as how we'd already spent a good bit of time eyeballing those Jap ships, they'd want our experience out there, looking for the Jap fleet."

Thach looked at a handful of papers, an aide standing by with a pen. He signed one paper and gave it to the aide, the man disappearing through the hatchway.

Three of Thach's other pilots moved close to Cheek and Baker, all of them with the same impatience for whatever kind of mission was coming next.

Thach said, "You know what that was? Those papers? They just officially named me commander of *Hornet*'s fighter squadron, and I'm still in charge of all *you* hopscotchers. You oughta know that they didn't give me this job because I'm pretty. The former squadron commander was Sam Mitchell. He went down. Nobody knows if he's still out there, or if he's gone for good. Regardless, they've told me to fill his shoes. I hate to have a new job handed me like that, but that's the way it is. So when Admiral Spruance tells me what he needs our airplanes to do, my job is to say 'Aye, sir.' He's an admiral after all.

"Look, this is all I know, and all you need to know. The enemy is busted to hell. Scouts report that most likely four of their carriers have gone down, or are so full of holes, they're worthless. And if they've got no carriers, they've got no planes. It's sort of simple." He stopped, and Baker knew the stare. It meant that Thach had more to say. "Our lady's gone. She couldn't hold up to all the wounds. They tried to save her, tow her back to Pearl, but there was too much damage."

Baker said, "What time?"

"What difference does it make? 0500, or so."

"It makes a difference to us, you know that. I just wanted to know. It's . . . the end of something, for all of us."

Thach looked at all of them, shook his head. "I'm not getting sloppy about this. Can't. You start thinking about sentiment and you make mistakes. We still have jobs to do, and we'll do them. I can't talk about *Yorktown* at all. You got that? There's Jap sailors out there who watched their ships drop like stones, and I guarantee, they aren't all mushy about it. They just want to see you dead."

They all responded with a quiet "Aye, sir."

Behind Baker, Adams said, "But they lost their carriers. They got no planes, you said so yourself. Why do we need to fly in circles up there if there's nothing to worry about?"

"I didn't say there's nothing to worry about. The Jap fleet is God knows where, and they've gotta be hopping mad. If you don't like being a CAP, then think about it like being scouts, lookouts, because sure as hell there are some big-assed battleships out there itching for a fight."

Baker said, "Well, there's something we oughta be doing. We oughta search for any of our guys out there floating around. There's gotta be life rafts all over the place, maybe some of 'em Japs. That'd be kind of a prize, don't you think?"

"What the hell are you gonna do flying past some poor Joe bobbing up and down, and you're going two hundred miles per hour? Your radios aren't good enough to call each other, much less give any accurate search information back here. They've got a passel of PBYs doing all the searching we'll need. They've already pulled guys out of the drink, so they don't need you to do their job." Thach paused. "Look, we already know what a torpedo or a five-hundred-pound bomb can do to a carrier, our *own* carrier. A fourteen-inch artillery shell can do just as much, maybe worse. The ship might be twenty miles away, so they'd hit us before we knew they were coming. Admiral Spruance knows what the hell he's doing. It's why Admiral Fletcher turned over command to him when *Yorktown* got hit. See? I know a few things too. I don't care what you know. I just expect you to do what you're told. And for the next few hours, you're gonna be airborne and make sure nothing happens to the two carriers we've got left. Clear?"

ABOVE USS *HORNET*—JUNE 7, 1942, 3:00 P.M.

He leveled off at twenty thousand feet, saw the others on both sides assuming a patrol formation, four sets of three, slight variation in altitude. The *Hornet* lay below them, a white foaming wake the only sign she was moving at all, and even now at barely half speed.

The skies were perfect, the seas below them gentle, no chance for any ship to intrude on the task force. The radar in the planes was ineffective at best, but Thach had a direct line open to the radar station on *Hornet*'s bridge, allowing ample warning should the Japanese manage an air assault from a carrier no one had yet to find. Far out around *Hornet* were the escorts, the destroyers and cruisers that kept their focus on the dangers that might come from beneath the surface. For now, the threat of any kind of menace seemed remote, the creeping confidence in all of them that this fight was won.

Thach led them in a sweeping turn, the typical CAP maneuver, a wide circle around *Hornet*'s position, all eyes meant to be trained on every part of the sky, every direction. But Baker was like most of the men around him: bored, restless, annoyed at the mundane assignment, looking for something dangerous to happen, when they all knew, even if Thach wouldn't admit it, that danger was gone. But Baker had begun to feel that it was never gone, the Japanese Zeroes beginning to chase him through his dreams, restless nights where he relived Bassett's death, so many of the bombers as well. He tried to ignore that now. After all, they were just dreams.

The formations around him spread out, another order from Thach. Since there was no need to assume a fighting posture, the CAP was more useful if their eyes could look past the planes around them. Baker followed his instructions, dropped back, then climbed, a hundred feet, then two, above the other two in his group. He scanned his gauges, but there were no worries about fuel consumption, his floating gasoline station straight below him. He adjusted his speed, stayed in line with Thach, who was well below him now, but even in a lazy formation, Baker knew that Thach would ream him out if he strayed out of line.

He saw a flicker above him, a quick sliver of reflected sunlight, and there was a burst of butterflies in his stomach. It was the familiar feeling, the sight of the Zero coming down toward him like a bullet. He jerked the yoke to one side, fumbled for the trigger buttons, pulled the Wildcat to the right, but there was nothing to see. The radio lit up now, Thach, Adams, more.

"What the hell?"

"Keep it straight."

"What's the damn matter with you?"

Baker tried to stay calm, his voice in the radio, "Sorry . . . cramp in my leg. I'm okay. Won't happen again."

He backed his hands slightly off the yoke, straightened his fingers, his hands quivering. He gripped the yoke again, slow movement, careful touch. He looked up now, where the reflection had been, but there was nothing to see except deep blue sky. Damn it all, that was a Zero. No, maybe it wasn't, you idiot. Maybe it wasn't a damn thing. You're all alone out here. Just the good guys.

The plane came in from one side, cutting through the formation, red meatballs, flashes of fire from the Zero's wings. He yelled a hard curse, shoved the yoke forward, a steep banking dive away from the others, in a frantic search for the Zero.

Thach's voice came through the headphones now, "Baker. What's wrong? Problem?"

He wanted to ask the question, urgent, terrifying. Didn't you see it? But he eased the yoke back, slid up slowly into the formation. No, they didn't see it. Oh Christ, what's going on? He took his time, said into the radio, "Yoke stuck for a second. Better have the plane captain take a look."

No one responded, and after a long moment, Thach said, "Yeah, we'll check it out. Be careful with her. Maybe you should return to the ship."

"No, sir, I'm okay. Just keeping a firmer hand on her."

He was still climbing, felt a genuine fear now, raised the Wildcat to a level flight above the rest of the formation. He tried to relax, find the boredom in the routine he had heard so much about. Minutes passed, his mind letting him relax, his eyes blinking, nothing to see but blue sky and Thach's airplanes. But he saw them now, a dozen or more, head-on, coming fast, guns flashing. No one around him took any action, no evasive movements, and Baker pushed back into his seat, prepared to fire at the lead plane. And now they were gone.

The drone of his engine surprised him, soft, calming, Thach's formations were still there, no one reacting to anything. Oh Christ, what's going on? He kept the question inside, and thought, I don't need anyone thinking . . . what? That I'm cracking up? But they were there, Zeroes. And then they weren't. He blinked hard, tried to see more than the sky and the Wildcats in front of him. But there was nothing else to see.

He was in his quarters alone, the others out on patrol again, a card game happening in the quarters next door. He saw the figure in the hatchway, Thach, who said, "Hey, Perk. Mind if we talk?"

Baker had a sinking dread, and said, "You don't have to ask, Commander. What's up?"

Thach sat down in a metal chair, and looked at him with a counterfeit smile. "So, how many did you see?"

"How many what?"

"Zeroes, I guess. If we were fighting Krauts, I guess they'd be Messerschmitts. That's sort of how it goes."

Baker was more uneasy now. "What are you talking about?"

"Look, I know what you saw up there. I've heard it before."

"You *seen* it before?"

Thach let out a breath. "Not yet. But scares hell out of me to think we'll never be able to let this go."

"Let what go?"

"Come on, Perk, don't play with me. You saw Zeroes up there, real as you and me. I'm surprised you didn't start shooting."

"I won't admit to it, Jimmie. Not to nobody. I'll lose my wings."

Thach was silent for a long minute, and Baker felt a small cold blast in his gut, knew what was coming. But Thach surprised him.

"I'm not grounding you, not yet. But I want you to stay down here for a few days. Let the others do the CAP. You know as well as I do it's boring as hell up there. We're spoiled, all of us. We've been fighting nothing but Zeroes and Jap bombers, while all those poor bastards in the Dauntlesses and Devastators were getting shot to hell. You know it just like I do. To us, it was a game, who's tough-est, fastest, the better pilot. Sometimes it was us, sometimes it wasn't. We lost good people and so did they."

Baker felt giddy relief. "God, thanks, Jimmie. I thought . . ."

"I know what you thought. You didn't need me to tell you that you might be grounded. You knew it up there, before we ever tail-hooked in. Look, I can't have you jeopardize a mission or another pilot. You know that. But this will stay between us for now. *For now.*" Thach rose, moved toward the passageway and stopped at the hatch. "How many did you see? Singles, or a formation?"

It was an odd, unnerving question.

"Singles, then a whole flock."

"Coming straight at us?"

Baker didn't answer and Thach said, "Just wondering if the Japs will ever leave us alone, even if we kill 'em all." He tapped the side of his head. "They're in here. They'd love to know that, even if they were on the bottom of the ocean. From all I've been told, we won this fight, and in a few days we'll head back to Pearl. But sometimes the winners of a fight can't shake what the losers coulda done to 'em, or what they saw. I think about Bassett, I think about Lovelace, hell, every damn minute.

"Oh, hell, forget about it. I'm no shrink. Just . . . clear your head, and I'll get you back up there. Right now, you oughta go get some chow. I heard they got meatloaf tonight. Not sure what kind of meat, but it's better than that crap the enlisted men have to eat."

Thach was gone now, Baker alone, sounds of the card game, a soft rumble beneath him from the massive engines powering the ship. How the hell did he know, he thought. You don't just guess about seeing things. He's seen it too. He's got as many missions, and he's shot down more of those bastards than I have, and he's gotten more holes in his plane than I have. I guess . . . somebody shoots at you long enough, they don't stop. You live with it. Oh God. I've heard of guys, foot soldiers, who crack up, who jump out a window when there's a thunderstorm. I'm too young for that crap. Maybe all I am is a privileged pilot. That's what some of these sailors call us. You hear it in every part of the ship. It's what Admiral Fletcher thinks, maybe Nimitz too. We're the *special ones*. *Yorktown* gets blown to hell, bombed and torpedoed, and instead of getting blown to pieces like some of the crew, we're up in the sky, watching it like it's some kind of glorious show. Now she's gone, sitting on the bottom of the ocean, and damn sure there are some of her crew still onboard. And the privileged pilots? They just move to another carrier, and bitch and sing sad songs about her, until it happens next time.

He rapped the bulkhead by his bunk. How long do you have, *Hornet*, old girl? Some Jap will get you too, but no sweat for me. I'll be up in the sky, and then they'll just stick me on the next boat. And for that, I am one lucky son of a bitch, and I'm supposed to be happy as hell about that. So, how the hell do I walk past some crewman here and not wonder if his number's up? No wonder they all hate pilots, more than they hate officers. Every damn one of them could be riding around in their coffin. Jesus. Stop this.

When you're up there, the whole world is what you can see out your windscreen. The crew here, the gunnery guys, the swabbies, the machinists, the guys dishing out Thach's meatloaf. They have their *whole worlds* too. My job is to keep somebody bad from blowing this thing to hell. Their job is to keep it afloat. So the next time you see a damn Zero, just shoot him down. If he's for real, you'll have done everybody a favor. If he's not, well, they'll probably send you back to San Diego. I can't get into too much trouble teaching idiots to fly.

He heard commotion from the card game, a loud whoop, laughter. Somebody hit a full house, I bet. Maybe I'll join 'em. He stood beside his bunk, his hand still on the bulkhead. No, not this time. Maybe Thach is right. I'll try the meatloaf.

ONBOARD USS *HORNET,* AT SEA—JUNE 11, 1942

Thach had gathered them in the ready room, stood up front, waited for them to sit, enduring the usual chatter.

"Quiet. You're gonna want to hear this. Just to show you how admirals think. Two days ago, we received orders from CINCPAC that we were to sail north, give assistance to some kind of stink that's going on in Alaska." Baker could see Thach's smile, his response to the loud groan that poured out from the entire squadron. "All right, quiet down. There's a bunch of islands up there, and for reasons no one's explained to me, the Japs are dropping bombs on one of our bases at a place called Dutch Harbor. It seems there's a force of Jap ships up there, and they're stirring up all kinds of trouble. I don't need to hear any more, for one very good reason. The order was rescinded by CINCPAC. It's somebody's problem, but it's not ours. It's possible all those admirals thought this crew might stage a mutiny. You fellows who weren't on *Hornet* from the beginning might not know that this crew has been wandering all over the Pacific for most of three months. I don't know about you, but I don't especially want some mechanic working on my plane if he's pissed off at the navy, or anyone else."

Baker spoke up. "So, what are the new orders, sir? They don't rescind anything without giving us something else to do. Are we going after the Jap fleet?"

Down the row from Baker, Adams said, "No chance. We gave 'em a hell of a head start. They're halfway back to Jap-land by now."

Thach held up his hand. "You're right. According to Admiral Spruance, that was never a good plan. The Japs outnumber us in ships about four to one. If they do have another carrier or two, we'd be in a mess. No, CINCPAC had a better idea. Call it a reward, to every damn man in these task forces. Not sure how many of you have noticed that we've changed course. Well, I have. And I can tell you why. Gentlemen, we're heading back to Pearl. We won this one, and we're going home."

TWENTY-SEVEN

Rochefort

"*Well, you were only five minutes, five degrees, and five miles out.*"

It was the first confirmation of the amazing success of Rochefort's near-perfect predictions, Admiral Nimitz's extraordinary compliments passed through Ed Layton, that the weeks of work deciphering the Japanese codes had been worth every bit of the sweat and sleeplessness.

Nimitz's words still followed Rochefort, embraced in some quiet place he just didn't need to talk about. The pat on the back had of course been first to Layton, Nimitz still wary, in the most benign way, of the odd ducks who labored in the hole that Rochefort generously called the Dungeon.

Once the actual fighting began around Midway, Rochefort found himself with very little to do. It wasn't that he was unwilling to offer valuable information about the Japanese movements, or unaware of what those movements were. There was a new handicap. Less than a week before the first assault on the island of Midway, the Japanese had changed their code, from the usual JN-25b, which Rochefort and his team had cracked, to the JN-25c. The code wasn't completely new, of course. Tossing one entire code out the window and inventing a new one could take the Japanese months. But the new code had just enough alterations that Rochefort's men did have to start over, even if they had minimal advantages from knowing the old code.

For Rochefort and his crew, information about the fights around Midway came first from Layton, who would happily provide any intel that CINCPAC was receiving. Added to that were the radio intercepts coming straight to the Dungeon from listening posts farther out on the coast of Oahu. And finally, Rochefort could listen in on exactly the same intercepts being received by the aircraft on both sides, as they engaged in the violent struggles for the lives of the aircraft carriers. The one area that Rochefort couldn't hear was radio traffic from the ships on either side. Radio silence was exactly that, and by the time Yamamoto, and then Admiral Spruance, opened up their communications, it was only because the fight was over.

Around Pearl Harbor, the celebrations were muted, if there were celebrations at all. The first had come on behalf of General Emmons, the army commander, who had so completely dismissed Nimitz's acceptance of Rochefort's and Layton's analysis. Now he came to Nimitz's office with not only his hat in hand, but an enormous bottle of champagne and a lengthy apology. It was Layton who quietly suggested that Rochefort be summoned, that he had earned more of that champagne than anyone else in Nimitz's command. The cork was popped and Nimitz had offered a toast to Rochefort, which he swallowed with uneasy pride, a growling ulcer, and a graceless thank-you: *"I'm just doing what I'm paid to do."*

THE DUNGEON, 14TH NAVAL DISTRICT—JUNE 9, 1942

He sat at his desk, looked across the brightly lit room, some of the men doing exactly what he was, allowing himself to take a breath. Faces were turning to him, some of them with the expectation that he would suddenly snap them to work, something new, some piece of information he had received at CINCPAC that would put them all to work. He held up a hand, ensuring their attention, and more faces turned to him.

"Since everybody's here, I thought I oughta mention . . . a couple days ago Admiral Nimitz gave us a big-time slap on the ass. Seems the army did too. Looks as though Midway is done, a victory for our boys. I'd like to believe that we helped, that we gave our people some advantage. The admiral was talking me up really nice, big words about our excellence, all of that. I couldn't really say what I wanted to, that nobody in this place right here, no *single* man in my command is responsible. It was all of us. I think you know that, and I'm not sure how to say that to the admiral. Hell, I have trouble telling him anything, except maybe 'Aye, sir.'"

Across the room, Dyer spoke up. "Maybe we oughta all go over there, one big parade, nifty formation, dress whites, the whole bit. You can introduce us to him, one at a time."

Rochefort looked down and smiled, a rarity. "I'm sure he'd politely thank every one of you, then he'd court-martial me. I'm a whole lot more comfortable staying out of the way of anyone whose name starts with *Admiral*."

He folded his hands on his desk and scanned the room. "Look, I'm not completely certain we *can* relax. I'm waiting for the radio intercepts to tell us a little more about the Japanese movements and just what their ships are doing. If we knew their damn code, we could pinpoint them pretty accurately. As it is, take whatever hints you can grab. Identify the ham-handed telegraph operators, as we've always done."

Beside him, Ensign Showers said, "Excuse me, sir. This just came down the pneumatic tube. There's a clear intercept that Admiral Yamamoto has ordered his ships to pull out and head west. It seems the order is going out to *all* of his ships. They're even calling some of the submarines, but there are others that will stay put. That's to be expected, I think, sir."

"That intercept is clear?"

"It's very clear, sir."

Rochefort stared at nothing for a long moment, could feel the energy in the room. "Listen up, dammit. We still have work to do, every day, every night. This was one fight, one good job by all of us. But there's still a war, and the Japs are going to find a new way to kick us in the ass." He stopped, could see the exhaustion on the faces, the smiles dulled by lack of sleep. "All right, here's an actual order. For the next three days, I don't want to see a single one of you in this room. Not one. I don't care what you do, as long as it doesn't involve the shore patrol or any army MPs."

Dyer spoke up again, beaming a smile. "Um, sir, I've got a rented house out on Diamond Head. I think the boys ought to come out there, bring what you want, although maybe not *who* you want. But if we stay away from the hotels, this'll keep us out of trouble."

Rochefort wasn't sure what he meant. "Are you talking about having a party? I thought you wanted to go to sleep."

"Joe, we haven't been to sleep in so long, we forgot what it is. But we damn sure could use a little festivity. Each of you, you're invited to my house out there. Bring food and booze, and try not to wreck the place. My landlord's a cranky rear admiral."

In the back of the room, Lieutenant Yardley stood, holding up an invisible glass. "I'll make the first toast right here. To Commander Joe Rochefort. He can be a real son of a bitch, and he can be a gem. Right now, he's two gems. Thank you, sir."

Dyer said, "All right then. We've got three days. Let's have a party."

14TH NAVAL DISTRICT, PEARL HARBOR, HAWAII—JUNE 13, 1942

The hangovers had passed, the men deep into the work of decoding and deciphering the new JN-25c Japanese code. Rochefort had taken a rare break, his chronic ulcer ripping through his stomach, a condition he had endured for months now. The men who knew him best understood that the ulcer kept him from most of the kind of drunken festivities they had just enjoyed, and even the single glass of champagne in Admiral Nimitz's office had been a challenge.

He climbed the steps away from the Dungeon, walked out toward the harbor and stared for a long moment, not really sure what he was hoping to see. It was a glorious sky, a single fat cloud drifting toward Honolulu, a hint of sound from the planes at Ewa. He thought, Training missions, I guess. They never stop. I suppose that's a good thing.

"Hey!"

He turned, saw the smiling face of Layton, who said, "What the hell are you doing out here? You're gonna get a sunburn, as pale as you are. How come you're not down in your hole?"

Rochefort absorbed the usual pat on the back from Layton, and said, "I had a little break. Or maybe I just needed one. I heard the carriers are coming in today. I'd kinda like to see that."

Layton stood beside him now. "Let's head upstairs. It's a whole lot better view. *Enterprise* is right outside the harbor. It's a sight when those big gals come in."

"I can see okay here."

Layton always knew when Rochefort was in a *mood*. "What's eating you?"

"Jesus, there she is. That's gotta be *Enterprise*. The tugs are moving her in. I guess it'll take a while to get her tied up."

Layton focused once more on his friend. "I said, what's eating you?"

Rochefort stayed quiet, a long minute, then said, "Three went out. Two came back. Hundreds of guys went down, or got shot down. Nothing I could do to stop it, but it doesn't make me feel worth a crap."

"You're an idiot, Joe. You know how many guys, maybe those guys right out there on *Enterprise,* are alive because of the work you did? Hell, Admiral Nimitz knows it. And in time, every one of those sailors will know it. They can't know it now."

"I keep secrets all the time, Eddie."

"Well, know this. There is another secret we have to keep, orders from higher up than CINCPAC. Nobody *outside* your immediate crew is to know anything about *Yorktown,* that she went down. Washington doesn't want any civilian newspaper reporting it."

Rochefort looked at him. "How the hell are they gonna keep that quiet? There are families, for God's sake."

"The families aren't being told yet, Joe. Those are the orders. You have a problem, yell into your shoe."

"Jesus, Eddie, that's cold as hell."

"It has to do with the Japs. We have to keep 'em confused. They thought they sunk two carriers, including maybe *Enterprise,* so that gives us a big advantage in the next fight, and you know as well as I do, there will be a *next fight.* Look, some of the destroyers are coming in."

Rochefort stayed silent for a long moment, stared at *Enterprise,* maneuvering to one side of Ford Island. "What's gonna happen to *Yorktown*'s crew?"

"Why you asking?"

"Hell's bells, Eddie, it's a couple thousand guys. They've probably got a hell of a lot in common, and a bunch of 'em have buddies who aren't coming back. I'm not the only one who'll be asking."

"All I've heard from the admiral is that a lot of 'em, the technical guys, machinists, gunners, and so forth, they'll be transferred to the battleships. The pilots, well, that's easy. Any new carriers that are coming off the line will need plenty of flight crews and mechanics."

"Good, I guess. A lot of those guys will hate the battleships, but at least they'll have duty." He looked out toward *Enterprise* again, and said, "It was a close thing, Eddie."

"What was?"

"The Japs came here in December to sink our carriers. They screwed up, and instead, took out our battleships. But still, a bunch of guys died that wouldn't have if we'd have done our job. It took us a while, but the Japs paid for that. I'm grateful for that. You maybe have no idea how grateful."

"Joe, what the hell are you talking about?"

"In December, my department missed it all. We had the clues about what the Japs were gonna do here, and we ignored it, and a hell of a lot of good men died for it. I hope, for those guys, we made up for it. I hope what the Japs lost at Midway maybe makes up for what they did to us here."

"Everybody screwed up in December, not just you."

"I don't care about anybody else. My people helped win this fight, just like we helped lose it in December. Right now my crew is down there in the Dungeon, working on the next problem, the next code, the next cipher. And we'll keep working until this war is over."

"You're making this personal, Joe. You told Admiral Nimitz you were just doing your job. Don't forget that."

"Nimitz makes me nervous. I was being polite. But as long as the Japs are killing our people, it *is* personal." He took a final look at *Enterprise,* more of the smaller ships maneuvering through the channel. "Why'd you come here, anyway?"

Layton stared at him, as though testing him. "I just wanted to see how you were doing. We might have a little bit of a lull, thought you'd want to take advantage of it. See some sights, do a little fishing maybe."

"There's never a lull, Eddie. See you later. I have to go back to work."

AFTERWORD

"Against overwhelming odds, with the most meager resources and often at fearful self-sacrifice, a few determined men reversed the course of the war in the Pacific."

—Historian Walter Lord

"The Battle of Midway was the most complete naval victory since Horatio Nelson's near annihilation of the Spanish and French fleets at Trafalgar in 1805."

—Historian Craig Symonds

"Pearl Harbor has now been partially avenged. Vengeance will not be complete until Japanese sea power has been reduced to impotence. We are about *midway* to that objective."

—Admiral Chester Nimitz—CINCPAC

THE ALEUTIAN CAMPAIGN

Coinciding with the Japanese assault on Midway, Admiral Moshiro Hosogaya commands a "mini-fleet" that sails northward with a number of smaller warships, cruisers, and destroyers, plus two junior aircraft carriers carrying eighty-two bombers and Zero fighters. They are to be reinforced by at least four battleships, sent northward from Admiral Yamamoto's main fleet. On June 3, 1942, the day before the massive air attacks that become the Battle of Midway, the Japanese reach their designated jumping-off position, and launch an assault on the only significant American base along the Alaskan coast: the port of Dutch Harbor. The attack causes a few dozen American casualties, and sends a significant warning that the Japanese have come north with serious intention. Admiral Nimitz, with the benefit of intelligence gleaned by Joe Rochefort's HYPO, believes the attack is a feint, the Japanese intending to invade and occupy two islands in the western Aleutians, Kiska and Attu. Admiral Robert "Fuzzy" Theobald, in command of the joint army and navy force around southern Alaska, is utterly unconvinced. Theobald believes the threat lies more around Dutch Harbor and Kodiak, some six hundred miles east of the two intended targets. Thus, Theobald does nothing to defend the smaller islands.

On June 6, 1942, two days after the fighting at Midway, the exuberant Japanese move ashore on the two islands. Expecting a stout military confrontation, they instead discover a force of ten unarmed American weathermen. As the American army and naval forces attempt to coordinate their response to the Japanese presence, Theobald's poor communication with army aircraft and troops at his disposal dooms any chance of effectively combating the Japanese ships or their aircraft. According to historian Craig Symonds, "So feeble was the attack on the [Japanese] carrier force that the Japanese commander may have been unaware he had been under attack at all."

The debates continue as to Japan's true purpose for the Aleutian campaign. Some historians believe the Aleutians, and not Midway, were the actual bait to draw the Americans out of Pearl Harbor. Many more believe the Aleutian campaign to have been a completely separate operation, with very different goals than were brought to Midway. This author believes the latter. First, based on intelligence that relies more on guesswork, the Japanese invasion of the two islands is meant to counter what they believe to be the upcoming invasion of Japan, which will originate from bases in the Aleutians. There are, in fact, no such large-scale American bases, and no such invasion is planned. Second, the two islands are considered an ideal location for the Japanese to construct airstrips, which will become a significant threat to the American mainland, from Anchorage to Los Angeles. Instead, what the Japanese engineers discover is that the ground on both islands is utterly unsuitable for the weight of heavy equipment, especially bombers. In addition, the minuscule amount of flat surface makes airfields completely impractical. It is a continuing mystery why the Japanese do not learn of these issues in advance.

Though the Americans and their Canadian allies bring air power to bear on the Japanese positions, the inclement weather, including dense fog, prolongs the occupation. Much of the fighting is a standoff, made worse by a winter climate that is particularly brutal for the unprepared Japanese. By mid-1943, the war of attrition takes its toll on the Japanese, now blockaded by a strong American naval presence. However, under cover of the fog, the Japanese succeed in evacuating several thousand men. By July 29, 1943, after more than a year, the campaign is over.

If there is one distinct benefit to the allies from this campaign, it comes during the first assault against Dutch Harbor, when a Japanese Zero, piloted by Petty Officer Tadayoshi Koga, crash-lands after damage from anti-aircraft fire. Koga is killed in the crash, but his aircraft remains virtually intact and is eventually swarmed over by American flight engineers. The enormous tactical advantages of the Zero are analyzed in great detail, and soon incorporated into American aircraft, including the Grumman F6F Hellcat, which proves superior to the Zero in almost every way.

THE AMERICANS

The Doolittle Raiders

"My cap is off to Jimmy and his brave squadron . . . Their flight
was one of the most courageous deeds in all military history."
—Admiral William F. Halsey

The utter lack of cooperation from the Chinese government or
their military means that none of the B-25s are able to land as
planned on Chinese airfields. As the planes crash-land in a variety
of settings, three of the crewmen are killed. Considering that
eighty men began the mission, that figure alone is astonishingly
small. However, their trial does not end with the loss of aircraft.
Contrary to Doolittle's orders to stay clear of Russia, one plane,
captained by Edward York, lands intact near Vladivostok. It is not
a wise move. York and his crew spend more than a year in Russian
custody, for no apparent reason other than that the Russians, os-
tensibly America's ally, have the power of imprisonment.

For those who land in China, eight land in Japanese-held territory, and thus are captured. Only four of those men survive.

Doolittle and his surviving crew are eventually returned to the
United States, and go separate ways. Several of the men do service
in the Burma campaign, some fly in Europe, while others serve as
training officers for young fliers.

Doolittle is awarded a Medal of Honor, and all of his men, including the deceased, receive Distinguished Flying Crosses. With a
push from Doolittle, each man receives a promotion.

Doolittle is promoted two ranks, to brigadier general, then
eventually to three-star lieutenant general, and commands the 8th
Air Force in Europe. Though he is often considered prickly and
difficult to command, particularly by General Dwight Eisenhower,

no one can deny Doolittle's status as one of America's most skilled and illustrious fliers.

Doolittle lives until 1993, and dies at age ninety-six.

Though receiving little if any publicity throughout the rest of his service and his life, Lieutenant Colonel Richard Cole becomes the oldest surviving member of the Doolittle team. He dies in 2019, at age 103.

> "It was, for me, a very sad occasion because, while we had accomplished the first part of our mission, we had lost all of our aircraft . . . and of course, we lost some of the boys."
> —JIMMY DOOLITTLE, 1962

LIEUT. J/G PERCY "PERK" BAKER

Jimmie Thach never reveals Baker's hallucinations, symptoms that today would be diagnosed as PTSD. Whether or not Thach believes the problem will worsen, he provides Baker with a recommendation to return to the States as a flight instructor. Baker gratefully accepts. He relocates to San Diego, and in 1944 is transferred to the newly commissioned Naval Air Station, Jacksonville, Florida. He is promoted to full lieutenant, then lieutenant commander by the war's end.

He returns again to San Diego, where he meets an army nurse, Penelope Tyner. They are married in 1947, and go on to have two children. Baker retires from the navy in 1959, and the couple moves to Galveston, Texas, Baker's hometown, where they care for his aging parents. Penelope retires from nursing in 1972.

Baker dies in 2012, at age ninety. Penelope dies seven years later, at age ninety-six. They are married for sixty-five years. Their oldest child, Jacqueline, serves as a lieutenant commander in the navy until 2010.

Gy/Sgt. Douglas Ackroyd

Despite the Marine Corps's need for experienced non-commissioned officers, Ackroyd feels he has done his time. He retires two months after the fight at Midway, after twenty-six years in the service. Never a man with complicated tastes, Ackroyd returns home to Alabama, but the quiet atmosphere of small-town America has lost its appeal. He moves to Mobile, and spends much time crossing the bay there to visit Pensacola and the training centers. But with the war, security is stringent, and even with his tenure, he can rarely visit the other non-coms. But they visit him. The local bars and cafes are havens for off-duty gunnery sergeants, and Ackroyd quickly becomes a favorite of many of the younger men, who appreciate his somewhat exaggerated stories.

In 1946, Ackroyd attends his first movie, the classic western *My Darling Clementine*, directed, of course, by John Ford. To his surprise, and extreme discomfort, the film is preceded by Ford's eighteen-minute documentary, *The Battle of Midway*. The film is all too vivid for Ackroyd to enjoy, and he will never again visit a movie house.

He reluctantly enters a social scene in Mobile, and meets but will not marry Francine Dolan, a widow whose husband has been killed in France. Ackroyd believes a widow still to be married to her deceased soldier husband. However, they maintain a relationship for twenty-eight years, until his death in 1974, at age seventy-six.

Lieut. Commander Joseph Rochefort

"This officer deserves a major share of the credit for the victory at Midway."

—Admiral Chester Nimitz

"He is easily the most consequential shore-based actor in the Midway drama."

—HISTORIAN ELLIOT CARLSON

"We knew the Japanese had been decisively defeated, but there was no great moment of exhilaration. Perhaps it was exhaustion, like that of a distance runner collapsing over the tape at the end of a long hard race."

—CAPTAIN JASPER HOLMES—MEMBER OF HYPO

"Things turned out well."

—LIEUT. COMMANDER JOSEPH J. ROCHEFORT

After his astonishing success in deciphering Japanese intentions throughout the Midway campaign, Rochefort returns once more to relative obscurity, though of course he is well known where it counts in Hawaii. His department continues to receive intense if discreet attention from Admiral Chester Nimitz. But Rochefort's success raises hackles in Washington among those members of the cryptanalysis teams who consider him to be both a disrespectful and annoying upstart and an unworthy rival. This view holds despite OP-G-20's miserable track record of misinterpreting Japanese coded messages and intentions. Thus, Rochefort is never received with the respect he deserves among the highest levels of the War Department, and of course he can never become a public figure due to the nature of his work.

In late 1942, Admiral Nimitz suggests Rochefort for a Navy Distinguished Service Medal, which Rochefort rejects, saying it will "stir up trouble in Washington." Though he understands the animosity between his crew at HYPO and their supposed partners at OP-G-20 in Washington, he does little to smooth over the bumps. His continuing success with the Japanese codes against those men who seem to fumble their way through the process makes him no friends. He doesn't seem to care.

But Washington does. In late 1942, at the urging of Admiral Joseph Redman, whose brother John is directly involved in Washington's woeful efforts, Rochefort is removed from HYPO and assigned to command a navy dry dock in San Francisco. While Rochefort accepts the assignment by keeping his emotions mostly to himself, his friends, including Commander Ed Layton, are outraged. But Nimitz is powerless to overturn the ultimate decision, made by Admiral Ernest King.

In the absence of Rochefort's hands-on management of HYPO, the new commander, Captain William Goggins, eventually employs more than a thousand cryptanalysts to do the work routinely accomplished by Rochefort's 104.

Rochefort retires in 1947, but is called back to duty in 1951 with the outbreak of the Korean War. Expected to be an asset in decoding and decrypting North Korean and Chinese messages, his lack of a free hand brings out the worst of his personality: the utter disregard for the code-breaking abilities of his superiors. His behavior is as it always was, rough around the edges, something unexpected by his new commanders. Though he serves until 1953, the experience is nothing like HYPO.

In 1975, Hollywood calls, announcing a production in the works for a film titled *Midway*. Rochefort's part is to be played by veteran actor Hal Holbrook, who seeks input from Rochefort. The portrayal offends all who know Rochefort well, as his role is often interpreted to be that of a carefree slob who spends time joyriding in a jeep with Admiral Nimitz. But Rochefort will never see the completed film. He dies in 1976, at age seventy-six, and is buried in Inglewood Park Cemetery in Los Angeles.

For years after his death, an effort is made to clear his reputation from the failure that allowed the surprise Japanese attack on December 7, 1941. It is partially successful, though Rochefort's friends, including Edwin Layton, know that Rochefort never would have accepted such a soul-cleansing whitewash. When asked to write his memoirs, Rochefort had refused, willing to accept responsibility for his failures and unwilling to argue that he should be recognized for his successes.

The medals he would not receive while alive are granted to him posthumously. In 1985, he is awarded the Navy Distinguished Service Medal, the Presidential Medal of Freedom, and the Legion of Merit. In 2012, a building housing offices of the National Security Agency at Hickam Field/Pearl Harbor, Hawaii, is named for Captain Joseph J. Rochefort. Thus do his accomplishments and the gratitude of the navy outlast those of his detractors.

"He didn't have friends in high places, [but] people liked being around him to soak up his smarts."

—HISTORIAN ELLIOT CARLSON

"He conducted cryptanalysis by hunches and intuition. He had the ability to take off in an illogical direction from a shaky premise and land squarely on a firm conclusion."

—CAPTAIN JASPER HOLMES—HYPO TEAM MEMBER

COMMANDER JOHN "JIMMIE" THACH

Thach is recognized and widely regarded as the navy's finest combat aviator. His design for confronting the far superior Japanese Zero, the Thach Weave, is used in aerial combat up through the Vietnam War, in combat between American jets and Russian MiGs, and it proves just as effective in those encounters. Thach is officially named a flying ace, with at least six confirmed kills of Japanese aircraft.

After Midway, the Navy pushes Thach and its other more experienced pilots to focus on training recruits rather than risking their lives against the enemy. Thach reluctantly accepts the challenge, serving at Naval Air Station Pensacola, and is briefly reunited with Percy Baker. But Thach is too well known to remain a flight trainer, and he is named to serve on the staff of Admiral John S. McCain (grandfather of the late U.S. senator). Thach's success and increasing renown result in an invitation from Admiral Chester Nimitz for Thach to be present onboard the USS *Missouri* in September 1945 to witness the Japanese surrender.

After the war, in a controversial move, the newly named U.S. Air Force attempts to bring naval aviation within its control. The navy lobbies hard for the idea to be rejected, Thach being one of the principal advocates for the independence of the navy's aviators. After considerable friction between the services, the Air Force's idea is dropped.

During the outbreak of the Korean War, Thach commands the escort carrier USS *Sicily,* supporting marine ground troops with a squadron of Corsair fighters, one of the most effective prop-driven aircrafts in U.S. naval history.

After the war, he commands the carrier USS *Franklin D. Roosevelt,* then commands a number of naval bases in the Mediterranean theater. In 1955, he receives the first of his four stars, the rank of admiral. He climbs an extraordinary ladder of success, from carrier division commands to command of the Pacific Fleet / Anti-Submarine Warfare. Promoted to vice admiral in 1960, he is appointed the Defense Department's deputy chief of naval operations (air). In 1965, Thach is promoted to full admiral and named commander in chief, U.S. Naval Forces Europe.

He retires two years later, in 1967.

For his service, Thach is awarded the Distinguished Service Medal, two Navy Crosses, the Silver Star, the Bronze Star, and two Legions of Merit, and, in 1958, is featured on the cover of *Time* magazine. The navy names a frigate in his honor, the USS *Thach* (FFG-43).

He dies in 1981, at age seventy-five, and is buried in the Fort Rosecrans National Cemetery in San Diego.

CAPTAIN ELLIOTT BUCKMASTER

As captain of the ill-fated *Yorktown*, Buckmaster assumes the worst about his career and the stigma that his name will carry. He is wrong. To his surprise, Buckmaster is almost immediately promoted to rear admiral, and is named chief of naval air primary training, the first man to hold that title. His new posting is the navy's training facility at Kansas City, Missouri. Buckmaster lobbies and is successful in having his former chief of staff, Dixie Kiefer, serve again in that role. Buckmaster, the *brown-shoe* sailor, recognizes the value of flight training like few of his rank, and he succeeds in changing routines and training manuals that had been mired in rigidity for years.

In 1945, Buckmaster receives a new posting to the South Pacific, as commander of the West Carolines Operations Area. As such, he is deeply involved in the search and rescue effort the navy undertakes after the tragic loss of the cruiser *Indianapolis*.

To this day there are critics who maintain that Buckmaster should never have abandoned *Yorktown*, or at the very least, should have kept his station until the very last moment. Almost unanimously, his officers and crew do not accept that condemnation. It is impossible to know just when that *last moment* might have been, given the carrier's precarious list, approaching thirty degrees. Removing his crew from the ship when he does possibly saves hundreds of lives. Indeed, the navy agrees, awarding Buckmaster the first of two Distinguished Service Medals.

He dies in 1976, at age eighty-six, and is buried in Holy Cross Catholic Cemetery, in San Diego.

ADMIRAL CHESTER NIMITZ

Nimitz serves as commander in chief—Pacific (CINCPAC) through major campaigns against the Japanese, including Coral Sea, Midway, Guadalcanal, New Guinea, Truk, Leyte Gulf, and the island-hopping campaigns of 1943–45, among many others. Late in 1944, Nimitz is promoted to fleet admiral, the equivalent to the army's five-star ranking.

On September 2, 1945, Nimitz, along with General Douglas MacArthur, signs the surrender papers with the Japanese onboard the USS *Missouri* in Tokyo Bay, though Nimitz is rarely given photographic or media credit for being MacArthur's equal in rank.

Considered one of the navy's leading experts on submarines, he is called to testify at the Nuremburg trial of Germany's Admiral Karl Dönitz, but rather than condemn the German submarine tactics, Nimitz acknowledges that the United States had engaged in the same type of warfare, the unrestricted use of the submarine (or German U-boat) to help the cause of victory. As a result, instead of a life sentence, Dönitz is sentenced to only ten years in prison.

In December 1945, Nimitz replaces Admiral Ernest King as chief of naval operations, accepting the position with the understanding that he will serve only one term, until 1947.

He becomes a powerful advocate for the development of nuclear-powered ships, especially submarines, and supports Captain (later Admiral) Hyman Rickover's efforts to develop what will become the *Nautilus,* the first submarine of that kind.

After his retirement, and after a number of diplomatic missions he accepts for Presidents Truman and Eisenhower, Nimitz and his wife, Catherine, retire to the San Francisco Bay Area, where he becomes a regent for the University of California. He is active in founding their Naval ROTC program.

He will never pen his own memoir, concerned about passing judgment publicly on his subordinates, saying, "History is best written by the professional historians." Indeed, his wife will burn nearly all of his correspondence to her, thus forever keeping his thoughts between them.

He dies in 1965 at age eighty, and is buried beside his wife and several good friends, including Admiral Raymond Spruance, at Golden Gate National Cemetery, in San Bruno, California.

In 1975, the navy commissions the USS *Nimitz*, a nuclear-powered aircraft carrier, which is in service to this day.

The National Museum of the Pacific War sits today in Fredericksburg, Texas, the home of Chester Nimitz.

JOHN FORD

Born John Feeney, the filmmaker, by being accidentally in the right place and time for the Japanese attack on Midway, does enormous service to those marines and naval personnel who endure the attack. What begins as a minor publicity gesture becomes an enormous tool of propaganda for the U.S. War Department. Ford's documentary, aptly titled *The Battle of Midway*, offers the American public a firsthand graphic picture of war that no studio special effects department has been able to capture. Ford himself receives a wound in his arm, which only adds to the public's perception of the legitimacy of the frontline action.

Though Ford's long and well-rewarded career is known more for his Westerns, including *My Darling Clementine*, *The Searchers*, *The Man Who Shot Liberty Valance*, *Stagecoach*, and many more, most credit his best work for films that have lasted in importance to this day, including *The Grapes of Wrath* (which is not about grapes), *The Quiet Man*, and *Mister Roberts*, among many, many others. He is awarded four Oscars for Best Director, and two more for Best Documentary, which includes *The Battle of Midway*.

He dies in 1973, at age seventy-nine, and is buried in Holy Cross Cemetery, Culver City, California.

Admiral Frank Jack Fletcher

With credentials that seem to pave the way for a career at the top of the navy's chain of command, Fletcher nonetheless has his many detractors. He is awarded the Medal of Honor for service at Vera Cruz, Mexico, in 1910, and in 1918, during World War I, he is awarded the Navy Cross. However, the *black-shoe* admiral is never completely accepted in a carrier command by the brown-shoe fliers and his command of Task Force 17, with his flag flying from the carrier *Yorktown*. Controversy seems to follow his every decision, and in early 1942, his failure to rescue the beleaguered marine outpost on Wake Island begins the loud talk against his decisions. In the Coral Sea, the decision-making process again comes under fire. Almost immediately, Fletcher has a strong advocate in Admiral Chester Nimitz, who says of the Coral Sea confusion that the Japanese "failed to attack Fletcher only because of a series of errors which . . . reached the fantastic." The Japanese are no less convinced that the fault lies in confusing decisions by both sides, and sheer good and bad luck. In 1943, the Japanese Naval Ministry concludes that "even today they are confusing."

Against this backdrop, it is to Nimitz's credit that he continues to place his faith in Fletcher, saying after the Coral Sea fight, "Fletcher's operations are remarkably well timed and executed." With the power of Nimitz's endorsement, most other criticism is muted. Thus, Fletcher is in overall command at Midway. Though the victory for the Americans is overwhelming, Fletcher still fails to receive the credit he has earned. That he abandons the wounded *Yorktown* and abdicates overall command to Admiral Spruance is seen by some as an act of cowardice, yet logic dictates that with *Yorktown* fatally damaged, Fletcher has no other alternative. Admiral Spruance agrees, and the smooth transition between the flag officers ensures the domination of the battle by the American fliers.

"If it had not been [for] what you did . . . I am firmly convinced that we would have been badly defeated, and the Japs would be holding Midway today."

—ADMIRAL RAYMOND SPRUANCE

Through all the back-and-forth and meaningless controversy, it is often overlooked that it is *Yorktown* whose dive bombers fare as well or better than the flights from *Enterprise,* while the bulk of *Hornet*'s planes never see the enemy, or are too late to the fight. While Spruance cannot directly be blamed, it is possible to attribute *Hornet*'s misfortunes to simple bad luck. The one possible exception, a source of further controversy, is Commander Stanhope Ring's *Flight to Nowhere,* which simply goes off in the wrong direction.

After commands through the Guadalcanal Campaign, Fletcher is assigned to command the Northern Pacific region, including coastal Alaska. As the war ends he assumes a role with the navy's occupation forces in Japan, and in 1946, becomes chairman of the Navy's General Board. He retires in 1947, at the rank of full admiral, and returns to his home in Maryland.

As most of his contemporaries prepare their papers for posterity, as well as the navy's official efforts to create a complete and detailed history of the navy's role in World War II, Fletcher, whose papers have mostly been lost throughout the war, will not participate. This energizes his critics, including Admiral Ernest King. Some believe he is covering up his mistakes, or even worse, has something to hide. There is no evidence to support either assertion. This author's judgment is that Frank Jack Fletcher is a man who will not promote himself in a culture of self-promotion. It is Admiral Chester Nimitz who ensures that Fletcher serves to his abilities, which are primarily responsible for victory at Midway.

Besides his Medal of Honor and Navy Cross, Fletcher is awarded the Navy Distinguished Service Medal, and receives a Purple Heart.

Fletcher dies in 1974, at age eighty-seven, and is buried in Arlington National Cemetery. He lies beside his wife, Martha, after fifty-six years of marriage.

THE JAPANESE

"The defeat of Japan's navy in World War II remains an unenviable monument to obstinate, outdated naval strategists."
—ADMIRAL TOSHIYUKI YOKOI, IJN

ADMIRAL CHUICHI NAGUMO

Nagumo is always a man who seems far older than his years since he is little different in age than his superior, Admiral Yamamoto.

Despite negative judgment of the aging admiral from Yamamoto and many of the younger men he commands, Nagumo's record prior to the Battle of Midway is exceptional. He leads *Kido Butai* to victories and destroys enemy shipping from Pearl Harbor to India.

With failure for Midway assigned to him by his command of the four doomed aircraft carriers, there is really only one major error for which he can be faulted: the confusion and indecisiveness regarding the arming of aircraft once the American fleet has been sighted. It is not a minor mistake.

Though a convenient scapegoat for the errors of others (including Yamamoto), he accepts his demotion with quiet grace, is given assignments to far lesser posts, yet still retains some command. Though given lofty titles, such as commander of the first fleet, he in fact supervises training vessels, and fulfills various administrative roles. He is rarely assigned to combat command until mid-1944, when the Americans engage the Japanese fleet at the Battle of the Philippine Sea, which results in an overwhelming victory for the Americans. Assigned to defend the island of Saipan, Nagumo and his army counterparts face an impossible task. Nagumo responds by taking his own life, but rather than the ritual *hara-kiri*, he shoots himself in the head with a pistol. He is fifty-seven.

I-168

The star-crossed submarine is the lone Japanese craft that shells Midway just after midnight, June 5. Unable to receive communication to that point, Commander Yahachi Tanabe has no idea his sub stands completely alone. Learning too late that there is no great armada of warships there to complete the job and pave the way for a massed invasion of the island, I-168 finally receives communication that she is instead to sail northward, to give the final and fatal blows to *Yorktown*. During that mission, Tanabe enjoys an astonishing run of good luck in evading, and in many cases sailing directly under, more than six American destroyers that are out to end her run. But Tanabe's luck runs out a year later, in July 1943, when I-168 is sunk by the American submarine USS *Scamp*.

ADMIRAL MATOME UGAKI

The loyal and efficient chief of staff to Admiral Yamamoto continues in that service until Yamamoto's death. His life is spared on that April day in 1943 only by the chance seating arrangement, where he flies in the second of the two planes, while Yamamoto is in the first, which crashes into the jungle. Ugaki survives the crash into the ocean, with two other crew members.

Ugaki continues to serve in combat onboard naval vessels, particularly the grand battleships of the fleet, and is the principal admiral in command during the disastrous Battle of the Philippine Sea. He is recalled to Japan to assume command of the Fifth Air Fleet, and is credited with ordering the first large-scale launch of kamikaze flights against the Americans at Okinawa. As the war draws to a close, Ugaki will not accept the emperor's decision to end the fighting, and on August 15, 1945, the day the emperor announces surrender, Ugaki insists he will make his own kamikaze flight. Along with ten other planes, he flies to the islands near Okinawa, but is shot down before impacting any American ships or troops.

Throughout his service to Admiral Yamamoto, Ugaki pens a lengthy and detailed diary. Oddly, he seems to focus first on each day's weather as much as the events going on around him. But the diary is a significant contribution to the understanding of the command structure and mindsets of the participants. At his death in 1945, he is fifty-five.

ADMIRAL ISOROKU YAMAMOTO

"Things are looking black for us now."

Every defeat seeks a scapegoat, and though most within the Japanese hierarchy, including the navy, will find no fault with Yamamoto or his strategy, it is that strategy that many feel is directly responsible for the grotesque failure at Midway. The plan is ambitious, to be sure, but with an overwhelming force approaching Midway, any direct assault against the Americans would most certainly have resulted in victory. Instead, Yamamoto violates one of the tenets of warfare—he divides his forces. His four fleets, combined, likely could have defeated any navy in the world. But the mission to the Aleutians serves an illusory purpose, and could have been mounted at any time in the future. The invasion fleet (Admiral Kondo) with battleships, a small escort carrier, and supporting ships could have been of enormous assistance to Admiral Nagumo's *Kido Butai*. To have grouped all four of Nagumo's primary aircraft carriers within only a few miles of one another invited the outcome that in fact resulted. But worse, in this author's opinion (and there are those who disagree) Yamamoto makes two egregious mistakes. He keeps his most powerful ships several hundred miles away from his valuable carriers, and he insists on radio silence, so that no flexibility of orders can occur. All of these factors are recipes for disaster, which, for the Japanese, is precisely what happens.

> "[He] was driven by his personal belief that the Americans were all but beaten and would need to be lured out to battle."
>
> —Historians Jonathan Parshall & Anthony Tully

> "The essence of his scheme was the supposition that Nimitz and his forces would behave exactly as the Japanese planned they should."
>
> —Historian Gordon Prange

However, none of this compares to the extraordinary value to the Americans in breaking the Japanese codes, so that Admiral Nimitz could lay his trap by sending the three American carriers close to Midway. It is hard to speculate how Admiral Yamamoto would have changed his plans had he known of that catastrophic intelligence breach.

Officially, Yamamoto remains commander of the Combined Fleet, but the Naval Ministry will no longer allow him to set strategy. For the first time in many years, Yamamoto has to accept that he must follow orders. He engages the allies in battles around the Solomon Islands, a mix of victories and defeats, none of which produce the powerful results of either Midway or Pearl Harbor.

In April 1943, Yamamoto makes the decision to bolster the morale of his troops who have been fighting a difficult struggle in Guadalcanal, an island off the coast of New Guinea. He plans a two-plane mission, which will embark from Rabaul, intending to land at an airstrip on a small island near Bougainville. The aircraft are light and fast bombers, with nine passengers in total, including Yamamoto and chief of staff Ugaki. On April 18, the two men board separate planes, since neither one can hold the entire complement. As is necessary protocol, the destination airstrip is notified of the admiral's itinerary, and a total of six Zeroes are to accompany, and thus protect, the two planes.

What none of these men know is that the Americans have broken this code as well, the itinerary well known long before the planes take off. In response to the intelligence revelation, Admiral Chester Nimitz confers with Admiral Bill Halsey, who makes the determination that this is a strike that must take place. Shortly after the two bombers leave Rabaul, more than a dozen American P-38 fighters intercept them. The Zeroes are no match, and both of the bombers are shot down. One crashes in the ocean, the other in the jungle on Bougainville. Admiral Ugaki survives the water crash. Yamamoto's body is found the next day after an exhaustive search by Japanese officers and troops.

In Rabaul, two of Yamamoto's most prominent staff officers, Watanabe and Kuroshima, are informed of their commander's death.

Yamamoto's body is cremated, and he is transported back to Tokyo Bay. Charged with guarding his urn is his longtime orderly, Omi. On June 5, Yamamoto is buried with extraordinary fanfare, a state funeral eventually attended by tens of thousands of citizens. His family is prominent among them, as are representatives of the emperor, and of course, Yamamoto's staff officers. As though to mock Yamamoto's many years of discretion, the crowd clamors for a view of his mistress, Chiyoko, but there is no sighting. Yamamoto's close friend Hori is the only one who seems to notice the lone woman who stays to herself to one side, standing with a hooded veil.

Immediately after the funeral, a number of local political officials float the idea of building an elaborate shrine in Yamamoto's honor. His friend Hori loudly objects, quoting Yamamoto: "However glorious his achievements, to make a god of a military man is absurd." Hori further says, "Yamamoto hated that kind of thing. If you deified him, he'd be more embarrassed than anyone else." The officials agree to accept that judgment. Today, the site of Yamamoto's home is a small and simple memorial park.

The death of Yamamoto has an effect on the Japanese people that no military defeat can touch. For the first time, it is understood that the Victory Disease that has plagued them all, that they simply cannot lose, has been shattered. While the Japanese public never hears an accurate assessment of just what happened at Midway, no one can hide that the great commander has been taken away. It is the beginning of the end.

ACKNOWLEDGMENTS

T he following graciously supplied me with insights or materials which aided greatly in the writing of this book. My sincerest thank-you.

RANDY EDWARDS—CONCORD, NC
DANIEL MARTINEZ—NATIONAL PARK SERVICE
    CHIEF HISTORIAN FOR WORLD WAR II VALOR IN
    THE PACIFIC NATIONAL MONUMENT—USS *ARIZONA*
    MEMORIAL
COLONEL JIM WILMOTT—USMC (RET)

The following have created diaries or memoirs that were essential in the writing of this book:

FIREMAN 2/C E. H. DOMIENIK—USS *YORKTOWN*
COMMANDER MITSUO FUCHIDA—IJN
CAPTAIN TAMEICHI HARA—IJN

COMMANDER W. JASPER HOLMES—HYPO—USN

CAPTAIN N. J. "DUSTY" KLEISS—USS *ENTERPRISE*

CAPTAIN EDWIN T. LAYTON—USN

CAPTAIN ZENJI ORITA—IJN

ADMIRAL MATOME UGAKI—CHIEF OF STAFF—IJN

In every book I've done, I recognize the historians without whose work my research would be woefully incomplete. The following have accumulated and crafted essential works, without which I could not have written this book.

HIROYUKI AGAWA

DAVID BROWN

THOMAS B. BUELL

ELLIOT CARLSON

ROGER CHESNEAU

ROBERT CRESSMAN

DAVID C. EVANS

STEVE EWING

MARK HEALY

SABURO IENAGA

RONALD LEWIN

WALTER LORD

JOHN B. LUNDSTROM

JEFF NESMITH

JONATHAN PARSHALL & ANTHONY TULLY

E. B. POTTER

GORDON W. PRANGE

THEODORE ROSCOE

DUANE SCHULTZ

CRAIG SYMONDS

IAN W. TOLL

Finally, I offer my thanks in the most personal way to my wife, Stephanie, and my daughter, Emma. The reasons are many, but in the end, it's simple: Writing can be all-consuming, self-involved mental gymnastics that can be hard to explain to someone who does not write for a living. Incredibly, they put up with it. That's amazing. I so love you both.

ABOUT THE AUTHOR

JEFF SHAARA is the *New York Times* bestselling author of *To Wake the Giant, The Frozen Hours, The Fateful Lightning, The Smoke at Dawn, A Chain of Thunder, A Blaze of Glory, The Final Storm, No Less Than Victory, The Steel Wave, The Rising Tide, To the Last Man, The Glorious Cause, Rise to Rebellion,* and *Gone for Soldiers,* as well as *Gods and Generals* and *The Last Full Measure*—two novels that complete the Civil War trilogy that began with his father's Pulitzer Prize–winning classic, *The Killer Angels.* Shaara was born into a family of Italian immigrants in New Brunswick, New Jersey. He grew up in Tallahassee, Florida, and graduated from Florida State University. He lives in Gettysburg, Pennsylvania.

JeffShaara.com

ABOUT THE TYPE

This book was set in Dante, a typeface designed by Giovanni Mardersteig (1892–1977). Conceived as a private type for the Officina Bodoni in Verona, Italy, Dante was originally cut only for hand composition by Charles Malin, the famous Parisian punch cutter, between 1946 and 1952. Its first use was in an edition of Boccaccio's *Trattatello in laude di Dante* that appeared in 1954. The Monotype Corporation's version of Dante followed in 1957. Though modeled on the Aldine type used for Pietro Cardinal Bembo's treatise *De Aetna* in 1495, Dante is a thoroughly modern interpretation of that venerable face.